# RESTORED

---

BONNIE LACY

FROSTING ON THE CAKE PRODUCTIONS

*To all who have gone before us.*

CONTENTS


Chapter 1                                               1
Chapter 2                                               9
Chapter 3                                              19
Chapter 4                                              25
Chapter 5                                              33
Chapter 6                                              35
Chapter 7                                              49
Chapter 8                                              53
Chapter 9                                              63
Chapter 10                                             71
Chapter 11                                             79
Chapter 12                                             89
Chapter 13                                             95
Chapter 14                                            101
Chapter 15                                            107
Chapter 16                                            111
Chapter 17                                            117
Chapter 18                                            119
Chapter 19                                            123
Chapter 20                                            127
Chapter 21                                            137
Chapter 22                                            141
Chapter 23                                            147
Chapter 24                                            151
Chapter 25                                            157
Chapter 26                                            165
Chapter 27                                            173
Chapter 28                                            181
Chapter 29                                            185
Chapter 30                                            187
Chapter 31                                            195
Chapter 32                                            201
Chapter 33                                            205

Chapter 34     207
Chapter 35     215
Chapter 36     219
Chapter 37     223
Chapter 38     227
Chapter 39     233
Chapter 40     239
Chapter 41     251
Chapter 42     253
Chapter 43     259
Chapter 44     261
Chapter 45     269
Chapter 46     277
Chapter 47     285
Chapter 48     291
Chapter 49     295
Chapter 50     301
Chapter 51     309
Chapter 52     313
Chapter 53     317
Chapter 54     323
Chapter 55     329
Chapter 56     337
Chapter 57     343
Chapter 58     349
Chapter 59     353
Chapter 60     357
Chapter 61     361
Chapter 62     365
Chapter 63     367
Chapter 64     371
Chapter 65     373
Chapter 66     379

Book Club Questions     389
Author Notes     391
Acknowledgments     395
Other Books by Bonnie Lacy     397

# ONE

"He's *mine!*" Phil Daynton slammed down his whiskey glass. The golden liquid erupted, splattered over his hand and soaked into the plush carpet in the warden's office at the Chicago prison. "Clarence Timmelsen thinks he can keep my little girl, Bea, from me." He stood, holding his hand away from his clothes. "Well, I'll cut him in half! And you can't stop me."

Warden William Ralston smirked as he sipped his drink, then quietly rested the crystal glass on his knee. Leather stretched and moaned as he leaned back in his chair.

"Don't look at me like that!" Phil stabbed his finger onto Warden's desk. "I get first crack at him!" Booze dripped onto the fine woodwork. His tongue flickered inside his mouth. Ohh. What a waste. He started to lick the back of his hand, but instead, wiped it on his jeans, then used his sleeve to mop the desk surface dry, bumping a family photo into another one right next to it. He caught them before they crashed to the floor. *Damn.*

Warden sat as calm as the calm just before dawn on every day. The calm before Phil knew his dad would be rising out of his drunken stupor soon. Just before the fear and chaos began. Just before the firing squad … fired.

Phil stomped toward the windows. Things had changed since Ralston had taken over the warden job.

For one thing, a new mahogany desk with leather bumpers had replaced grey metal government issue furniture from the last warden. Phil tapped the leather bumper, as he passed the desk. Should have been a pool table—it would have been a better use of beautiful wood and leather. The ceiling fan quietly sliced the heated air; the brass blades reflected the green desk lamp below.

He scanned the grounds outside, as he leaned against the rich wood framing the window, sipping what was left of his drink. Inmates lounged in the fenced-in commons area. *Must be break time.* Most sat at picnic tables or on the sidewalk, leaning against the brick building. Only a couple seemed to be running laps along the fence.

The fence wasn't your everyday-white-washed picket fence. Razor wire topped off the chain-link mesh in endless circles.

Phil shook his head. *Who would try to escape over that?*

*What a kingdom.*

The office wing formed its own three-story lookout tower, and crowning it was the warden's office on the third floor—with a view of the prison yard, parking lot and entrances in three directions.

Maybe after Clarence was dead and he had Bea all for himself, Phil could get his own warden position and they'd be set for the rest of their lives. He'd show this pansy-faced warden how to take control. Kill or torture off the weaklings and create his own powerful legion of cold soldiers. He straightened, chin jutted. Then he'd rule. Then he'd be the kind of leader this place was worthy of.

Warden stirred the ice in his glass with his finger, his gold rings glinting on his brown skin. "You'll have to get through me, first." He sucked the liquid from his finger and licked his lips.

Something was ... was Warden mocking him? "You think you're so damn smart." Phil faced him and folded his arms across his chest. "I used to be dead drunk, but I ran circles around you—got the girl *and* the drug money. And *still* stayed ahead of the cops."

Warden slowly lifted his head, his eyes locked on Phil.

Something tickled at the back of Phil's neck, like a fly had landed there. Or a feather drawn across his skin. He tried to lift his hand to brush it away, but he just trembled.

He couldn't move his hand.

He turned.

Someone had snuck up behind him.

But no one was there.

Cold chills traced up his back and shoulders, like the caress of a lover, only this was no lover. It was a sinister presence he had only encountered once before. Memories cut through his mind. Hot hands from his past raked over his arms and squeezed at his neck, teasing and taunting him into submission.

Warden was still staring at him—eyes piercing.

Phil tried shaking it off—residual twinges skittered in places he couldn't scratch in public. His face burned as he turned away too late.

"Reliving your past?" A deep voice spoke, but it wasn't the warden's. The voice vibrated every cell of Phil's body with an evil frequency.

Phil shivered and faced the warden. He couldn't help himself. The past pressed into ... now. He was that little boy who had been harshly disciplined—picked up physically and planted in front of his dad—knowing what came next.

All the Warden had said were three words, but Phil knew the voice. Same one from every time he'd been hurt, taunted, or abused. Those deep gravelly words accused him, pulled a tarp over the truth, and buried the trail of pain.

Phil shuddered, shaking himself out of the sensations and sounds. "Get outta my head." He kicked the desk.

Warden snarled.

Phil dropped onto the chair across the desk from the warden and tossed the name plaque to the side. "That man. Clarence Timmelsen." He swung his arm wide. "You have hundreds of men to torture. Why do you need *him*?"

Warden's eyes narrowed. A glint of raw emotion, Phil guessed pure hatred, poured from those dark pools. They turned from black holes to blood red.

Phil's eyes locked on him. The walls, the ceiling fan, desk, even the carpet blurred, until all Phil could see in the room was Warden Ralston.

With each breath Warden blew out, the air grew thick, like 4th of July firecracker smoke. His whole appearance seemed to change. Were those faint outlines of scales and horns materializing through the smoke?

Phil shuddered and rubbed his eyes. His empty glass found its way to his lips, like a baby's thumb finds its way to her mouth.

A sick grin twisted Warden's lips. He sucked in a deep breath and the smoke disappeared. "I want Timmelsen, because he killed my brother. It doesn't matter how it happened." He shuddered, shaking off whatever had enveloped him, like a dog shakes off water. "He killed my brother, Lewis, and I want Clarence Timmelsen dead."

The door burst open and a skinny weasel of a guard entered. His filthy grin turned to horror as he realized his blunder. He quickly backed out, closed the door and knocked. "Um, Warden?" He cleared his squeaky voice. This time a deeper voice came out, only it wasn't the effect he had obviously hoped for.

"What a dork." Warden shook his head and shifted his shoulders, adjusting his tie. "Enter, Blockhead."

"I've told you and told you. Don't call me that." The guard glared at Phil. "It only undermines my authority."

"Okay, Tay. Baby Tay. Baby Brudder." Warden grinned, his teeth sparkling. "That better, Tay? Tay?"

Warden's brother, huh.

Tay's brown face turned red. His eyes clouded over. "All I want to tell you is," he straightened, "we are ready to go get that ... that Clarence guy." His chin jutted out when he glanced in Phil's direction. "Van's all gassed up and Randy is getting the paperwork fixed."

Warden snorted. "You have any brothers, Phil?"

"Nope." He might have had a brother, but the kid wouldn't have survived his father. How had he, himself lived? How had Bea slipped through?

Tay's chest caved in like a popped balloon. His naturally dark skin took on a gray hue, his eyes appeared wet, but he gulped in a deep breath and his eyes turned hard. "You are a b-bastard!"

He turned and tripped on the expensive oriental rug, falling into the desk. His hands bumped the whiskey carafe. He desperately tried to keep it upright and he almost saved it, but a last grab sent it flying, soaking the paperwork on the desk and sloshing onto Warden's expensive suit.

Phil jumped away to avoid the flood, but Warden's anger activated more scales, this time visible to all. No smoke or mist to hide behind. They shimmered green and gray and gold. Flickered and reflected light. Warden's whole face changed. His eyes bugged out, cheeks stretched flat and his nose grew to a snout.

But those teeth.

Quickly, it all morphed back into Warden's handsome but cruel dark features.

Phil lifted the empty glass to his mouth again, fingers trembling. The booze must be affecting his imagination.

From the look on Tay's face, he guessed he'd seen those scales, too. Growing up with the Warden must have been quite interesting.

Warden smirked. "I'd fill that glass for you, Phil, but as you can see, I'm all out." He calmly tapped his ear and spoke. "Carmile, please bring the necessary equipment."

Interesting. No earpiece. No wires. Must be some sort of implant.

Someone knocked on the door and Warden nodded.

A striking person entered. Almost air-brushed light brown skin. Smoky dark eyes perfectly outlined—resembled an Egyptian goddess. The suit was tailored to fit her ... his body. Hair dangled long around a woman's chest. But lower there was—

"Thank you, Carmile. We had a little mishap." Warden stepped away from the desk, brushing at his pants.

Phil couldn't take his eyes off the secretary.

Tay couldn't either.

She moved with the grace of a woman, but with a man's stride. Lifting one end of the solid wood desk, she sopped the whiskey from the carpet.

What was ... he? She?

Warden cleared his throat. "Time to roll. Gather in the Timmelsen man. Bring him to me." He glanced out the window. "Tay. Load up the van. If you leave now, you can drive all night and get there in the morning."

"Yeah." Tay turned to the door. "Whatcha say we don't drive all night, Bro, and get a motel halfway there?"

Tay's hand seemed to freeze on the doorknob.

"You will do as I say, Baby Brother." Warden's voice grew softer, with a growl, his eyes still on something outside. "You will leave now and drive all night. Gather Mr. Timmelsen and bring him to me by morning."

"Yeah. Okay, Bro." He stood, hand still frozen on the knob "You can let me go now. We ain't no kids in the backyard anymore." He squealed. "Let me go!" The door opened and he leaned into the opening but appeared to be suspended mid air— as if held by some unseen force—like a rubber band stretched tight, ready to shoot its missile. Suddenly, the force holding him seemed to release and he shot into the hallway. He picked himself up and ran.

Phil snorted a laugh but restrained himself. He stood and followed where Warden stared. One inmate was out of line, weaving back and forth. A guard abruptly turned toward the window where Warden stood and stared back. He then signaled for the other guards to handcuff the inmate. They took him out of Phil's line of vision. A sharp pop made the others in line jump, but none looked away from the guard in charge. All stayed obediently in line, eyes straight ahead. Intent on staying at attention. The other man never came back.

Phil disengaged himself from the scene outside to find Warden smiling at him. Eyebrows raised.

And a plan dropped into his mind. Why not let Warden *have* Timmelsen? Why fight over him?

If Warden arrested Clarence ... then Bea and Katty, but especially pretty little Bea, would be unguarded.

And vulnerable.

## TWO

Noell Carpenter sighed. Day off. Weekends were so long.

She stretched. Nice not to go to the Roads Department, but she missed the guys. She missed the camaraderie and the joking. The family atmosphere. Even Rat.

The family.

She supposed everybody had questionable members in their family. One might be nice, another maybe from a different culture. And everybody had a Rat. Her work family had one; he had tried more than once to interest her in his idea of love.

Ick. Hence the name.

Her room upstairs was pristine, as always, but today it seemed empty. She liked the clean feel—just a couple things on the bedside table—her Bible from Gamma, the "Osceola Times" cup from the porch and her baby bracelet. She rolled over and picked up the bracelet. So tiny. The smallest pearls she'd ever seen and little pink beads mixed in. A small round locket out of what looked like silver, created a center showpiece.

When she opened the locket, a photo of herself as a baby was on one side and Mommy's picture was on the other.

Noell hovered her finger over both photos, letting the

emotion flow until she snapped the locket shut. Even though she had touched the bracelet many times, still she could discern other voices—Gamma's most of all. "My baby girl. You are so precious."

She blew out a breath and blinked back tears.

Before Gamma died, when grief and fear pulled her down, she could run downstairs and snuggle with Gamma and everything would be all right.

But not anymore.

Gamma was gone and so was Grampa.

And so was Mommy.

Loneliness.

Noell had never known Mommy by any other name than ... Mommy. She couldn't remember her face, except from photographs like the one in the locket.

And the nightmares.

Gotta get up and focus on something.

Anything, other than loneliness.

Anything, other than nightmares.

As soon as she got dressed and went downstairs, more emotion flooded her. The stairway descended into the living room and Gamma's beautiful red leather sofa sat front and center. Her empty spot still ... empty. Even though one end was piled with magazines and old mail, and boxes surrounded the sofa, Gamma's spot was always open. Waiting.

A sob rose in Noell's throat and she swallowed it. She didn't need to go down that road now, with no one to pull her back from the edge of pain and nightmares.

Get busy.

Do something.

Breathe.

The room was stuffed. Barely space to walk from the bottom of the steps to the dining room in front of her. Or from Gamma's sofa to the enclosed front porch or to Gamma's bedroom at the back of the house. At least from the bottom of the steps, it was just a right turn into the kitchen. She had used that well when freshly baked chocolate chip cookies still cooled on the counter. Just nab four or five, whip around the corner and zoom up the steps. Gamma never saw. But she knew.

She leaned around the corner now.

No cookies.

Books piled to the ceiling against the back kitchen wall, framing the back door. Gamma had always said they were good insulation.

Noell shrugged. Maybe.

She loved to read and was forever checking books out from the library or buying softly used books from Mrs. Bertrand's thrift store. Seemed like Mrs. Bertrand always found some that spoke to Noell. She loved that store.

Maybe she could give back. Her eyes skimmed the walls. Give back stacks and stacks of books to Mrs. Bertrand.

When Gamma was still alive, Noell had tried to get rid of some of the clutter by sneaking items out. She had donated them to the thrift store. Mrs. Bertrand and the other ladies working there promised to never tell. Anything to try and clear the house out.

She shook her head. Hadn't helped. She couldn't tell if it had made any difference or not.

She blinked. Really emotional today. She wiped her face with her sleeve.

Breathe.

She could go to the Roads yard and rake, whether they were open or not. She knew how to get in. Anything but stay here. It felt like every box and stack in every room had tumbled down on top of her.

Maybe Fletch could come over later after he got off work and they could ... go for a walk or watch a movie at his house. There was no room here to do anything.

What if she cleared away clutter around the TV? They could watch a movie together.

If she picked up the magazine piles on the sofa and moved them to the kitchen, that would help clear room for one more person on the sofa. Cozy.

She hauled the magazines to the kitchen but when she got to the back door, she realized there were two more piles she'd put there yesterday. One pile was already sliding into the narrow path to the backdoor. She slid them as best she could with her foot, but the other stack started sliding until there was a mess of magazines covering her feet.

She needed a recycling bin. No, she needed one like at the dump for newspapers, magazines, cans, everything.

Good idea. Note to self. Call Monday and see if they could pull one here.

Noell had been working for an hour before her stomach growled. Breakfast. Taking the steps two at a time, she went up to her room for a book to read while she ate.

Two more doors opened off the landing hallway and Noell became distracted by them. It had been a long time since she had explored.

This house was all hers now, so she ought to find out what she owned.

She jiggled the doorknob to the first room, but it was locked. What?

She dug around the boxes on the floor, felt along the doorjamb, the baseboards and finally produced a key stuck in a crack between the doorjamb and the wall. What on earth? What would Gamma have had that needed to be locked up?

She examined the key—a little bread wrapper twisty looped through the hole. Gamma used those for everything—from hangers for keys, to tighten an old screw. The twisty had been barely sticking out from where the key was hidden—just enough to be able to slide the key out. What if it had fallen further behind the wood?

Flipping the key one way and then the other, Noell inserted it in the door lock. Wrong way. She flipped it again, wiggled it back and forth and the lock clicked.

The door opened a crack—purple rug. Noell had to give the door a kick to get it open all the way. Cobwebs hung as if protecting the entrance, until she swung her arms, breaking through.

A bedroom. The bed was still made up with a pretty quilt, splashes of yellow sunflowers and green leaves outlined in purple and lavender.

Oh. No.

Just leave. Just close the door and pretend she'd never found that key. Go downstairs and cook. Go outside to the camper and forget this house was here. Some people actually did that.

But she couldn't. Her feet were stapled to the floor. She glanced at her feet. No. To purple carpet.

Deep breath.

Stay here.

Don't run.

Her hand still grasped the doorknob.

She knew where she was.

A movie of people played in her mind—a much younger Gamma, Grampa, others she didn't know or recognize. All moved together through time—through this house. The same house, the same rooms—only no clutter.

No boxes or stacks of books.

Anywhere.

The steps were beautiful, all cleared off and newer supple wood, instead of tired and dried out. And dirty.

She blinked.

Time dropped her back into the current day.

This room—she knew instantly whose room it had been, and that knowledge dropped her to her knees.

The quilt pattern blurred. The photos on the bedside table swam before her brimming eyes.

Mommy's room.

Breathe.

She couldn't move.

The movie played again.

Someone was crying. Dishes clattered. Telephones rang. A deep voice, "I'm sorry. We can't talk right now. We've ... our daughter ... " A little voice, "Where's Mommy? Gamma? Where's my mommy?"

Oh God.

Why had she never explored? Had Gamma told her not to— to protect her—to keep her out of Mommy's room?

A stronger will pushed her to her feet. Gave her strength to inch slowly to the bed. The old quilt was soft under her fingers. She traced the pattern of leaves and stitching. Gamma must have made this.

Or Mommy?

Noell held her breath as she sat on the bed. No springs squeaked. No sounds.

Just soft.

And comforting.

She willed herself to lie down, then curled on her side, hugging the pillows. Pulling the quilt around her shoulders, she breathed it in. A little musty but somehow so fresh.

Mommy had slept here.

As the quilt warmed her shoulders and back, the love she had longed for from her mother's arms surrounded her. Tears held back for so long spilled out.

This was not how she had expected this day to start.

"Mom. Gamma. Grampa too. I feel you all here somehow.

Something here is so warm and comforting." She wiped her face and sat up. "Why Gamma? Why didn't you … "

Noell realized for the first time why Gamma had left this room intact. The pain had been too real. And as the years crawled on, grief grew into a formidable monster that Gamma couldn't fight by herself.

As she began to explore the room, she realized something else. Maybe this room had been preserved … for her.

For now.

She picked up a small framed photo and plunked herself back down on the bed.

Mommy.

Her nightmares were still there, slithering into her sleep, flooding her tormented nights. Mommy's face still screamed out at her, her hand still reached for her.

But this photo …

Mommy had been pretty.

Noell combed through her own hair as she noticed Mommy's long blond hair.

Her eyes. Kind. Loving. Same clear blue as her own.

Mommy's eyes in the dreams were terrified.

Mom, what did you go through that day?

She lifted her head to study the room.

Gamma … and Grampa, what did you go through that day?

Noell still had the nightmares, but her grandparents had lived with the cruel daily reality of that pain. Their daughter had drowned.

She pressed the photo to her chest as she wandered about the room, touched curtains, sniffed a bottle of perfume.

She reached the closet and paused, her hand on the doorknob.

No voices. No visuals.

Deep breath as she opened the door, not knowing if she wished it would be full or empty.

Creak.

Full.

So many revelations hit her as she explored—Gamma, to keep her own sanity, had held onto everything, so she wouldn't have to part with her memories.

Oh Gamma.

Noell gently touched each garment, releasing the fragrance of her mother. She closed her eyes, waiting for the onslaught of powerful visions and voices.

What she heard instead was laughter so melodic. Bubbles of it.

Dancing and laughter.

"You're so pretty little one."

"Look at your curls dance!"

"I love you."

Oh God.

Blinking back more tears, she slowly closed the door.

Turned into the room again. No clutter. No hoarding. Almost as simple as her own room.

She was beginning to understand Gamma even more.

While Noell had struggled with her own problems—germaphobia, nightmares—Gamma had been in such pain.

She treasured seeing this intact room and felt it was meant to be. She needed to experience her mother's things and let the voices speak to her heart.

Someday she would need to take all this down.

Just that thought was enough to make her heart hammer in her chest.

Pictures flooded her mind of the rest of the house and she gasped. Struggled to breathe. She closed her eyes.

In that moment she knew she had to face what Gamma wouldn't.

Couldn't.

She had to clean out this house and get rid of it all. Sell it.

She couldn't let it be a noose around her neck. She couldn't let it trap her and paralyze her whole life, like Gamma had.

She knew now that Gamma had been trapped by her grief, but Noell realized she couldn't let herself do that.

She had to find release and get free.

She had to sell this house. Clean it out and sell so she didn't end up the same way.

She walked to the door spurred on by those thoughts, the photo of Mommy cupped at her chest.

She could do this.

Until she saw the steps. Each step had stacks on it. Books. Magazines. Boxes.

How on earth ... ?

# THREE

Katty yawned. Good to sleep in today. She checked her phone. Wow.

Bea slept in too? It was seven o'clock and she wasn't begging for cereal and juice. Maybe she was growing up. Oh, for when Bea was sixteen and slept till noon.

Katty slipped out from under the sheet and stretched. So much she should do today.

Laundry. Always laundry.

What she really should do was work with Bea—let her practice writing her name. While she did that, Katty loved to draw. Bea always wanted to draw too—cute trees and sunshine, but Katty made her write her name several times before she turned her loose.

She glanced at all the drawings Bea had taped up in the living room, as she zipped up her hoodie.

Everywhere. Above the doorjamb. Down the legs of the kitchen table.

Well, she had taped the ones above the door. Bea had done all the rest. Tape was cheap.

She opened the refrigerator door. There was even a picture in there. Oh, so cute. A belly laugh rose up from her toes. A drawing of a cow was taped to the milk jug.

That Bea!

Katty took the milk and juice out. When had Bea done that? She left the drawing taped to the milk. Wouldn't be long till the tape got too wet, but for now—

"Mommy! Look!" Bea raced to Katty. "Look! I drew a Mommy cow and her baby! Can we go to a farm and see them?"

About a dozen paintings were scattered on the dining room table, the floor and on each chair. "How long have you been up, Bea?" She placed the milk and juice on the table.

"I just got up!"

"Right."

Katty picked up one picture and put it on the stove to dry. "Reminder. Don't turn on the burner without moving the picture." She pulled out bowls and spoons, muttering to herself. "I remember a day, not so long ago, when I started a fire doing just that and the fire department—"

"What, Mommy? Fire?"

"No Baby Bea. Just talking to myself." She poured cereal in both bowls and then the milk. "I also remember the days when we were always out of milk and cereal and you, my beautiful child had to fend for yourself."

She cupped her hands around Bea's full cheeks. "I would wake from my drunken stupor to find you eating peanut butter on stale, moldy bread." She wiped her eyes.

Bea stood up on her chair. "Mommy. You're crying. Can we have peanut butter?"

Katty hugged Bea. "So thankful, Baby. So thankful." She checked the cupboard.

"Yeah. Thankful." Bea nodded. "To Jesus. To Clarence. To the birds. To God—"

Katty burst out laughing. "Oh, I love you!" She moved some cans around and mumbled. "I don't see any peanut butter."

"I love you too, Mommy." Bea slurped her cereal. "I love peanut butter too."

"We'll have to get some, okay? Sit down and eat and I'll go out and get the mail. I forgot to get it yesterday. Be right back."

Katty peeked outside to make sure no one was outside. There had been a day also, when she wouldn't have cared, or even realized that she was outside in her pjs. She used to go to the store in these same shorties. Just roll out, grab Bea and go. She cringed, hoping people had either forgotten, or they had forgiven her.

She opened the door and stepped outside on her beautiful new wooden deck. Clarence was so generous. He had said they needed to be safe and to be honest, the old deck had been falling apart. New pots of lavender drew her, and she pinched a leaf, sniffed it as she went down the steps to the mailbox. She opened it and pulled out more than a days worth of mail, when she noticed a little red bike with a huge bow the size of a dinner plate tied around the handlebars.

She gasped. So shiny. She walked around it and patted the seat. "It's beautiful, but—"

Bea screamed from the door and ran down the steps. "Mommy! Is this for me? Did it come in the mail? How did they fit it in the mailbox? Mommy, it's beautiful!"

Katty shushed her. "It's seven o'clock in the morning." She glanced at the neighbors across the road and next door. Ugh. *He* was up. The guy next door had never done anything to them, but he still gave Katty the willies. He waved from the window. Shirtless. Ick.

"Did *he* give me this bike?" Bea pointed.

"No!" Katty shushed her again and gripped Bea's pointer finger in her hand. She lowered her voice. "No. I'm sure he would like you to think he did." She pulled at the bow, revealing an envelope.

She handed the envelope to Bea, shoved up the kickstand with her bare foot and pushed the bike to the deck. Bumping up each step, she steered it to the door.

"Mommy! *My* bike?" Bea followed her. "In the house?" She grinned. "Cool!"

Katty slammed the door. "Open the envelope Bea. See who it's from."

Bea tore it open and squealed as a ten-dollar bill floated to the floor. She held up the card for Katty to read.

"To Bea—"

"Bea! That's me! That's my bike!"

"Wait! There's more." Katty grabbed the card. "I can't read it while you're jumping up and down." She squinted. "To Bea. From your Secret Admirer." She flipped the card over and over. "Who on earth would do this?"

Bea stopped bouncing. "Clarence! He would. It's from him!" She started dancing around the bike. "Clarence would do it! Can I take it out and ride it? I rode Alexander's bike ... one day."

"You rode his bike?" Katty leaned over and looked into Bea's eyes. "After I told you not to go over there anymore?"

"Well ... only once." She brightened. "But I could ride it!" She hopped on the seat. "Can I?"

"No! We have to call Clarence first and make sure it's from him. Otherwise we don't know who did this. And if we don't know who gave it to you, then you can't ride it. Or keep it."

"What?" Bea's lower lip trembled. "The card. It said to me." She pointed to her chest. Her face crumpled and she stomped her feet.

"Bea!" Katty's hand swung but she drew it back. "Bea! Stop that right now!" She realized she had left the front door open and just her luck, a cop drove by.

God!

She slammed the door and scrambled for her phone. "I'll call

Clarence and find out." She checked the time. "Almost eight o'clock. He'll be up."

Bea hopped on the bike, almost knocking it over.

Katty steadied the bike. "Hello Clarence?"

# FOUR

Clarence Timmelsen tilted the coffee carafe toward Harold. "More?"

Harold shook his head and covered his cup. "Naw. Takes me too long to get to the bathroom. Sure is good, though. Better than down at the dining room. Theirs is like pee water."

"The very reason I make my own." Clarence filled his cup. "Coffee at prison was sludge. You didn't need a spoon to stir sugar in, you needed a concrete mixer."

Harold laughed and tipped his cup way up to get that last drop.

Old geezer. Wore his upside down American flag pin everyday. Did he have one for every shirt or did he take it out every night? Bet the nurse did it.

Clarence reached over and righted the flag.

"Bothers you, huh." Harold tucked his chin down to try and see the flag. "I do that every morning."

"What? What do you do every morning?" Clarence picked up his cup.

"I turn it upside down just to piss you off." Harold chuckled.

"I know it bothers you, so I make sure, before I leave my room, that I turn it upside down."

Clarence slammed his cup down. "Isn't there something about that in the Bible? You'll go to hell for doing that." He bounced his head up and down.

Harold choked.

"Whoa!" Clarence patted him on the back. "Don't die on me." He looked toward the hallway. "Nurse!"

Harold waved him back, laughing. "I'm fine." He blew out a breath. Chuckled again. "Thanks for telling me that."

"Telling you what?" Clarence cupped his hand around one ear.

"I don't want to go to hell." Harold laughed again. "Damn. We're like a couple old ladies. Can't hear. Can't breathe."

Clarence chuckled, too. Good to laugh these days. Good to have a friend to laugh with. Sigh.

They settled back and watched the morning traffic pass Clarence's open door in Hillcrest nursing home.

"Do you really turn it upside down every morning?" Clarence peeked at Harold.

Harold broke out laughing, slamming his hand on the desk.

Clarence wiped his eyes. Belly laughs. He coughed to clear his throat.

"Everyday we can have one more laugh is a good day." Harold nodded and glanced out at the hallway.

People in wheelchairs, either being pushed or self-mobilated, headed to the dining room for breakfast. Nurses rushed past the door with med cups or charts or bedding.

Busy. Busy.

Clarence turned to gaze out the window. The maintenance man crouched in the corner, digging in the brightly colored chrysanthemum bed. Weeding? The guy was always quietly digging somewhere. In fact, he'd been there before—digging. Clarence leaned forward and pointed. "Wha—"

"Hey!" Harold waved at someone passing by in the hall. "We should start an agency together."

Clarence swiveled in his office chair. "A what? A government agency, insurance agency? We could run one better than that bastard Pete ... Pete—"

"Pete Malovitch."

"That bastard Malovitch." Clarence shook his head. "One bad dude. Almost killed me." He leaned his head back against the headrest. "Thank God for Sheriff. That man saved my life."

"No. An agency. What if—what if we started with who we are? You're a lawyer and I'm a detective—still have my certification."

Clarence lifted his head. "You do? That's ... awesome." He leaned forward and peered at his framed law certificates. He pointed. "Those haven't expired. I renewed that just before I was kicked out of prison." He shook his head again. "You think we could really do that?"

Harold shrugged. "Why not? We ain't dead yet. People hide from life and the law in small towns. Why not in a nursing home?"

"Yeah." Clarence jutted his chin and nodded. "Why not?"

"Think of the damsels in distress we could save." Harold flicked his eyebrows up and down.

The door pushed open.

"Clarence!" Carol rushed in. Her eyes appeared red; black smudged her cheeks. She was a beautiful woman normally, but right now, something had either scared her or hurt her, and it gripped his heart.

Clarence jumped up and grabbed her shoulders. "Is Joe okay? Carol, what happened?" He searched her face. "What happened to Joe?"

"Joe's like always ... he's worse ... but it's not him." She gulped. Tears spilled from clear green eyes onto fair cheeks. "It's you, Clarence—" She pushed past him to the TV and turned it on. The screen flashed. She flipped channels and Phil Daynton and

Lex Forte's faces filled the screen, with a byline below looping their names.

Clarence pointed. "What are they doing on TV?" He leaned closer, reading. "And when did they become prison consultants?" He fumbled with the remote and volume blared. He punched it down.

The camera panned to the announcer interviewing Phil. "And Mr. Daynton, when did Mr. Timmelsen escape from Chicago prison?"

Clarence growled. "I didn't escape. Judge Green had it set up way back ... he had me kicked out."

Carol shushed him.

A photo of Clarence flashed on the screen.

Every cell in Clarence's body went rigid. His jaw dropped and he grabbed at his coffee, only to knock it over.

Carol rushed to pull paper towels, but stopped and stared at the TV.

Harold pointed. "Look! They have a picture of you, Clarence!"

Phil looked full into the camera. "He was kicked out—"

Clarence nodded. "There you see? Damn right I—"

"—by mistake. He killed a man while incarcerated."

Clarence slowly lowered himself onto his chair, his fingers massaged the scar on his cheek. "I killed ... it was self defense." He pointed at the TV. "He was going to kill me and ... and—"

The announcer had asked Phil another question.

"Oh, he'll pay all right." Phil looked straight into the camera. "A posse was sent out overnight to the nursing home to bring him in."

A small crowd had gathered behind Phil and Lex on screen and they began murmuring. "A posse?"

"Where?"

A woman right behind Lex gasped, her hand over her mouth. "He's in the nursing home? A murderer loose in a nursing home?"

Loud voices could be heard from the hall.

Clarence's phone rang and he picked it up. "Hello?" He listened for a minute. "Katty. Hi. It's crazy here right now." He pointed to the TV. "What?" He listened again. "No, Hon, I didn't give her a bike. Why?"

The voices from the hall grew closer.

"Turn on your TV. That bastard Phil Daynton and Lex Whathisname are on." He nodded. "The same. They are saying they sent a posse out for me and they're gonna take me back to prison." He leaned forward. "What? It's awfully noisy right now."

Sheriff Dennison pushed through the door, talking to someone behind him. "He's innocent. I've read his files." He stepped in front of Clarence. "You have to have papers. Authorization."

Harold set his chin. "Sheriff's here. He'll straighten things out."

A puny, dark-skinned prison guard followed through the door. Full prison uniform. Hand at his gun. Face stern. Another followed close behind, double the size. Same evil.

Clarence stiffened and backed his chair up, pulling Carol with him. Six months since he had seen a guard. Six months!

Randy Gerald followed, a brown envelope in his hand. Same guard uniform stretched over an expanding belly. His brown eyes determined.

"Randy!" Clarence dropped his phone and started toward him. Something else lurked in Randy's eyes. Frustration? Embarrassment? Yes, but something more. Randy almost growled.

"Clarence—" Randy handed the envelope to Sheriff.

Miss Oster, Administrator, flew into the room and butted in front of Randy and the guards. "I knew it! I knew it was a bad idea to let you live here, much less open your law office here." She planted her feet in front of Clarence and Carol.

"Clarence?" The phone spoke.

Clarence tightened his grip on Carol's arm. "Randy, what is all this?" He stepped in front of Carol and pushed Miss Oster aside.

The skinny guard flinched and drew his gun. The other guard followed suit.

Sheriff dropped the paperwork and drew his.

Everyone in the room immediately raised their hands in surrender, except Clarence and Randy.

The door pushed open to the tallest guy in Osceola, Nebraska and probably this side of heaven.

"Michael!" Clarence breathed a sigh of relief. Good timing, Buddy.

"Clarence. How's it going?" Michael ducked through the doorway and scanned the room. "This a party?" He slid around the guards to Clarence. "A costume party." He patted the guard's hat and tapped his gun. "Realistic. Guns look real."

The guard jumped. "Who's Michael?"

"Stand down." Randy stepped between the guards and Clarence and Sheriff.

The phone again. "Guns? Clarence, what is going on?"

Clarence bent to retrieve the phone, but the guard kicked it away.

Someone knocked, pushing the door open.

"You boys need any ... " Lisha Hall stuck her head in, surrounded by three more aides. "prune juice?"

"Eek!" An aide pointed. "They have guns!"

Randy hefted his large chest and planted his feet, pointing at his guard. "Stand down! This is a nursing home. Old people live here!"

The guards backed down and holstered their guns.

Sheriff holstered his and gathered the papers.

Clarence pointed his crooked finger at Randy. "Randy, what gives?"

"I'll take some prune juice." Michael piped up.

Harold started to stand. "I'm a detective and I'll—"

Tay pulled him up by the collar and shoved him out the door. "Detective. My eye. Shut-up old man."

"Excuse me ladies." Randy escorted Lisha and the aides out the door. He bumped into Miss Oster as he turned into the room. "Ma'am, excuse me. This is private business." He shoved her out the door.

She stomped her foot. "I am Administrator of this nursing home and I have a right—"

Randy stood firm. "I have jurisdiction here. Clarence is my prisoner."

Clarence froze. Every vein turned to ice. "P-prisoner?"

FIVE

Katty switched the phone to her other ear. "Phil? And Lex? Posse? What is going on?"

"It's awfully noisy right now." Clarence's voice sounded tense.

Someone—sounded like Harold—said, "Sheriff's here."

Katty held onto the bike. "Sheriff?"

Clarence had obviously forgotten all about her and their conversation. "Randy!" Then clunk.

Katty jerked her head up and stared at the phone. "Sounded like he dropped the phone." She put it to her ear again. "Clarence? Clarence? What is going on?"

Bea climbed off the bike. "Mommy? Clarence dropped the phone? Is he—"

"Shh, Baby." Katty checked her phone. Still connected. She slowly sat on the sofa. "Clarence?"

Voices she had never heard before. A deep voice—Michael?

"... guns ...."

Katty froze. "Guns? Clarence what is going on?"

Bea climbed onto her lap and leaned toward the phone. "Clarence? You there? He's playing with guns? I want to!"

"Shh. Bea, stop!" Katty listened again. Sounds of sliding, scraping along a surface and a bump into something.

She kept listening in spite of Bea pestering her.

"Did you ask him about the bike?" Bea slipped off her lap, almost knocking the bike over.

Katty steadied the bike, phone still at her ear. "More guns?" She stared at the phone. "At the nursing home? Oh my God!"

Bea, back on the bike, feet on the pedals, set the bike in motion, rode around the kitchen table and down the hall toward the bedrooms.

Crash!

Katty jumped up. Prune juice? "Bea? You okay?" She ran to see the damage.

She got to Bea in time to see her in the bathroom, crawling out of the toilet, splashing water onto the floor. "Bea! Are you alright?"

Bea was grinning. "I rode the bike, Mommy." She pointed. "Into the potty."

Katty put the phone to her ear. "Clarence?" She wiped her cheeks and hugged Bea. Then pulled away. Clarence's voice was shaking. Prisoner? "What? Prisoner?"

"What's a prisoner, Mommy?"

Katty tried to suck in a breath but couldn't. She blew out through her mouth.

*Breathe!*

"We've got to go!"

# SIX

Click!

Clarence stumbled. The room blurred. Breakfast oatmeal fought its way up. Cold metal encased his wrists. Handcuffs.

"Michael! Help!"

Michael just stood there beside the door, head bowed.

The guards backed away a step but kept a tight grip on his arms. "Who's Michael?"

Clarence swallowed and cleared his throat. "Randy. What the hell?" He coughed. "Randy. Why are you doing this? What did I do?"

All three—Randy and the two guards—blended together. They wore the exact same uniform: drab brown with patches on the sleeves, ball hat. Same old uniforms Clarence had stared at for the past sixty years in prison.

One guard's eyes flitted to everything in the room but Clarence. The skinny one glared, eyes boring into Clarence as if he had a personal vendetta against him. An evil amusement. Name tag: Tay Ralston.

And Randy. His voice was firm, almost sharp, but his eyes

betrayed him. Wouldn't look Clarence in the eye. He pulled out papers and unfolded them, reading, making it official, "I have been sent to retrieve one Clarence Timmelsen—"

"One Clarence Timmelsen! Randy, it's me, Clarence!" He struggled with the handcuffs. "What do you have against me?"

" ... to be brought before the Chicago State Prison Board on the matter of the death of inmate Lewis Ralston."

Something in Clarence shifted. His right cheek prickled where Lewis's knife had sliced his skin. That had been almost twenty years ago.

Clarence read the guard name tags again.

Ralston's glistening eyes glared pure evil. Something else. He had a vendetta, all right.

Clarence struggled against the guards. "He was your ... your—"

"He was my brother." Ralston grew taller. A mist enveloped him, like steam off a boiling kettle. An unmistakable sour stench filled the room.

Randy stepped between them, paper at his side, facing Ralston. "I told you if you became a problem today, no matter your relationship with Warden Ralston, I would report you." Face to face. Randy's barrel chest touched Ralston's belt. "You understand?"

Ralston didn't nod. He didn't relax. "I understand." His eyes still pierced with evil intent, voice mocking. "Sir."

Randy turned to face Clarence, still scanning the document. "The case went before the board and they determined—"

"They determined that you killed him in cold blood." Ralston finished with a squeak.

Ralston hadn't moved, but Clarence's skin crawled.

"It was self-defense. His brother was there. He saw it all." Clarence's voice rose in pitch. "They attacked *me*." He tried to point to his right cheek, but the handcuffs held. "D-Dirk was there. He saw."

"Dirk is dead."

Clarence stumbled back. The atmosphere took on an icy chill. "He's dead? Can't be!" He searched each face.

Ralston confirmed it, nodding his head, chin jutting out.

"This can't be happening." Clarence glanced at his rooms, one for the office—desk and all—and one for a bedroom.

*How had this become home?*

"Let's get going. It's a long way back to Chicago." Randy doffed his ball hat.

"But I'll need my stuff, my—"

"You'll get all prison issue again, just like before." The evil guard laughed. "Only this time, you ain't gettin' out."

"Enough." Randy pocketed the papers. "We don't know that. We have just been ordered to bring him in."

"But why didn't this come up when I was sent here? The warden didn't have a problem with it."

"There's a new warden in charge."

"In the last few months?" Anger began to boil. Clarence's old friend, rage, punched him in the gut. "He just figured this all out in the last few months?" His voice broke.

Ralston hooked Clarence's arm and towed him along. "Like the man said—let's get going."

Randy stood firm. "I have been delegated to bring you in Clarence. But be assured, you are under my care. Nothing's going to happen to you. This will be over soon."

"Oh it'll be over. I'll be back here tomorrow night."

A deep chuckle sliced through the silence. "I wouldn't count on it. If you have any hot dates, you'd better cancel them for the rest of your life because you're not go—"

"That's enough, Ralston. He'll be back here. I guarantee it." Randy opened the door. "Now let's get going. Lots of miles to drive."

Michael stepped aside.

"Michael." Clarence choked and leaned toward him.

"Who's Michael?"

Michael bowed his head. He seemed to diminish in size.

Clarence tugged at the handcuffs, looking up into Michael's face. "Michael. Why can't you help me?"

No answer.

No movement. Curly brown head still bowed.

Clarence waited.

Ralston pulled at his arm.

Randy pushed from behind.

Oatmeal threatened.

Michael looked away.

Clarence shuddered.

As they dragged him out the door, his eyes never left Michael's bowed head until the door silently swung shut.

Down the hall.

Carol hovered. "Clarence. You'll be back. You'll see." Her chin quivered.

A light touch on his back. Her touch tingled, sending a vibration through him, ending at his soul. Hit its mark.

Residents had gathered in the long hall, in the living room, on their way back to their rooms after breakfast.

"There he is." One pointed. "I knew he was no good."

"This mean our pool game is off?" No one laughed.

"Clarence ... "

No.

Mrs. Hatly. She was openly weeping, standing next to Harold. Her glasses were off, in Harold's hand. Her skinny arm reached to Clarence.

He choked and gasped a sob. And another. "Harold ... please ... "

Harold nodded. "I'll watch over her." He cleared his throat. "Until you get back."

The guards pushed him toward the door.

KATTY PLUNGED her hand into her bag, digging, throwing tissues onto the floorboards of her car. "Where are my keys?"

"Mommy?"

Out flew her make-up bag and a half-empty pack of cigarettes. "I didn't know I still had those." Out went a brush.

Bea kicked the back of Katty's seat. "Mommy?"

"Bea! Not now!"

"But—"

Katty turned in her seat, her hand swung wide to strike.

Bea, wide-eyed, opened her mouth, but no words came out. Her pointer finger slowly lifted off her leg, arm rising. Eyes still wide open. She continued to raise her arm, finger pointing above Katty's head.

Katty sputtered. "What?"

"You told me you were going to keep them in the sun shade thing, so you wouldn't loose them." Her arm straightened, finger trembling.

Katty faced the windshield and looked up. There were her keys dangling from the visor—right where she had put them.

She wiped her eyes, started the car and hesitated. She turned to Bea. "Bea. Baby. I'm sorry." She could barely reach Bea's cheek to caress it.

Bea leaned into Katty's hand and kissed it. "It's okay Mommy. You didn't hit me. You haven't in a long time. I'm proud of you."

Katty wiped her eyes again. "You. Are so good. You. My Bea." She blinked. "Now we have to go to Clarence. Guns. Prisoner."

She backed out slowly. A cop was always patrolling their little trailer court. Must live close or have a girlfriend nearby.

At the highway, they waited for three semi-trucks and five cars, one pickup. "Good grief. Hurry!"

She crossed the highway and drove into Hillcrest parking lot. A huge white van was parked out front.

She got out, released Bea's carseat straps and lifted her.

"What's that van for Mommy?" Bea pointed. "What's it say?"

"It says, 'Chicago Pri … .'" That would break Bea's heart.

"What, Mommy?"

"Umm."

---

MICHAEL STILL STOOD in Clarence's room behind the open door. He and the angels around him were the only beings there.

Awful visuals of what had just happened swarmed his mind.

"P-prisoner?" Clarence had blinked.

The guards had each grabbed Clarence's arms and stretched them behind his back.

"Agh!" Clarence grimaced and almost fell to his knees.

"Sheriff! Do something!" Carol pointed to Clarence. "They're hurting him!"

"Guys. He's eighty years old." Sheriff shook his head. Papers dropped at his side.

"Stop them!" Carol pulled at Sheriff's sleeve.

"I can't." Sheriff held up the envelope. "It's all here. I'll have to go to the office and get this cleared up." He shook his head. "But for now—"

Clarence shook his head. Arms behind his back. Eyes wild. Jaw jutting.

Michael wiped at his eyes. That moment had been the worst. Clarence's eyes.

"No! No!" Clarence had wrenched one hand free and slammed his fist into the guard's jaw. "You can't do this!" He screamed. "Michael!"

Michael flinched. His warrior buddies tightened their grip around his huge arms.

One guard popped Clarence on the head with his beat stick and wrestled his hand behind him.

Clarence had pulled loose and punched him in the chin, pushing him into the wall, knocking a couple framed pictures and law documents to the floor. Glass shattered and the balloon frame with Bea's photo in it flew apart as it hit the floor.

Michael flinched and tore at the other angels.

The three muscular angels, bigger than he, circled him, pinned him to the wall, smothered him with their fragrance. Fresh from Father.

Electric jolts zapped his body, electrifying the human skin, the whole body, until he shuddered.

Restoration. Crucial for the ever-present evil on this earth.

One angel, Zahab, blond and full of Golden Light, spoke in his ear. "My brother Michael. Listen to the voice of the Father. Go not against Him. He has a divine plan and you are a part of it. If. If you will obey and not interfere. We know not the future but can minister with the humans to bring in Father's plan. Help Clarence now by walking alongside, bringing messages to him, flowing strength from above. If he receives, all well and good. If he does not, that is not your concern."

Noises filtered in from the hallway. Gasps as people must have seen Clarence in handcuffs.

A shriek.

Mrs. Hatly. Poor precious woman. Michael didn't need supernatural powers to discern her love for Clarence.

Michael ached inside. "Father. Let me … " He shook his head. "I will not disobey. Please, Father." He wrestled his own will. Wanted to rush down the hall and throw the guards to the floor, freeing Clarence—but desperate to obey Father.

Zahab and the other angels released him. Sounds of an army preparing for battle—clattering swords and shields, horses stomping—layered over sobbing from the hallway.

The battle was on.

His sword slowly extended out of his right hand, as his

human body deferred to the angelic. A shield appeared from his left. Powerful wings unfurled from his shoulders and back.

Head still bowed, he commanded the center of the room.

As he kept his head bowed, he grew even taller, through the ceiling. Feet apart, sword and shield above his head.

His face to the heavens, he cried out, his sword pointed heavenward. A tear tracked down his rugged cheek. He bowed on one knee and pounded his right arm across his chest. "Not my will, Father."

As soon as he said it, he appeared beside Clarence.

"Gonna go with me after all?" Clarence glanced sideways at Michael. "God, I need you."

"I'm with you for the long haul, Buddy. Only this time, it's not repairing old buildings." Michael's hand hovered just above Clarence's shoulder. His brother angels surrounded them as they walked.

All except for the guard, Ralston. He had his own entourage —demons, hissing and spitting at Michael and the other angels.

Clarence shifted his shoulders. "I can't believe I'm going back." He choked.

Residents gathered in the dining room. Wheelchairs glutted the entrance. Some stood by the beverage counter, dispensing their cup of watered-down coffee.

Every manner of supernatural creature hovered, each claiming rights to its assigned human.

Gnarled demons hissed and spit as Mrs. Hatly and Harold entered the room, their angels brandishing swords on both sides.

The demons covered the eyes and ears of their charge.

Michael shook his head. If movie goers could see *this*. Made Star Wars look like a church pot luck supper.

As Clarence and his guards marched by, one woman dropped her coffee cup. It shattered, pieces scattering across the floor.

Voices buzzed. One old woman chattered loudly into her

phone and pointed. "Yes, he is. And there he goes. Back to prison where he belongs."

Michael braced for the explosion from Clarence. Clarence stared straight ahead until he saw Mrs. Hatly. His chin quivered—just barely holding it together.

A demon jumped loose from its human, wielding a jagged dagger that clanged against Michael's sword. It rotated in the air, swung its weapon, landing on one leg, the edge of otherworldly steel tight against Michael's right cheek.

Michael's angel brothers closed in, ready to restrain him if necessary.

The demon hissed and howled. He pranced about Michael, flicking his sharp talons at Michael's arms, his sword trailing about Michael's neck.

Michael didn't counter, his sword held in check.

"Ha! This angel's bound." The demon turned to the horde and roared, raising his sword. "This one's bound!" Its raucous laughter bounced off the chasms of hell, ending with a squeal.

The floor opened up revealing hideous yellow eyes in the underground flickering in excitement. All on Michael. The monsters sniffed the air, lust aroused.

The prison guards opened the way for Clarence and Randy into the reception area, unaware of the taunting and tension in the invisible realm.

"Strike him! Strike him down!" the hordes screamed.

Mrs. Hatly leaned into Harold, crying and reaching out to Clarence.

Michael edged closer to Clarence.

Connecting to Father, Michael sent a prayer. He could still help Clarence, only not interfere. One of the hardest assignments ever in eternity. His heart wanted to stuff all the guards back into their van. He'd even drive them back to Chicago—in a fiery chariot.

Clarence slowed as he neared Mrs. Hatly. His feet moved in

slow-motion. He stopped between each step, dragging the guards to a slow gait.

Ralston flicked Clarence on the ear.

His demons roared, raising their weapons in celebration. "Finish him! Now!" they roared.

Clarence flinched.

Michael flinched with him, his own ear stinging.

He turned to see a demon lowering a bow and arrow aimed for the kill. Grinning, growling, its yellow eyes poured hatred Michael's way. Brownish scales covered muscular arms and legs. The creature rose to its full height in defiance, roaring, its thick tail pounded the ground. "My master is pleased. Your human is defeated! His destiny is decided!"

Michael held his weapons in check. He trembled with righteous anger, ready if only the Father released him.

Mrs. Hatly grasped hold of Clarence's sleeve and pulled him closer. "You don't need to go. You have been freed." Tears flowed freely. "Please Mr. Michael. Please help him. Don't let them take him."

Zahab leaned in. "How does she see you?"

"I don't know. She always has." Michael nodded. "She has a pure spirit. I bet she can see Father too, she just doesn't realize it."

Ralston perused the room. "Who's this Michael? She keeps talking about Michael. I don't see anyone who can help you, Clarence." He guffawed. "Unless it's this guy with a walker."

Harold stiffened and stood taller, one arm around Mrs. Hatly, totally unaware of the invisible forces in battle. Tears ran unchecked down his wrinkled cheeks.

Michael nodded at the angels surrounding Harold and Mrs. Hatly. Shields up, they blocked darts meant for Mrs. Hatly from the enemy.

Michael leaned down to Clarence. "You'll be all right. You'll be back."

"I'll be all right Mrs. Hatly. I'll be back." Clarence struggled to break his hands free of the handcuffs.

Ralston pointed to Mrs. Hatly. "Is this your girlfriend?" He squealed and pursed his lips. His voice cracked in glee. "How touching. I'm so moved." His face was inches from Mrs. Hatly's. "He won't be back. He—"

"Enough, Ralston." Randy reached for his beat stick. "I never would have brought you if the warden hadn't insisted." He glared at Ralston. "I'm in charge here and I'm telling you to back down."

Ralston rolled his eyes and withdrew from her.

She bopped him on the head with her cane.

Ralston lunged at her, his demons rushing in, but Clarence knocked Ralston off balance, and he stumbled to the floor.

Michael started to grab Clarence's shoulders but was pushed away by a demon flying full-force at him. The demon hissed in his face and screamed, "You are bound! You can't cover him. Obey the Father!" Other demons dropped in, pinning Michael's arms.

Residents close by screamed and ducked.

One man hit Ralston with a cane. The man's angel spread his wings, covering him. Gutsy humans.

The dietary aide pushed the residents back, his arms outstretched. "Get back, or you'll get hurt." He took the cane from the old man. "Get back." The angels surrounded him and the residents.

"That's enough!" Randy pushed past, his beat stick just above Ralston's head. "Get outside! Now!"

Ralston shoved off the floor and kicked at Mrs. Hatly, narrowly missing her.

Demons laughed, darting in to stab at her.

Michael struggled to get free.

Zahab and his brothers swooped in, swords raised, searing the demons that were restraining Michael. The stench of their rotten, burning flesh choked them, their eyes watering.

The other guard pushed Ralston toward the door. "Stop! She's an old lady. Treat her with respect." He saluted Mrs. Hatly. "No offense, Ma'am."

Randy stepped in. "Enough, people!" He escorted Ralston out the door and pushed back in for Clarence and the other guard. "I never thought we'd have to use tasers in a nursing home. And on my own men. Let's go before we cause a riot!"

Michael scanned the heavens. "I think you already did." The clash of swords and shields was deafening.

Zahab and his brothers were spread thin: one taking on monsters twice their size, another rushing into the battle both arms spinning swords, severing heads and limbs.

Zahab held back, hovering over Michael and Clarence, ready to enter in as needed.

"Go!" Zahab glanced behind him. "Now is the time! Go!"

Michael pushed Clarence out the door.

Helpless.

Michael hated helpless.

*Father, Your will.*

---

SUNLIGHT BLINDED Clarence as they stepped onto the sidewalk. He blinked tears away, struggled to wipe his eyes but the handcuffs held ... along with a guard gripping each arm.

"Clarence!" No mistaking that tiny voice.

Little arms hugged his leg.

No!

Bea, followed by Katty.

He blinked again and there was her precious face upturned next to his knee.

What was this? Just like sixty years ago when he said goodbye to his dad. And Annie. The town. His whole life.

Clarence tugged at the handcuffs. "Don't let them see me like this!" His voice came ragged. Hot tears blurred his vision again.

"Clarence!" Katty's eyes darted from the guards to Randy to Michael, who had stepped out the door. Back to Ralston. Then to Clarence.

Bea bounced next to him. She didn't miss a thing either. "Why do you have handcuffs? Who are they? Where are you going? Is this a movie?"

Naked.

"Clarence. What's going on?" Katty stomped right up in front of him. Planted her feet on either side of his, blocking his way. Her wide eyes dug deep into his. "Where are you going? Who are these people?"

Ralston edged toward her, hand on his gun. "Who wants to know, baby?"

Her look could have killed thousands. Hadn't taken her long to go back to who she had been—druggie, hard woman.

Clarence growled. "Leave her alone. Leave them alone!" He struggled with the handcuffs, managed to rip one hand free and slug Ralston in the jaw.

A gun went off and Bea fell to the sidewalk.

"Bea!" Katty screamed and covered her with her own body. "Bea!"

Clarence roared. "You shot my Bea!" His other hand went for Ralston's neck, handcuff dangling, both hands squeezing.

Another gunshot.

Pain. Deep. No.

Randy dragged Clarence off Ralston. He rolled Clarence onto the concrete and pulled up his T-shirt. "Good God, no."

Clarence gasped. He lifted his head. Blood on his belly.

No.

Six months ago, yeah.

But not now.

Six months ago, he'd wanted to go to the hills and die. Six months ago, he would have done the deed himself.

"Get Ralston's gun, Anderson. Get him restrained!" Randy yelled.

A nurse ran out the door.

Clarence's eyes blurred. He reached his hand to her, handcuff bouncing off her shoulder. "Carol. Ambulance." His head dropped to the sidewalk. "Bea."

SEVEN

"She won't come over." Lex smirked into his whiskey, pushing down the ice cubes with his finger. "She's one of the elite—stalks the bars for rich old guys, hoping for a hit and a marriage." He lifted the glass and slurped his drink. "High-dollar, believe me."

Phil squinted and picked up his pen, not looking at Lex. Hardly looking at the note he'd just signed. He didn't need to. Fold it and slip it in the envelope. He'd already addressed it and stamped it. Didn't even need to look up the address. He stashed it into his pocket to be mailed later.

He wished he could be there to see Katty's face when she figured out who had sent the note. He could just imagine. She'd go all crazy with fear just like she probably had when she found the bike. He knew that face of hers. He'd caused much of that panic in her, himself. Visions of ... he almost shuddered when he thought of what he'd done to her.

This note would keep Katty in check, especially since the old man was probably on his way to prison by now. She was vulnerable, just like a naked baby bird falling out of a tree into a pack of cats. Almost made him shiver.

Now on to the business at hand.

Every part of that woman's body was delicious—from her glossy reddish-brown hair, pale shoulders to red-enameled toenails flashing from open toed heels. "She knows. She senses us." He gulped down his drink. "It's the frequencies I give off that turn her on."

Lex rolled his eyes, but Phil ignored him. He rose from the table and walked to the bar, signaling the bartender for another whiskey and whatever she was drinking.

As he walked to her, she shifted onto her other foot, her hip swaying, making her already short red dress ride up even more. She didn't tug it down.

*My kinda girl.* No need to prime the pump.

He stopped behind her. No panty line. He moaned a little too loud and she turned.

Her hair brushed his cheek as she swung around. Blue eyes questioned his and she half-smiled.

*Tease.*

He reigned in and held his eyes to hers, but worked his peripheral vision hard. Natural young curves. Mountain climbing was his best sport. Red was definitely her color.

She glanced at the drink in his hand and raised her eyebrows. She followed to his whiskey in his other hand. "Heavy drinker? Or are you meeting a date?"

"I just met her." He pushed the extra drink toward her, still keeping his eyes on hers. Women loved it when he took them seriously.

She raised up on her toes and hovered close enough for him to be able to sniff her perfume. Her chest brushed against his arm, sending tingles to his nether regions, his breathing quickening. "Really? Where is she?"

Oh, playful, huh? Something else lurked in those blue eyes and they flickered to the right just a second, almost imperceptible.

Before he could turn to check it out, she leaned in again and accepted the drink. Her long red fingernails clinked against the glass, just as an arm circled his neck from behind.

He dropped his glass and it bounced against the carpet, splashing whiskey up onto her pale legs.

She never flinched, but licked her lips and sipped the drink he had just handed her. "What's your name?"

"Phil." The arm tightened, and his voice gurgled. His eyes never left hers, even as his body was dragged backwards. He sputtered when the grip on his neck grew tighter, choking out air.

"Nice to meet you, Phil." She held the glass up in a toast. "We don't want to waste the booze now, right?" She tipped her beautiful head back and slugged the drink down.

He felt and heard a deep chuckle from whoever dragged him, until he was swung around and punched in the gut. He doubled over and bounced back against a table, then face-planted onto the floor. Drinks and popcorn slid off, sprinkling him.

When he opened his eyes, Lex's face was an inch away. Phil could almost count every whisker and pore.

"Told you she wasn't in your league." Lex tossed his head in the direction of raucous laughter.

Phil twisted and rolled to his stomach.

Lex snickered. "Rich old men, huh?" He shook his head. "That guy has got to be a prize-fighter. Look at him. Gray hair, wrinkles. He has to be eighty. But, that body. Good example of a head transplant. Wonder where the guy's real body is."

Phil rubbed his throat, coughed and sat up. Opened his mouth to comment when his phone notification went off. He struggled to get to his feet, then to a nearby chair. "It's Facebook. I have it set to alert me when Bea's mom posts anything." He snorted. "She got the bike." He laughed. "Look at this picture. My Baby Bea is sitting on the bike." He showed Lex. "She looks like a little doll on it."

Lex read the post. "How'd you do that? She'll know who you are."

Phil rubbed his neck. "I faked my picture and name. She'll never catch on."

Lex raised his eyebrows and nodded. "Yeah." His eyes lingered on the photo. "You should leave them alone. They don't deserve what you want to do." He signaled the bartender for two more drinks.

"Her momma done me wrong. She escaped and I didn't even know about the baby—Baby Bea. She hid her from me until you heard through that dealer—Harsden." He scrolled through the posts. "I might never have known I had a daughter." He stopped at a message. "Aww. Katty says here, 'What will we do without Clarence?'" Phil mimicked in a high falsetto. "What will we do without Clarence?" He tapped his phone. "Oh baby, I'll show you what to do."

Lex shook his head and laughed, handing a drink to Phil.

The beauty and her fake boyfriend slipped past them. The old man shoved his arm behind his back, a certain finger waving at them.

Phil stood up and adjusted his jeans. The door closed behind the couple and he clinked glasses with Lex. "Clarence is getting tucked away in prison just in time."

EIGHT

August skies were so beautiful. The clouds were huge, white fluffy blobs floating against that startling blue—the most beautiful blue Clarence had ever seen.

Tears slid down the sides of his face as he was carried, or rather jostled, to the van.

"Get the first-aide kit." Randy clicked the key fob and unlocked the vehicle. "Warden will kill me if Clarence dies now."

Clarence almost laughed at that. Someone else's life depended on him living.

Another guard pushed open the doors from inside and stepped to the ground. The guy with the goatee looked familiar. But the other guy—that awful red patch would be unforgettable. Angry red thing sucked into the whole left side of the guy's face. Clarence remembered his own clenched hands. Same red ropey scars—now with a little fresh blood. Maybe it wasn't a birthmark.

"Here. Get him in the van and lay him down." They lifted him onto the seat and strapped him in.

God it hurt. Clarence had been knifed, beaten, gored with a screwdriver, and penetrated in every other way, but seeing Bea fall, knowing she had been shot, hurt just as much as losing

Annie. Tears brimmed, but he would not let them see how badly he hurt and feared for her life.

"Really?" Randy unhooked the straps. "You think he's gonna escape with a gunshot wound?"

"We were warned." Goatee Man climbed in and sat on the bench seat across from Clarence. "They say he's as strong as an ox."

How Clarence wanted to lash out. The nursing home had relaxed him, softened him. But self-preservation kicked in. Not crying. Not opening his mouth. Rage boiled. Either he would break out and escape—get back to Bea and Katty, Mrs. Hatly—or he'd die trying.

Goatee Man, the name on his shirt read Ralph—but Goatee Man fit him better, clicked Clarence's handcuffs to an armrest bar. "Seems he can fight his way out of any handhold." He turned to Randy. "Killed one of the baddest guys on the cellblock." He sat beside Scar Man.

The back door opened behind Clarence and a struggle ensued. Grunts and scuffles.

"You, my man, are in deep trouble." Randy growled. "If Warden wasn't your brother, you'd be fired." Seemed Randy had changed. The real Randy was hopefully still there, layered under this gruff, growling man. "Gimme that!"

"Not my gun. My brother gave—"

The back door slammed on Ralston's words.

Randy opened the side door, checked Ralston's gun and stowed it in the waistband of his own pants. "Baby Tay won't ever be fired. He's got a job for life."

Tay Ralston kicked the back of the seat Clarence was on. His foot dug into Clarence's back—must have just fit between the back of the seat and the bench. Figured. His whiny voice sounded like a string of prayer words Mrs. Hartsen prayed at the nursing home, only Tay's words weren't prayers.

Randy crawled in beside Clarence. His belly was even bigger than Clarence remembered.

Clarence tried to reach toward him, but the handcuffs stopped him. "Randy. Get help for Bea." His voice sounded gravelly and strained. His hand fluttered like Mrs. Hatly's.

Oh, Mrs. Hatly.

A sob tried to burst from his throat but he swallowed it back down.

"That nurse called 911. I heard her." Randy pulled up Clarence's shirt. "Damn." He opened the first aide kit and stirred the contents. "Poor excuse for a first aide kit. Not much left." He dug until he found tape and bandages. "Clarence, it wasn't supposed to go this way. We were told to bring you back. That's all."

Funny, the wound didn't hurt that bad now. When he was shot it had, but not now. Must be a flesh wound.

How was Bea?

Then pain hit inside his belly, like a punch to the gut. Groaning, Clarence doubled over. Didn't help that Randy was pressing tape onto the bandage to his skin.

"Blood inside your gut hurts bad." Goatee Man talked like he knew. "It's meant to be inside your veins. That's the point of all our blood vessels." He rubbed the back of his hand and sat back in his seat. "It'll get better once it dissipates."

Clarence gasped. The pain was sharp and almost made him nauseous. He looked around on the floor. *Breathe.* Felt like he could fill somebody's boot.

The van rocked as Randy stepped out.

Heavy van.

Heavy man. Randy slammed the side door shut and climbed into the drivers seat.

"Timmelsen. You look green." Goatee Man scooted his feet out of the way, against the van door.

"Oh no." Scar Face glanced under the seat. "No bucket." Behind the seat. "Nothing."

Ralston kicked the back of Clarence's seat, giggling.

*Breathe!* He would not puke here. Suck it down. He swallowed. Belched. Tasted the vile stuff that wanted to come up. Swallowed again. His face burned, mouth watered. The guards eyes bored into him—Randy's too through the rearview mirror.

"We'll get you to the infirmary just as soon as we get back to prison." Randy inserted the key and started the van, put it in gear. "Keep a lid on it."

And it all came up. All over the guards—Scar Face and Goatee Man.

The van lurched as Randy stomped on the brake.

"Ha ha!" Ralston kicked the seat. "Good shot."

Goatee Man opened the van door, hands spread wide, away from his dripping clothes and ran into Hillcrest. Back in the van with towels and wipes—staples in a nursing home—he and Scar Man mopped themselves and the seat, the floor. "Dude! This stinks!"

Clarence's eyes stung. His throat burned. He tried to wipe his mouth only the handcuffs wouldn't let him reach. He looked down at his T-shirt. He had missed his own clothes and hit everyone else. Good thing. His shirt seeped blood again.

Randy pulled out of Hillcrest Homes parking lot and turned onto the street.

Clarence strained to see Bea, Katty. Carol.

Anybody.

*God help them.*

It had only been a couple months or so since being transported *to* Hillcrest Homes. Kids waited in line for the school bus —backpacks loaded, bright new shoes—as the van drove past. The swimming pool was closed after a hot summer.

He squirmed in his seat—every time he moved, blood seeped. He might bleed out before they reached Des Moines.

Different van—not the old musty, cigarette smell. New car smell ... and now ... he'd baptized it well.

Randy was the same guard that had driven him from the Chicago prison to Osceola, Nebraska. The other guards were a new addition. Did the new warden think he'd bulked up at Hillcrest Homes? All that ice cream.

Goatee Man leaned forward. Click!

Scar Man snapped the others. Click!

Shackles.

Clarence sighed. Tears threatened again.

Randy glanced over his shoulder and he caught Clarence's eyes.

"Warden ordered shackles." Randy turned onto the highway. "Not my doing."

Ralston tapped Clarence on the shoulder from behind and snickered. "Cozy, huh, Clarence?" He dragged cold hard metal around Clarence's shoulders. Click!

Clarence jumped.

Ralston must have cocked the gun. "Real cozy." Ralston's whiney voice.

Cold sweat ran down Clarence's back. He shivered.

So much had changed.

He'd changed.

He did not want to die. He didn't want to go back to prison.

Goatee Man braced himself against the seat. "Knock it off, Ralston. Holster the gun!"

Randy swerved. "He has *another* gun?" He pulled over at Terry's Dive Inn and hoisted his bulk around in the seat. "Ralston!"

His booming voice hit Clarence like a sledge hammer.

"I'll put *you* in shackles next!" Randy shook his finger. "You are on detention. Holster the gun!"

Ralston slid the gun from around Clarence's shoulders, down his arm, and into his side. Lingered there.

It had been a long time since the hard muzzle of a gun was aimed at Clarence, much less stuck in his side. His thin T-shirt was no protection from the cold metal. He held his breath. In a short second, it'd all be over. Wouldn't even matter that the first gun wound was bleeding around the bandage.

When Randy had transported him to Osceola, he'd just wanted to find a hill and die. But now, faces flooded his mind: Bea, Katty, Mrs. Hatly, Harold, Carol—

"HOLSTER!" Randy roared.

Ralston slid his gun into his holster. Snapped it in and whispered, "I'm keeping my hand right where I can reach it, Clarence."

"I see your lips moving, Ralston!" Randy didn't miss a thing.

After spending time with little Bea, that precious four-year-old girl, Clarence had realized what purity was. Yeah, she got ornery. What kid didn't? But her heart. Clarence could almost smell her sweetness.

Here, Ralston oozed evil.

Clarence blinked.

It had a distinct stench ... like sweaty, oily, filthy socks. Or worse.

Blatant difference between Bea and Ralston. Never had Clarence seen good and evil so clearly. So glaring.

Thinking back on his sixty years in prison, he realized he had accepted the gray between good and evil. Prison lived by its own standards, and those standards sat just this side of evil.

A powerful silence hovered between Ralston's last threat and Clarence's next breath.

Clarence cleared his throat. "Why am I being taken back to prison?" He leaned forward, stopped by the seatbelt and Goatee Man's hand on his shoulder. "Randy!"

Randy swerved back onto the highway and took a deep breath. He adjusted the rear-view mirror and looked Clarence in the eye. "We were told to come get you, not why. They will fill you in when we get back to Chicago."

"But—"

"Sit back or I'll stick my gun in your side again." Cold metal against his neck gave him goosebumps.

"Ralston!" Randy swerved off the highway again, came to a stop on a side street. "Get his gun and shackle him. Now!"

Goatee Man and Scar Face jumped up and opened the side doors.

Rear doors burst open.

"Gotta be handcuffs. This back seat doesn't have shackles."

Clarence guessed by the scuffle behind him that Ralston wasn't giving in easily until metal clicked on metal.

Doors slammed.

They jumped back in and Randy pulled away, leaving Scar Face to pull the doors shut.

"I am a lawyer and I know my rights!" Clarence cleared his throat. "This is pure harassment and I don't have to take this! Sending me to Hillcrest Homes was set up by the judge back then. You know that! That's by a court of law!" They didn't need to know he hated Judge Green who had set it all up.

Randy gunned the engine, head and eyes forward. "All I know, is that we were directed to bring you back."

Emphasis on the word directed. Like he didn't have a choice.

Clarence shook his head. Like *he* had a choice. He looked down at the shackles. The guards in front of him vibrated—ready to pounce at the first chance. Maybe Clarence should give them cause.

"I don't want to go back!"

Randy slumped. "I have no choice. It was go get you, or my job. I have three kids in college now."

"What is the just cause?"

Ralston snickered. "We don't need just cause." He lowered his voice so just Clarence could hear—maybe Scar Face could hear too. "Warden has the prison all wrapped up. The last warden was a loser. This guy's sharp. You'll like him. He don't put up with no crap." He hissed in Clarence's ear. "He pays real good, too."

"You mean, he's bought and paid for." Clarence shivered.

Ralston laughed. "Oh he's paid for all right. And so are the rest of us ... or most of us." He snickered. "Remember Will? My other brother? Not the one you killed."

Clarence froze. He stopped breathing. His chest felt as if Will was still standing on it like he had ... what thirty years ago? That had been the fight of his life. Or one of them. His right cheek prickled where Will had sliced him.

No! When he had walked out of prison back then, Will had still been incarcerated, still angry, even flipped him off, but he had been locked up.

"He's like family to me, the warden." Ralston giggled like an excited girl just about to dance her first dance. "Oh, wait!" He leaned forward. "He *is* my family. He *is* the warden."

Randy yelled from the front, "Ralston, I swear, knock it off!"

Ralston released his seatbelt and leaned into Clarence, his face just within Clarence's peripheral line of sight, his gun out of Randy's line of sight. "See, when you beat Will up back then, it kinda ticked him off. So he got word to the outside—to Daddy—and well, it's all history. Daddy is a big-time lawyer ... even bigger than you, Clarence. And he got Will the warden's job." Ralston's black eyes got big. "I only hope that the old warden is okay." He grinned. "He was never heard from again."

Goatee Man laughed. "He was heard from, but not like in a letter or email."

Ralston snorted. "Well, right. He was heard from ... like in a humble apology ... from a hospital." He clucked. "He'll never walk again. Too bad. He had a nice wife and some grandkids, I think." He tapped Clarence's shoulder with the gun. "Oh, and you are gonna get reunited with some old friends of yours, too. What were their names? Yeah. Phil was one. I think Lex was the other.

They kinda have a bone to pick with you, too. Seems you made some enemies along the way."

Clarence met eyes with Randy in the mirror. For a spit second, was there a grimace? Remorse?

Clarence's fingers went cold and numb. Hard to breathe. The smell of his own blood, compounded with Ralston's stench, sickened him.

Where was Michael? Why wasn't he doing some angel thing —like taking this guard that shot Bea down or helping Clarence escape before they reached the prison?

Goatee Man grinned.

Ralston popped him on the head with the gun. "Oh, you're gonna like the changes they've made."

## NINE

Noell shivered. The walk to Hillcrest Nursing Home wasn't far—just a couple blocks—and it was still summer, technically, even though school buses had been dropping off kids at the corner for a few weeks now. The kids always looked so tired as they walked home. Book bags. Homework. One kid always carried his trumpet case too.

She knew trumpet cases. She had begged to play, knowing Grampa would never deny her anything that was legal. But her band teacher only had a seat available for a flute. He had a whole row of trumpet students and only one flute player. Even saxophone would have been good but there were five—in a middle school band of thirty. Flute would have been just okay, except for the fact that the one and only flutist was Mary Jane Brixton, their papergirl, who one day when the newspaper had gotten lost, glimpsed a peek into Noell's world and home. Never would she sit next to someone for a whole period who knew some of Gamma's hoarding secrets.

She had loved school at first. People must have been nice to her right after Mommy drowned, because she remembered moments when the kindness of people overruled the bullies. Her kindergarten teacher, Mrs. Townsend, always had a hug for her and a "you can do this" when she helped Noell with her coat. She must have lost her mom young, too.

But once Noell entered middle school, things changed. She was different from the other small town kids. She didn't have a mom, or dad. Gamma tried to be the mom who baked treats for the class or invited little friends over after school, but once their mom picked them up at the door and saw the ceiling-high clutter, they didn't let their child come back. The one-and-only mom that did let her daughter come back made it clear that the girls would play outside or just in Noell's room where clutter was against Noell's rules.

In high school, students treated her just like every other classmate, except when it came to social time. They never invited her anywhere. No mother pushed her child to include her in anything.

The Peters and Pauls at churches must have thought she needed saving because they were all over her—inviting her to youth conferences and hayrack rides. She had gone on one hayrack ride. Never again. Those sweet Christian kids were vulgar and crude.

Startled, she realized she was almost at Hillcrest. Why had she gone back to those awful memories?

Clarence would be able to help her sell the house. He was almost becoming that Grampa she missed so much—someone she could talk to, confide in. When he hugged her, she felt like she had been snuggled in a warm blanket on his lap. Just like Grampa.

Sigh.

Strange though, that she was so shivery today. She rubbed her shoulders and arms. Should have worn a hoodie. The sun was out and there was no breeze. But goosebumps popped up on her arms. No time to get sick.

Mrs. Carton stood outside the dining room door at the

nursing home, smoking a cigarette. Ick. She looked to be more than a hundred years old, instead of eighty or however old she was. Amazing she was still alive after smoking all her life. She said it calmed her, when her neighbors drove her crazy. The woman half smiled as she blew smoke and gave a wave with the fingers not holding the cigarette, then flicked the ash into the bushes.

Ick.

Noell stepped up on the curb, just as a deputy and the sheriff pushed open the front door from inside. They barely nodded to her, then stooped to examine something on the sidewalk in front of the entrance.

As she walked past, they wiped up something with a rag. When they lifted the cloth, it was dark red. They quickly hid it.

Too late.

Someone must have fallen on the sidewalk and the home had to report it according to policy. It broke her heart to see the elderly age and go through trials. Disease, handicaps, injuries robbed them of these sweet years. Hope it wasn't Mrs. Hatly.

As she opened the entrance door, sounds of people sobbing and screaming pierced her like a bolt of lightning. Her mind exploded with visuals of guards overlaid with pictures of evil mist, like a trailer of the newest horror movie.

Noell hadn't done that in a long time. She had been so distracted with whatever the Sheriff and Deputy had been wiping off the sidewalk, that when her skin had come in contact with the metal door handle, she had forgotten to protect herself.

Pictures popped in and out of her mind. Faces. Homes. Restaurants. Animals. Layer on top of layer. Chaos of people and their lives, the horror, the good times and bad. The noise was deafening.

Goosebumps tracked down her right leg. Involuntary shivers.

From just one door handle. Multiply that one handle times millions of people—day-after-day, over many years.

She quickly slid between the door jam and the door, as it closed.

Inside Hillcrest, the noise and chaos continued, only it wasn't her visions. This was real. Curiosity overcame her need to run back home.

What was going on?

Nurses flurried in and out of the office. People stood with their walkers or sitting in wheelchairs down both sides of the hallways, as if a parade had just gone by—the most heart-warming parade, even to the point of affecting them to tears. One woman in a wheelchair blew her nose.

Harold. He'd fill her in. Where was Mrs. Hatly? Mrs. Monson was sobbing and mumbling something about a little girl dying.

What?

Noell tried to catch someone's eye as she passed them, but they seemed deep in conversation, so she hurried to the nurses' station.

Carol was charting, writing almost frantically. She glanced up at Noell, grimaced in recognition. Her chin quivered and she wiped her swollen eyes. Other nurses busied themselves with meds. Lisha leaned in a corner, sobbing.

What the?

Noell walked on down the hall to Clarence's room.

Residents in the neighboring rooms either hid with their backs to anyone passing their doorway, or one or two babbled, pointing, shaking.

Confusion.

As she passed Mr. Harold's room, all he did was look up at her and nod. His eyes appeared to be watering. He wiped them with one hand, eyeglasses hanging from the fingers of his free hand. He raised his eyebrows and shook his head.

What?

He cleared his throat and attempted to speak, then shook his head again. He motioned and pointed toward Clarence's room.

She walked to 204 and knocked on the door jam.

No one hollered, "Come on in!"

As she stepped inside his room, something crunched under her shoe. Shattered glass. All over the floor. Pictures had fallen, or been knocked off the wall and frames were broken apart on the floor. She picked two up—one was his law certificate and the other was the photo of Bea. The decorative frame had broken—red, blue and green balloons scattered on the floor.

*Oh my God.* Tears filled her own eyes.

On the desk, Clarence's cup was tipped on its side. Coffee stained the newspaper and other papers underneath.

She pulled a string of paper towels out of the dispenser above the sink and mopped up the coffee.

A visual of the deputies out front, wiping what seemed to be blood from the sidewalk popped into her mind, as she soaked up the coffee on Clarence's desk. She lifted the paper towels, and the coffee stains merged with her memory of the blood on the cloth in the Sheriff's hand. "Oh my goodness."

"C-Carol?" Noell glanced down at the broken glass again. "Carol? Lisha?" She felt gut-punched. Her heart pounded in her chest as she ran out the doorway and down the hall to the nurses station.

Carol bumped into her at the entrance. Lisha was still crying, only now she was standing and wiping her face with her brown hands.

Carol took one look at Noell's face and the paper towels in her hands and drew her into the station. She sat her down at the desk and pulled up a side chair, wiping her own face. Then took Noell's hands in her own. "I know you have become good friends with Clarence, so ... there's something I need to tell you."

Lisha's sobs erupted again from behind Noell. She squeezed between the back of Noell's chair and the counter and started to leave the nurses station but stopped and cleared her throat.

Noell swiveled toward her in the chair, Carol's hands still on hers.

"I know I had my problems with dat man." She blew her nose and wiped it. "But I love him. See, he and I are alike. Stubborn." She swallowed, pointing her finger at her chest. "Angry. I gits him." She turned into the hall, but rotated back to face them. "That man'll die in prison. He is strong, I know. But he is old and they will kill him." She walked away, another aide's arm around her shoulder, side-by-side.

"A-hem!" The administrator stepped into their line of vision, hands on her hips.

"Screw privacy regulations right now!" Carol stood her ground.

Noell blinked. "P-Prison?" She turned back to Carol and checked her eyes, then glanced back at the administrator. "Lisha ... said prison." One-by-one, the med nurses scooted out and left Carol and Noell alone. Even the hovering administrator left. "What did she mean?"

Carol bit her lip, her wide eyes brimming.

Noell's own eyes filled. "And there's blood out front. When I walked up the sidewalk, two deputies were wiping up what looked like blood. And at the door handle ... " She caught herself before saying too much.

Carol sucked in a breath and blew it out. "This morning Sheriff called me and said the prison where Clarence used to live had put out a warrant for his arrest, to bring him back."

"But—"

Carol shook her head. "I know. He doesn't belong in prison." She blinked. "Guards—they must have driven all night—almost immediately came in and handcuffed him and dragged him out. One guard was awful—ranting about Clarence killing his brother —waving his gun."

"Gun?" Noell's mouth dropped open. "Here?" She pointed down the hall. "With all these people?"

Carol nodded and swallowed. "They got him outside and Clarence was fighting them all the way. He hit that guard in the mouth and knocked him against the wall in his room. His pictures are all broken."

Noell nodded. Her hands shook, still holding the paper towels.

"Anyway, when they got outside, Katty and Bea had just driven up and ... there was a scuffle and the guard shot Bea."

Noell shrieked. "Bea!" She pulled her hands away.

Carol caught them, threw the paper towels away and gripped Noell's hands tighter. "Clarence went crazy. Slugged the guard." She broke down. A sob escaped, but she got control. "And the guard shot Clarence!"

"Oh God!" Noell slipped her hands from Carol's, her fists covering her mouth. "Clarence." Noell jumped up. "We have to ... " She sat back down. "Where's Bea? We have to get Clarence back. Is he ok?" Her hands gripped the armrests. "Oh God!"

Carol placed her hands on Noell's shoulders, her face inches from Noell's. Her beautiful green eyes swollen and red. "We have to pray—that somehow this is all a mistake and he'll come right back to us. That Clarence and Bea will heal and be ok." She shrugged. "We have to pray."

Noell nodded, coming to her senses. "God ... help."

The phone rang and she jumped.

Carol picked it up. "Hillcrest. This is Carol." She listened then curved into the phone. "Okay." She nodded and reached for Noell's hands again, her face toward Noell's. "Bea is going into surgery right now."

Noell's face crinkled. "Oh, God."

Carol pushed a finger at her. "Hang on." Into the phone, "What? Okay. I know. We're fine here."

Lisha sobbed behind them. "We're *not* fine. We need a posse, or sumpthin. Is that Sheriff?" She reached for the phone. "Gimme that. We need to go get Clarence!"

Carol pushed her away and spoke into the phone. "No. She won't. But that's what we all want to do." She straightened. "Call the governor?" She glanced at Noell, then Lisha. "It's a start. But there's got to be something more. I know." She closed her eyes while listening, nodded, tears streaming down her cheeks. "I ... Thanks. Bye." She turned her face away and blew out a breath, wiping her eyes.

Noell stood. Hesitated.

Carol came to and stood with her. "I don't know how." She reached for her hands, feet on either side of Noell's, her body almost curving into Noell's. "And I don't know when. But I know he'll be back." She reached one hand to Lisha, gripping hers, too. "He might have to go through some things. That guard was evil." Her eyes darted from Noell to Lisha and back. "But the other one —Randy, I think—is good." She tried to smile, but it only brought more tears to her eyes. "Clarence has been through a lot, and he is strong. He will be okay."

An aide rushed up. "I'm sorry, Carol, but it's Mrs. Hatly. She's in distress. I ... I've never seen her like this."

Carol nodded, dropped Noell and Lisha's hands and pulled her stethoscope from around her neck.

To Noell, "Go to Katty." She paused. "She needs you now."

## TEN

Katty watched as two nurses in scrubs guided the gurney through the double doors marked surgery. A white sheet covered Bea's tiny body.

Katty hugged the teddy bear to her chest, wishing she was hugging Bea.

When a volunteer had tucked a soft, pink teddy beside Bea, the woman looked up at Katty and had slipped her one too. Katty's was exactly the same as Bea's only a smaller version.

"Look Mommy. They're the same." Bea had compared them. "Same eyes. Same color."

Then she had been hit with a spasm of pain and blacked out.

Katty wiped her face. So many thoughts raced through her mind. Thankful she was off drugs, so she could really be here for Bea.

A random thought—where was Clarence?

Back to Bea. Horrible to see her in pain. Would she be ok? Would she live? Where was Clarence? He was always with her, ready with advice or hugs or ... love.

Tears started again. She blew out a breath and ducked away

from a Housekeeping lady. Must be strong. Must keep the stiff upper lip.

"God, she looks tiny." Katty unconsciously followed the gurney, step by step, even after reading the painted sign on the doors. "No Admittance Beyond This Point."

A nurse spotted her and met her at the double doors. "Honey, is there anybody with you? To keep you company?" She gently shook her head, her wide brown eyes concerned. "Because you can't come in here." She glanced behind her at Bea. "I'll take good care of her—just like she was my own."

Katty could only nod and watch the nurse walk away.

The doors began to close when the nurse did an about-face. She quickly slid between them and grabbed Katty in a bear hug. "She's gonna be all right. We pray for healing in Jesus' name." The woman let out a sob but staunched it.

Katty gasped and held on like the two had become one. "Oh, God. Help." She burrowed her face into the woman's neck and shoulder.

The double doors opened again. "Beth?" The nurse hesitated. Her eyebrows slowly pinched together. Eyes filled and she took two steps toward them, her arms open wide and enveloped them both. "Baby. She's gonna be okay."

Nurse hug—Oreo style. The nurses were the strong, outside cookies and Katty was the sweet, soft center. She could hardly breathe, but didn't want them to let her go.

She swallowed when they finally did. "Th-thanks." She held in the emotion so hard, her head and throat hurt.

They slowly let her go and without a word, stepped to the doors, pushed the open button and walked through.

Katty could still feel them against her skin, pressing into her back, her arms. Fragrance of sweet woman and antibacterial soap lingered on her skin, swirled around her. Almost tangible.

She blinked.

Had she really seen ... ? For a split second, a ring of creatures? beings? surrounded her.

She blinked again. Must have been the soap smell, the stress.

The doors closed, but Katty didn't move. She scratched the teddy bear ears. Her feet were planted till they wheeled Bea out again.

Until someone gently touched her back.

Katty didn't turn, but Noell peeked from around her back. Her blue eyes were wide, eyebrows raised slightly, mouth parted. Not smiling, but face open. She continued to touch Katty's back.

Katty blinked. As Noell continued to caress her back, gentle tingles raced across her skin. She shivered.

*Oh God. Can't break down.*

Noell tipped her head toward the hall behind them. "You want to go sit down? I think they have coffee."

Katty hesitated and shook her head. If she didn't move, then maybe Bea would come back through those swinging doors. If she—

"Or we can stay right here." Noell nodded, glancing up and down the hallway.

Katty sighed. Turning her back on the double doors felt so wrong, like she was turning her back on Bea.

"I'm sure they'll keep you informed about her."

A receptionist close by nodded. "We sure will." She patted the phone beside her and smiled. "We have a direct line, but usually someone comes out. In person."

Deep sigh. "Sure. Let's sit."

A loud group of four commanded the small waiting room. They were laughing and eating, playing cards. One was chasing a small bouncy ball. He retrieved it and bounced it so high, it hit the ceiling and they all laughed again. They stopped and looked straight at Noell and Katty.

"Uh ... " Noell smiled. "Hello."

One woman smiled. The others sat down on a row of chairs against the wall.

Noell stuck her head in another room and motioned for Katty to follow.

This smaller room was unoccupied. The sun was warm and welcoming through long windows. Four chairs circled a small table. Two more chairs filled a corner.

Noell shrugged. "Here okay?"

The other people could still be heard, but the receptionist desk and hallway created a buffer.

Katty sat. "Thanks Noell." She rubbed Teddy's ears again.

"The hospital give you that?" Noell pointed to Teddy.

Katty held it out and nodded. She retied the flowery bow and swallowed. "Bea has one too, only bigger." She fiddled with one ear, then hugged it. "What if this is all I have to—"

"She'll be fine, Katty." Noell reached for her hand. "Such tiny fingers."

Katty watched as Noell caressed each finger, outlining each one with her own, like her finger was a pencil and she was going to make a Thanksgiving turkey picture.

A thought blinked in—a neighbor had faithfully taken her, as a child, to Sunday School and they had made the turkeys in class. That had been the first time Katty could remember that someone's touch could be sweet and comforting, rather than painful and bruising.

"You had a grandma, didn't you? Did she do this with your fingers?" said Katty. Oh, she hoped so. With everything she had been through, she hoped some little girl had experienced this soft touch.

Noell nodded, her eyes misty. She glanced down at their fingers, clasped together.

"I'm sorry. She just died, didn't she?"

Noell flinched. But nodded.

"I'm sorry." Katty gripped Noell's fingers. "I didn't mean that to sound so ... I'm not used to being ... and talking ... I'm not sweet like you."

Noell stared, wide-eyed. "Who raised you? Did you have a mom? A dad?"

Katty nodded. "Yeah ... yeah." What could she say to this beautiful, sweet person?

"You know, I have to use the restroom." She stood and faced Noell. "I'll be fine and I'm sure you have stuff to do." She shrugged. "They say she'll be fine, so you don't have to wait."

"Oh. Okay." Noell glanced at the exit door. "Are you sure?"

Poor Noell wanted out anyway. She would never be back. Even though she was a friend of Clarence's. They were too far apart—too different to even be kind-of friends.

"Yeah. I'm sure. I'll ... just go to the bathroom and then I'm sure they'll be done." She started down the hall, toward the nurses station and looked behind her at Noell and waved.

Poor girl. She probably wasn't used to being snubbed or lonely.

Katty spied a housekeeper. "Can you tell me where the restrooms are?"

The woman dumped the contents from a trash can into her cart dumpster and pointed down the hall. "Last door on your left."

"Thanks." Katty let her peripheral tell her if Noell had left. The chair was empty. She knew she might have hurt Noell's feelings but Katty never had a friend that stuck. She'd always hidden her family and life away from the world. Anytime kids or neighbors had tried to pry or get close, she closed—no slammed—the door on them. Same thing now.

If you didn't allow people in, you didn't get hurt.

But somehow, she had let that jerk Phil in. She had thought he was rescuing her from her abusive home life, but instead, he had opened up a whole new dimension of abuse. Visuals flashed before she could stop them. She found the bathroom and closed the door softly and locked it. She leaned against the door, shaking her head. Would not cry.

She had trained herself well. No crying. Her mom could punch her hard in the ear, right before they entered the principal's office, and Noell would enter the room like a queen waltzing to her throne. Mama knew where to throw a punch so it never showed, unless you had x-ray vision. One little old neighbor lady could always tell when Katty was having a bad day. She'd invite her for cookies on her porch. Katty would go, but learned to hide so her mom wouldn't see her when she drove past on her way home from work.

She stared at herself in the mirror. Truth. It was a miracle she was alive. Another truth. It was a miracle Bea was still alive.

Oh-oh. The face in the mirror was soundlessly sobbing. Katty watched as if the face was someone in a movie and not ... her. The face was red, wet. Eyes swollen. Mouth scrunched up. Snot everywhere. Ugly. Ugly.

She rushed to use the toilet but threw up instead.

*Oh God.*

She leaned over the sink.

*Breathe.*

She washed her hands and face, then slipped into the hallway.

Surely they would be out from surgery by now. She'd better get back.

The noisy bunch were now playing cards. Still noisy.

She peeked around the receptionist desk. Noell's chair was still empty.

Funny. She'd sent Noell away, but ... reality. She wished she'd stayed. Katty wished Noell had been rude back to her and told her to take a hike—that she'd never leave. That she'd be there through thick or thin, through every bad word, every hurt, every joy. Who'd tell her to shut up when she was being stupid.

Katty needed a friend like that.

Nurses smiled at her. She knew what they were thinking. *Poor girl. What a bad mom. Your daughter got shot. She needs a new mom.*

She tapped her phone. Maybe Clarence had called or texted. Where was he? In all the scuffle, she hadn't seen where they had taken him. Sheriff had scooped Bea up and they all jumped in his squad car and rushed to the hospital.

No texts.

*God.* Don't cry. Keep it in. Don't look up when someone walks by.

Like now.

Oh no. The person sat down. Right beside her. And pushed a steaming cup-to-go under her nose.

Katty peeked up.

Noell.

# ELEVEN

Clarence moaned. Something was wrong. Something was off. Lisha must have given him the wrong meds.

Wait.

He never took any pills. He tried to roll over in his bed but something literally punched him in the gut. He must have gotten out of bed in the middle of the night and run into a chair or stumbled into—

"I think he's comin' round."

Something cold and hard touched his ear.

This wasn't the nursing home.

He opened his eyes.

A van. Not just any van—a prison van. Randy was driving. Goat Man was snoozing on the bench seat facing him, and Scar Face sat beside Goat Man, eyes on Clarence.

Clarence floated somewhere between knowing he was in some sort of horrible nightmare and the reality he saw before him.

It all rushed back. He must have been dreaming. He looked at where his hands had been resting. Dried blood.

A cold, hard object slammed into his left ear. Again.

"Ralston!" Randy yelled from the drivers seat. "I told you to holster your gun. Now!"

Ralston tapped him again from behind.

Cold hard steel against his temple. He held his breath. There had been many moments like this in prison: another inmate had him in a vise grip—an arm choked around his neck from behind, or three inmates closed in on him in a shower, each one wielding some sort of homemade weapon. Every time, Clarence had remembered that life was precious and could end in a second.

"Ralston!" Randy yelled, making Goat Man jump awake. "Guys! I don't care if he is a guard and that he's Warden's baby brother. Keep Ralston in check! Got it?"

Goat Man and Scar Face nodded and leaned forward, seeming to invite combat with Ralston. Welcoming it. "How the hell did you get out of cuffs?'

Ralston snickered. "Always hated begin skinny as a kid. Not anymore."

Goat Man shook his head. "You are a dork."

"Got it?" Ralston chuckled and tapped Clarence on the ear again. "Just so we're clear."

Clarence clamped his mouth shut. *This* should have been the bad dream, the nightmare.

And Lisha giving him meds should have been reality. He never thought he'd want to go back to the nursing home. When he was kicked out of prison more than a couple months ago, he'd wanted to go back to prison, but now that he was, he was terrified. Terrified of prison, when it had been his home for sixty years. Didn't make sense, except that he'd learned a whole new life at Hillcrest, in just a few months.

And right now, this very moment, he wasn't sure he'd ever make it back to Hillcrest alive. This moment felt like his last; no more Bea or Katty or Noell. No more Mrs. Hatly.

His heart lurched. He hadn't realized how much—

"Stopping for gas and pee break." Randy flipped the blinker on and turned into a truck stop. Neon lights flashed even in daylight. "Open, Fresh Coffee, Sandwiches To Go, Clean Restrooms, Showers."

Each guard on the facing seat unbuckled their seat belts, then leaned forward, unsure of what to do with Clarence.

Scar Man cocked his head toward Randy. "What do we do with the prisoner?"

Clarence froze. He had become so used to freedom in Osceola that the very word chilled him. The shackles on his arms and legs told the story. Prisoner Timmelsen. He had to get used to that sound once again. Interesting how short a time it had taken for him to be used to freedom and never being referred to as an inmate.

He blew out a breath. He hadn't realized how well he had adapted to freedom and thinking of himself as a man, a man with a future—however short that might have been. Now, he guessed by the constant tap of Ralston's gun against his head, he had no future, except a few bitter, painful days.

Randy opened the side door and handed Goatee Man a credit card. "You get the fuel while I check Clarence."

Goatee Man and Scar Man stepped out onto the concrete and proceeded to get the gas pump started.

"Let's see how you're doing Clarence." Randy stepped one foot into the van and reached several places before he found a strong handhold and pulled his bulky body into the van. Two men had stepped out, but one big man replaced them. His bulk filled the bench seat. The brown uniform was stretched to its limit across his wide belly. Aftershave wafted from him.

What had happened to this man in just a few months, other than a huge weight gain? If Clarence remembered right, he himself had been mean and abusive when Randy drove him to

Hillcrest, and Randy had done everything he could to smooth things over for the nurses and residents. When Clarence would cuss, Randy had gently touched his arm, warning him to settle down.

Now, here they were, going back to prison. And Clarence wondered if he'd even be alive when they arrived.

"The pain bad?" Randy lifted Clarence's shirt and grimaced.

"Just let me die, Randy." Clarence shook his head. "We both know if I'm going back to prison, I won't live long." Clarence swallowed.

"It's not that bad."

"No, Randy. You know it won't be this that gets me."

Randy stared at Clarence for a long moment, then lifted the bandage and peeked. "You'll be okay. We just have to get the bullet out." He looked behind Clarence at Ralston. "You should have your gun confiscated— shooting a little girl and a prisoner without cause. I don't care if the warden is your big brother, I'm still writing you up."

Ralston growled from the back seat. "He won't do anything. He's scared of me. He's scared of Mama. If he hurts me, she'll come after him."

Clarence's eyes widened but he didn't say what he was thinking. He was tired of being pounded on the back of his head for so many miles.

But Randy wasn't afraid. "Mama's boy, huh?"

Ralston hovered over the back of Clarence's bench seat. "Be careful. My bro—"

"Yeah. I know. Your brother's the warden." Randy pulled Clarence's shirt over the wound. "I've heard it over and over, by now." He raised his eyes to stare down Ralston, "And I'm sick of it. I don't care if he is your brother, I'm reporting you."

Ralston snickered into Clarence's ear, "Yeah, well I think this time he'll see it my way." The gun tapped Clarence's head harder with each tap. "My brother hates this man so much, that he will applaud anything I do to him, in honor of our brother, Lewis." He faked a sob he obviously didn't feel.

Randy swallowed down any words or anger he wanted to spew. "Clarence, I'm taking you into the truck stop for a bathroom break. Think you can move around a bit?"

Clarence glanced at this shirt and then the shackles. He nodded as he looked toward the store. A visual flooded his mind of the last trip he'd made with Randy and how mean he'd been, kicking him in the shins when Randy had unshackled him. "I'll be fine." It wouldn't be fun to be seen in this condition but for Randy, he'd make the effort to be civil. "Let's go."

Randy unhooked Clarence as Scar Man stepped to the back of the van, his hand on his holster.

"You are all gun-happy." Randy moved out of the van with one motion and held out his hand to Clarence. "What did Warden tell you that he didn't tell me? Huh?" He glanced at Scar Man. "Help Ralston out."

Clarence reached his hands to Randy and tried to scoot forward in the seat, expecting major pain, but it wasn't bad. Surprised, he edged his foot out the door and onto the ground. When he brought his other foot out and onto the concrete and straightened, the pain hit his abdomen and he doubled over, groaning.

Randy caught him before he went all the way down and steadied him. "You okay? You've been sitting there for hours and the wound kind of cramped you. You'll be better off the more you move around—just as long as the bleeding doesn't start all over again." He put his arm behind Clarence's back and braced him to take a step.

Clarence sucked in a deep breath as Ralston stepped out behind him and came around to his side. He moved first one foot and then the other. Everything hurt—his back, his shoulders from the way he'd been snoozing. Odd that the wound didn't hurt that much right now. It had been terrible right when he'd been shot but now it wasn't too bad.

He'd been knifed, abused, violated, but never shot—until today. It still didn't even come close to how bad he hurt for Mrs. Hatly, Bea and Katty. And Noell. Carol. Even Lisha.

Lisha had been his enemy for the first month at Hillcrest, but not now. Oh, they spat a lot and argued everyday, but something had changed.

Randy and Ralston urged him toward the entrance to the truck stop just as a young woman about Katty's age was leaving with one, two, three kids following behind her like baby chicks. She took one look at him and gasped.

He glanced down. His Led Zeppelin T-shirt was bloody and had a hole in it now. On down to the shackles. He had slept in the van so he imagined his hair was a mess, too. He guessed he looked frightful from the look on her face, plus each little kid looked terrified.

"I'm sorry." He tried to smooth it over even with the guards on either side of him. "I'm sorry for what they see." All he could imagine was Bea and how frightened she would be, seeing him or anyone in his condition.

The mother gathered the children behind her, but made room for Clarence, Randy and Ralston to pass in front of her. Her dark eyes scanned everything, from blood to shackles, then straight to his eyes. Clarence read fear there, but something else. Fear. And sympathy.

As they stepped past her, she bowed her head, her eyes still on Clarence's face. "We're praying for you, Sir."

Sir?

His knees crumpled under him and Randy had to heft him up again.

"Praying for—?"

Randy interrupted. "Please, Ma'am, we can't allow any contact between him and you." He looked into Clarence's face and stopped.

She spoke even stronger, still keeping the children behind her.

Little hands gripped the seams of her jeans and wisps of black hair flowed from behind her knees.

He took another step as the guards pushed him forward into the store.

A hand touched his arm and stopped him. She stepped in front of him, her little brood bouncing in line behind her. Now one small, dark eye peeked.

She hesitated. "I saw you."

He stopped. "You saw me? I—"

"Yes. I saw you in a dream." She gathered his whole body in her glance. "Just like this."

He looked down again.

"You were surrounded."

He guessed he was. A guard on either side.

"No. Not them." She hesitated. "Oh they were there, but ... there were others."

"Others?"

Randy interjected. "Excuse me Ma'am, but we need to keep going."

She became more determined, and focused even more on Clarence. "You were, *are* surrounded by ... " she seemed to be looking behind him and around him, "by hundreds of angels."

His skin tingled and he barely breathed. He would not cry.

Ralston started to laugh but she shushed him. He blinked, like he'd never been shushed with such respect, but total authority.

"Angels?" Clarence looked around. *Michael?* He wasn't there. Or maybe he was and Clarence just couldn't see him. No way when he was being transported from prison to Hillcrest had he ever thought there had been angels, but this trip? Already was different.

"Yes. Hundreds. With *you*." She pointed at his chest. "And you will survive this ... uh, trip." She hesitated. "More than survive. You will go ... back to," she looked directly at him, her face questioning. "Back to a nursing home? Your home."

A child quickly burst out from behind her. A small girl with black eyes and hair. "And you have a girlfriend!" She giggled.

"Hush." The woman pushed her behind. "Yes. There is a woman, a tiny gray-haired woman with a pink ribbon in her hair."

Clarence blinked and his legs buckled again.

*Mrs. Hatly?*

Oh God. What was this?

Randy and Ralston lifted him away, into the store, but Clarence stared behind him at the woman and children, who were now stepping from behind her. One. Two. Three.

"Wait." Clarence put on the brakes and looked at the kids. All bright and shiny. They almost sparkled, they were so pure. He pointed, even though his hands were in cuffs. "There is a fourth kid." He'd never done this before. "You left one in the store?" What was he saying. How did he know that?

But he did.

Her chin quivered but she regained her composure. "Yes. There is a fourth—in heaven with Jesus."

The little ones all nodded. "She is playing with Jesus!"

Were these people crazy? Or was *he* crazy? As he walked away, he couldn't help but stare behind him until he couldn't see them anymore and he almost tripped over a huge man's boots who was waiting in line at the cashier. The man growled as they stepped around him.

Randy smoothed it over. "Excuse us. We're a little bulky here. Excuse us."

Clarence shuffled forward as best he could in the shackles,

but his heart was still with the woman and her children. He had never felt so disjointed. He was one place in the natural, but another place in his heart. But when he thought of it, he'd lived his whole life that way—his body was in prison but his heart was with Annie, wherever she was.

Restrooms. Women's. Men's.

Randy sent Ralston in to clear the area so they could take Clarence in.

A young man in a suit rushed out, still zipping up, a wild look in his eyes. When he spied Clarence in all his bloody, shackled glory, he edged around them.

Ralston held the door open.

"What?" Randy pointed at the young man. "What did you do? What did you say to him?"

Ralston chuckled. "I just told him that a murderer was needing to use the premises and that he needed to cut it short and zip it and git out." He smirked, his hands on his hips.

Randy shook his head, but pushed Clarence into the restroom. "Let's get this done before Ralston gives anyone else a heart attack."

Humiliating. His own hands in handcuffs. He couldn't even pee by himself. Old anger climbed from his gut to his throat as Randy zipped him up. Steam had to be misting off his face, it was so hot. This was way more invasive than Lisha in the nursing home when she was being ornery. She would knock on the shower door, wait one second, then yell "Get done or I'm comin' in!" Then she'd rattle the keys. There was never a long hot shower there and he remembered it would be the same in prison. Get wet. Get soaped. Rinse. Get out. Hopefully with everything intact.

Back in the van he was both exhausted and exhilarated. The young woman and kids were gone when they walked out, but Clarence still felt the impact of what she had said. He looked around him. Maybe Michael had shown up.

"There ain't no angels around you." Ralston squeaked. "There's jus demons, and a whole lot of 'em." He sniggered.

Clarence was determined to not lose the feeling, the rising up of something he'd felt only a few times in his life. An undeniable knowing that something, someone, was on his side. That someone had his back.

Maybe he wouldn't die in prison after all.

## TWELVE

Noell handed Katty the cup, but her expression was puzzling. "I couldn't remember if you drank coffee, so I got hot chocolate instead. Hope that's okay." Maybe she shouldn't have—

"I ... " Katty's chin quivered and her eyes brimmed. A ragged breath escaped her lips. "I love hot chocolate." Another breath. "Thanks."

What do you say to a mommy who has just seen her child shot down? Noell fiddled with her hair braid. Did Katty like being touched? Did she hate it? And what had she seen? Her daughter had been shot. Had she been bloody? Was she awake? Crying in pain?

What had Gamma seen when Noell's own Mommy died? Mommy had drowned, so was she ... bloated? *Oh God*. Had she closed her eyes? All Noell could see in her nightmare was Mommy's eyes wide open in terror. Had they ever closed in peace?

Oh Gamma. What you must have gone through—losing your own daughter. Grampa too.

Noell hadn't been born with a bank account attached to her name, although because of Gamma's investments, she was now a wealthy young woman. But she had grown up with constant nightmares of her mother drowning. Plus Gamma's own pain of hoarding. Losing Grampa. All they had was each other—Gamma and Noell. A hard life. Never having friends over because of Gamma's hoarding.

And now Noell was alone. No Mommy. No Gamma. No Grampa.

No one to share her life with. No one to care whether she came home or not. Not one person to have dinner with.

Noell stopped.

But Katty's most precious possession in the whole world was across the hall in surgery. And her best friend in the world, Clarence, had been literally kidnapped back to prison.

Noell shook her head. She swallowed and reached for Katty's hand.

Katty jumped, her eyes on their hands, as Noell slowly wove her fingers with Katty's. She slowly looked up at Noell and nodded, her hands clasping Noell's even more firmly. She continued to nod, until a tear dropped on Noell's hand.

Noell gently rubbed her thumb against Katty's knuckle. She blinked a tear away and swallowed. She didn't care how long they had to sit like this, she would never take her hand away.

Katty blew out a ragged breath just as the door to the surgical wing swung open. A youngish doctor walked toward them, untying the mask from the back of his head, letting it flop loose at his chest. He seemed confidant and pleased.

Oh please, God. Please let Bea not only survive, but thrive.

He nodded at Noell, then pulled a chair directly across from Katty and sat. "She's going to be fine. She will recover without any complications." He held up a bullet. "This is what we took out of her. We were able to repair the site closed and I am confidant she will heal completely and never miss a four-year-old beat."

Katty placed her cup on a table, but she didn't reach for the bullet, so Noell did. She started to put it on the side table, almost tucked it into her jeans pocket but instead held it in her other hand.

"Can I see her?"

"They are taking her into recovery and it will take them a few minutes to hook her all up, but then someone will come out and get you." He nodded at Noell, "You can come, too."

Noell nodded.

She looked up as Carol pushed the open button from outside and squeezed through the automatic doors before they were open all the way, followed by Lisha.

Reinforcements.

Carol winked at Noell and nodded.

Upon seeing the doctor, Carol stopped and stepped away to a respectful distance.

The doctor glanced up and smiled. "Carol. Lisha." He stood to shake hands.

Carol took his hand in both of hers, her eyes never leaving Katty's face. "How is she? How is our Bea?"

The doctor nodded and backed away. "I'll let you all visit while I go check on our tiny patient." Directly to Katty, "I'll keep you informed, especially the next twenty-four hours or so."

Katty stood to thank him and after he left Carol and Lisha embraced her. Lisha peeked over and pulled Noell into the group hug as Carol murmured, "She's going to be okay. She will be alright. She's a strong little girl."

Katty collapsed just then.

Lisha held her and kept her from falling.

There was no way Katty would fall as she was held up by two strong women who were used to lifting residents in the nursing home. Their training kicked in and they gently sat Katty back down, finding chairs for themselves.

No one spoke for a few seconds until Lisha broke the ice, a grimace on her face. "Nobody in my family ever been shot." She shook her head.

Noell leaned forward. "This is all too crazy to believe."

Carol checked Lisha's face, then Katty's. "I know. In our little town of Osceola. Everyone was so upset—the residents most of all. But those guards—pushing and shoving Clarence and—"

"Yes. They was brutal. They had him handcuffed." Lisha shook her head. "I had problems with that man from the beginning, but ... " She didn't finish her sentence.

Carol glanced at Lisha's face again and continued, nodded to Katty. "When you and Bea ran up—she was asking questions as only little ones would." Carol sighed. "She doesn't miss a thing—the handcuffs, the guards." But when the guard said something to you, Katty—"

Katty shook her head, her eyes wide. "He came on to me. Said something like 'Who wants to know, baby?'" She imitated his slimy voice. "I had stepped in front of Clarence," she added, "and asked what was going on. I think I asked him where he was going." She stared at the wall. "Bea was right in there, asking him stuff. That's when that skinny weasel of a guard said what he did." Her forehead wrinkled and tears began to flow. "And that's when Clarence broke loose and slugged the guard." Her other hand flew to her mouth as she realized the truth. "Clarence was protecting me—us. He slugged that guard in defense of me, of Bea and me." She choked. "Never has anyone done that before. My dad, my mom, my brothers. None of them ever stood up for me." She made it a point to look into Noell's, Carol's, and Lisha's eyes. "Ever. Until Clarence today."

Noell glanced away. Grampa had always stood up for her. He had always been the one to rush into her room when she cried out in her nightmares. He had always come to school to take the principal to task over someone bullying Noell in the lunch line or at the lockers when the teachers weren't looking.

Until he had died, Grampa always had Noell's back, except for one time when he had let her stand up to a bully herself, and he supported her. She had come home crying one last time. He must have been fed up. He marched her back to school and stood behind her as she punched the bully in the jaw. He had grinned all the way home. She never knew she could hit that hard. And the kid had become a friend all through school until graduation. Where was *he* now?

Noell realized she had been gripping Katty's hand hard and relaxed her hold. She also realized something she really down deep knew—her growing up years had been sweet—despite the hoarding, despite loosing Mommy at a young age and despite the nightmares.

The doors to the surgery wing opened and a perky nurse walked through. "Katty? Katty Randolph?"

Katty rose. "Can I see my Bea?"

"You sure can." The nurse gauged the others around Katty. "Family? Friends?" She realized who Carol and Lisha were and grinned. "Nurses."

Carol looked at Lisha. "Oh, we have to get back. We just wanted to come and check on Bea and you, Katty."

"Yeah. I gots to give a bath and ... " Lisha trailed off.

Neither seemed ready to leave, torn by duty to job and wanting to stay.

"We'll try to come back after work." Carol tried to smile. "We knew the residents would want an update on Bea. Even the Hate Clarence Club wanted to find out how she is." She popped her hand over her mouth. "Said too much. Wipe that from your memories, girls."

Lisha stood. "If those biddies start in on Clarence, I might have to drown one of them today." She grinned.

Carol stood too. "Well so much for the privacy act!" She leaned over and hugged Katty, then Noell. "Bye, Katty. Let us know how we can help." She raised her eyebrows. "Okay?"

Katty nodded. "Sure. Thanks." She stood and reached for Noell's hand. "Ready to go in?"

Felt like family. Noell nodded and slipped her hand into Katty's. Almost felt like sisters. Almost. Cousins maybe.

Carol and Lisha waved as they pushed the open button to the automatic doors.

Noell waited for Katty to take the first step. When she did, she seemed conflicted. She had to be eager to see Bea, but—

"W-what will she look like?" Katty took a deep breath. "I-I guess we'll have to go find out. She might still be asleep."

Noell nodded and pushed the open button.

Katty linked her arm in Noell's and stepped through the doors as they opened. Odd. It felt so right.

The nurse waited for them near an open door and ushered them inside.

## THIRTEEN

"I can't believe this." Randy flipped on the blinker and made a slight right turn into a truck stop. He glared into the rear view mirror. "We are literally," he pointed at the windshield, "less than fifty miles from the prison. You can't wait?"

Ralston growled from behind Clarence. Growled again. "No, I cannot." He kicked the back of Clarence's seat like a child. "I gotta go."

"Grrr." This time growling came from Randy up front. He pulled into a parking spot and opened his door.

Goatee Man stroked his goatee. "This is stupid. This is when things happen."

Clarence had been thinking the same thing only with a different twist. If only he wasn't shackled. He could push out the back door while it was open and make—

Scar Man leaned forward. "You were thinking the same thing, weren't you Timmelsen?" He grinned. "Weren't you."

Was he that transparent? He hadn't even turned his head. But the wheels had been turning. He cleared his throat. "Since we're stopped, I have to go, too."

Both Scar Man and Goatee Man groaned.

"Told ya."

Goatee Man tapped on the window at Randy and pointed at Clarence.

Randy opened the side door. "What?"

"He's got to go, too."

Randy dropped his head to his chest. "Alright. Let's get going. We are almost there and I want to be done with this whole ordeal." He twirled his finger in a vortex. "Get him out. Make it snappy."

Clarence scooted to the edge of his seat as Goatee Man and Scar Man unbuckled the shackles. He had a sharp memory drop in of when Randy had taken him to Osceola. Randy had hoped to trust him and had unshackled him, but Clarence had kicked Randy in the shin. Clarence had deserved to be completely shackled. He had settled down and they came to an understanding. The last half of the trip, Clarence rode in front.

He had tensed at the thought without realizing it. Settle. Relax. Because it isn't happening this trip. Goatee Man and Scar Man *and* Ralston and Randy. It had just been Randy from prison to Osceola.

Not happening.

"Easy Cowboy." Goatee Man positioned a hand on his holster and unsnapped it.

Clarence grimaced. "I'm just an old man who has to pee. Give me some slack." Somehow, they'd slip up—somehow. Just one guard might turn his back and Clarence maybe could slip into the trucker area and catch a ride with one of them. He looked down. Blood on his shirt might be suspicious, but it was worth a try.

Prison this time would kill him.

Scar Man stepped out and turned to help Clarence down.

Clarence slid over to the door.

Goatee Man held out his hand to steady him and Clarence stepped down.

"Damn! Hurts ... to stand." Clarence slowly straightened, breathing in shallow breaths through his mouth. "Wow. Wow." He grabbed at the air and finally his hand found the door handle. Yeah, he'd be able to run and escape. He was a damn pansy.

People parked next to the van gave him sideways looks. Everyone of them gasped at the blood on his T-shirt. Then to the handcuffs on his hands. Then the leg irons.

As they walked inside, people seemed to part on either side to let them pass, like magic. Must have been impressive. A guard on either side of him. Humiliating. In spite of the pain, Clarence stood as tall as possible, head held high, eyes kind.

As he passed people, they'd first glimpse the blood, handcuffs, then quickly look away. They were horrified.

Him too. Embarrassed by the attention, by the guards seriousness ... and it was serious. Embarrassed by the curiosity of the children. They poked their heads from behind a parent or pointed.

He must have looked like a common criminal.

God.

Clarence couldn't even smile. He tried to seem pleasant, but after awhile, it grew tiring and he assumed a cold hard stare which he guessed was more fitting for the occasion.

Surely he'd been exonerated and released. They were making this long trip for nothing—a waste of time and gas and manpower.

Goatee Man stepped into the restroom and cleared it out. Clarence almost laughed at the expressions of the men and boys racing from the room. What had Goatee Man told them?

Play the part of the con man. Put on the terrible face. Cold, hard eyes. Act out the part that people believed without knowing the facts.

The fact—these guards had literally kidnapped him, taking him against his will to prison for defending himself against a thug years ago.

His cheek *still* tingled as he remembered the scene when Lewis Ralston came at him with a knife and four more, equally vicious inmates surrounded him.

He still couldn't figure out how he'd gotten a knife in time to defend himself against Lewis. When two guards had busted into the shower room with beat sticks and guns, the others thugs had dispersed, leaving Lewis and him to duke it out with knives. Lewis had sliced Clarence's cheek and Clarence hadn't even hesitated. He knew he had to strike, seeing the guards were on Lewis's side. Roaring, Clarence plunged into him and the knife flew. Before he knew how, the knife was in his hand and it hit its mark in Lewis's neck, slicing open the artery. Lewis still lunged into him, but a second later, collapsed. The guards yelled for help and backup. None came and Lewis died on the spot, blood everywhere. His body—legs and arms—splayed at odd angles. How could Clarence be held responsible when five men came at him with knives?

Clarence used the toilet, with the help of the guards.

Humiliating.

They turned to leave the restroom when a man with a trimmed, long pointed beard, wearing a strange cowboy hat, entered the restroom.

The guards, on either side of Clarence, stiffened. Their hands gripped his arms even tighter, ready to reach for weapons if needed.

The man seemed to absorb everything in one glance—from Clarence's bloody shirt, handcuffs, guards ready to beat him away if he appeared to be threatening in any way.

Strange. The man seemed to know Clarence. He looked him straight in the eyes in a friendly way—kind of like Michael did.

Where on earth was Michael, anyway?

This guy made Clarence feel like Michael had.

Michael always made Clarence feel like he had a purpose, like he was strong and could do anything. This guy knew something. Or was someone important without looking like it. Who was he and what did he want? Was he one of God's creatures or an angel?

Hard to even walk by the unlimited displays of candy, snacks, chips and drinks. He had gotten so used to freedom. Walk to the grocery store any day of the week and spend money. Buy candy bars from Mindy or John who worked there. Be harassed by John—a far cry from what he was going through right now with the guards. Oh, to have John threaten him right now.

They made it to the cashiers and the man was there—face-to-face. He smiled. His plaid shirt was odd too. Odd hat. Odd beard. Odd shirt. Odd smile, or odd that he smiled at Clarence and the guards.

The guy had to be an angel.

There was no way even six months ago, Clarence would have thought that. He'd have shooed the man away, insulted him. Thinking he was a pest, or a scammer. Or gay.

Back in the van. Back in shackles. The longest day of his life. Again.

The last thing Clarence wanted to see was the entrance to the prison—Maximum Security Prison in Chicago. The front gate security guard waved them on. As they drove through the gates, chills ran up and down Clarence's spine, so much that he hardly felt Ralston's gun tapping his ear. He shuddered repeatedly.

Ralston whispered, "You're gonna love the changes here. He's waiting for you."

Didn't even faze Clarence. Those whispers were only background noise to the louder voices shouting in his own mind. "You'll never get out of here. You'll die a horrible death in here."

"Ralston!" Randy's eyes glared from the rear view mirror. "How many guns do you have? Holster your gun!"

Ralston continued to tap Clarence's ear. Cold, hard metal slid across his throat, then rested at his temple.

Ralston knew they were in home territory and he was Warden's baby brother.

Clarence held his breath and squeezed his eyes shut. Not crying. No tears.

A garage door opened and Clarence blinked in the bright overhead lights. Every cell sweated. Every cell vibrated with fear. Radios squawked with the news—"Timmelsen is on the property. Timmelsen has arrived."

Ralston leaned in. "See? You're famous. Timmelsen is in the building. Timmelsen is here." He chuckled. "Kinda like Elvis." He laughed even harder.

Clarence shuddered at the sound of his laugh. This move was going to be the toughest of his whole life. Losing Annie, his dad, seeing the townspeople at the train station for literally the last time and entering prison at nineteen years old—everyday since.

This would undoubtedly be the worst day he had ever lived through. If, he indeed lived.

His heart wanted to cry out to God but even Michael had abandoned him. What god would ever help him again?

His dad always used to remind Clarence that God never turned his back on a person and that was from a man who had never entered a church since his wife's funeral.

But God had turned His back today.

# FOURTEEN

Bea's hospital room was right across from the nurses station. Katty guessed they put the serious cases there and she guessed that Bea's case was pretty serious. She prepared herself for the worst. Seeing Bea from surgery, tubes all over, white as the sheets.

"Ready?" Noell's hand hovered over the door handle, waiting.

Katty nodded. "Yes."

Noell slowly slid her sleeve over her hand and pulled the door open.

Odd. Noell's expression was odd, too. Like expectant fright. Katty studied the door. She couldn't see what might be so terrifying.

They stepped into the room. Bea faced the wall, away from them. She must still be out from the anesthesia. Baby Bea.

Katty's eyes filled with tears at the sight of her, pale against the pillow. She swallowed back a sob. All she wanted to do was pick her up and snuggle her. To keep her safe. Awful how she used to be drunk all the time and leave Bea all night and a good part of the day, alone. She had cared more about partying and drugs than her own daughter.

Awful, awful.

She tip-toed toward the bed and Bea turned her head, a grin on her face. "You're awake."

"Look Mommy. Can you see them?" Bea pointed at what seemed just the air. "They're sparkly. They have eyes and wings." She sighed and leaned back against the pillow. "I think they're angels. I think they saved me, Mommy."

Katty raised her eyebrows and hugged Bea. "Where do you hurt? Is it okay that I hug you? Are you okay?" Now she sounded just like Bea did. Asking every question in the book, five times each.

Bea sighed.

"Are you tired? Do you hurt?"

Bea shrugged. "Kinda. But the nurse said I'd be okay and better in no time. She was nice. She said that the lights would go away when I woke up more." Bea searched the room. "They're all still here, so is it okay that I can still see them? I don't want them to go away."

Katty glanced at Noell. She was searching the room, following where Bea pointed. Damn. How could she ever talk to Noell with a straight face again? "Baby, maybe the nurse was just trying to make you feel better."

"Don't you see them Mommy?" Bea pointed. "You did before in the car. Remember?"

Katty blinked and leaned her head toward Noell. "She's just sleepy, I think." The lights were beautiful. Maybe it hadn't been a good idea to bring Noell in with her. Because she really wanted to talk to Bea about them. She could almost see a face. Wings for sure. So beautiful that Katty could feel her knees buckling. No. She had to stay standing and strong. Light reflected from some-where. She didn't see any except for the light fixture over the bed. They seemed to have light from within somehow.

Beautiful.

Noell was silent.

Katty peeked at her and blinked. The expression on her face

mirrored Bea's. Rapt. Awe. Tears. There were tears in Noell's eyes. She was definitely seeing something.

A nurse pushed the door all the way open, carrying a tray. "Hi, Little One. Just a light lunch. You are so tiny, you need to eat fairly often." She placed the tray on the table and pushed it closer to the bed and leaned to Katty. "My name is Candy and I'll be your nurse today and maybe tomorrow. Is she still talking about seeing things?"

Katty raised her eyebrows. "Uh—"

"She seems determined that there are angels in this room. Or at least lights." Candy lifted the cover revealing broth and jello. Apple juice sat beside it, with utensils and a napkin. A tiny stuffed pig decorated the tray. "Just so you know, she could be hallucinating from the anesthesia and other meds they gave her in surgery. It happens."

A light swooped around the nurse's head and landed on her shoulder. She fussed with the bedding and the tray, checked tubes and the IV drip, totally unaware of anything going on around her.

"You have a great room here, too." She nodded out the door. "Right close to the nurses. And it's so peaceful." Deep sigh. "It's ... peaceful."

Bea giggled.

The light flickered from Candy's shoulder, almost waving at them. If the nurse felt peaceful with it there, Katty figured maybe that's what these lights were for, what they were supposed to do —bring peace.

Bea reached for the tiny pig. "What's this?"

Katty stepped in. "It's a tiny pig. Maybe a toy. Cute." She moved the juice closer. "Maybe take a sip—just a sip—to make sure your tummy is settled."

More lights flew in and circled the nurse's head and shoulders. They seemed to hover around her. Almost putting on a show.

Bea pointed. "See, Mommy? Look at all of them around her head." She giggled and blinked. Still sleepy.

"We'll watch her and chart it and if she doesn't come out of it, we'll alert the doctor and see what he wants to do. He has kids so he gets them." She smiled and tucked in the sheet around Bea's feet. "Are you still cold, Honey?" She pushed the table right up to Bea's chest. "Want to be careful for where the wound is in her tummy, around her belly button."

"Do I still have a belly button?"

The nurse stopped and stared at Bea. "Why ... of course you do, Sweetie! You just ... well there is kind of a bandage over—"

"Is it a pretty one?"

"Uh ... what?" The nurse evidently didn't have kids.

"Is it Star Wars? Or a—"

"I think it's white." The nurse shook her head. "Or maybe blue."

"That's okay." Bea leaned up a little to the tray and tapped the jello. "What's this? It's green."

Katty came to Candy's rescue. "It's jello." She shook the bowl. "See? It wiggles." She moved her shoulders and hips in a dance. "It's dancing! Shake it baby!" Things were definitely more fun when the lights were around.

Bea tapped it again. "Fun!" She reached for her spoon. "Can I eat it?"

Noell laughed. "Sure." She took the spoon from Bea and tapped it. "Fun!" She scooped up a tiny spoonful and aimed it at Bea's mouth. "Taste it?"

Bea stared at it, then up at Noell, then Mommy. Then Candy. "Okay." She opened her mouth.

Noell fed her and put down the spoon. "Good?"

Bea's eyes opened wide. "It's good! Tastes ... green. Or like ... green." She hesitated. "Grass is green. Broccoli is green, but it doesn't taste like that." She picked up the spoon and took another bite. "Tastes like—"

"Lime?" Noell took the spoon.

"What's lime?"

Katty perked up. 'It's what you put in ... uh. Maybe it's apple flavored."

Bea nodded. "I think it *is* apple. How do they do that? Put apples in there and make it all jumpy?"

Noell laughed. "Well, they put a bunch of apples in a bowl and tell them to dance. When they dance, the skins all fall off and juice runs out. And they put that juice with other stuff to make the jello dance."

Candy rolled her eyes.

Katty chuckled. Noell got kids. She should be Bea's nurse.

Noell shoveled another bite into Bea's mouth.

"Well ... I think you have this covered. I'll go make rounds." Candy seemed to come to and took a deep breath. "She is coming out of it, so I'm not too worried about what she was seeing anymore."

Katty bit her lips. A grin slipped out and she bit her lips again.

The angels were swirling again—almost making a joke—only Candy didn't know about it. Candy could chart what she wanted, but the lights and angels were more than ever. More flew in from ... where? They appeared at the walls, in the doorway.

Candy checked her watch, evidently wanting to get away from the crazies. "Let me know if you need anything." She pointed to the tray. "Try to eat something else. Try the broth. It's great." She waved as she left the room.

Katty nodded. "Yeah." Broth to a peanut butter and jelly girl. Right.

Noell was still seeing them too, because her face was joyful. She covered her mouth, trying to be deadpan.

Katty's face wanted to burst. She was grinning from ear to ear! Bea had just been shot and had to have surgery and Clarence was ... gone. But her heart was full and bursting with ... joy? Never. Never had she felt this way. When the lights had appeared in the car a few weeks ago, she had felt peace, but something more. She had known that in spite of what was going on, everything would be all right. She just knew, somehow.

This was kind of the same, but even more so.

Out at the nurses station, Candy could be heard talking to someone. "I don't know what Bea's background is, but her mom stares at the air too. We maybe should chart that something runs in their family. Like they're all seeing things." She seemed to pause. "Still, it's so quiet in there—peaceful somehow."

Noell snorted.

Katty shut the door and giggled, covering her mouth.

"Mommy! They're dancing around your head, like the jello!" Bea grinned an all-teeth grin.

Katty looked at Noell, her heart bursting.

Noell looked up and laughed a delightful laugh, wiping tears from her eyes.

Poor Candy.

## FIFTEEN

Harold tapped the cell phone and shook his head. Rubbed his eyes.

A list of phone numbers was written neatly on a pad of scratch paper beside him on the table—neatly for him anyway. The pad was a freebie from the hospital. He had a stack of them to use just for moments like this.

He shook his head again and combed fingers through his hair.

He used to be good at contacting people when he'd had the detective agency. Never hesitated—just dialed the number. Talked to many kinds of people: women and men who were influential or poverty-stricken, all cultures. Suspicious wives. Criminals. People hiding from life. Even people who had been given asylum. Interesting business.

He missed it. And yes, he had worked long hours. Lucille, his wife, had complained once-in-a-while, but for the most part, she was very patient—knowing his love of the job and how much he helped people.

That was it—the whole reason for doing what he did—he helped people in tough seasons.

Seemed so long ago. Hell, he probably should have quit sooner than he did.

He stared out the window. The trash dumpster was his mountain view. He didn't care. Clarence teased him about it because the view out of Clarence's window was the rose garden.

Harold gulped. They'd had many laughs over that.

Damn, he missed that man. He glanced at the dumpster again, the lines blurred.

Who would help Clarence if he didn't?

Lisha poked her head in. "You okay?" She checked his water carafe. "I'll get you more. Be right back."

He wiped his eyes. Now he had an excuse to delay the call. Lisha said she'd be right back.

And she was, carrying his water carafe and a cup of coffee. Good girl. She was worth gold to the residents.

"Thanks Lisha." He sipped the coffee. Wasn't like Clarence's but it'd do. Damn, he missed that man.

They'd started out kind of rocky, but he'd not had a friend like Clarence since Lucille had passed away.

Lisha smoothed the bedcovers and re-arranged his toothbrush and toothpaste on his sink. She pulled the blinds down then released them back up.

"Say it, Lisha."

She turned to him. "Who me?" She shook her head, long dreadlock ponytail bouncing. "Just cleanin' up a bit."

"Right."

She sat on the bed. "I was just thinking. Since you were a detective and all—"

"Go on."

"And since you have your phone out and all." She folded her arms across her chest. "Can you call somebody about Clarence? Didn't you used to know somebody, who knew somebody else, who could git him out? Somebody that could help him?"

Harold dropped his chin to his chest, his eyes closed. Lord, you send 'em when I need 'em. This woman.

He tapped the pad of paper, underlining one phone number with his gnarled finger. "This one is the governor. I knew his dad real well—good man. This one is Sheriff Dennison." He had racked his brain to come up with names, but other than the governor and Sheriff, he couldn't think of anyone. "I'm trying to think of people I used to know or work with." He picked up the pen. "Help me?"

Lisha nodded and blinked. "Okay. Well, let's see." She stood and paced. "Clarence wasn't in the military. The governor is a good one. Maybe just call him and he could give you names." She snapped her fingers. "What about our senator or representative? I don't know their names, but … "

Harold clapped his hands and pointed his pen at Lisha. "Good one. I used to know someone from back in my day." He stared out the window. "A couple of them. Good men, too."

"Can you get hold of them? Would they remember you?" She caught up a stray braid into her ponytail.

"One would remember me. We worked together on a murder case for years. Didn't crack it, but we tracked down every lead. He had a brother too, that had a high-profile business. He'd come on board and help. Now what were their names?" He snapped his fingers. "Somebody else. I don't know if this one is still alive, but there was a woman, Eva Trumble, who was a senator back then." He chuckled. "My Lucille was jealous until they met. They became good friends."

He wrote her name down. "The other one was Stan … Stan Martinson? I don't know how to find these people now." Felt good to be doing something. This detective thing was still in his blood.

Lisha held up her phone. "I know how we can start."

## SIXTEEN

These guards were going all out. Were they really that afraid of him, locking everything on him from his hands and feet to his head? Every shackle, every handcuff, every bit of armor—locked.

Clarence blew a breath out. He pulled against the handcuffs, without letting on—not moving a muscle. Tight. Everything was tight. His hands had begun to tingle.

But as Clarence scanned the people gathering, maybe the extra protection was for *him*. Men gathered in every allowable place that inmates could gather. It had only been a couple months since Clarence had been shipped off to Hillcrest Nursing Home, but these people seemed more evil than he remembered. He knew he hadn't changed that much in such a short time.

Their eyes were more evil—squinting, but more than that. The eyeballs were black. As Clarence passed each man, they almost growled, teeth showing in a snarl. A low growling.

Was this a pack of wolves? Smelled as bad.

Clarence's skin prickled. The sounds and faces and eyes gave off some sort of frequency that bombarded every cell of his body, making him shudder and shiver.

In just a couple months the whole atmosphere had changed.

Oh, it had been bad before—very evil, prisoners always fighting, threatening. But right here and now, it felt like the prisoners were in charge, not the guards.

The more Clarence studied the people as he was pushed through, the more tense he became.

"Bring him here." A huge man standing at a counter, wearing the typical brown uniform, pointed at Clarence. His fat finger flipped over and beckoned. "He has to sign here." He tapped on a paper. "He doesn't go anywhere else, until he signs in."

They unlocked one handcuff so he could sign the paper. He put the pen to it, but caught sight of the words, "for life," and quickly withdrew his hand and protested. "I'm not signing that." His law degree kicked in.

Four guards pressed him into the counter. He gasped. Right on the wound. Someone popped him on the head. Two held him planted there, while one slipped a cable around his neck and kept him tethered. The other grabbed his right hand, cupping his own hand around Clarence's, making him sign his name. "How you spell it? C? T-i-m?"

Clarence watched as his scrawled name appeared on the page, the words flowing out of the pen that he himself grasped but had no real control of. He was able to read part of the document, since he didn't have to think about what was being written.

"What is this?" he yelled. "That says—"

The big man, his name tag read Teddy, growled at him. "None of your damn business. Warden wants you to sign it, that's all."

"None of my business! It says I signed over to Warden my whole life. My savings. My family. My future."

The guards all laughed.

Clarence blinked. Bea would be Warden's. A vision of her, dressed up in gold, a huge gold bow in her hair, flowed through his mind. Katty. What would happen to them? The whole town of Osceola that Dad had spent years quietly buying. This couldn't be happening.

Warden walked to the railing from upstairs, grinning. He waved. "Howya doin' down there, Clarence?" He spread his arms wide. "Welcome back!"

Clarence froze. He couldn't take a breath. Felt like Warden was standing on his chest, *plus* the huge man in front of him.

The guards around him laughed even harder. All in on the little joke. Joke's on Clarence. Funny. Funny.

The cable around his neck pulled tighter. The shackles on his ankles burned through his jeans.

Clarence grimaced. He would not let on ... the pain.

The guard dropped the pen and the others replaced the handcuff, only this time his hands were in front. Strange. They had enjoyed tearing his arms out of the sockets to pull his hands behind his back.

Pain in his hands. His wrists were burning red. The handcuffs were cutting into his skin. How on earth? They hadn't cut into his wrists until now. Felt like little blades were on the inside of each one. He looked. There were ... little ... how?

This was all his imagination. Had to be. But how could it hurt so bad if he was in a dream?

Nothing in the nursing home had compared to this. God, this was not going to be good. He was in good shape but no time in working out or running could have prepared him for this.

It was almost ... .

Michael. Where was Michael?

He looked where he had seen Warden standing. This had to be a ... nightmare.

Warden was standing there, grinning, but behind him or morphed over him was ... something moving. Outlines of ... something ... .

Every cell in Clarence's body screamed, "Run!"

The mist rose above Warden at least ten feet. Seemed to be a part of him, but had scales, horns.

Satan?

Clarence blinked. He started to bring his fingers to his eyes, but a guard grabbed the handcuffs and yanked his hands down.

Warden had almost become one with the ... creature. His body and face grew and glowed. He still grinned until he stretched and then he stood alone.

The guy was nuts.

Something still flickered in Warden's eyes. Clarence stood in awe and fear as he watched. Had they slipped him drugs?

He shivered. Whatever it was that moved in Warden's eyes was worse than that devil. It could see into his very soul. Clarence tried to back away. It knew things. He could almost feel it inside him.

Even the guards cringed and backed away. So they saw it too.

Randy stomped. "This is rubbish." He might have been the only sane person there.

Two men standing to the side of the Warden looked familiar.

*God.*

Phil and Lex.

Clarence had known they were evil but never guessed they were connected to Warden.

He tried to move. Tried to move his feet and run away, but the shackles were glued to the floor.

Even the huge man looked like he wanted to run, but he just stood there.

Randy turned, took one apologetic look at Clarence and ran.

Chicken.

Clarence was doomed. This must be hell. He never figured he would die in the pit of hell. Why had Michael been his friend from day one at the nursing home? He had never been a great person, but never figured he'd go here. How could a prison turn into the very picture of hell?

The reality of where he probably was, hurt more than any burning shackles or handcuffs.

Clarence's eyes blurred. The whole place was on fire. He squinted through the smoke. This couldn't be real.

Inmates seemed free to roam and revel in the pain of one man —Clarence. They danced around him along with the guards. They played on the same team.

This was worse than dying.

Where was Michael?

"Michael, please. Help."

Warden must have heard him for he tossed back his head and roared. "Michael won't save you! Your Bea, can't save you! She's dead. Poor baby. Tay shot her and now she's dead." He turned it all the way up. "You weren't there to save her, to protect her. You're a cheat and a liar and a loser."

With each accusation, Clarence bent lower and lower until he was on the floor. Each person pounded him on the head or worse, where he was burning, as they danced around him.

# SEVENTEEN

Phil stared at Clarence.

The man was formidable. Even though he was old—eighty something—when he came in, he stood almost a foot taller than the guards and even though he was fully shackled, he still walked upright and strong.

Hadn't the report said he'd been shot?

But here he was. His white hair was long and he had a full beard. He looked better than when he'd been in prison before.

Phil had an inside track even before that. Working as a dietary assistant in the prison kitchen gave him access to the needs of staff but also the inmates. He'd been around food and grocery stores all his life. When he'd been hired at the prison, he realized he would fit in with the community of inmates, although he'd never served time. And just because he'd never served time didn't mean he didn't deserve to.

He grinned. He just hadn't gotten caught, like all these other yayhoos.

The atmosphere in the rotunda exploded when they dragged Clarence in. Every cell, except the maximum security cells, lined the space, so every man could see them. Something changed in the inmates. A definite beat could be heard as they pounded on any surface near them—bars, doors, walls, floors. It was thunderous. It was darkly powerful.

The beat grew stronger and louder and all united in a chant.

Faces grew more vicious.

Eyes turned yellow and black.

Someone shouted, "Bea is dead."

Phil started. "W-What?" He leaned closer to Warden, but even he had changed. Something, a mist or film, a transparent layer of a creature, demon or dragon rose around him. Warden's eyes ... shadows or tiny sparks flitted inside, like firecrackers. Something behind him pounded the floor in time with the beat.

Phil backed away. A tail?

Warden had something going on, alright. Just like his own dad.

Phil looked around for the stairway. Where was the whiskey?

Again, the crowd yelled, "Bea is dead."

His heart lurched. "Warden! What is that?" Phil tried to talk to the man. "Bea is dead?"

Warden grinned. The mist cleared but he didn't look any better. Sweaty. Flushed. Eyes hard. "Oh, she isn't dead. She's just wounded."

He raised his arm toward Clarence, who was kneeling under the attack and roared a sick laugh, shaking his fist. "Break him! Break him!"

# EIGHTEEN

Michael was allowed in the prison but only at a distance. Demons were posted on every corner, every hallway, keeping any creature from the Kingdom of Heaven out.

The demons always thought they were in control, but Michael knew differently. Father was always in control and he had a plan—even here.

He followed the guards, who escorted Clarence, as close as they would let him. His army followed close behind him, weapons raised.

He could see Clarence. They were going to kill him if they kept up that torture. He was in great shape for anyone, but if they kept it up, he'd be gone from this earth.

Michael didn't think that was Father's plan for Clarence, yet. There seemed to be much for Clarence to do back in Osceola. So many lives to touch, especially Katty and Bea.

Making Clarence sign his life away, literally, was a big mistake. Maybe Clarence didn't remember, but Michael had been with him since his birth and he couldn't sign his life away. He was Blood-Bought. A member of the Blood Family. Not that one couldn't resist and turn away. Michael knew every decision Clarence had ever made. He had them in a book.

The demons and Warden, his guards were liars. All of them.

Humans needed to learn the Truth.

Michael cringed when the shackles became red with fire and the handcuff blades cut Clarence's hands.. He had lived in a human body, himself. He knew pain. He had pounded nails into his hand, not to emulate Lord's death at the cross, but because he was terrible with a hammer.

He checked his army—all kinds of angels, from different cultures, different colors, different ranks—all willing to follow Father and to guard Clarence. All willing to go into battle alongside Michael. All hard-core, seasoned warriors from eternity.

Jarrel leaned into Michael. "Randy is splitting. He is no longer with them. How do you want us to handle him?"

"However Yeshua would. Gather round him and minister according to Father's plan." He held his sword up. "Let Randy dictate. He will learn to direct you. Some are learning even now to be kings and sons. Let him grow into who he is to be." He glanced at where Clarence stood. "Just as Clarence is learning and growing right now. Learning that this is real."

Jarrel bowed low and backed away toward Randy.

On other days, Michael might have tripped Jarrel or maybe started a tussle—an angel wrestling match—but not today. So much hinged on this one battle here at the prison. The future for Clarence, but also for Katty and Bea, Noell, many residents and staff at the nursing home, community people who would possibly be affected by whether Clarence lived or died here. This battle could end now—this moment. Or last for months, even years. There were no time restrictions in the Kingdom.

This battle was Clarence's personal Armageddon. What he did here at the prison held the destiny of many future generations. Father was in control, but Clarence had the opportunity to change history.

They couldn't afford to lose focus. The battle was on and they were in enemy's territory. They had to stand no matter what the humans did.

Michael cringed when Warden stepped out onto the bridge. The man was crazy. Infested with every demon. He was sold out. He had progressed to a very high level in the enemy's camp. Only Michael outranked him, even though the Father was in control.

Warden had held such promise for the Kingdom when he was a boy. His mama worked hard to provide, his daddy, too. They had struggled with three little boys to raise and provide for. But one night's decision gone wrong had changed everything. Daddy had taken a job in another state for more money than what he was currently making. Mommy had decided to stay put, keeping the boys in school, not wanting to leave her friends. She had just started back to school to become a nurse. Commitment in the marriage had fallen apart and one thing after another, that old word divorce became more and more part of conversations until the papers were signed.

Michael could never figure out if since the demons all knew, every one of them, that Father was in control and the plan set forth in the Book was still the plan, why they even put forth such effort to try to win. Why didn't they all go on vacation to the Bahamas or the mountains? They knew how the Book ended.

Satan knew he had to work every moment to try and draw each and every human away from the Light. To fill his hell, he had to use every tactic to win souls to his side.

But it wasn't hard work. Plant a seed here and there and the humans ran with it. Discontentment. Rejection. Materialism. Consumerism. They deserved it. More. More. More.

And then they wondered how all this had happened. If they'd just go back to the roots, they'd figure it out. And some did.

If the humans only knew. If they only read the Book, they would know that the devil is a liar. That the enemy had no hold over them. The Destroyer had no power unless the humans gave it to him.

The humans gave their power that Jesus had died for them to have, to the Enemy.

Michael shook his head when Warden rose up and displayed his real self. Amazing that they were taking a chance in opening up their realm so the humans could see everything.

Even the angels.

But the humans were now so deceived and intoxicated with the Flow and Magic that they couldn't even see the angels. Or they could but they didn't think they had any power. They didn't care. Again, if they had read the Book.

Or believed.

Wait.

What?

Clarence was crying out. "Bea! My Bea!"

Again. Lies flowed from Warden. Warden was raising his fist, yelling with the throng.

Oh, how Michael wished he could take Clarence and just show him Bea. That she was engaging with angels, even now at the hospital.

Show him that simple faith in Jesus ...

The stage was set, though. The plan was set forth in the Book.

They couldn't interfere unless the Father directed.

So Michael stood steadfast as Clarence crumpled to the floor.

# NINETEEN

Clarence snored himself awake, but slowly drifted back into dreamland.

The bed seemed hard. He rolled to his side, but couldn't quite make it all the way over. Maybe the other side would be more comfortable, but something stopped him, restricted him.

Lisha must have played a joke on him and put up his side rails. She could be very sneaky when she wanted to be.

He chuckled. Lisha was never quiet except when she wanted to play a trick on him.

He blinked his eyes open, knowing she was standing over him, that toothy grin wide and an ornery quip to start his day right. He'd follow with his own and the banter would take off from there. Carol usually rolled the med cart by in the hall and would come in to join them. She always just laughed with them, because no one bantered like Lisha.

He opened his eyes again, a thought coming to him, ready with his smart remark.

His vision of her massive body, dark-skin, black eyes, hair swooped up in rope-like dreads layered over a man, and by the looks of him, a doctor. He had a white doctor coat on and a stethoscope looped around his neck. White hair, green eyes and skinny as a rail.

The vision of Lisha evaporated and reality hit hard.

He must have had an accident and was in the hospital emergency unit or some physician's office. The walls were lined with cabinets, a sink area and a desk workspace. Fluorescent lighting make him blink.

He raised his head, intending to sit up and get out of bed, but something restricted him. Shackles. But more like a straight jacket/shackles combination. Some sort of macabre kind of torture suit. His arms were in a sleeve crossed over his chest, hands each handcuffed to the opposite side of the bed. No bed—but a table. His legs were treated the same as his arms in pants of sorts, but all attached to the table. Little zippers opened everywhere.

"What is this? Where am I?" The suit began to close in on him. He lifted his head. "Get me out of this!"

The doctor smirked. "Oh you'll get out soon enough but not to where you'd like to go." He pointed to the floor emphatically. "*This* is your home now. You'll end your life here, one way or another."

The doctor had something going on in his eyes that made Clarence think of doctors in Nazi Germany at the death camps. He'd read where they invented all kinds of morbid and gruesome experiments.

"Let me show you around a bit." The man took hold of the gurney and gave it a shove, sending Clarence and the table in circles. "We have everything a regular hospital has and more." He walked to a cabinet and opened it, revealing strange looking equipment with all kinds of dials and knobs. "We offer a complete range of treatments, aimed at benefitting every need."

And in an instant, Clarence was in a different realm. Same doctor. The same cabinets. Not the same torture suit. Only handcuffs locked to the table, ankle cuffs too.

The man was examining his hands when he noticed Clarence

looking at him. "You're awake." He smiled. Nothing macabre about him. Same white hair. Same green eyes. He lifted his narrow reading glasses off his nose, letting them drop to his chest from a cord and took Clarence's pulse.

"Where did the torture suit go?" Clarence tried to point. "There was a different feel to this room and you." He lifted his head. "You twirled the table around."

The doctor smiled. "You have been unconscious for quite a while and to wake up in the infirmary has to be confusing."

"Infirmary?" Clarence lifted his head again. "Where am I?"

"Don't you remember the van trip here from ... " he read the chart lying beside Clarence's leg, "Osceola? You don't remember the trip here?"

It all came crashing back. But more than that.

"Where are the fires? Where is the Warden and that beast he changes into?"

The doctor shook his head. "You have been hallucinating in your sleep about demons and angels and fire and burning shackles." He smiled.

"But I—"

"When a person has been through a distinct life change— change of location, loss of relationships—it becomes hard to grasp what reality is." The man put down the chart. "Reality. You are now residing at Chicago's own MSP. Maximum Security Prison. You will be here the rest of your life. You most likely will always be in some sort of restraints—hand cuffs, shackles, leg cuffs. You are never going back to ... Osceola, Nebraska."

Clarence heard the words. He comprehended each one. But grasping the full meaning eluded him.

Never going back to Hillcrest. Never seeing Katty or Bea. Or Mrs. Hatly. Carol. Lisha.

He had wanted to die here before the warden had taken over. The old warden was nice enough. He'd never turned into some sort of dragon, that's for sure.

"What about when I came in here? There was fire. There were creatures—"

"You were dreaming like I said. Sometimes dreams or hallucinations appear so real, we can't discern between reality and the dream world." The doctor smiled, opened his mouth to speak again, but didn't.

Something felt off. The dreams were so real. He could almost feel the pain from the burning shackles. The blades piercing his skin from the handcuffs.

He raised his head and tried to hold up his hands, tried to turn them in the handcuffs. Before the doctor could stop him, he pushed his arm farther into the cuff and twisted so he could see his wrist.

His wrist was circled with pierce marks. Black dried blood at each point. "See? See there?" Clarence raised up, his shoulders off the table. "What are those?"

## TWENTY

"I can't believe how fast she is recovering." Katty walked alongside Bea as Candy, the nurse pushed her in the small wheelchair.

"Little ones seem to heal fast and get over sickness and injuries much faster than adults." Candy patted Bea's shoulder. "I think it's because they move around so much more. They are always fidgeting or playing, bouncing."

Katty rushed ahead to the car. "I know. She is always bouncing to some kind of music in her head." She opened the car door. "Especially when music comes on the car radio or the TV at home." She laughed and wiped her eyes. She couldn't believe how emotional she was. Bea was okay, and would be fine, but—

Candy touched her arm. "You've been through a lot, too. Seeing your own child shot. Then surgery. It has to be scary."

Katty straightened.

Candy's blue eyes were so intense and concerned.

Katty couldn't stop the tears when Candy hugged her.

"Mommy, look! I left my candy in my car seat!"

Katty looked down. Bea wasn't in the wheelchair. She was already in her car seat. "What? Bea! How did you ... " She wiped her face.

Bea was kicking her feet, happily munching something, her mouth already smeared with brown chocolate.

It felt so good to laugh. "Well, Candy, I guess you're right. She can move around better than I could." She found a wipe and began to clean Bea's mouth.

Candy grinned. "We're gonna miss you, Bea!" She leaned in the car and waved to her. And to Katty, "Call us anytime if you have any questions. Don't hesitate and really, let me know how you're doing, too. I have tomorrow off and I could come over and check on her."

Katty immediately got a visual of the trailer court and her trailer—falling apart, tacky trash—wait! Clarence had helped her replace that crumbling deck and the warped fake paneling inside. She tossed the dirty wipe onto the front seat of her car and nodded slightly. Her humble little trailer actually looked cute. "Uh, sure." Deep breath. She truly didn't know how to do this friend thing, if that's what this was. "That'd be fine. If you want to."

"Sure! I'll call before I come over to see if you need anything." Candy hugged her again. "Gotta get back to work." She spun the wheelchair around to face the hospital. "And you obviously don't need this thing anymore!"

Her laugh sounded like bells tinkling.

Katty buckled Bea in. "Does that hurt your ow-y?" She loosened the straps. "We won't make it as tight as those people told us to. Just for a couple days. Then it's back to making it so tight you can't breathe!" She tickled Bea then thought better of it. "Does that hurt?"

Bea kicked and finished the candy. "No Mommy." She giggled. "I love you Mommy." She pointed. "And the angels are laughing too, just like if you tickled them."

Deep sigh. "I wish I could—" A sensation of pure joy and peace overwhelmed her. "Never mind. I think something ... I think ... " She shut the car door and hugged her chest, walked around the car to the driver's door. "I think ... I just ... they're here." She looked into the air, not sure what to look at, or what she'd see. In the hospital, she had seen something more than the beautiful lights.

She sat in her seat and looked at the hospital door. Candy waved. She waved back. She'd never had a friend. A friend that would come over and ... what? Have a drink? She wrinkled her nose. Not going there, ever again. A cup of coffee? She could learn to like coffee if that's what friends did together.

A friend that would care enough to check on her and Bea?

The people who she used to do drugs with were not friends. They were people in the same trap and prison, same pain that Katty had been in. Users, abusers, willing to do whatever it took to get whatever they wanted, from whoever they wanted. And what they had wanted most was to numb out and forget their own past and pain.

But a friend, a real friend who would give as much as they took? Or give as much as Katty gave? A give and take relationship.

Doing healthy things together. What would that be?

Uh. She tapped her finger on the steering wheel.

Coffee.

Katty grinned and started the car, waving once again at Candy. Candy had already moved to her next task on her job.

Shopping. Maybe friends shopped together.

The only time she'd ever shopped for anything other than groceries, had been when Phil took her shopping to fussy her up —show her off to his friends when they had first lived together. After that, it had been all downhill.

The times when she'd meet Clarence in the park. They'd watched Bea play or they pushed her on the swings.

Together.

She sighed as she turned into the grocery store.

Friendships were going to be a new experience and it would

take time to learn how to do it right. And to trust anyone with seeing her home and her life—who she was.

Bea kicked the back of Katty's seat. "Mommy! Can I have some Bubbly Pebbles cereal? And ... and—"

"Sure Bea. I think we can do that." Interesting. Clarence had just paid her the day before yesterday. She actually had money in her account to buy groceries and sugary cereals. Something kicked in at the same time. She'd never lived extravagantly—never had much of her own, and if she had any money, she'd spent it on booze and drugs—groceries always came later.

But now. She had money. Some anyway. Clarence had been so good to her.

"Oh, Clarence." She put the car into park. Even this car wasn't new, but it was all in one piece and ran like a top. Clarence had made sure of that. He'd had it all gone over at the auto shop. They'd washed it and detailed it. She ran her hand along the steering wheel. "Beautiful." She leaned her head into the steering wheel. "Clarence. Where are you? Are you okay?"

"Mommy. Can we go see him after this? I want to show him my cereal."

She didn't know. *God*. There had been such craziness at the nursing home when Bea had been shot, that Bea hadn't seen Clarence get shot. Thank God she hadn't seen that. But what now? How could she tell Bea?

Katty turned in her seat and opened her mouth and immediately shut it. What could she say? Deep breath. "Honey, I think he's busy. Maybe we can go ask Carol if he's there. He might have a client."

Bea knew what that meant, since Katty had become his paralegal. Bea knew that meant go get the coloring books and color or draw. And be quiet.

"Okay. We can get some ice cream then." Bea clapped her hands. "Can we go in now?" She yawned. "I want my cereal."

"Time to get our shopping done and go home for a nap before

anything else." Katty unbuckled her. "You just got out of the hospital! So we need to get home and get some rest!"

She helped Bea out of the car and onto her feet. All those times when Katty had been drunk and had just left Bea home alone. Once, Katty had actually been partly sober by the time she'd gotten home around noon. She had looked everywhere for Bea and become terrified. Finally, when Katty was about to give up and call the police—which would have been bad—she saw Bea's foot sticking out from under the old rocking chair. She had rushed to it and found her, all wrapped in a little tent of her own making under the seat of the chair. Still shuddering and sobbing, but asleep, sucking her thumb. Bea never sucked her thumb, but she had then.

Katty got her purse and ran after Bea to the store entrance where a man who was coming out, loaded down with bags of groceries, held the door open for them.

"Hey little one." He looked up at Katty. "Is she the little girl that got shot? How is she doing?" He didn't stop talking long enough for Katty to answer. "That old man—shooting innocent kids. Awful. I'm glad he is getting locked up. What did he need a gun at the nursing home for anyway?"

Wait. What?

"Clarence didn't shoot her!" Katty ran after him to his car. "He didn't shoot her!" She caught hold of one of his bags and stopped him. "The guard shot her and him!" She was yelling. "Clarence got shot too!"

He yanked the bag out of her hand and opened his car door. "Not what I heard. He shot her and then shot himself."

Katty stomped her foot and snapped at him. "He did not! Clarence is our friend. He is like a grandfather to me—to us!" Emotions boiled over. Frustration at this man and the gossip-mongers of the community. Lies. Pain of seeing her own daughter shot. Terror—would she die? The pain and horror of Phil's abuse, her own parents abuse. Fear of being alone with those voices.

Everything rose up at once as she pounded the hood of his pickup. "The *guard* shot Bea and Clarence."

"Mommy?" Bea sang out from the open door of the grocery store, Mandy Ashton standing behind her, holding the door open. "Are you coming?" She held up a box of cereal from behind her back. "I found my cereal."

Mandy grinned. "She's ready to eat it and that's okay. I just wanted to make sure it was okay that you buy it before I let her open it."

Small town grocery store.

Katty watched as the man backed out of the parking space. She stepped off the curb following the truck out of the parking place. She flipped him off, then caught herself. Some habits took longer to break.

"Mommy!" Bea was persistent and Katty didn't want to tire her.

She wished she could follow that man to wherever the other gossipers were and set them straight. Where was Clarence right now? Maybe Sheriff would know how he was.

She walked to the store. Bea was so cute, waving the cereal box at her.

"Can we buy this Mommy?" Bea shoved the box in Katty's face.

Every bright color, especially red, exploded in front of her eyes. Crazy figures and characters ran across the picture and a graphic of the cereal came close to jumping off the box.

Katty laughed. "Are you sure this is the one, Bea? I mean you seem a little unsure!" She scooped her up into her arms and squeezed her tenderly. "I love you!"

"Let's get a cart. We might need one."

"No doubt." Katty broke a cart free and sat her in the cart. "I think you should ride today, okay?"

"Okay, Mommy." Bea grinned. "That way I can see everything."

"Thanks Mandy for corralling her." Katty pointed outside. "That man out there was saying that *Clarence* shot Bea and I had to set him straight."

Mandy nodded. "That's what everybody is saying. I don't know what they all have against him except he was in prison before. He's a good man." She hugged Bea. "Is she okay? We all heard she was dead."

Bea patted her chest. "I'm not dead. I'm alive!" She stretched her arms up for emphasis.

Mandy hugged her again. "You sure are alive! And we're glad you are."

John Potter sauntered to the check stands. "She *is* alive!" He bopped her nose. "We heard that those cereal balls," he tapped on the box, "kidnapped you and carried you off to ... Cereal Land and made you queen of their clan. You get to eat their cereal all the time and live happily ever after." He bowed low. "Queen Bea." He chuckled.

Bea's eyes popped. She looked at Katty and Mandy, then back at John. "Really? I dreamed that I think."

Katty wiped her eyes. "Oh you guys. You make me laugh when I need it."

"That's what the sign outside says. Didn't you see it?" John spread his arm wide, as he said the words. "Blank blank blank— the place where the employees make you laugh." He pointed outside. "It's up there ... or it was yesterday."

Bea looked outside wide-eyed as Katty wheeled her away.

"Let's buy our stuff and get home, Bea." Soup. Crackers. She'd only been gone from home twenty-four hours, but couldn't remember what they needed.

"'Roni." Bea pointed. "Shells." She started to stand but one word from Katty and she sat down. "Cookies, Mommy."

Oh no. The toy section.

Bea stood up in the cart without any struggle or pain and began to inspect every toy.

Mandy was stocking gum in the same aisle. "She's doing good, isn't she?" She stood and adjusted her apron and retied it. Her round belly filled it out. "She moved easy enough. Is she going to be okay?'

"Yeah. They did surgery and took out the bullet. It was right next to her liver, but didn't do any real damage, other than to make a hole in her."

Bea didn't miss a thing. "There's a hole in me?"

"Yes. It's so we can feed you cereal right there instead of wasting time feeding you through your mouth," Katty laughed. "We'll just pop it in that hole and ... " Bea's face was so funny— her mouth dropped open and eyes perked up bright and happy.

"Really?"

"No. I'm just teasing. They fixed it all up when you were in the hospital. No holes!"

Bea wasn't listening. She was reaching for a doll, then a stuffed kitten. And a ... oh how to say no to her today. With what she'd just been through. It had broken both their hearts when Katty had said no to the beautiful red bike. Seemed like a million years ago.

If it wasn't from Clarence, then who?

"Mommy. This? And this? Can I have this one too?"

Bea was so cute. So pretty. Flashback to when she came out of surgery, all hooked up to machines and pale as the white lights.

"Sure. Put them in the cart. We need milk and bread."

Bea broke in. "And peanut butter. Remember we were out."

Katty tapped her on the nose. "We were. Good job remembering."

They picked up a few more things and hit the check stand.

"Look at all this fun stuff, Bea." Mandy handed the toys to John. "Can I come over to play, too?"

John bagged the groceries and toys and held one up. "What's this? They didn't have this when I was a boy."

Mandy chuckled. "You *are* a boy!"

Bea grabbed it from him. "It's a cubic rube. A round one." She flipped it to the backside, all encased in a clear plastic cover. "See all the pretty colors?"

She didn't have a clue how to twist it to make the game work. Katty bet she'd figure it out fast though. Bea was so smart.

"Okay Bea. We have to get you home to rest." Katty picked her up out of the cart and let her walk. "Thanks Mandy. See you."

"Yeah, Katty." Mandy followed her to the door. "And don't let those people in the gossip factory get to you. You know the truth." She nodded. "We know the truth about Clarence. He's our friend."

"Yup. He's a good guy."

Katty drove into her driveway and helped Bea to the house.

By the time she had unloaded the groceries, Bea had the packages opened and the toys all around her on the floor, playing. Cereal boxes surrounded her too.

Katty'd given into every whim. She'd made Bea give up that red bike from nowhere so she guessed some cheap little toys and cereal would be okay.

"Look Mommy. This doll's eyes open if you sit her up and close when you lay her down. She's so pretty."

"So are you!" Katty picked up the trash. "Bea, I'm going out to get the mail and I'll be right back."

Bea hadn't even heard her, she was so immersed in her playing.

Now that Katty was assured that Bea was all right, all she could think about was Clarence. She'd forgotten to go to the Sheriff's. Maybe she could call.

Not much mail—a newsletter from the hospital, she must be on their mailing list now. A flyer from the grocery store—she should start reading those and shopping by them. Two credit card applications.

And a note. To Bea. Weird.

She flipped it to the back and then the front again, as she

walked into the house. Dropping the rest of the mail on the counter, she examined the envelope.

That handwriting.

The way the sender had written the capitol R in Randolph. It curled to a tail at the bottom of the R, then swooped it around under the rest of her last name.

Her heard pounded. She swallowed.

Only one person made his Rs that way.

# TWENTY-ONE

Phil had raised his hand in the air, chanting with the inmates. "Bea is dead. Bea is dead." Even though he was as much in the flow of evil as anyone there, he'd had trouble saying those words.

When he had tried to say the words, he couldn't, even though Warden had assured him Bea wasn't dead.

He must really be her father and not some slime-ball Katty had gone to bed with. Otherwise, saying those words wouldn't get to him.

It was startling the way everyone had been engaged with the beat and the words. Lex, right next to him, backed away to the wall behind them. He'd done his share of battles and stupid, but even Lex seemed shocked.

Phil had watched as every face in every cell had become his own dad.

Ew.

The face and time was imprinted in Phil's memory. He'd been just a kid, like maybe ten.

His dad had been such a fake. Meat cutter at the local grocery store by day and priest of the local cult by night. His day job served him well—he was the everyday neighbor and friend.

People confided in him and women flirted with him, which helped fill an already long list for his harem. He was King Pin in his own life and mind.

But the deeper he got into his night life, the harder and more abusive he became. A man at the store called him High Priest, which earned the man a fierce look from Dad. Phil hadn't known what that meant until later.

The expressions Phil had witnessed on all the faces at the prison as they frolicked, was the same as he'd see on Dad, when he'd come to the store after school. Dad was supposed to pick him up and he'd waited thirty minutes before he started walking.

At the store, he'd pulled the heavy door into the meat room open and greeted his dad, but his dad appeared to be zoned out —in some sort of ecstatic state. Chunks of meat were all around him on the counter, on the floor. Blood dripped off the cutting table. His eyes were just staring, and he was licking blood from around his lips.

Phil had hated the stench of the meat room anyway, but the acrid smell that day had made his eyes burn.

He'd tried to wake his dad. Called his name several times. Phil hadn't wanted to go near him. Only when the store owner tapped Phil's dad on the arm did he start awake again, lost in the horrible dreams he must have been in. He had been holding the meat knife in one hand and when he woke, startled, he just about stabbed the owner in the chest. Phil was mortified at what the owner had seen of his dad, but at the same time he was titillated and entranced, drawn into the ecstasy.

His father's blood ran through his own.

That had been the expression on every face at the prison.

He'd tried to join in the revelry and wanted to, especially when one of the women danced near the stairway downstairs. He'd found himself drawn down there, but when he glanced back at Lex, the expression of fright on his face stopped him.

Lex had been scared? What a baby.

If Phil had admitted it, he had been too. But he'd also been excited.

From Dad's face to the real faces, from Warden's face to Dad's face.

A woman had slipped upstairs and run straight to Warden, only he'd rebuffed her, taken her hand and placed it in Phil's.

"For you, Brother."

The video that played in his head at that moment was the same one as when his own dad had done exactly the same thing at a cult meeting.

Dad had led a young woman to Phil, placed her hand in his and said, "For you, Son."

The only time he'd called Phil anything but Bastard.

TWENTY-TWO

Noell walked home from the hospital. What a strange day, outside and inside. Her heart was full after all she'd seen in that hospital room with Katty and little Bea.

What was that? What were they? They looked like little Christmas lights, only they moved! By themselves!

Had to be real because Bea and Katty kept talking like they saw them too. Like they'd seen them before.

Noell thought at first they were reflections from outside, like a car driving past and the sun beaming off the car and then it flashed inside, along the walls. Only the sun wasn't out much. The cloud cover was complete. Odd for a late August day.

Or if the sun had been shining through the windows, they could have been dust specks floating through a sun beam. Gamma used to call them angel dust.

But the sun hadn't been shining in.

What would science call them? She opened the browser on her phone. But what should she google? Sun beams? Angels?

She stared into the distance and stumbled over a curb. The sparks of light seemed real, seemed to be something or someone.

Someone?

Yes. Because they interacted with Bea. They moved around her and Katty. Not Katty as much as Bea. They had landed on Bea's hands and head. Even on her nose, which Bea said tickled. She had held out her hand and three landed there.

Noell smiled. They were real. A real *something*. Noell saw the lights flitting here and there. Katty saw them too.

Her newly awakened science mind wanted to find answers. But the rest of her wanted it to be real, not something that could be explained away. Spiritual. Real, but God. No matter if they were angels or God. Whatever else He had up His sleeve, she wanted it to be Him. Real.

She was automatically heading home but as she crossed the highway from the convenience store, and looked both ways at the railroad tracks, her heart fluttered.

The pool.

She didn't want to go home. Nobody was there. It had become a lonely place. She hadn't seen her neighbor, Fletch, for a long time because he had a full-time job now. Were they becoming adults? He had a full-time job and she was a home owner.

Before she had gone to the nursing home and found all the chaos and then to the hospital, she had made the decision to sell that old house and all its contents and live in the camper.

Maybe that would have to get put off—at least until Clarence came back.

She shook her head and found herself stepping over the embankment. Since all that had gone on at the pool, the park board had deemed it necessary to build a short wall around it to prevent kids from wandering in. But she still knew how to get in.

Looking behind her, she checked to see if anyone was watching. Houses lined the park border on the west and north. Railroad tracks lined the south and a road on the east.

But that was stupid. There was no one about and how could she expect to see if someone was watching from a house? Always so afraid of what people would see. Always concerned with what would people think.

Nobody cared. Nobody.

Except for the gossipers. They seemed to have a radar for seeing and hearing about people, to have something to gossip about. She knew all about that. She'd been the butt of jokes and gossip all her life.

"What happened to your mom, little girl?"

"Why do you live with your grandma?"

"Why doesn't she ever have company?"

"The mailman says that when he hand delivers mail, he sees all the junk in her house."

The junk. The clutter.

And no Mommy.

Made the junk even more visible when there wasn't a person to see or talk to.

That might be the real reason she wanted to put off going home.

She stepped down into the cave where the pool was. She hadn't been in there since she rescued Clarence that day. She had told herself she would come back often to research it. To study it. But what did she know about doing that?

All she knew right now was that this place made her feel peaceful. She could breathe here. She could think and dream in here, no matter that the place made some people creep out. She should have felt that way too, what with her nightmares and all.

She sat on the rock next to the pool. She'd study that too. Nightmares and dreams.

Next time she'd bring her notebook. Maybe Dr. Steven's journal from the camper. Let him help her research this cave and pool.

She dangled her necklace—the same necklace she had dropped into the pool. Only this time she didn't fear jumping in after it.

She loved how the simple but limited light caught on the necklace as it twirled, casting reflections onto the rock walls of the cave. They resembled letters, maybe a different language. There was stuff carved into the walls in places and the reflections seemed to highlight them.

The water felt just like she remembered it—silky and oily at the same time. She hooked her necklace around her neck and trailed her fingers in the water again. It almost felt like baby oil, only thinner. And cleaner feeling. It had more substance than the water out of her tap at home.

She wanted to go in, and she would again, before it got cold. Reminder: bring extra clothes and a towel. That journal and her notebook.

She stuck her fingers in again and it felt like it went through something. Like when she combed her fingers through her hair and they scratched her head. Through the hair strands.

She glanced at her phone beside her. What if when she tapped the glass screen, her finger went through? That it went through the glass but to another realm or another place?

She picked it up and tapped it. An app opened. That was it.

But what if it could go through and enter somewhere else?

Like in a sci-fi novel. Or movie, when a portal opened up and the character ran through it to another dimension.

What if she stuck her fingers into glue? Stupid. They'd just get glue all over, not go through to anywhere. To the glue dimension. Duh.

When she was little, she had been entranced by TV, the scenes, the characters in the program. Gamma and even Grandpa had to pop her on her fingers because she'd always go to the TV and try to touch the trees or people she saw there.

What if she could have gone in there and touched them?

Or better yet, what if she could have gone into the TV, her whole body, through that glass and lived in the story?

It was the same feeling she had felt when she laid down on

the carpet in the living room and imagined herself walking on the ceiling—a whole new world. Her bed could have been over there. Her chair in the corner above Gamma's red leather couch.

She forgot about her phone in her hand and almost let it slip into the water. It hadn't but what if she could have gone in after it and the whole pool was the open door to a different realm?

She was getting excited.

Back to the lights in Bea's room at the hospital. What if they were real and part of another realm that humans could access.

She dangled her finger into the pool and wondered.

The water was just molecules, right?

That stopped her.

Right?

She was just a bunch of molecules zooming around each other. Some were for skin. Some for inside organs. Maybe?

Science class seemed ever so much more fun right now than it had in high school.

She knew she had been led here. Definitely to the camper to find the journals and then to explore this place. Maybe this pool, this cave was a place where people had felt close to God. She certainly did. It made her think of Him and think of the eternal, but wonder what He had in store for her, her life.

She tapped on the rock that she sat on.

That was made up of molecules, right?

She stabbed her finger there again. "Ow!"

She sucked on her finger. What if there was another realm through there? If she was made of molecules and the rock was too, why couldn't she stick her finger through the rock?

That stopped her.

What if she couldn't get it back out?

# TWENTY-THREE

Michael watched as Noell unhooked her necklace. He nodded at her angel, Jasper.

There was freedom from the Father for Noell. Freedom to explore this part of her life. Freedom for her in this time of her life.

"Father is pleased she is here and we are to support her in this journey of exploration." Michael nodded at the pool. "This pool has been one of pain and loss. Of people being robbed of their destiny, but no more." He pointed at Noell. "She will take it back for what Father really intended."

Jasper nodded. As Noell's angel, he had the mandate to protect and guard her. He had been assigned to her from her entrance into the Earth realm at her birth. He stood by her, ministering to her from the Father's heart.

Jasper smiled as Noell tapped on the rock. "She's gonna try it sometime and when she does the whole world will open up to her. She has the Einstein heart and spirit, doesn't she?"

Michael chuckled. "Yes she does. And more." He shook his head. "They all have so much more to explore, but they just tap on their phones."

They watched as Noell stood and stretched. "Note to self—bring notebooks and Dr. Stevens journal next time." She wandered next to the cave walls and shone her phone flashlight onto the rock. "Things are written here." She tapped her phone to the camera and snapped a few photos. "I should find Gamma's old camera and take pictures of each drawing or words. I love that old camera." She traced the lines with her finger. "Something else is here. Before I felt evil at times, but now it's different. I wonder why."

Jasper started to open his mouth but shut it. He motioned to Michael. Pointed to his own chest, then his mouth, then to Noell.

Michael slowly shook his head. "We're not opening up that portal, brother. It's not our call. She has to initiate it. Plus, Father's plan is in place. He is opening up the humans to this realm, but they have to learn to storm heaven."

Jasper nodded. "I want that interaction."

"We all do. But it can't happen until time. Time when all is in place. Time when the sons of God are ready, and some are more than ready. Doing everything that Yeshua did on earth and more."

"But some?" Jasper raised his eyebrows.

"Some are not even realizing they are sons of God. They are still ... well, let's just say they're not ready." Michael smiled at Noell. "She hasn't had any training along those lines—wondering if she can push her hand through rock—but she is just about there." He squinted. "She would never say that though."

Noell broke in, still unaware of their presence. "Gamma always used to say she felt close to God on her red leather sofa." She grinned and wiped a tear. "I would too. It's beautiful."

She gazed at every crevice, every chunk of rock. "I feel close to Him ... " She paused and tried again, looking up. "I feel close to ... You God, here. Right here in a cave." She grinned. "Why a cave and not that church where Gamma's service was?"

Jasper nodded at Michael. Precious moments only an angel could witness. And the Lord.

Noell spoke the answer to her own question. "That church belongs to something or someone else. You God, don't live there."

She touched the rock wall, rotated and scanned the cave again, her fingers connecting with the rough, damp surface. "When I think about it, I think some people would have a problem with me saying You live in a cave when ages and years have been spent building massive and gaudy churches for ... not You." She sighed. "For them."

Michael pointed at Noell. "She is closer to Him right now than most humans."

Jasper nodded and grinned. "In a cave."

Noell lifted her hands, eyes closed. "I want to know *You*." Her eyes blinked open. "Who You really are."

A cloud drifted into the cave, filling every crevasse, every crack.

Michael blinked as Noell knelt onto the cold, hard floor, her arms still extended high.

Jasper swallowed and closed his eyes, his wings unfurled.

Michael bowed his head, hands open. His body and wings expanded along with Jasper's.

"Lord, I love You." Noell whispered.

Michael nodded as another angel dropped in, his hand across his chest. The angel nodded in acknowledgment.

Another flew in.

And another.

Soon, there were many and the cave was crowded.

All surrounded precious Noell, as she worshipped, totally unaware of anyone but the Lord.

## TWENTY-FOUR

Clarence waited while Ralston unlocked the cell door. Two other guards stood behind them, ready to beat him down if he tried anything.

Clarence could have found his way there himself. For some reason they put him in his old cell—the one he had been in when they had kicked him out, months ago. Up the steps and half-way down the corridor.

As he stood there, it felt like he had never left. Only, a chill swept around his shoulders, a ghostly presence engulfed him, a faint howl echoed through the corridors.

He shivered when the door slid open and Ralston pushed him inside the cell.

The noise must have triggered the neighbors, because inmates on both sides rattled the bars on their doors and began to heckle him.

"Hey baby. Welcome home."

One man close by must have remembered Clarence. "Clarence, we killed Dirko for you! He didn't like it without you anyway."

Another man piped up. "Yeah baby. And we helped staff make

your new bedroom very comfy. We painted over your love notes to that bitch, Annie."

Clarence held his breath.

Ralston laughed. "Oh, you big meanies. That's not nice." He pushed Clarence onto the pull-down bed. "Here you go. Home at last." He rapped Clarence on the head with his beat stick. "Now don't go redecorating the walls or nuthin. You won't last very long in here, so don't make no more drawings. Otherwise we have to repaint and we don't want to. Got it?"

Clarence literally remembered every drawing, every word he'd written or carved into the walls. He could close his eyes right now and visualize them all. He could read the walls from inside his imagination—Annie and hearts, Dad, every important person in his life, words of encouragement, a calendar of days, months, and when time had stretched—years. He could read it all.

Ralston slammed the cell door with extra vigor and inserted the keys with a flourish.

Damn guard loved putting him back into prison.

Damn him!

Clarence stood too fast. The wound and bandage stretched and pulled. He stumbled to the bars and pushed against the door before Ralston had it locked. "You are a bastard! I don't belong here!"

The door knocked Ralston off balance and back into the cell block railings. The guards pushed him upright and tried to scramble around him to get to Clarence.

Clarence had already pushed his way down the walkway to the end of the cellblock. First one inmate yelled, then another, until the whole cellblock was in an uproar. Most were on Clarence's side for the first time since he'd been back. They wanted to be the one to be running free, even though there were three guards running up the steps, ready to capture Clarence as soon as he ran down the steps. One minute they taunted him, the next minute they cheered him on.

The bandage had torn off when he broke through the two guards upstairs and he could feel the T-shirt fabric rubbing against the wound as he ran. He was going to pay for running. He was going to pay for breaking through the other guards. He'd pay for pushing Ralston against the bars. He'd pay big.

But he couldn't let them think he'd gotten soft and wimpy. He had to be tough.

Or die.

"Cla-rence! Cla-rence! Cla-rence!" The inmates chanted just as they had when they chanted "Bea is dead. Bea is dead." Two-faced bastards. Hypocrites.

The guards just stood and waited for him to get downstairs. They weren't even focused. Lazy bums.

Just as he got halfway down the steps, a dietary staff pushed a fully loaded cart out of the hallway to Clarence's right. It was loaded with cases of soda, blocking the guards from Clarence. Blocking Clarence's escape.

He thought.

He turned right into the same hallway and pulled the heavy cart in behind him. He had no idea how to get outside or if he even could.

He'd die trying.

But he wasn't going to be a pawn or sissy or lily-livered. They'd have to work to keep him in check and locked up. Or kill him.

He almost ran into another kitchen staff. He remembered her. She was the one who gave him the hand knitted scarf!

"In there!" She pointed to a door. "In through there, Mr. Clarence!"

He slammed into the door, right into the kitchen—right into supper prep—pans and loaded carts everywhere.

He couldn't stop his momentum and overturned several carts, meatballs flying everywhere. Seemed like the kitchen staff was all on his side, because carts and equipment parted, clearing a path through the chaos. A door opened at the far end of the kitchen and Clarence ran toward it.

A semi truck was parked right outside the door, the delivery man was checking his clipboard just as Clarence jumped from the building. His eyes popped, seeing Clarence running toward him. He stepped aside.

How had he gotten this far?

But three guards ran from the back of the truck to the loading dock and two more ran from the front end, surrounding Clarence.

The kitchen noise behind him was deafening, the inmates working in there cheered him on. But when they saw he might get caught, they threw pans and utensils—anything they could get their hands on.

The guards drew their guns.

A tall inmate from the kitchen pulled Clarence back inside and slammed the door. "Dude. You're gonna get killed. You can't get outa here. You don't have a gun and you're bleeding."

Clarence glanced down at his shirt. Yup.

Three guards skidded in behind Clarence and grabbed him just as a pot of hot spaghetti sauce flew through the air and landed on one of the guards. "Gaaa!" He screamed, trying to wipe it from him. "I'm burning!"

Clarence jumped back, just in time to land into the arms of a guard who was prepared with handcuffs. The guy was quick. He had them over his wrists and clicked before the other guard had quit screaming.

Clarence shuddered.

He was dead. His heart pounded.

Whatever made him think he could escape?

The guards shoved him back through the kitchen. The kitchen staff cheered him on, but they weren't the ones that would be beaten, he was sure of it. They wouldn't feel the brunt of breaking away. They were thrilled right now, but he would pay for their thrill soon enough.

The guards marched him through the kitchen and past the scarf woman—"Dorothy" her name tag read. She wiped her eyes. "I be praying for you, Mr. Clarence."

He nodded. "Pray for my little Bea. She got shot too."

Dorothy's eyes widened. "They shot you?"

He nodded and lifted his shirt.

She covered her mouth with her hands. "You-you need a doctor."

The guards dragged him away, but he turned them all back toward Dorothy. "Thank you for my scarf. I still have it in my room at the nursing home. Maybe I'll even get to wear it ... I hope."

She nodded as they marched him away, her hands together at her mouth.

The closer the guards got to his cell, the fiercer and unrestrained they became, giving him a punch here and there.

When they reached his cell, the noise was thunderous. Inmates stomped on the floor which made the whole floor shudder and creak.

Ralston squealed. "We gonna break the prison!" He gripped the walls. "In here. Git 'em in here now!"

In that single second before they shoved Clarence into the cell, he glimpsed Warden at the end of the cellblock, surrounded by several men, hit men Clarence guessed. Warden had a smirk on his face, like Clarence was playing directly into his hands. Doing exactly what he had foreseen and getting exactly what Warden had wanted all along.

The breath went out of Clarence's chest, like a beast had just butted him. What had he been thinking? What had made him think he could outrun guards who were half his age? That he wouldn't suffer any consequences— like beatings and maximum lockdown?

Stupid. Stupid.

This was probably what had happened to Dirk. Huge, dark-skinned, friendly Dirk. Prison had been his only family and that was his only crime.

As the guards pushed him into the cell, they descended on him, like gnats on dying fruit. Pummeled him. They punched him over and over in the wound, till he didn't feel anything anymore.

He would not die. He had to make it back to Bea and to Katty. Mrs. Hatly.

His last thought before he lost consciousness—he loved his little family in Osceola, and he might never see them again.

## TWENTY-FIVE

Katty shuddered as she let go of the notecard and watched it flutter onto the counter beside the cereal box.

Bea sat before the TV, watching her favorite show—The Gummy Family. Why that was her favorite, could only be explained by her love of the candy. Otherwise the show had no merit at all.

Back to the note. Katty had thought Phil was dead after he had left Bea to burn on the slide in the park. *She'd* almost burned to death because of him. Surely Phil had been locked up somewhere. Sheriff hadn't told her he was loose. Maybe she had just … hoped he was dead.

Well, she'd march over to the sheriff's department and make sure he knew Phil was still stalking them.

She tapped her fingernails against the cereal box. Bet the bike had been him too. So like him. Make others believe he was a saint.

Bea loved that bike and thought whoever dropped it off, tied with a big red bow, was the best person in the world.

And Katty looked like a bitch—a crabby old bitch—because she had made Bea give up the bike.

Grrr!

She was glad they hadn't kept it and hoped that whoever had it now was happy, but she wavered back and forth. Should she have let Bea keep it or given it away?

Gravel crunched. A vehicle had driven in her driveway.

She peeked out and froze.

A cop.

Her old mentality kicked in, until she realized she didn't have anything to hide. She hadn't done anything bad.

Whew.

Maybe it was from the shooting and they needed more information. Or maybe Sheriff wanted to make sure Bea was okay.

Ha. Ha. Like that'd ever happen. He was a nice guy and all, but why would he worry about her and Bea.

The deputy replaced his radio and opened the car door, stepped out and walked to the deck.

Glad the deck was fixed. It looked so much better.

Still, her breathing was coming in gasps. Her face felt hot and she was sweating.

She opened the door just as he reached up to knock.

He stood there poised, eyes wide, mouth open. "Uh, hello."

"Hi." She looked behind him at his patrol car. "Nice car. All nice and shiny."

He glanced behind him and let his arm drop. "Thanks."

No distractions. Back to her. "Are you Katty Randolph?"

"Yes." She cleared her throat. "Yes I am." She tapped her fingers against her leg. Evidently he wasn't going to start the conversation. "I just re-upped my car registration—last week—as a matter of fact." She kept on tapping. "And my bills are paid." Thanks Clarence.

He brushed his hand at her. "Oh, no. That's all good. Um. I'm Officer Scott and that's not why I'm here." He checked inside. "Mind if I come in?" He slowly fished his identification out of his back pocket and showed it to her.

"Uh-okay." Officer Scott. She stepped aside to let him in.

He smiled as he entered the house and removed his ball hat. "I see you have a little girl."

Katty glanced at Bea and swallowed. "I probably shouldn't let her watch so much TV, but we just got home, and I was putting groceries away." Truth. Well kinda. She had really been wanting to kill Phil Daynton, so maybe her murderous vibes had reached the police department.

"Oh no. She's fine." He cased the kitchen area. "Is there someplace where we can talk?" He tipped his head toward Bea. "Someplace more private?"

Katty frowned. Didn't sound like a true cop request to her. "Private?" Was this a come-on?

He shook his head. "Someplace away from your daughter."

"Oh." She shrugged. "Outside?" She pointed to the door. "On the deck?"

"She'll be okay?" He pointed over his shoulder at Bea.

"Yeah. We won't be long, right?" She opened the door. "Bea, this kind man wants to talk to me a minute. I'll be right outside."

Bea didn't move or turn her head.

"She'll be okay."

He chuckled. "Must be a great show. I should find out what it is and watch it myself."

She stepped to the deck.

He closed the door partway, checking to make sure Bea was still watching TV and that they could still see her from there.

He cleared his throat and glanced at the neighboring trailers.

Katty began to lose patience. "What is this about? And why all the secrecy?"

He reached into his pocket again and pulled out a paper.

She'd seen those before. "A summons for my arrest?"

"No. Just a complaint filed against you."

She fumbled with her thumb, her fingers circling it. "A-Against me?" That old presence of fear sat on her chest.

"Yes." He took a deep breath and watched her face. "Someone reported that they felt you were abusing your daughter."

Katty stopped. "Uh ... when was this filed? Because she just got out of the hospital. Today. There was stuff going on just these last few days."

He checked the paper. "This was from three days ago."

Katty blinked. She wanted to cry. "Did they say what I did?" She fell back into the defensive druggy misfit character. The lines she used to feed the cops then, wanted to flow out of her mouth.

"Look. This is just a complaint." Officer Eddington waved her to the small table and chairs. "Can we sit?"

Katty nodded. She motioned for him to take a chair and she sat in the other one, taking time to glance inside. Bea hadn't moved. She had to be so exhausted.

"Is she okay?"

"Yeah. She just got out of the hospital and we needed to get some food, so she is really tired."

"I won't make this long." He folded the paper. "I just need to make sure you two are okay and see if there is anything we can do."

One of the neighbor kids rode by, younger siblings running along, their laughter barely broke through Katty's fog.

Who had turned her in?

Something clicked on though as she continued to squint. The sun glared off of ... a red bike. A brand new, red bike. A spanking shiny new red bike!

She stood up and waved at the kids. They were so happy. Laughing and yelling. "My turn." If Bea couldn't have it, those kids deserved it.

Bet Mrs. Crabbyface had seen her with Bea when she'd discovered the bike. Katty had walked the bike to the huge trailer court dumpster with Bea following behind her, crying all the way. "Mommy, I'll be good. If you let me keep it, I'll pick up my room everyday ... and and—"

Katty remembered her response and she had yelled the words, "Bea, you are in no way keeping this bike, if it's not from Clarence. I don't care what you do, you aren't keeping this bike."

Bet Mrs. Crabbyface had heard every word. She probably even pushed her window open just a little bit more so she could hear every word they had yelled.

But what Katty remembered next made her skin crawl. Cold shivers ran up her back.

She had spanked Bea.

And that must have set off the do-not-abuse-your-kids siren in the trailer court. Mrs. Crabbyface had seen her spank Bea and for her accusing heart, that was enough for her to call the cops on Katty.

Whew.

Katty sat down hard. "It was Mrs. Crabbyface, wasn't it? She is always spying on us." Katty turned to Officer Eddington and really saw him for the first time since he had knocked on her ... door. Blue eyes. Short, sort of military cut blond hair. Kind of skinny, but not super tall. Freckles? Kind of cute.

"Mrs. Crabbyface?" He brushed his hand against his mouth. "We don't ever report who filed the complaint. We just follow up on it." He seemed to get uncomfortable. Blushing. He was blushing.

Katty realized she had been staring at him. She averted her eyes, but not before she caught him checking her out. Or was he assessing her like a good cop should? Checking her eyes for any sign of drugs or booze. Were her eyes bloodshot? Or did her breath reek of booze? Did her hands shake when she brushed back her hair?

Sigh. "You know Mrs. Crabbyface used to be nice."

"Nice?" He tilted his head toward that trailer.

That's who filed the complaint for sure. "Yeah. She really tried to help us back then. She was really sweet—bringing us sweet rolls, cookies. Tried to be friends or at least neighborly." She shook her head. "I was okay with it at first. Thought she'd make a good babysitter for Bea when I ... when I went out." Katty looked away from him. Dang. Why had she gone there?

"Out?" He shifted on the chair.

She always managed to make guys uncomfortable, especially since she had quit using. "Yeah. I used to ... I did ... a lot." Courage girl. If she could ever have a relationship with a guy again, she'd have to start with truth. "Yeah. I did drugs. Booze. Everything."

He nodded and swallowed. "Me too."

She built up steam. "I did every party drug. Every hard drug. Booze."

"Me too."

"I ... wait. What?" She stared into his face. Open as her Bible had been lately. "You too?"

He nodded.

"I started abusing her." Katty pointed toward the trailer. "I'd leave her all night alone. And part of the morning. Out all night." She wiped her eyes. "My parents did the same thing to me. No, I haven't been as bad as they were. They were ..." She wiped her nose.

He just stared.

Why was she telling him all this? "But that's when Clarence came around pulled me out of that stuff."

"Clarence?" He pointed at her. "You mean the guy who got shot when your daughter did? That Clarence?"

Her nose began dripping. She grabbed a leaf of the lamb's ears in a pot nearby. Soft. She wiped her nose. Then blew it. On a leaf! "Yes, that Clarence. He happened to be sneaking back into the nursing home through the park. I was ... and I almost ... Bea." She choked. "Thank God he ... got there when he did." She unconsciously waved as the kids rode by again. "I'll never forget the feel of his rough old hand in mine, as I took a swing at Bea—

and I don't mean a park swing." She covered her face with her hands and sobbed. "You must think I'm awful."

"No." He shook his head and started to cover her hand with his, but removed it. "I don't think you're awful. We all have stuff. Junk." One nod. "Only most aren't as honest as you are." He adjusted his ball hat. "But Clarence. Is he a relative? Grandfather?"

Bea slipped out the door, carrying the box of cereal, shaking it. "Mommy, you should taste this! It's so good." She stopped. "You're crying." She glanced at the deputy, then climbed onto Katty's lap, placing the cereal on the table. She peeked at Officer Eddington from under Katty's arm. "Mommy? Why is he here? Are we in trouble?"

Katty peeked at him. "Well—"

He smiled at her. "No, you aren't in trouble. Some nice person told us you might need some help is all."

"Yeah. I got shot."

"I know you did. But you're better now, right?" He held out his hand to her.

Bea hesitated a minute. She walked over to him and crawled onto his lap. "I'm better. It still hurts. Some." She lifted her shirt. "That's where I got shot." She looked at Katty. "Mommy, we forgot to go see Clarence."

Officer Eddington straightened and glanced at Katty.

"I ... I know we forgot Bea. But. Well. Clarence isn't at the nursing home right now."

"Did he go get groceries, too?" She shook the box again. "I should let him taste these. He'd like them."

Officer Eddington continued. "So Clarence is your relative?"

Katty shook her head. "No. He's a friend." Stress took its toll and she forgot about Bea. "And can you believe that a guy at the grocery store was saying that Clarence shot Bea?" Her jaw jutted out. "The guard shot Bea, then he shot Clarence."

"Who shot Clarence, Mommy?" Bea's eyes were wide. "Who

shot him, Mommy? Did he get shot like me?" She stared at Katty then at Officer Eddington. "Is that why he's here?" She pointed at the officer and her chin began to quiver and her voice broke. "Mommy, where is Clarence?" She winced as she walked to Katty. "Mommy, why is he here?"

God.

The look on her face. It must have looked the same back when Katty was still using and trying to talk her way out of a jail sentence. She'd sweet talk the officer and when that didn't work, she'd throw a fit. Katty couldn't remember what Bea's face must have looked like back then, but it must have been exactly like it was now—terrified eyes wide, mouth open, tears running down her cheeks.

Katty gathered her in her arms. "Sweetie. We haven't done anything wrong. It's not like it used to be." Katty plunged in further. "And Clarence was shot trying to save you. And me."

## TWENTY-SIX

Clarence couldn't remember where he'd been. He'd been somewhere, like a dream or existence. Another realm maybe. Another dimension. Felt like he'd been asleep for years instead of overnight. Lisha must have turned on the overheads. She must have drugged him.

He blinked and his eyes started watering. He reached to wipe them, but his hands wouldn't move. Couldn't move.

Man, whatever Lisha had given him had him slammed. His couldn't even make his body move, his hands move.

The more he tried to shift positions, the more he realized he was in pain. And deep pain—so deep that he couldn't feel until he moved. The pain as he tried to move woke up another pain and another and another until his whole body screamed.

Someone moaned.

Voices. Voices heard in the distance. Sounded like his head was in a can. When he was growing up, he had a friend who would always walk the distance to his house from town, just two miles or so. But Clarence could always hear him coming. He'd sing and throw rocks into the water in the ditch. Or he'd holler for Clarence when he was at about a mile from his place.

Voices from a distance. Another room. Another mile. Another time.

"He can't possibly live through all that."

"I told you to beat him, not kill him. I had future plans for him." A sick laugh followed.

"And you may kiss the bride." He shivered. She was so beautiful—had that glow about her.

"That kid'll turn out just like his dad. They both have sawdust for brains."

"Dawes Timmelsen has had his hands on every building in this town."

Voices.

"It'll kill him."

Clarence jolted. Nobody from Osceola, Nebraska had ever been sent to prison before him.

Tears wanted to break free.

No.

Judge Green had found him guilty and had shipped him off to prison without a thought for his future, his welfare. He just wanted revenge. Revenge for Clarence marrying Annie instead of what Judge Green had set up.

Well, he got it.

Maybe nobody from Osceola had ever been incarcerated before, but no one had ever lived to tell about it either. And he would. He was still young. He could rise above. It would take everything he had in him, plus what his dad and mom had put there, to survive. But he would do it.

Lights felt brighter.

Clarence blinked. Tried to open his eyes, only the light was blinding. Like a dentist light aimed directly into his eyes. Or piercing sunlight in winter.

His eyes watered. He tried to wipe the tears away but he still couldn't move.

Something, a cloth or tissue wiped his face. "There you go,

Clarence."

He opened his eyes. Closed them.

Opened them to see a woman with the tissues in her hand. "That better, Clarence?"

A man stepped forward. "Don't baby him. He needs to get used to prison life."

Clarence moved his legs. Tried to sit up. To get up.

Nothing worked.

He looked down.

No.

Memories shifted with memories and they all collided. He wasn't that young man first convicted and sent to prison.

He was old Clarence back in prison. "What happened to me? I know I got shot, but—"

"You, sir, had the worst beating I have ever seen. I'm surprised you're not dead." The nurse shook her head and she tended to his IV. "Makes no sense to beat a guy to death, then give him medical attention to do it all over again."

Someone back against a wall cleared his throat. "That's enough. You take care of his needs and nothing more."

"Where am I?" Clarence looked around the room, then down at his body. "And what hap—" Then he remembered. All too clearly. They had taken him back to his cell after he escaped and beaten him. He must have blacked out at a certain point.

A black man in an expensive suit and tie stepped alongside his bed. Warden. "We're going to let you experience what you did to my brother, Lewis. No mercy. You killed him without giving him a chance to live." He half laughed and half growled. "We're just going to let you experience that over and over and over … until you can't heal or get back up. Just like Lewis."

Chills skittered through Clarence, making every injured cell scream.

This was it.

He'd never get back to Mrs. Hatly. Katty or Bea. That old

saying was true. Distance made the heart grow fonder. Or something like that. Because just the thought of never seeing any of them again, made him hurt more than any beating. He'd started to let himself dream of the day he could walk one down the aisle —especially Katty—maybe even Bea if he lived long enough.

That probably wouldn't happen now.

Another man stepped from a darkened corner. Deep chuckle. "And while you are being well taken care of here, I'll be heading back to dear Osceola, Nebraska, to take care of two ladies for you."

Phil.

Lex stepped up beside him.

No.

Clarence's whole body went cold, from his feet to his head. He didn't even feel the old gunshot wound. Not even the new wounds, whatever they were.

Katty and Bea.

God.

Rage began to boil within, making his stomach tighten.

"You can't." He choked. "You-You ... " He tried to move. Every part of his body that could be mobile, was shackled down to the table. Something had to come loose, even a finger to point into that evil man's chest. "You'll never get away with it. Too many people know them now and care about them. I'll kill you first."

Laughter erupted. Deep guttural laughter echoed off the walls. It was only a hospital size room, but it sounded like a huge cavern. The laughter expanded and filled the space, like thousands of people laughing together. The laughter turned taunting, then raucous.

Phil leaned close to Clarence's ear and growled. "Even if you do manage to get out of here—and I don't know how that would be humanly possible—your girls—Katty, and especially little Bea —will be different when you get back to them. I'll make sure of that." He tapped Clarence on his forehead. "Oh, I'll take good care of them for you, Clarence."

Clarence's insides wanted to explode. Every cell, every emotion, his whole gut wanted to chop Phil up in pieces and never put him back together—just like a horror version of Humpty Dumpty. Chop Phil up, so no one could put him back together. So he could never hurt his girls again.

He'd kill Phil Daynton. He'll rip his arms and legs off if he so much as touched Bea or Katty. He'd take his insides and ... feed them to the hawk. Where had that hawk gone? Was he still at the park? Oh, that park—he missed it too.

If he ever got back to Osceola, he'd have to try to find that bird. It had been around when he'd first gone to Hillcrest —always.

What if that hawk had been an angel, too?

When Clarence had first been shipped off to the nursing home, all he dreamed of was to come back here—to prison—the only home he'd lived in that long—sixty years.

But now.

"How are you doing, Clarence?" That doctor with the googly eyes. He must be infested with about thirty demons to make his eyes dance like that. Must have played dominoes too much when he was younger. Dad always said that the game of dominoes was demonic, hence the name—demonoes. That was how Dad said it.

"We are moving you today, Clarence, so pack your bags."

He didn't have a thing of his own here with him. They'd ripped him out of his room and shot him and bussed him here. No bags. No toothbrush. Guess the prison would have to pay for one.

"Where are they moving me?" Clarence guessed after all the trouble he'd caused, he'd get to live out his life in death row. He'd at least caused supper to be late.

"Back to your cell. You cost the prison too much money to

keep in Maximum Security. Besides there are friends there who would like to get reacquainted with you."

Clarence could only guess that reacquainted meant beat up again.

He had almost never prayed during his eighty years. He had no idea why he should start now. Did God ever listen? He knew God had never answered one way or another the last sixty years. He'd spend sixty years in prison with the love of his life dead.

That's the way God answered.

But at this moment in time, Clarence had no one else.

Where had Michael gone? Weren't angels allowed in prison? He guessed not, because even Michael had deserted him.

He wanted to wipe his eyes.

But there was something about God today.

Here.

Now.

The doctor had left the room so now was his chance.

Gulp. He literally had no one else. Carol always said she could feel people praying for her. Right now, Clarence could only feel his body waking up from the beating.

Tears threatened.

"God?"

It almost felt as if the Man upstairs was pulling on him. "God? You there? Where is Michael?" Did he really expect an answer?

He was beginning to hurt.

A lot.

"God, I don't know how to do this but ... please take care of Katty and Bea. And Mrs. Hatly. And Carol. And Harold." He paused. "And Lisha." A sob surfaced but he swallowed it down. "And me, God. Help me."

"Aww. How sweet." That squeaky, voice.

Damn.

Tay Ralston looked over his shoulder at the guards following him through the door. "He's praying." He laughed. "That God of yours must not be listening to you because you are still here!"

Nasty laughter. Loud laughter.

Served him right. He should have known better. Never talk to God. Why would God have anything good for him? He'd lived eighty years and nothing good had ever happened in his life. Except Annie. And God had taken her away too.

He had given Clarence Katty and Bea and others. He was taking them all away.

God didn't care.

TWENTY-SEVEN

Noell woke, the sun streaming in through her window. She stretched and yawned. So good to have a day off from the Roads Department. She loved her job and pretty much liked, even loved the guys working with her. But today to sleep in and have the whole day to … wait. She had informed herself last night that she was cleaning the porch today.

Shoot!

Well. She would do it. No matter what.

She stretched again. Felt good. Slept well, except for the usual every-night-nightmare. If only she could have one night without it—one night!

You'd think for as many times as she'd experienced it, she would be used to it by now—that it wouldn't affect her.

Until she thought about it.

Everyone had dreams.

Everybody had nightmares, too.

But did everybody have the same nightmare over and over for … fifteen or so years?

Every night?

Every damn night?

She sat up. Maybe she should go to a doctor. A therapist.

She lay back down across the bed. For some reason this time, this morning, she didn't want to run away from the dream.

She only wanted to be rid of it forever.

And the more she thought about it, the madder she got.

Why couldn't she have some peace? If she couldn't have any family, why couldn't she have one night when that stupid dream didn't show up.

How does a dream happen anyway? What started it?

*Who* started it?

Did some demon sit there with a movie reel and hit start? Play the nightmare over and over? Must be how it happened.

Only this morning, she was getting angrier and angrier.

Somehow this had to stop because she didn't want to go to bed anymore, knowing she would have to face the dream again and again.

That first drip of water followed by a deluge, pouring over her.

Terror.

She couldn't breathe. She gasped, but she sucked water in. She was drowning.

That was bad enough, but then Mommy ... Mommy appeared, her eyes wide, her mouth open in a scream that sounded like it came from every direction, wrapping Noell in more terror.

Even stranger—there were times during the day that the dream attacked and when it was over, water dripped, from her nose, her hair, her clothes. Real water. Really dripped. More than once, she had lied to Gamma about water dripping as she leaned to kiss her. Gamma had enough to worry about.

It was just a dream.

Probably nothing she could do, but what if there was?

Time at the cave yesterday had made her question everything. Even to where she tried sticking her hand through a rock!

So what if she could go back? Go back into that nightmare.

Wait. Why not go into Mommy's room. Would that take her closer? Would being near Mommy's clothes, her bedding and smells and keepsakes ... would that make it easier for her to go back in?

She sat up.

She wasn't sure if that was a good idea. Would she find herself trapped in some sort of time warp? Another dimension?

That'd be better than getting trapped in some rock.

Maybe in another dimension, she'd wouldn't have bad dreams.

She hesitated. then hopped out of bed, grabbing her flannel shirt and almost ran to Mommy's room. She'd never locked it back up and enjoyed seeing the door open when she came upstairs to go to her own room.

She turned on the light.

Flipped it off again and opened the shades and curtains, letting in natural light. Somehow she was sure that Mommy had loved sunlight when she had been alive. She even opened a window to freshen the air.

Then she turned into the room.

Beautiful. The sunlight zapped the yellow in the bedspread and it reflected into every corner of the room. Maybe she should move into this room.

No. She loved her room.

She sat on the bed and then slid onto the rug. She had no idea how to do this, but she knew for sure that somehow she was mad enough at the dreams that no matter what she had to do, she was going to take her life back and never let those dreams terrify her again.

She closed her eyes and prayed. "God?" She tried again. "God? If this is okay to do, please help me. Let me go back into that dream and make it stop!"

Quiet. She didn't move. She pictured the beginning of the

dream when the water burst in on her. She had no trouble doing that. Visuals were clear. Every day when she closed her eyes, she could see that. When she wiped her eyes, when she put on mascara, when she blinked.

Here it came. The torrent of water.

Only this time, it was different.

This time she was in her mom's car in the back seat. The two of them were jabbering away about something. Making up and singing goofy songs about dinosaurs. She even remembered some of the words, "big fat tail, bang, bang." And, "tiny pea brain." She wasn't sure if she'd just made that up or if that was the way they sang it.

She just remembered a jovial time. It had been raining all day, but they still went shopping. At first it was cold and uncomfortable, but she remembered Mommy making it fun. They jumped over puddles that were getting bigger by the hour. Mommy had to help her over one by the curb. When they decided to stop for supper and watched it continue to rain while they dipped french fries into a shared ketchup container, Mommy called Gamma and told her they were on their way home—that it'd be half an hour or so.

Noell remembered the sound of Gamma's voice as she told them to be safe. They piled into the car, Mommy buckled her into her car seat and off they went, never realizing how much rain had fallen by that time.

Grampa once said since then that if he'd realized how much rain they had gotten, he'd have driven his pickup to get them. Or told them to find a motel room—a little hideaway retreat for the two of them.

They still sang songs, but Mommy seemed distracted. After awhile she just drove and Noell almost fell asleep until Mommy cussed. Mommy never cussed—at least not around Noell.

And that's when Noell noticed water over the road. Mommy tried to make up a song about driving through water but the words weren't as much fun as the dinosaur songs. Mommy leaned closer to the steering wheel maybe to see better. Noell had a clear view of water on the road.

Then Mommy's voice shook. Was she crying? "I can't see where the road is." The real words Noell would never forget and she still heard them in Mommy's voice. They were not anything she might have made up, "Oh no! I think we're in the river. I think the bridge is out!" Then a whole tree floated right for the car. It slammed into Mommy's door and shattered the glass.

Next thing Noell knew Mommy was floating and not talking. She must have gotten knocked out but when the cold water rushed in, she probably came to and realized the extreme danger they were in.

That's when Mommy swam over the seat like the car was in the bottom of the swimming pool, not just on a road covered with water.

Mommy's face would haunt Noell forever. Her eyes were huge and her mouth open, "Noell! Noell!" Her arms reached toward her, fingers fluttered like she was already unbuckling her. That's when the car must have slammed into the bridge and Mommy disappeared.

Even though Noell was a little girl of four years old, she would never know how she got out. Somehow her seat belt unbuckled and as she let herself go back into the memory, she remembered some hands lifting her out of the seat, then the car, then the river and she woke up higher on the river bank, lights blinding her and Grampa screaming their names.

Then she was safe in his arms. He trembled and shook.

When Noell looked up into his face, he was crying. Sobbing.

He had saved Noel.

But Mommy was lost.

Her last memory of Mommy was her terrified face.

How could Noell go back and change that? How could she do

that? If she could, she'd go back and save Mommy. Someone had saved Noell, so why couldn't they have saved Mommy?

But what if … Noell tried to breathe, only the air stuck in her throat. What would make that nightmare just a dream and not something terrifying? What if she could change it and see Mommy smile? Feel her touch of love.

God.

Her throat tightened.

Noell laid back and stretched out on the rug, with Mommy's pillow under her head. All she wanted was peace. She didn't want to make God mad or stir up any demons. She just wanted to live in peace somehow.

She closed her eyes again and prayed. "God, if you are really who Gamma used to say you are, could you please help me see Mommy smile?

A photo of Mommy and Noell popped into her mind. She sat up. Mommy had been smiling and so had Noell in that picture. She even remembered where it had been taken. Just out in the back yard after they had picked strawberries from the garden and Noell had her mouth full. Red strawberry juice on her lips made it look like she had lipstick on.

Noell jumped up and ran down the stairs, jumping the last three just like she had as a kid. The photo was on the mantle across from Gamma's famous red leather sofa.

There!

Exactly as she had remembered. Right after Mommy drowned, Noell had practically slept with the framed photo. She had even taken it to school a time or two until the teacher sent it home with a note, "Please have Noell keep this photo at home. It is lovely though."

And right now, Noell could almost go back to the day it was taken, hearing the laughter, tasting the strawberries, the color so rich, the day so warm.

When Noell looked at the picture now, Mommy's expression

was terrified just like in the nightmare. Eyes wide. Mouth open in a scream muffled by all that water.

"No!" She shoved it aside. "It's not like that! How did it change? She was smiling! I've looked at it all my life and she was smiling!" Noell almost screamed.

Just that fast, the vision started like it had everyday when she came through the front porch door. She'd open it and the clutter seemed to slide toward her off the piles. Then it would turn into water in the vision. The water was always real—again she'd lie to Gamma and tell her that somebody had their sprinklers on and she'd gotten hit.

This time the water crashed toward her in the vision, more violently than it ever had, almost knocking her over physically. These visions were too real. She hung onto the railing as she waded up the stairs that she'd just run down. The water rushed down the steps like a waterfall might over huge boulders. It took all her strength to hang on and pull herself up the steps.

She would not let this beat her. She had to stand firm.

When she reached the landing, the railing was bending under the weight of the water. Thunder! She heard thunder—like a storm had hit in her house—flashes of light startled her. She looked toward the windows and the bright day had turned into a dark sky.

Impossible!

Whoever had taken over her dream had now raised the bar. The terror ramped up a notch or two. Not only was the water even more violent but there was wind.

She grabbed the doorknob to Mommy's door. As she passed her own door which was open, her own room seemed undamaged, unaffected. No rain. No wind. That was tempting, but she plunged on into Mommy's room and crawled the rest of the way to the bed.

She dove for the middle of the bed, clutching the photograph to her chest. She could feel the sides of the car around her and her car seat under her bottom.

Mommy was in the front seat.

If the dream had been a nightmare, then this reality was a horror movie.

The car lurched just as it had when it hit the bridge. Mommy seemed unconscious, but then slowly turned to Noell.

Noell covered her face. She didn't want to see this. It would be some sort of ghoulish face, a Halloween horror mask.

Noell screamed.

She peeked through her fingers. It wasn't an awful mask. It was Mommy, beautiful Mommy, reaching out to Noell, a sweet expression on her face, eyes full of love and her mouth open but in a kiss. Noell could almost hear Mommy crooning to her, to be a good girl, to help Grampa and Gamma.

Had Noell pictured Mommy wrong all along? Had the sweet smile from the photo switched with reality in her nightmares?

She lifted the frame from her chest.

Ohhh.

The smile was back in the photo.

Noell closed her eyes and focused on Mommy's face—the last visual of Mommy—sweetness, full of love.

No terror.

No fear.

Just love.

TWENTY-EIGHT

Clarence could barely move, but pushed himself to flop his feet over the side of his bed and sit upright. He began to sweat with the exertion, his vision blurred. The bars swam in front of him.

Didn't matter when he'd eaten last. Whatever was still in his stomach was working its way up.

"Take deep a breath, real slow." A voice from his past? A voice inside his head. That made sense. He had to be crazy to still be alive.

Clarence looked up and realized the voice had come from a man standing at the bars. "Yeah. Real easy considering they probably broke my ribs." He tried it though. Helped with the blurring. His stomach contents went back down where they belonged.

"I'm new here and I just realized that you are new, too." The man reached his hand through the bars. "I'm the Chaplain here —been here three weeks."

"Three weeks. That would explain why you think I'm new here." Clarence didn't want to sound rough or rude. He just hurt.

Chaplain looked at his clipboard. "Says here you just arrived."

"Well if you look deeper, you'll find that I've been here for sixty years. Then one day they decide to kick me out—according to the decision of my judge back then, who was a bastard. Sorry, Chaplain. Sent me to a nursing home. But ... I don't even know what day it is ... they sent out four guards to bring me back because—"

"Because you killed my brother in cold blood. Knifed him, cut him, then inflicted several wounds on me and you think you should get away with it."

That voice.

Strange scratching noises at the window. Was that—?

Warden stepped up to the bars, edging the chaplain aside. Right behind him stood Phil and Lex.

Clarence stared at each one, then at the chaplain. "See, the people in charge here have their facts wrong. It was self-defense. Five men surrounded me, each with a knife—and let me tell you they were not kitchen knives. They pushed in closer. Me, I didn't even have a kitchen knife. They start swinging when what's his name ... Lester, a guard, stepped in, his own life in danger. He pounded one with his beat stick and I got one guy's knife, when Mr. Warden, here—only he wasn't the warden then—closes in. Nice for their Mama that both her sweet boys were here in prison, so she knew where they were at night, right?"

Warden growled.

"Well, then, Mr. Warden's brother rushes me and slices me on my cheek." It still stung, even though it had been—

"That's enough Timmelsen." Warden put his arm around the chaplain and escorted him to three guards standing behind him. "Sir, we are thankful for your service, but right now, Mr. Timmelsen needs to get his facts right."

"Oh. I forgot. You're right. He sliced my cheek open and in self-defense, I aimed my knife at anything I could and it happened to be his neck. Kinda stopped the attack." Clarence shook his head and stood. Shaky knees. Sweat running down his back. But he stood and faced the men. The chaplain was still there. "If I remember right, you, with all respect Mr. Warden, ran.

Like a dog with its tail between its legs. Left your brother to die alone on a cold concrete—"

"Enough!" Warden's eyes bugged out and his voice echoed off the walls of the cell block canyon and slammed back into them. His face, even though he was dark-skinned, was bright red. He stepped forward to the bars, just like the last warden had when he had kicked Clarence *out* of prison to the nursing home. He gripped the bars in the same way.

Clarence couldn't quite pass up the opportunity. He was gonna die anyway. "Feel good to be holding onto those bars again, huh? It's where you belong."

Warden vibrated, the bars rattled as he pounded his fists into them.

Silence.

Even the neighbors were quiet.

The scratching started up again. It was a bird ... a huge bird, right outside his window.

Warden pulled out his phone. "What is that?" He tapped his phone. "Tower, shoot that bird."

Voices echoed. "What bird? Where?"

Warden pointed. "Outside Timmelsen's window. Shoot it down."

Clarence realized too late. "No! No."

The chaplain broke in again. "This should go before the board."

Warden glanced over. "None of your business, Chap." He signaled the guards. "Get him out of here."

"Y-you can't do that." The chaplain protested all the way down the steps.

Shots.

The bird flapped its wings against the building, clawed at the window.

More shots and it fell away.

Warden shook his head at Clarence. "Back to the bars—at

least I'm on this side and not that side." He was back in control. "Oh, and here are some friends you need to say good-bye to."

Phil and Lex stepped forward, one on each side of the warden.

Phil smiled a sick smile. "So we're on our way." He trailed his fingers across the bars. "Back to Osceola. Since you're here in prison, Katty, and especially little Bea, are all alone. No one to protect them."

Clarence stepped close to the bars and grabbed them. He shook the cell door, making the warden and all step back. He roared. "You wouldn't dare!" The noise he made shook the entire cell block—every inmate was listening. The atmosphere was electric—lightning could strike at any moment and blow them all up.

As Clarence gripped the bars, he envisioned first Judge Green. Phil's face morphed with Judge's—both evil men. God, he hated the man who had first sent him here.

At that moment, Clarence knew he was a father, a grandfather, a protector.

But at the same time, he knew he was trapped and might never get out of this prison. He might never get back to protect them, to embrace them and who he had become.

Trapped where he didn't want to be.

And terrified for Katty and Bea.

He had to find a way out of prison.

## TWENTY-NINE

Michael knew the surge was coming. He could feel a rising, a shift in focus, in intensity.

In power.

He had to remain steady and firm for just a short time and then all hell would be cast out of this evil prison.

After all hell broke loose.

Even though he was in human form, he could still access the heavens as needed. He could still float back and forth from dimension to dimension, realm to realm.

And when he accessed the heavens, he literally felt every weapon loaded and revealed. Every angel and creature banded together for one purpose—to engage with the evil there in the prison and release the captives.

The comrades were getting excited and as they readied their weapons and armor, sparing broke out. They loved a good fight and this was no exception.

Battle cries rang out. Sword clanged into sword and shield.

Horses stomped as they were brushed and saddled. They snorted and danced, hardly letting their rider capture and harness them.

Chariots lined up, each one equipped and polished, wheel spokes woven and lined with victory streamers.

Excitement pervaded all and as Michael walked among them, he was saluted and hailed from every side.

The hubbub echoed throughout the heavens and mountains.

The Master, at his throne, watched and laughed, enjoying the Kingdom preparations, following His words and decrees.

Michael grinned.

Father's laughter.

Ahh.

Melodic. Deep. Stirring.

Powerful.

And soon, Michael knew … soon would come the moment when all would stand in readiness. All would be accomplished and each warrior and steed would stand at attention. Every creature, every chariot ready.

A deep quiet settled in, every eye of every angel, horse, and creature locked onto The One Who had made them.

Locked on for when He gave the command to ride.

THIRTY

Katty wandered into Hillcrest, feeling like a lost lamb. Her own little lamb followed her a few feet behind.

Bea had gone back to dragging her blanket along everywhere. And while it was extremely annoying—shutting it in the car door every time they got in the car and a corner trailing into the toilet —Katty realized why Bea needed it. Her only source of wellbeing and stability was gone.

Katty hadn't realized how much they both had grown to depend on Clarence.

And to love him.

She turned to see how far Bea was behind her. Five resident doors. And she was dragging the blanket. Ah. She could wash it.

Katty sighed. Her own heart ached. Maybe she could find a blanket of her own.

Harold. He was saying something to Bea from his doorway and she stopped in the middle of the hallway. Head down. Blanket at her feet. He tried to reach for her and he couldn't. His head bowed and he kept bouncing it up and down, until Katty realized he was crying.

She turned to go back when Lisha showed up. She gave

Harold a long hug, her lips moving. She wiped her eyes and stood.

Bea hadn't moved, except to bend over even more.

Lisha glanced up at Katty, then scooped little Bea up in her arms, like a newborn baby. She gently covered her with the blanket and hid her face with it, standing just like that. Just swaying. Just hugging.

As Katty stepped closer, she could hear a deep, soft humming and tears filled her eyes. Lisha reached out an arm to Katty and drew her into that hug.

"My babies." Lisha cried too. "We miss that old, ornery Clarence." Her massive chest rose and fell with each ragged sigh. "Oh Lord, you gotta bring him back to us." She started walking. "You heading to his room?"

Katty nodded. "There's probably some work I could do." She broke again. Wiped her face. "I just want to be here." She took Bea. "And so does she." She swallowed. "When I used to do drugs and was gone all night, she used to hide under my old rocker." She hesitated. "She's doing that again. So I thought maybe it would do her good to come here and see the people she loves— you, Carol, Harold." She turned toward Harold's door and took a step in that direction.

"It's okay. I'll git him." Lisha nodded. "He's takin' it hard too. They had become buds. Gonna start a detective business with him a detective, and Clarence a lawyer and all." She handed Bea and blanket to Katty and waved them on. "You go on and I'll git him."

Katty nodded. Her heart broke to see Harold sob like that. Lisha too. She hugged Bea harder.

She passed the nurses station and heard someone blowing her nose. Carol looked up, wiping her face and threw a wadded tissue into the trash.

Carol walked to Katty and Bea and enveloped them. "It's rough." She turned and blew her nose again. "Blow your nose.

Wash your hands. Then do it all over again."

Katty nodded. "Have you heard anything? Is he ... is he okay?"

"Sheriff is doing all he can to intervene, but the prison is kind of closed to inquiries right now. Really odd." Carol rubbed her arms. "We have to pray."

Katty nodded. "Sometime, could we ... pray?"

Carol hugged her. "You bet." She turned back to her desk. "I'll be down later."

Katty sucked all the air out of Clarence's room as she and Bea opened the door. Someone had evidently cleaned things up because she'd been told that frames on the walls were broken and the desk messed up. She walked in and sat her bag down on the floor. The desk was always a mess so that wasn't new.

If she could just keep things going here for when he was released, that might help. And it would give her something to do, instead of sitting at home thinking too much. She began to make piles and organize a little and came across a picture Bea had colored for him. "Bea, we should tape this one up. We forgot." She turned. Bea was still at the door. "Come on Bea. We have to be strong. I'll help you and you help me. Okay?"

Bea looked up with the most forlorn look on her face. Her eyes were swollen and red and her chin quivered.

Katty walked to her and picked her up again, careful of her tummy. "What do you say we get some ice cream."

Bea shook her head. "I just want to stay here."

Katty blinked. "Y-You don't want ice cream?" She sat down on Clarence's office chair, Bea on her lap.

Bea settled in and leaned against Katty's chest.

They sat that way for a long time, just looking at the room, the pictures, out the window.

Bea took a breath. "It smells like him here."

Katty blinked. "It does." She continued to breathe him in. What if he could feel them, right now? All of them—Harold,

Lisha, Carol, Katty and Bea. What if he could hear them, feel them all crying for him to be safe and come back to them?

"Bea, we need to pray."

Bea immediately folded her hands, still resting against Katty. "God help Clarence come home." She leaned carefully forward. "And help his shot place."

"What? His shot place?"

Bea held up her shirt and pointed to the bandage. "His shot place. This."

"Oh. Yeah. His shot place." Katty nodded.

"Amen."

"Amen."

Another amen came from the doorway. Carol walked in with cookies and juice. She set the tray down and hugged Bea. "Good praying, Bea. That's exactly what I wanted to pray for him."

Bea climbed down and sampled a cookie. "Yum." She wandered to the TV. "Can I watch?"

"Sure." Katty nodded. "Funny. Since he isn't here, she is being so respectful. She would have just turned it on like at home if he had been here." She stood and picked up a box. Set it on the desk and opened it. "Clarence doesn't belong in prison and I'm thinking there might be something in one of these boxes from when he was there before that might help get him out."

"Might be. Good thinking." Carol walked out munching a cookie.

"Better than sitting around." Boxes and boxes from Pete's Insurance Agency. Clarence had never wanted to go through any of them. And she couldn't blame him but while she was here she might as well do it.

She opened the flaps and fished through the papers. A new yellow envelope was on the top. Might as well start there.

"Huh."

"What Mommy?" Bea was more tuned in than usual. She

always zoned out to the TV; Katty usually had to set off a bomb to get her attention.

"Nothing, Baby." Adoption papers. She glanced at Bea again. For her? She read more. Several names were listed. Bea Randolph. Katty Randolph.

*Oh God!*

She slowly sat and began digging into every word. "Adoption process."

Bea climbed onto her lap. "What's 'doption, Mommy?"

These were adoption papers for her and Bea to be adopted by Clarence!

Bea tapped on her arm. "Mommy, what is that 'doption stuff?"

"Oh baby, it's when a person takes on the care of another kid when it's not really their kid. Like when they love a kid so much they want to have them as their own."

"Is Clarence 'dopting us?" She pointed first at Katty, then herself. "Me and you?"

Katty hugged her. "I'm not sure yet, Bea. The papers say so, but I have to check first." It was like Clarence had left these here for her to find, but maybe not with him gone to prison. Maybe he'd planned a party to announce it.

Was this even possible? How was it possible if she had a mom and dad? Or kind of? She didn't even know where they were and better yet, didn't care.

Wait!

And somebody named Noell Randolph Carpenter.

Who was that?

"Noell?" Katty sucked in a sharp breath. "Noell."

Bea climbed on her lap again. "Noell too?"

But Noell Randolph Carpenter?

Randolph?

That was Katty's name.

Katty jumped up and began to flit from box to box, then back to the desk. She dug into the box there, into the papers under the manila envelope.

Whispered the names she had discovered—Dawes Timmelsen, Dawes Retrieval Systems, Judge Green.

What if she could help Clarence from here? What if she could find information in these boxes that could help get him home?

She cleared the desk of anything that didn't have something to do with getting him out of prison. Old stained newspapers. Daily devotion and activity sheets from Hillcrest Homes—he had quite a backlog of those. Used napkins.

The trash can was going to overflow today.

Every paper she picked out of the box, she placed on a pile, sorting them according to dates and themes.

Bea was asleep on Clarence's bed. Good. She needed the rest.

Katty walked to the bed and watched her daughter sleep. Her thoughts went back to before all this when they'd discovered the red bike and how naughty Bea had been—demanding to keep it, stomping her feet to get her way. But here she was curled up on Clarence's bed, recovering from a gunshot wound.

Today.

Katty realized that her day could have been so very different than right now—just watching Bea sleep and working at the desk. She wouldn't let herself go to what might have been, but.

She pushed Bea's hair away from her face. So sweet. So pretty.

She walked to the window and drew a deep breath, hugging herself. What if those papers were real? What if Clarence had really adopted them all—even Noell?

A tear trickled down her cheek and she wiped it away with the back of her hand.

Please God, bring him back so they could actually live like he was their relative. She had never realized how much she depended on him but ... loved him.

Back at the desk, she picked up the envelope again and

flipped through the adoption papers. No one but her and Clarence knew about this.

Wait.

The court house had to know. He was a lawyer, but he had to have filed something at the court house.

When Bea woke, they'd take a little drive and see what they could find out.

Time to get into all these boxes and find out the mystery. She felt like she was snooping and in fact she was, but she knew in her gut that Clarence would totally approve.

She dared not hope or dream about what all this could actually mean for her and Bea.

Noell too.

So many things: someone would have their back first of all, Clarence had already helped them immensely, but might there be more, financially. Maybe they could move out of that crappy trailer court where Mrs. Crabbyface always reported them for child abuse.

Stop!

She had no right to even be thinking that.

Clarence was in prison. He had a gunshot wound himself. And He might never get to come back to Osceola.

Don't think that either. She wiped away another tear.

Back at the desk, she picked up one pile of papers. The Dawes Retrieval System agreements. Clarence's dad had been a very smart man. His son gets ripped out of his life because of lies and he goes in and gets back at the judge by secretly buying up all of the available land and real estate.

And leaves it all to Clarence.

Brilliant.

# THIRTY-ONE

"Sure." Noell nodded at Fletch. "Let's just go for a bike ride." She checked the windows in the camper. "It's really nice out."

"I'm sorry I can't afford much right now." Fletch hung his head. "I didn't think my car would take so much money to fix."

"That's why you should ride a bike and not drive cars." Noell smiled and winked. "They are really cheap annnnd ... uh, good exercise. Double plus!"

He continued to hang his head, only this time his dimples showed.

Noell jutted her chin. "That's why I'm selling this old house and living in the camper forever. It's cheap and mobile and—"

"Good exercise for when you don't have a car to pull it. You just pull it yourself, right?" Fletch scratched his thick dark hair. "Do you have straps for it? How do you h-hook on for when you want to move it to the park?" He grinned.

"Pretty proud of yourself, huh?" She popped him on the shoulder. "Smart aleck. Really. Let's go for a ride." She walked to the old garage and pulled the slider door open. It was like a small barn.

Barn. That would be fun. Get some animals and ... she had no idea how to do that.

She mounted her bike and headed toward Fletch's house, two doors down.

He jogged along beside her and tried to talk. "So ... what have you been doing lately?" He started to pant. Must be out of shape, now that he wasn't a high school jock anymore.

Oh, that small talk. Should she tell him about the cave and how she wanted to stick her hand through a rock? Or maybe about how she was going back in time to change her nightmares? Yeah. Or—

"Hey, did you know that guy that got thrown back in prison? What was his name?" Fletch slowed to catch his breath.

"Yes. Clarence Timmelsen." It was the first time anyone other than the nursing home had asked her. No one cared about her like Clarence had. She peeked at Fletch and slowed to a stop. They were in front of his house.

Fletch's house was a cute white bungalow style with black shutters and a black trimmed front door. Simple but cute.

"Yeah. Sounds like he's in a lot of trouble for shooting that little girl." Fletch unlocked the detached garage and rolled out his own bike. "Pretty awful. I hope she's okay." He steered it toward the park. "And to think he was a lawyer and all."

Noell just stood there and shook her head. However could people get the facts straight if they hadn't been there? If she hadn't walked to Hillcrest right after it happened and talked to Carol—who had been there, she'd think the same thing.

Only this time she did know the truth. "Clarence didn't shoot her." She followed him down the sidewalk, walking her bike. "Carol was there." They waited for a car to pass. "They had Clarence in cuffs and outside—they were taking him back to prison—when Katty and Bea got there. Katty isn't shy and demanded to know what was going on. A smart mouthed guard got in her face, flirted with her, calling her baby and Clarence came unglued. He got one hand out of the cuffs and slugged him and the guard or one of the guards shot his gun and it hit Bea."

"God. He shot her." Fletch stopped his bike on the other side of the street. He turned to her, his eyes wide. He loved kids.

"Yeah." She caught up to him. "Clarence went crazy and slugged him again and the guard shot Clarence, too."

"Wow. Was Sheriff there? How's Bea?"

"She's going to be fine. They did surgery and removed the bullet. They already dismissed her from the hospital." She wiped her cheek. "But nobody knows how Clarence is."

"Wow. You okay?"

His concern touched her. He was cute, too. He really reminded her of someone but she didn't know who.

She nodded. "It was hard to see Katty so scared. Her little girl shot down." She circled around the playground equipment. A little boy waved, and he zoomed down the slide. She smiled. "And she is really close to Clarence. She says Clarence saved Bea's life when Katty was on drugs."

They followed the path down to the cave under the bridge.

She opened her mouth to tell him about the cave and pool, but closed it again. Wait for a better day. She still wasn't sure of what had really happened down there. But, she *was* sure she wanted to go back.

He stopped riding and walked his bike to the big bright blue sign. "This is really a show stopper. I love the way you can read 'Osceola' from the highway."

She pulled her bike beside his and leaned it against the huge cottonwood by the creek. "I should have brought a blanket but I guess the grass is its own blanket." She sat facing the creek. Crossed her legs and patted the ground next to her. "Come and sit. The grass is soft and ... like green pastures." She cocked her head back. "Where did I hear that? Green Pastures."

"'You make me to lie down in green pastures.'" Fletch recited as he sat beside her. There were those dimples again. "Um ...

Mom says that one all the time. It's in Psalms, but I'm not sure where." He dropped his chin to his chest. "She would so have my head if she was here now!" He mimicked her, "What do you mean, you can't remember where that's at? I speak those verses to you all the time!"

Noell laughed but then retreated into her own memories. So that's what a mom would do, if she'd had a mom. Her thoughts went to Katty. Maybe not every mom had that in her upbringing to give to her own children. Fletch had a mom who spoke Bible verses. Katty was a mom that had abused, but was now trying to be that Bible verse mom.

But Noell had had Gamma, a Bible verse grandma. And Grampa.

Fletch waved in front of her face. "You still there?"

Woo. Her cheeks puffed. She rubbed her forehead and tried to hide behind her hand. "Yeah. I just was thinking about what it was like to have your mom speaking Bible verses to you."

"Must seem kind of dorky, huh."

She stared at him. "No." She shook her head. "Not dorky." She picked up a twig and began to skin it, peeling the outer bark. "I just never knew or thought about what that would be like. My mom ... " She trailed off.

"I'm sorry." Fletch swallowed. He started again. "Your mom." Hesitated. "She drowned, right?" He faced her. "How old were you?"

"Four." The twig was just a naked toothpick by now.

"Do you remember much about when she drowned?"

Oh man. Did she remember? Should she tell him about when it happened? The nightmares? Her mom's face as she drowned? Her life since then and when she touched a handle on a door, she heard and saw something of every person who had touched it before her?

Did she dare tell him that?

He'd think she was crazy. And right now as she was hesitating, he probably was thinking he had intruded, when in reality she wanted—she *needed* someone to talk to about it.

About it all.

She maybe could tell him some of it, but he would think she was crazy if she told him about the creepy vibrations she had when she touched stuff.

No, better left unsaid.

## THIRTY-TWO

Clarence tried to find a comfortable position. He didn't know if the wound in his side was better or if he was just getting used to it, but it hurt when he rolled to his side—either side.

Sleeping on his stomach was totally out.

His back was the best, although it still hurt. What if he had some sort of infection and no one was aware of it. The doctor seemed incompetent, like he was half crazy with those rolling eyes. Maybe the guy just had a twitch.

Or maybe he was evil like everyone else here in prison.

But if there was infection, they weren't doing anything about and Clarence knew from experience he could die.

Fear stole every bit of breath he had left in him.

He couldn't die in here. That would not happen. Even if he became sick, he had to get out of here somehow. Even if infection was inside of him, he would somehow get out and go home to Osceola.

He had planned for so much. Those documents still were legal no matter what. He had dropped them into the box where his dad's papers had been. There were a lot of boxes still in his rooms at Hillcrest, waiting to be unpacked or burned. But that one box held his very inheritance—his proof of ownership, other than what they now had proof of at the court house. His dad had been so smart in buying up most of the town.

Clarence knew that what his father had done was all for revenge. Revenge against Judge Green who had sentenced Clarence to life in prison for killing his daughter.

Interesting how life happened and the seasons rolled away and then back again. Back when Clarence was young, he had been in love, married the love of his life, only to have her ripped out of his life in an accident that he had been framed in. After all this time—sixty years of blaming himself for her death—he had just learned in the last few months that he himself was supposed to die in that accident and Annie would have been free for Pete's dad to marry, making *him* the son-in-law of Judge Green—not Clarence.

Spending sixty years in prison was pretty much dying in Clarence's way of thinking.

Something tapped against the bars on his cell.

Phil Daynton.

Evil man.

Probably the devil himself for how he had abused Katty. Thank God he had never gotten his hands on Bea.

Yet.

"Mr. Timmelsen. I just stopped by to let you know that I am taking a long road trip. And I suspect that you have an idea of how far it is."

"I don't give a damn about where you go or what you do. Just stay away from my girls."

"Your girls?" Phil smirked. "How do *you* get to claim them?"

Clarence almost burst out about his last visit to the court house but clamped his lips shut. That bastard would never find out about the adoption until they switched places and Phil was on this side of the bars instead of Clarence.

Clarence turned toward the wall. It hurt to move, but he

didn't want to look at that damn devil's face. Evil seemed to ooze from him. Hard to tell, but Clarence was sure there was something like another being that hovered over Phil. Something that licked at every part of Phil. Almost like flames or a massive tongue of fire.

Unfortunately, he might have turned away too late, because the visual was stuck in his brain.

"Clarence." That voice laced with syrup. Reminded Clarence of when Dad had tried to give him medicine from old Doc. He had told him it was juice with honey in it. That it was a treat. But as soon as the liquid hit his tongue he knew he had been deceived. There was no juice in it. Honey maybe.

"See Clarence, I'm going back to Osceola. You just came from there, so's you remember the road. Or parts of it." Phil trailed his fingers along the bars. He made a sort of choking sound.

Clarence flinched.

"I'm going back to bury my daughter, Baby Bea."

Clarence froze. He had known Bea was Katty and Phil's, but—

Phil suppressed a sob. "You shot her. And I have to go back to take care of my family. To bury my own blood daughter."

Clarence winced as he rolled onto his back. "You are a liar. She isn't dead. I know it." He tried to sit up and pushed through the pain. He swung his legs over the side of the cot and stood. "She isn't dead." He roared. "I know it in my veins." He stomped to the bars. "She is more my blood than yours. She'll run from you!"

"Well, I guess we'll never find that out will we." Phil squinted. "You are here." He tapped on the bars. "Locked in. And probably going to die here, with the way you are bleeding."

Clarence glanced at his shirt.

Damn!

"And Bea is at a funeral home as we speak, lying in state. Her little limp body waiting for Daddy to pay his respects and then get tossed into the ground."

Clarence froze; the visual was too clear in his mind. He could feel his face wanting to fold in on itself. A picture popped into his mind—Bea's sweet body lying in a casket lined with pale pink satin, a rose tucked into her clasped hands.

*Nooooo!*

He backed to his cot before his legs gave out and landed hard.

No. No, no. Don't let that be true.

Phil walked away tapping against the bars, but stopped while he could still see Clarence. "So tell me, Mr. Timmelsen. How does it feel to have everything ripped away from you ... again?"

In the past, Clarence would have rushed the bars, hoping to somehow mangle the man. Reach through those bars and choke out his life.

But today.

The life had been ripped out of Clarence. The rug of truth was pulled out from under him. He wanted to cry or throw up.

His shirt was becoming wet with sweat, either from infection or fear for himself and his girls.

His Bea might indeed be in a coffin.

## THIRTY-THREE

Michael leaned against the cell wall, watching the transformation of Clarence as the man lay on the cot. The dark stain on his T-shirt grew and spread as his chest rose and fell with each gulp of breath. Tears tracked down into his hair, his ears. He wiped his face then cupped his hands over it.

Michael tried to remain distant, to not let emotion get in his way, but experiencing this metamorphosis was the best thing he'd seen in all eternity. Well, besides when Father revealed his creation of mankind, or when Yeshua was born into this Earth realm.

And the worst thing he'd seen lately—he bowed his head—was Clarence locked in the cell.

Okay.

Michael breathed in deeply, connecting with Father for strength.

What was happening with Clarence was good, but nothing surpassed when Yeshua burst through sin and death, crashed into the Earthly realm, baffling every demon in hell by his resurrection to life and took his rightful place at the right hand of the Father.

**Nothing.**

## THIRTY-FOUR

After Fletch left, Noell puttered around the house. She picked through a box; there were so many and she was always overwhelmed. Would anyone want this pretty little jewelry box? She didn't.

Another box. What about that box of notecards? Again, pretty, but she didn't want them. She never wrote notes to people. She didn't have anyone to write notes to.

Where was the trash bag she'd had out yesterday?

She kicked away a half-full box, picked up the box that had been underneath and parted a stack. No trash bag. Even if there was one started it was definitely easier to just go get a new one.

In the kitchen she got distracted by all the cookbooks lining the walls. One stack was from the floor to literally the ceiling. She shook her head. How on earth had Gamma done that? Must have been when Grampa was still alive, but she doubted he would have allowed that.

Gramps and Gamma had gone to auctions together and bought treasures at each one. But they had kept it to a low roar when he was still alive. When Grampa died, Gamma had gone into another level of buying and hoarding.

And this mess was the result.

It was hard not to be mad at her, when Noell was left with it all. She couldn't live like this anymore. Either sell the house and everything in it—even the red leather sofa—or clean it out.

Neither option satisfied her longing to just be herself. That was her dilemma. She just wanted to find what she wanted to do in this life.

Most people her age were going to college. No, most kids her age partied and drank and had a good old time. For just a split second, she let herself imagine what that would be like.

Carefree.

No worries.

She'd seen girls from her graduating class at another town, when Gamma had needed to go to a different doctor. The town was big enough to have a shopping mall with some of the popular stores. Each girl swung several bulging bags, chattering and laughing. Two had looked her way but pretended they didn't see her, but the third one kept glancing at Noell, then staring down at her purchases.

Would that be fun?

Maybe.

Just someone to have a coffee with or go to a movie with. Maybe.

There. Dang. She'd been past that kitchen counter three times and hadn't seen the trash bags sitting there. She pulled one out then knocked over the pile of books stacked there from yesterday and had to start over with those.

She had never thought of herself as an angry person, but the frustrations of today were turning into a lit fuse that would explode if she didn't squelch it.

She had to get organized.

Somehow.

The counters all had stacks of books and bowls, There was not one vacant space.

The kitchen table just had junk piled on it. Instead of putting an object in a box or the trash bag, she'd get frustrated and dump it there.

She didn't use the table for eating. She ate in the living room on Gamma's red sofa, sitting in Gamma's spot, watching TV.

She swept everything off to the floor.

Wow.

A clean surface.

Everything went on pause as she snapped a mental photo of that cleared table. A clean surface. A blank space. No clutter. No piles right there on that one spot. Nothing on that piece of furniture.

Something inside released and she found she could relax as she captured that image of the table cleared off. Even if everything that had been on top was now in a heap on the floor or on top of the piles on the floor.

Just that one image was enough to give her hope.

She kicked aside the clutter on the floor, clearing space to stand at the table and either pack or go through a box. She'd start where she was, which was in the kitchen and not go onto another room, another space until the kitchen was cleared of junk.

Her eyes scanned the kitchen. Whew. This was just one room. The cookbooks lining the walls. Every surface was loaded. You could no longer see the granite countertops Grampa had installed years ago; the space was all covered with boxes, spices, canned goods, and junk.

If all that was on the counter, what was in the cupboards.

Her breathing started to come in short gasps as she allowed herself to take the whole kitchen in.

Never.

Never do that again.

Just take care of what was in front of her.

She cleared a path between the table and the back door, pushing everything to the sides, making it wider so she could use the back door. She vowed to take whatever she had gone through —whether it be trash or give-away—she vowed to dispose of it that same day.

To the dump each day if they were open. Note to self: find out when they are open.

Or to the thrift shop or Mrs. Bertrand's shop. Or to another town if they didn't have room for all this stuff. Somewhere someone had to need some of this stuff.

Or she'd host the biggest marshmallow and hot dog roast in the history of this town ... or nation. Force each person to take a box home. A sort of grab-box event.

She sat on one of the clear kitchen chairs. That was a good idea. Wonder if it was legal.

Note to self: go to the court house and check when and where she could have a fire. She could invite her neighbors ... except Mr. Grimes. No way would she invite him to anything but his own funeral.

She grinned at that thought. That would make a great story.

But there was that young family across the street and down at the end of the block. And Fletch's family. Fletch. Maybe some of the road guys. That would be fun. She actually did know someone she could invite, especially with the guys from work.

She cleared space off next to the box of trash bags and arranged the tape, scissors, box cutters and markers there.

Which box? Didn't matter. Just pick one.

Just the next box.

Then the next room.

Then ... no.

The box in front of her was all she would allow herself to see. No more scanning the whole room and getting overwhelmed. Just one box at a time. And the next box. Or the next pile.

And carry it all outside to the ... where from here?

She walked to the back door and spied Grampa's old truck.

Did it run? Wait. He used to have a pickup box trailer to haul stuff to the dump ... tree branches and trash. Where was that?

She ran outside and there it was—behind the old garage—an old pickup box, white chipped paint and a few dents, but very usable. Now she just needed to make sure the pickup started and hook it up.

She knew where the keys were. Grampa always told her and reminded her again and again, "Now where did I tell you I put my extra keys in case your Gamma loses hers?"

She'd giggle and run for the old radio on the stand beside the back door and lift off the cover and there they were—always safe.

She ran back inside and did just that.

There they were!

Back outside to the old truck.

Please start. Please.

A visual of Grampa's foot pumping the gas pedal up and down reminded her do the same thing. Then she turned the key, foot down on the gas and boom!

It started.

Grampa had always said that it was the most dependable vehicle he had ever owned. Before now, Noell had planned to sell it, but not now. Not if she could start it after this many years.

Gamma had started it right after Gramps died because she too had trash and give-away stuff to get rid of, but that was what five years ago? Didn't cars or trucks get all gummed up after a while of not being driven?

But here was this fantastic truck and it started right away! Well, fantastic old truck with a few dents as well, the red paint was now kind of a rust color and not very shiny anymore, but it ran! She slid her hand over the glovebox. It was a Chevrolet. Spelled out.

And it started!

It felt like Noell had won a marathon! Or the lottery.

She ran around the truck. Funny colors. Each part, from the

hood, the doors, even the tailgate, were all different colors—brown, green, black, red—all unified by the rust and worn patina. Gramps used to drag parts home from junkyards or farm sales. This must be where he put them.

Gramps.

A lump formed in her throat. He had been such a good man. Literally raised his granddaughter, along with Gamma.

She shook her head..

Onward.

She inspected the hitch and whatever that thing was called. Just like on her camper. She had helped hook that up.

She could do this.

Once inside the truck, she backed until she heard a bam.

Oops.

Shouldn't have given it that much gas. Now there was another small dent, but the hitch was right over the ball.

Now what?

Maybe Fletch could help her the rest of the way with it.

She had done it! She was in business. She could throw the bags into the old trailer and get them out of the house at least.

She ran inside and grabbed a box. Into the trailer.

And another box.

She cleared space around the table floor. The trailer already was a fourth full.

Just having a plan and a system was enough to fuel Noell's day.

Back in the house, she stood over the sink, drinking a glass of water. Katty and Bea kept popping into her mind. Maybe now would be a good time to walk to Hillcrest and check on them. See how things were at the nursing home too.

The walk did her good and as she pushed the automatic door button and watched the door open, she thought of Gamma. She'd never had to live here. She would have been fine with it, only her red leather sofa had to fit in a room.

Noell grinned as she walked down the hall toward Clarence's room, envisioning the sofa jammed in one of the rooms. Wouldn't fit in that one. That one either.

Then Clarence's room. Maybe Clarence's room would work.

She knocked.

Katty looked up from the desk and Bea on the bed.

Oh-oh.

Katty's expression literally changed when she saw Noell.

Before, she had almost been smiling—pleasant expression at least.

When Katty realized Noell was knocking on the door, her face changed to ... fear?

## THIRTY-FIVE

"Hi guys." Noell swallowed and waved. Still stood in the doorway.

Bea popped up. "Hi." She rubbed her eyes.

"Shoot. Did I wake her up?" Noell pointed at Bea.

Katty glanced over at the bed. "No. I think she was awake before you knocked." She kept busy with the box on the desk. Her hair hid her face.

Noell glanced down the hall. Both ways. Shoulda stayed home. This was awkward.

Katty glanced up. "You can come in." She smiled, then glanced around the room. "Doesn't seem the same without Clarence, does it."

Okay. Maybe Noell had misread Katty just now.

Noell stepped in.

Bea smiled at her.

"How are you feeling?" Bea was so pretty. Brown eyes were huge, framed with dark lashes.

"I'm good." She patted the bed beside her. "Want to watch Daryl and Dumpty with me?"

"Uh, sure. What is Daryl and Dumpty?" Noell smoothed the covers and sat beside Bea.

"It's that."

The TV showed hundreds of colorful fish swimming around a little girl, who was wearing a rainbow stripe swim suit.

"Her name's Daryl. And she swims with the fish in the pond. The fish are learning their numbers, so Daryl counts the fish." Bea took a breath, like she was diving underwater. "One. Two. Three."

Katty smiled, looking at Bea. "She'll go on and on. She goes past five hundred, so if you get bored, you can take a nap." She pointed at the bed.

Noell chuckled. "I can count to four hundred."

Bea sat up. "You can?" She clapped her hands. "Good girl!"

Noell laughed. What a cutie.

Katty cocked her head and pulled Noell away from the bed. "Hey Bea. I'm going to talk to Noell for a little bit. Just stay here and watch TV."

"Okay Mommy." Bea watched them as they slid out to the hallway.

"Ha." Katty smirked. "She knows something is up. If Daryl is on, she never hears me. I could tell her that I'm going for ice cream, and she wouldn't even move or look my way." She shook her head. "Today, she is on high alert."

"Mommy, don't forget about the book fair. Okay?"

Katty shook her head. "And there's that."

"Book fair?" Noell raised her eyebrows.

"Yeah. They're having a book fair here this afternoon. With all the ruckus going on around here, everybody forgot about it. I guess the people sponsoring it walked in this morning, loaded with boxes and boxes of books. Surprise!" Katty shrugged. "Hey, do you think you'd be able to stay with Bea for a little bit." Katty pointed behind her toward the desk. "I need to check on something I found on Clarence's desk. At the court house."

Babysit?

*It'd been awhile.* Noell glanced at Bea. "Sure I can. I was tired of … doing what I was doing at home."

Katty grabbed her purse and some envelopes and waved good-bye.

Bea hardly waved back.

"Can we go to the book fair? They brought us face paints. Can I paint your face? Can I paint you a lion?" Bea hardly stopped for a breath. She had a plan.

Noell sat in front of the mirror as Bea painted her face. Why had she agreed to be the lion? Cool idea to bring books alive at the nursing home. Not so cool to let a four-year-old apply orange paint.

They had barely just met, but Katty had needed a babysitter so she could go to the court house, so here they were.

This was for sure going to strain her germaphobe habits. The sink was her savior.

## THIRTY-SIX

Katty parked the car and walked to the building. This court house was amazing. A new one could never match the beauty of it. Why didn't they build new buildings like this one? She turned. Well, the new bank was close. Really close. But it had to be hard to mimic the architecture of these old buildings. She should look up its history and find out how old … oh yeah, the year was right there. 1922.

The minute she walked through the doors, she gasped. "This is huge."

The walls were smooth and cold to the touch. She traced the pattern in the stone with her fingers. "Beautiful." The railing was made out of marble. Steps were too.

At the landing, Katty read all the signs.

County Treasurer. County Clerk. Assessor. Where to go?

County Court. She vaguely remembered having to go there with Phil over something he'd done and he'd dragged her with. She'd stumbled into the court room and lost her balance, knocking over a couple chairs in her drunken state. But she wasn't too drunk to be unaware of the shame and humiliation, especially when Phil didn't even try to help her. He made it seem like she was the one at fault—which she was, but before she knew him, she'd never had a drop of booze or done drugs. She hadn't been pure, but …

She didn't think the Treasurer was the place. Or Assessor. Maybe the Clerk. She'd had to come here about something before, only she couldn't remember what it was.

A little bell dinged as she pushed the huge door open.

Katty opened the manila envelope and drew out the papers. "I don't know if I'm at the right place or not." She bit her lip. "I'm not even sure I should be doing this."

"Why not start at the beginning?"

"Okay. I'm Katty Randolph." How much should she tell this woman? She didn't know her. Would she tell the whole town? Dive in. "I am friends with Clarence Timmelsen and well, I am his paralegal."

The lady wasn't going to help her at all. Katty plunged in. "He was shot and taken back to prison and I have been going through some of his papers in his room—trying to find something to help get him back home and I found this. I just wondered if it's real and legal."

"Well, first, do you have a valid driver's license?"

Katty nodded and dug it out of her purse, setting the purse down on the floor. She held it up for her to see. Thank God she had kept hers up to date through all the drugging and boozing. At least there was one thing good out of that time.

"Okay. Thanks." The woman took a look at the documents and smiled. "I remember when he came in to do these. It wasn't that long ago." She checked the date on it. "Yes, just about two weeks ago." She scanned it, looked at the second page. "Yup. It's all here." The woman's name tag read Shirley. "I take it he didn't get a chance to tell you about it."

Katty shook her head. What on Earth was she doing? What made her think she had the right to snoop?

What made her think this was real? Had Clarence really adopted them? She swallowed.

"No. I was just trying to find something ... something that could maybe be used to get him out of prison and back home and this was on the top of the box I was going through."

Shirley nodded.

"Well, is it real? Is he really—"

"Adopting you?" She nodded. "Yes he did."

## THIRTY-SEVEN

Thanks to a friend he still had contact with, he had been able to secure a car—a four-door Grand Marquis—a late 80's model. Phil didn't need to know much about cars, only that they ran good enough to get away in, but also to become part of his disguise.

Some people might remember him from when he was in Osceola before. And they might not like him back here after almost killing little Bea on the slide. Someone, especially the sheriff or maybe the deputies, might have a problem with him driving around the town, scouting things out. No, spying.

He had a plan and part of that plan was being seen in many different towns and places so that when he did land in Osceola, he would have some alibis. They didn't need to be hard core, like in exact timing but he needed to be seen several places other than Osceola.

So. First stop was Wahoo. He could have skimmed around the town on the by-pass but he made a point of driving through.

Coffee shop first. It was more high-class so had a different clientele. Those rich old women who were lonely.

"Hey there, Sweetheart."

The woman finished pouring water into the coffee brewer and looked up at him. "Can I help you?"

"I would love a real man's cup of joe. None of that foo-foo stuff. No flavorings. Just raw courage." He flashed his I'll-get-you-in-bed-before-you-realize-you've-been-had smile and pulled out his bundle of cash.

Her eyes widened as he pulled several bills from the clip and she blushed. Her skin took on a radiance—partly from embarrassment—but a light sheen covered her skin maybe from sweat.

Priming the pump.

Maybe he could create a vacuum when he left Wahoo, so that when he drove back through here with Bea, this little coffee barista would be drawn in and ready to roll. Fun times in the old Wahoo tonight.

"Look at those muffins." He licked his lips, tilting his head so the old ladies at the neighboring table could get an eye full. "I probably don't need any, but how much for the stud muffins?"

One of the old ladies tittered. Another gasped.

"Stud muffin." The youngest of the group who looked to be about eighty, laughed. "I know what that is." She had something going on what with her red lipstick perfectly applied.

"Stud muffin? Raspberry and blueberry are all we have left." She tapped on the counter with her fingernail. "And they are two dollars apiece."

Another lady snorted. "A piece."

Phil burst on the inside at what he had started. Dirty old ladies. But this young thing in front of him. Hmm. She was as fresh as the muffins and needed some—

A gnarled old hand reached in front of him for a blueberry muffin and flaunted it right past his nose. She chuckled. "Sonny. Seems you think you are God's gift to woman." She tilted her head toward the table of her friends. "We could teach *you* a thing or two."

A cackle from that direction almost made his skin crawl.

Those ladies were terrifying—even to him.

"Where do you live?" The muffin floated in front of his nose again and he couldn't help but smell it mixed with her perfume. His stomach rumbled.

She laughed.

He'd never been one-upped by a bunch of old ladies. If the old ladies were this horny, what about the younger set?

He glanced at the barista around the muffin. Her face was as red as the "I Love Coffee" poster with red hearts all over it on the wall behind her.

He cleared his throat. "I'm just driving through ladies and had the unexpected pleasure of meeting you all."

They giggled again. Two high-fived each other. These ladies didn't miss a thing. His own grandma was younger, he thought, and didn't know what stud muffin meant. Of course, he'd never had this kind of discussion with her so ... maybe she did.

The barista slid the muffins and his coffee across the counter. "That'll be six dollars and seventy five cents." She wouldn't look at him. Or at the old ladies either. They'd totally embarrassed her to the point of wanting to die where she stood.

He counted out the money and made it clear he was leaving a substantial tip. One pile was payment. The other was the tip. Maybe that would relax her so she'd—

She scooped the payment pile across the counter and put it in the cash register. The other pile, she left on the counter and turned, walking into the back room.

Huh. Guess he'd gone too far with her. Win some, lose some.

He picked up the pile of money and scattered it on the table where the old ladies all sat. At least they appreciated him, screaming and laughing. He pushed the door open with his arm, coffee and muffin in his hand, and could still hear their lewd comments. "Wonder what he'd give us if we—"

The door closed before he could hear the end of that sentence. He never got embarrassed but he almost was now.

Next stop—get gas. The windshield washer fluid in the container was out, so he had to go in. "Hey there, Sweetheart. How's it going today? You're looking beautiful."

She looked up at him from what she was doing. She was squinting, a hard look in her startling blue eyes and her right eyebrow twitched. Her skin was over-tanned and wrinkled before its time. Her beer themed T-shirt hung off her shoulders.

"My name's not Sweetheart." She pointed to her name tag. Audrey. "And I know I'm not beautiful, so cut the shit."

He swallowed. Women in Wahoo were hard to read. "Well. My mistake." He held up the windshield squeegee. "Just was wondering. If you have time and all. I don't want to trouble you—"

She slammed the cash drawer. "I said, cut out the shit."

A couple men at a near by table grinned. "You better treat old Audrey good. Otherwise, she'll haul out her bazooka and blast you with it."

"Got more windshield cleaner out there? You're all out."

"That's better." She cocked her head toward the pumps. "Get your ass back out there and use one of the others."

Phil stood there, the squeegee up in the air and so was his proposition. Had he lost his touch? Never had he met such a diverse pack of female products to shop from. Wahoo would definitely be on his hit list.

"Okay." He dared not look at the men's table. They were already chuckling, obviously knowing her better than he did. Tail between the legs time as he walked out to the car and cleaned his windshield. Even that was humbling, but he knew if he drove into Osceola with a car like he wanted, a Mustang maybe, that the cops would be alerted to watch him.

He started the car and drove away.

Next stop.

Osceola.

He'd have his daughter soon enough.

## THIRTY-EIGHT

Noell glanced down at her T-shirt when Bea dipped the brush for more paint. Not cool to apply paint to her favorite shirt. The Escher design would never be the same. Hopefully it washed out. At least there wasn't paint on her boots—yet—her thrift store treasures.

"Sit still." Bea sighed, her rosebud face flushed. "It's really hard for you to sit still, isn't it?" Her husky voice had the ring of a mom's exasperation. She had learned well.

"Uh, yes. Yes, it is hard to sit still."

Bea closed in, her sweet breath on Noell's face. The brush tickled. Goosebumps zinged up Noell's spine as Bea lightly touched her, bracing her hand against her cheek.

"You smell good."

"It's the paint."

Detective Bea sniffed closer, then smelled the brush. "No. It's you. Did you just have ice cream?"

Noell burst out laughing. "No-o." Her face itched already.

"Cimmamon rolls?" Bea got really close and squinted her eyes. "They make them right here."

Clearly, Bea had been around. Tough little girl. She had to be, with her mom's drug habit.

*At least she had a mom.*

Whoah. Where'd that come from?

*Maybe she's been neglected but she's only four—she has a chance at life with a mommy.*

"Are you crying?" Bea lifted her hand from Noell's cheek.

*No. I just see my mom drown—every night in my nightmares.*

"I must have something in my eye." Noell leaned in to check the mirror. "Yeah. See?" She wiped a speck away. "There. Better." She opened her eyes wider so Bea could paint around them.

"You need to practice your roar." Bea dipped the brush and roared a baby roar. "Like that. Can you do it?"

Noell tried it.

She hadn't signed up for this.

"No, louder. Your voice is too soft. Don't roar like you talk. Roar like you ... roar!"

Noell stared at Bea, then at her lion self in the mirror and roared so loud the paint shimmered in the jar. Something dropped in the hallway, clattered to the floor.

Bea laughed and laughed. She grabbed at Noell's arm to keep from falling off the stool. Amazingly, she kept the paint brush from making anything orange.

A nurse stuck her head in the room. "You okay in there? I heard some jungle sounds."

Noell caught Bea this time before she fell.

She stared into the mirror. Her thick blond hair roped back in a ponytail. The orange paint on her forehead and cheeks made her blue eyes pop. Blue like the sky.

*Roar!*

Something ... something changed in those blue eyes. Snapped. Sparked. Her flesh trembled. Chest wanted to burst.

This was a foreign emotion. Power. Strength. Like the lion in the book.

*Roar. Roar like a lion.*

She'd never realized how prominent her cheekbones were or how her jaw jutted out. Or maybe it was the red circles Bea had painted on each cheek.

The paint flowed freely on her smooth skin. She needed to wash this off. Now. How long would she have to walk around in the lion costume someone had donated? She swiveled to see it on the other chair.

"Hold still." Bea groaned. "I painted orange where the red was 'posed to go."

Oh-oh. This would take forever if Bea had to start over.

Picky little girl.

*Lucky little girl.*

Katty walked into the room just in time to save Noell from further embarrassment. Her eyes popped wide, like she was in shock, but her chin quivered.

Noell was sure Katty didn't want to break into tears on seeing what Bea was doing to Noell, but maybe she did. Noell and Bea had to look pretty funny—good for a belly laugh.

Nurses walking past the room either looked shocked or burst out laughing, then walked away, their hands over their mouths.

Katty slowly laid the envelopes she had been carrying on Clarence's desk. She was still staring at them, shaking her head.

"Um. Uh." Katty couldn't seem to speak.

Noell had been ready to scream before Katty walked in, but now a belly laugh was working its way up in her too.

"Hold still. I'm just about done." Bea waved the paint brush in front of Noell's face.

Carol knocked at the door, a big smile on her face. She was barely under control. "Can I take a picture of you two? Since it's for the book fair, we will need a few pictures for the bulletin board and the newsletter."

"Uh, no. We don't need our pictures in there, do we Bea?" Noell hopped up and checked the over the sink mirror by the door. "Holy moly!" she needed to watch her words. Bea was so excited that Noell had let her do this. "That's a lot of paint, Bea."

Bea jumped down. "Please? Please can we get our picture taken together? You and me?"

Noell turned toward them. Katty and Carol both had tears in their eyes and were having trouble not laughing.

She shook her head. "I guess." This wasn't what an introvert ever wanted to be doing. She just wanted to actually go home and get back to work cleaning and pitching stuff out.

She let Bea drag her back to the sink. "Okay if we stand here where we painted?"

Carol was biting her fist and she turned her back on them, her shoulders were bouncing up and down.

Katty was having the same problem, but she was used to Bea's antics and she had a huge grin on her face—not at her daughter but at Noell's face. "Noell, I can't thank you enough for watching Bea for me. It was something I had to check on for Clarence and—"

"Yeah." Bea butted in. "Clarence is 'dopting us."

Noell bounced on the chair. She could barely talk with all the paint on her face. She checked Katty's face again, then Bea's. "He's adopting you?"

Had to be true because Katty got tears in her eyes right away. She slowly nodded, glancing at Carol too.

Carol nodded back. "He's been talking about doing it for awhile now. I know he hasn't been here all that long, but he is so attached to you girls." She snapped a picture of Noell and Bea, then scooted Katty beside Noell and took another one.

"You too, Noell. Clarence 'dopted you too." Bea grinned up at her, wiping paint from her fingers.

Noell jumped. "Me?"

Katty looked at her with a sweet smile on her face. "If you are one Noell Randolph Carpenter." She raised her eyebrows.

That needed to soak in. "I am. I mean that's my name." Why would Clarence be adopting her? "Wait. What is your last name?"

Katty, standing right beside her, turned and looked at her. Eye to lion eye. "My and Bea's last name is Randolph." She raised her eyebrows. "Same as yours." She smiled a tender smile. "I did some checking while I was over at the court house." The orange paint covering Noell's face must have gotten to her because she grinned, then let out a laugh. She tried to be serious but wasn't successful. She laughed again. "Your grandmother was my grandmother's sister. Your grandma was my great-aunt or something like that. Shirley at the Clerks' office tried to explain it, but all I know is your name is my last name and that makes us cousins somehow."

Noell blinked. "How come we didn't know each other till now?"

Katty reached for a paper towel and wet it. She gently proceeded to wipe the paint around Noell's eyes as she talked. "Because my grandma got into trouble. She chose a different life and that's one that my mom and then I chose, too." She wiped her eyes with the backside of her hand. "I know your grandma tried to figure things out and get the family back together, but my grandma wouldn't hear of it. She called your grandma a goody-two-shoes. Which wasn't true." She dropped her hands to her chest. "I remember your grandma. She would bring sweet rolls for us or a casserole. My grandma would throw it all away." She wrinkled her nose. "I climbed into the dumpster to get the sweet rolls once and ate one behind it until Grandma caught me and made me throw it out. It was so good."

Noell smiled. "She was a good cook. Her rolls and cookies were so good." Her eyes started to sting, and not from the paint.

"Well, I should leave you girls to get acquainted." Carol patted their shoulders. "Clarence always wanted a family. And now he created one of his own."

Katty leaned in. "We have to get him out of prison."

"But is this really true?" Noell checked her face in the mirror.

Katty nodded. "I asked the same thing at the court house and what's her name ... Shirley I think, said yes. We are actually adopted." She folded her arms across her chest. "It's true."

## THIRTY-NINE

Bang!

Clarence jumped!

Powerful dreams wouldn't let him wake.

Bang!

He blinked.

A guard stood directly above him.

Where?

His eyes were open, but he couldn't completely tear himself out of the dreamworld of mountains and green pastures. Beauty. Light. Creatures.

"Git up!" The guard raised his beat stick for another whack, only this time instead of hitting the cot Clarence was sleeping on, he threatened to pound Clarence.

He'd been lying there all night and when he tried to move quickly, like he used to, he couldn't. He was stiff. Everything hurt. No surprise there. He'd been beaten on every part of his body.

The guard had his beat stick ready. "Get your lazy ass up and get dressed. Day's a wasting."

He shuddered as he pushed up from the cot and lifted one foot at a time to get to the facilities. The guard gave him some time to clean up: wash his face and brush his teeth, but when he started to comb his hair, the guard had had enough.

"Come on. Get moving. We have work to do."

Clarence followed him out to the walkway and down the steps. Each step down felt like his bones were breaking apart. Like they were moving in ways never intended. Must be how football players felt after a game. It would help if he could have breakfast, but he guessed that wasn't on the schedule for today. Grin and bear it.

The guard led him to a closet that held housekeeping carts and cleaning supplies. He showed Clarence what he needed and pulled a cart out into the hall. "You'll need this and this."

Toilet cleaning supplies.

"And this."

Shower sprays and sponges.

Great. He'd done this detail many times when he was first incarcerated back sixty years. It had been dangerous back then and he was sure it would be just as bad now, or worse.

At least the prison building itself hadn't changed all that much. He could still remember the layout.

"Come on. Let's roll. I have lots to do before my shift is done." The guard pushed him into the cart and it hit his gunshot wound. He winced but wouldn't let himself cry out. No sense calling down more trouble than it was worth.

He glanced down at his shirt.

Bleeding.

Again.

He remembered this shower and bathroom. It was *the shower*. The one where he had been attacked. Where he had killed Warden's brother, Lewis, in self defense. Loud voices echoed from inside. Evil laughter. Someone screamed just like Tay did—high pitched girl scream—from a guy.

He parked the cart right outside the door and picked up the cleanser spray and mop. He knew the drill. Evidently the guard was staying with him—showing him the ropes, or making sure no one killed him on the first day. He'd wasted several days in the infirmary so he hadn't had a chance to set up a day count in his cell. Hash marks worked well. Tonight he'd try.

As he stepped into the shower, several huge men stood around another puny young kid. They were poking him and yelling at him. The kid was stripped naked and his towel was in the hand of one of the larger men.

But when Clarence entered the room, all eyes turned to him. They forgot all about the kid, which he took to his advantage, grabbed his towel and ran past Clarence and the guard.

Clarence had been in the same situation when he'd first been incarcerated. He hoped the kid appreciated it because Clarence was obviously going to take his place in the grand scheme of things. Didn't really matter who, just that they had someone to taunt and beat.

Or worse.

The guard looked the other way and backed out of the room.

Clarence had been set up.

He skirted around them and kept his distance. At least he had some weapons—just a mop and cleanser spray but that might not feel too good in the eyes or mouth. He hoped.

"Oh, Mr. Cleaning Man. Sorry. We left a little mess for you to clean up." One of the men glanced over his shoulder and nodded. "You might want to bring in a shovel." He grinned a greasy, evil grin. "And some sweet smelling spray because it really stinks in there."

Clarence held his breath as he walked to the toilet area.

The smell brought tears to his eyes. He put his arm over his mouth just when someone pushed him from behind and he landed right in the middle of the most shit he'd ever seen in one place, except for a feedlot back home. Smeared all over the floor and the fixtures, the mirrors.

They shoved his face in the muck just as someone ripped his

pants and underwear down from behind. Lewd comments. He was in for the prison initiation. He'd been a lot younger the first time. Didn't matter. If he lived, he'd kill every one of them.

As soon as Clarence had that thought, he found himself on a rocky cliff.

No more men.

And no more shit.

Just him high above a drop-off. He tried to step back, only to find he was at the very top of a knife-edge precipice, with only enough room to stand.

Gasping, he stumbled. A chasm dropped below on all sides. It extended farther down the longer he looked. Soon he couldn't see the bottom—only rock walls of the canyon, ever stretching away.

No river. Just dry rock.

"God! What?"

Sweat broke out on his forehead, his neck.

His chest constricted. Each breath became more difficult to draw.

Tears broke from the corners of each eye.

"Oh. God!"

A quiet enveloped him.

"This is it." He lifted his eyes, his head rigid. "God. This is it, huh? I thought we just flew into heaven. Maybe Michael ... "

As he blinked, a cloud appeared in front of him.

No.

Not a cloud.

It flowed closer.

Took shape.

A head. Shoulders. The body. Legs.

A man?

He floated close.

"God? 'S'at you?"

The man smiled and held out a hand. "Come."

Clarence glanced down then barely moved his hand at his side, pointing to the drop-off. "Y-you see this? Am I the only one seeing this here? Like … I die, Jesus."

The man smiled.

"Damn. This is getting annoying. I'm freaking out and you're smiling? Saying come?"

Jesus held out his hand again.

Those eyes.

Clarence had seen those eyes before.

At prison—Lester.

Carol.

Bea.

"Come."

Clarence searched the edge right below. No ledge. No place to …

"Come."

Tears burned.

Clarence swallowed. Slowly nodded. "Then this is it, Lord?" His heart pounded in his chest. "No more Lisha."

Jesus smiled and beckoned with his fingers.

Clarence lifted his hand.

Tried to reach.

A rock broke loose and tumbled, bouncing off ledges. He lost sight of it as it crashed outside his peripheral vision.

Where it landed didn't matter. Not looking down.

A tear escaped and ran down his cheek.

Sob.

Deep in those eyes.

"Come."

No worse than drowning, right?

No worse than …

He sucked in a breath and stepped off.

FORTY

The road, as Phil drove into Osceola, was decidedly very pretty. It curved into town from the veterinary clinic, past that Dollar Store. You could see the cemetery from the road. Grave robbing would be an interesting and profitable job. Bet some of those graves had valuable stuff buried with the bones.

He'd spent time there, hiding out with Lex. Too bad Lex hadn't come along, but they'd decided that both of them would draw too much attention. He might have to fly in later. Buses ran through these small towns.

He shook his head. But right now, all he had time for was kidnapping his daughter and doing whatever he had to do, to make that happen. Just the thought of her sweet tender skin, made him itch.

The implement business had added some little tractors in front. Bet Bea would like riding on one of those. Wonder if the guy Lex had bribed with a beer, was still working there. They'd have to reconnect.

And there was Phil's favorite place to hide behind, next to the implement dealer—the drive in. The guy there was always nice, even though Phil had caught him staring as he had jogged up the hill to his stake out car. Suspicious. Some people couldn't let things alone. They thought they had to be the look out, ready to report any suspicious goings on.

If that guy could see him now. He'd have to stop in for some ice cream while he was here. Better yet, he'd bring Bea in too, on their way out of town. Unless, of course, she was tied up.

He turned off the highway into town and headed to the trailer court. Better be careful not to get noticed by Katty, but even the neighbors might know who he was. He dug in his bag for a ball hat and sunglasses. Bet if those little old ladies from Wahoo lived here he could get them to watch out and spy for him. Wouldn't take much to buy them off.

Phil choked. Gross.

Not much had changed here. Same tumble down trailers. Oh, some were nice, but Katty's was ... nice. Fixed up. The deck was new. Potted plants. A new skirt had been added around the base of the trailer and it looked like it had been painted. Bet old man Timmelsen had sprung for all that. Katty had a good thing going.

Her car was gone so he slowed. Windows were the same—so good possibilities for entry some night.

Oh-oh. Old lady alert.

A woman about the same age as the elderly ladies at the coffee shop hobbled from around the end of her trailer and waved at him.

If he didn't wave, she'd get all mad and remember it later, probably talk to her phone buddies, ripping him. So she'd remember him.

But if he waved, she'd remember him for being a nice guy, friendly, willing to engage.

He was cooked both ways.

He waved a normal wave. Not too friendly or over done, but not too sissified either.

And he shouldn't look too interested in Katty's trailer or anything else here. Being a criminal was hard work.

Especially kidnapping.

He didn't see the red bike he'd sent Bea, so he guessed it caused the right amount of stress and arguing to cause a rift between Katty and Bea.

He drove to the park next. Touring the town. Typical family playing on the equipment. Mom sliding down the slide. Dad pushing a kid on the swings. Nothing out of the ordinary.

Hillcrest seemed the same. He'd have to find a way to scope that place out without causing any suspicion.

He checked Facebook on his phone. What was Katty posting lately? Huh. And who was this Noell that commented on her posts? Noell Carpenter. Huh. Must be just a friend, but they seemed to know each other pretty well from the feed.

He'd have to check her out. He logged her name into memory. Maybe she would be a way into Katty's life. Maybe he could use Noell to set Katty up and steal Bea away.

He parked on the square across from the bank. It was new and very well done. He nodded in case anyone was looking his way, as he slowly slid the gun from under his leg to behind him and into the waistband of his pants.

The streets surrounding the court house were bordered by pickups and cars. Mostly county 41 which was Polk County Nebraska. One or two other counties.

Amazing building. Those pillars could support the Empire State building or at least the prison. Marble. Whoever had built this place was rich. It was well done, and the builder and city builders had spared nothing with materials.

Sign on the entrance door—no guns allowed. Right.

Country Treasurer. Assessor. He guessed the County Clerk would know. Now what angle?

"Hello. What can I help you with?" The woman in front of him had a name tag but it was on edge so he couldn't read it. But he could see that she was the clerk. He had the boss lady.

"Hi. I am looking for some property." He still wore his hat and glasses so he hoped his identity was secure. "Only I'm not sure of the address." He took out his phone and did a quick search. You had to love internet. There was Noell *and* her address. "Ridge Street." It also had that her grandmother had just passed away. How convenient. "531 Ridge Street."

The woman wrote it down on a scrap of paper and walked to a back room. If only he could think of a good reason to go back there with her and snoop through all those old journals. He'd have to think about that. He knew they were part of public access, but he guessed they would frown on him if he just asked to snoop around a bit.

She returned with her paper and a huge book. She dropped it onto the counter and flopped it open where her finger had been holding a place. She pointed to the line. "It's right here. What did you need to know?"

"Well, for one thing, is it for sale? And who owns it?"

She shook her head. "Not at this time. It is owned by Gwendolyn Randolph Carpenter. She passed away a short time ago, so I'm guessing it was inherited by her granddaughter, Noell." She handed him the scrap of paper with her scribbling on it. "Anything else?"

"No. No. That looks like everything I need." He tapped the paper. "Just to make sure I got this right—Gwendolyn—that's quite a name. Then Randolph Carpenter?"

"That's what the book said. I think they called her Gwen."

"Oh. Right. Gwen." Randolph? That was Katty's name. He tipped his hat. "Thank you for your time and trouble."

"Oh, no trouble." She smiled. "Just like to help out. Are you moving to the area? Because there are other properties that are available. The property on Ridge Street might not be available."

"I'm thinking about it. Yes." Not on your life. It'd be a cold day in—

"Well, if there is anything else I can help with let me know."

He opened the door. "Thanks. I'll do that. Have a good day." He saluted and left.

Ridge Street. He remembered driving past here not long ago as he looked for hiding places. He hadn't remembered the house though. It was nice enough. A front porch that had been built in. Camper in the side yard. He slowed.

If this kid, Noell, was living there, she'd likely have a car. Should have found a way to check that at the court house too.

Randolph, huh.

Seemed pretty dead right now. He might not have much time. He drove around the block and found an alley that bordered the property. Who did the camper belong to?

Back on the street, he found a place to park his car in the parking lot at Hillcrest. There were always lots of cars and people coming and going at shift ends and during the day with visitors and such. He guessed no one would get suspicious for a few days.

Yup. 531 Ridge Street. He needed to sneak around back and break in.

First he'd try the legal way.

He knocked.

No one came after waiting several minutes. He knocked again and tried the doorknob.

Unlocked.

Don't open it. Find another way.

He walked around to the back of the house. No one seemed to be around.

A little shed sat between the old camper and a garden—or what used to be a garden. An old pickup and a trailer. Trailer had some trash and boxes in it.

The camper was locked, although if he really wanted to, he could jiggle the knob enough to break in. If he wanted to. Or if he really thought there might be something in there. He kicked the step. It was just an old junky camper.

The shed might be different. It was pretty well kept, like maybe there was something going on in there. Phil could almost feel the next scam on its way to his mind. He just had to open up to it.

He checked the doorknob. Locked tight. Even with more jiggles, he couldn't open it. What was in there?

He was getting so engrossed in the mystery, he forgot to be scrupulous and act like a neighbor.

Which of course was happening.

An old man limped with a walker a few doors down, to his back shed. He stopped and waved to Phil.

Caught.

He waved back.

He'd have to scope the neighborhood at night.

This Noell probably didn't matter in the scheme of things anyway.

He walked around the house acting like an inspector. That might fit since the old lady had just died. That window had been fixed. A shutter was needing to be repaired.

Back at the front door.

Don't look behind. Don't see if anyone is about. He'd go on in like he was a relative or friend.

"Hello?" What would he say if her knew her? "Noell? You home?" He pushed the door open but something was keeping it from opening all the way.

Whoah. Holy shit. Did the kid even live here? The something that was against the door ... was a whole household of crap.

He tripped over a pile of magazines, into a stack of boxes.

It was still light out so he could see relatively well without turning on lights, but this was a maze that no one could navigate, unless you knew the map.

Wow. Every room was piled high with boxes and junk. He'd seen this on TV once. A hoarder show, where they tried to intervene. But this was even worse than on TV.

He opened the refrigerator. Pretty skimpy. A container of leftovers. He opened the lid. Spaghetti.

His stomach rumbled. He hadn't eaten all day.

Smelled good but he put it back. Just the minute he stuck a fork in, she'd come back and interrupt his dinner.

He pushed the door shut and scanned the kitchen. He picked up a butter dish and slid his finger along the top of the butter stick and licked it. Tasted okay. Seemed like she'd been here recently. So maybe she lived here.

The old lady's bedroom probably looked as she had left it when she died. Tons of junk. Only one side of the bed could be slept in. Bibles piled up on the other side of the bed. Religious old lady. Probably the same as the little old lady who kept inviting Phil to Sunday School when Dad was in the cult. Never in a million years.

He opened a door revealing a stairway going up. Might be where the kid slept. He'd find out more there. If she came home while he was upstairs, he'd have to jump her or jump out an upstairs window.

He clomped up the wooden steps. No carpet. Noisy. He tucked his shirt behind the gun at his back, as he peeked in one room first. It was very simple and clean. Austere. Like a hospital or library. He pushed the door all the way open, just to make sure she wasn't hiding behind the door.

---

NOELL OPENED THE BACK DOOR. She congratulated herself as she glanced back at the old pickup box trailer. Good girl, Noell. It was already a fourth loaded with trash and boxes. She had gotten a great start on decluttering and it invigorated her to keep on going.

After being somewhere like the nursing home, though, it was hard to come back here. The nursing home was so clean.

In her own home, she never knew what might be lurking under or behind all those boxes.

---

A LITTLE BIBLE, a cup and a tiny bracelet were all that sat on the bedside table. Phil picked up the bracelet. It was he guessed, a baby bracelet, with tiny beads and pearls that spelled out Noell.

He had never had one himself, he was sure. His bloodthirsty father would never have saved such an heirloom. When Phil had been kicked out to the orphanage, they had even taken his stuffed turtle away.

An angry growl surfaced from somewhere inside Phil. His past wanted to surface. The things he had seen and done. Abuse. Atrocities.

---

NOELL SHOOK HER HEAD. Don't look at the rest. Just focus on the next box or the next pile.

Maybe she should call Mrs. Bertrand and ask her if she'd take all those cookbooks. Surely someone would want to collect some. A new bride might want them for her kitchen.

She had no idea of what could be in all these boxes here in the kitchen—spices? Canned goods?

Sigh.

She had some idea of what might be on the porch. She'd dug in those boxes searching for work clothes for the Roads Department. Actually saved her a lot of money.

Maybe she should have a sale. Sell it all. Hire an auctioneer and maybe they'd help set it all up. She had no idea how much money it would take, but at least she wouldn't be left with all of it.

---

THE GROWL and pain in Phil's gut grew larger and louder. He stretched the bracelet until the old and weakened elastic broke, releasing the tiny pearls and beads.

They seemed to be suspended in the air, all across the room like tiny soap bubbles floating.

Voices were released with the beads. Words of kindness and love. "My sweet baby. Oh, you are so cute."

Words he had never heard directed at him in all his life.

Then words of pain and horror. "God, help! Save my baby!"

Pictures too. He cringed as he saw a woman caressing a baby. The same woman screaming underwater.

Who was this Noell?

Who was the woman?

He knelt at the bed. What was happening? How could an object speak? Or store pictures?

He'd never had anything like this happen. Why now?

He had to get to Bea.

Something was happening to him—trying to take him over. Something he'd never experienced before. He'd always known demons and spirits but this was different. This was ... pure and holy.

---

NOELL SLID a box over to the table and started to lift it onto the work surface.

---

THIS WOULD NEVER DO. Phil needed strength to counter these voices.

He roared.

BOOM!

She dropped it back onto the floor. Super heavy. She opened the flaps.

Books! More cookbooks.

The box was gonna stay there. Cleaning this house out didn't mean she needed to hurt herself. Maybe Fletch would help with that one.

———

ALL THE PEARLS and beads immediately fell to the floor and bed.

Felt good.

At least felt like himself again. Which wasn't saying much. It had taken him a long time to embrace his dad's level of evil, but now he'd never go back to that wimpy little boy he'd been before.

———

KITCHEN STUFF WAS HEAVY.

She lifted the next box the way the guys at the Roads Department taught her. Butt in, feet apart, back straight. Lift with the legs.

This box was even heavier.

She dropped it on the table. Boom!

———

HE ROARED AGAIN.

He needed to be strong. He needed to keep with the plan.

Get Clarence killed. Get his Bea.

Soon.

Before he gave into these ... these—

Soon he'd have help.

Lex would be here soon.

———

THE TABLE SWAYED.
Noell sidestepped.
Oh-oh!
Crash!

———

PHIL FROZE.
Someone was downstairs.
He drew his gun and stood still, barely breathing.

———

NOELL OPENED THE BOX FLAPS. No wonder. Cast iron pots and pans.

"I broke Gamma's table." Noell still had trouble calling things hers. "I broke *my* table."

Time to quit. Time to call it.

She stopped. If she had quit every time she had felt like it, she might not have made it past third grade.

The kitchen walls wanted to push in at her.

Well, she could push back. Maybe she couldn't fix the table or lift every box, but she could keep on going.

She stooped to open another box.

Just someone's old household goods. Smashed boxes of plastic zip style storage bags. Aluminum foil. Every one of the boxes was smashed.

She gathered the box and stomped out the door. She had to be strong. She had to get rid of all this stuff. Enough, already.

She gave it a heave into the trailer.

Felt good.

---

PHIL INCHED TO THE WINDOW.

Must be her. Must be Noell. Long blond hair, pulled back in a ponytail.

Down, boy. You came for Bea.

He stood and watched her as she pushed some boxes together.

Now was his chance.

He stumbled down the steps, two at a time, almost turning into the kitchen.

Front door. Dumpy porch.

Out the door.

Slow down. He turned back into the doorway before shutting the door. "Okay. Everything looks okay." Lady at the court house said the grandma had just died. "Sorry about your grandma passing."

Perfect.

He quietly closed the door and walked down the sidewalk in the opposite direction of his car. Hell, from here, he could walk to anywhere in this town, it was so dinky. And walk back later for his car.

## FORTY-ONE

Back in the house, Noell checked the cupboards and sure enough there were two rolls of foil and several boxes of bags. This was stuff that people bought in the store, though. Her too. She should probably keep stuff like that. It would save her money.

She opened another box. Spices. When she checked in the cupboards, there was more of everything. She didn't have a clue how to use them. Did a person use sage in tacos? But it would save her money to keep them.

Noell went through several more boxes.

She glanced up, knowing how good it felt to see things cleared, but there wasn't anymore space than before. Boxes were stacked on the keep pile and where she always dumped them to go out to the trash trailer was clear.

What?

"Oh man. I ... "

She wasn't getting rid of anything. She had just done the same thing that Gamma had always done. What if she needed this or that? She'd have to buy it and keeping it would save money.

She looked at the pile she'd already done. It was bigger than before. She was doing the same thing. She was following in Gamma's footsteps all right.

She sat on the chair hard. She needed help.

What if Katty could use some of this? Katty was a single mom and had endured, from what Noell had heard Clarence say, a rough life. She'd seen the trailer they lived in and it wasn't much.

A picture of Mommy's room upstairs hit front and center. It would be so cool to let Katty or Bea have that room. This was way too much house for Noell alone. She could share it.

She had family.

Katty and Bea were her family.

She wasn't alone.

What if she had them come over and go through stuff—find things they might need? It would help both.

She glanced around the room. What would they need?

Her chest wanted to burst. She had family. It hadn't been that long since Gamma died but the pain and loneliness that was left behind made it seem like years.

She had family!

She should call Katty and have her over and ...

She looked around at the stacks of boxes, books, junk. What would she think? Katty didn't have a lot, but Noell was sure that she was not living in a mess like this.

Noell could show Katty her own room and she would know it wasn't Noell's fault.

Silence.

No.

Katty and Bea would never set foot in this house.

## FORTY-TWO

Katty wasn't sure Noell was so thrilled to have them as family. With all that orange paint on Noell's face, it was hard to read her.

Katty checked Bea. She was on Clarence's bed watching TV, so Katty stepped to the window. The leaves were beginning to change color. Even the rose bushes out front had a different hue.

It couldn't be fall already. School had just started..

Clarence had a great room. He had a view of the park, the parking lot, the rose garden. He could watch people come and go if he wanted. She'd never seen him just stare out the window like some people here, though. He was just too busy. And she loved the idea of him and Harold cooking up a detective-lawyer business. Maybe that would keep those two out of trouble.

How was Clarence?

She was so scared for him. He had told her stories of his time in prison, especially at first, before he became a lawyer. He'd been just a kid.

People were leaving, waving to their loved one as they walked down the sidewalk. They must be able to see into the resident's room. She'd never checked to see if Clarence was waving when she and Bea left. She'd have to do that.

Sigh.

When he got back.

Tears threatened. Not going there. Bea would ask.

A car drove into the parking lot but parked clear on the edge of the other side of the parking lot.

She was so worried. Carol said to pray and they had.

Would God hear?

Bea stretched on the bed. "Mommy can we have ice cream?"

Katty smiled. "Sure. You have't had any yet." She held out her hand, "Let's walk down together and get some. Maybe even take Harold some. Or Mrs. Hatly."

Mrs. Hatly. She and Harold both were suffering so badly with Clarence gone. They had both sent Bea a get well card with money in it. Sweet.

Katty looked down as Bea slipped her little hand in hers. So soft. Tiny. She hoped she could keep this closeness they had right now. Stupid that it took a tragedy to kick her in the butt, to be a better mom—to care more.

At least Bea was better. Funny how little kids healed faster than adults.

She looked up as Harold raced toward her, walker or not.

Bea ran to him. "Harod!" She hugged his leg, but stopped. She had learned not to trip anyone in the nursing home. They were so unbalanced sometimes. Katty and Carol, even Lisha, had worked hard with Bea so she didn't knock anyone over.

"Katty!" Harold shook as he walked to her. "Katty!" He started stuttering. "You-you-you."

She caught up to him and he was trembling.

"Harold?" She grinned. "Are you okay?"

He didn't laugh. His face was serious. "N-no. Don't ... ice cream. Don't." He gripped Katty's shoulders. "No!"

His eyes bored into her. She held his arms. "Harold? What are you trying to say?"

He began stuttering again, like he did sometimes when he was tired.

"Harold, we'll be okay. We'll bring you back some, okay?" She grinned. "Unless we eat it all. Then we'll have to bring you some tomorrow."

Katty released his arms, but he wouldn't let her go. Lisha came down the hall and helped walk him to his room.

"Poor Harold. I don't know what got into him." She looked behind her as Lisha steered him into his room. He was still reaching for her. And stuttering.

"Mr. Harold. What's the problem?" They could hear Lisha's loud voice well and still even hear Harold—he was so upset.

"I-I-I bad men. I-i-ice. No ice. No-no ice. Bad men."

Lisha leaned out the door. "You know what he's talking about?"

Katty shook her head. "He just came at us and grabbed us."

Lisha nodded and looked past them down the hall. Then back in the room. They could hear her page Carol. "Carol. I'm on a hunch but Harold has gots something up his ... no. No. Not that. He is—"

They rounded the corner. "Huh. The machine looks like it always does—inviting, right Bea? We want ice cream!"

They could still hear Lisha. "Carol call—"

Bea laughed. She could almost reach the ice cream cone holder. One more month and she'd be tall enough.

Katty pulled a cone out and handed it to Bea. She'd gotten pretty good at serving up this stuff. A perfect curl at the top every time. She pulled the handle down and the soft creamy ice cream slowly filled the cone.

A voice behind her. "Mmm. That looks good. You've gotten really good at that. You need to be a soda jerk."

Katty looked behind her and smiled. Mrs. Hatly was up and around. Since Clarence had been gone, she had taken to her bed but especially her room. Katty hadn't seen her since. "You want one, Mrs. Hatly?" She turned, holding the perfect cone out to her.

"Give that one to little Bea. Then I'll take a tiny, tiny one." She sat on the loveseat across from the ice cream machine and leaned her cane against her legs. Her twinkle was not as twinkly, but her smile was still sweet. She had definitely suffered with Clarence gone. There seemed to be something special between them— love maybe? So cute.

Wait. Why was it cute when little kids had a love thing going on and when old people did, but when just adults had it, it wasn't cute anymore. It was serious.

This might be serious for Clarence and Mrs. Hatly. They only had maybe a few more years to live. This was serious for them.

Bea sat down beside Mrs. Hatly and Katty handed her the ice cream cone.

"Be careful."

"I know." Bea heard this warning every time someone handed her anything to eat. And she always was careful. Just things happened that were out of her control. She licked it and smacked her lips. "Yum."

Katty smiled. "How come it always tastes so good? You have it several times a week. Or more! Why is it always so good?"

Bea's face took on wisdom. "How come the booze always tasted so good when you had it every night and got sick from it every morning?"

Katty held her breath. She didn't get angry. Just blew out a breath. She stared at Bea, then looked at Mrs. Hatly, who was happily licking her cone.

Mrs. Hatly glanced up and licked her lips. "Me too."

Katty filled her cone and sat on the chair nearby. "You too?"

Mrs. Hatly nodded just as Sheriff Dennison and two deputies rushed in through the entrance. They were red-faced and breathing hard. Guns were drawn.

Katty dropped her ice cream cone and it landed ice cream

down. She jumped up and stood in front of Bea and Mrs. Hatly. "What is going on? Why are you waving guns?"

A deputy checked the door they had just come through. "Sheriff. There they go. They must have gone out another door."

"There are too many entrances in this place. Needs to be secured."

They all three slammed out the door, shaking the walls as they pushed it open.

"There who goes?" Katty followed them to the door and checked outside. Sure enough there were two men racing toward ... that car ... she had seen earlier through Clarence's window. As one turned around to get into the drivers seat, she got a glimpse of his face.

Phil!

"Oh God!" She backed away, stepping on the ice cream. She slipped and started to lose her balance but before she could land on the floor, a strong hand gripped her arm and caught her.

The cute cop. "You okay? You look like you saw a ghost!"

Carol gathered paper towels and wiped up the ice cream cone and Katty's shoe. "You okay?"

Katty glanced from her face to the cop's. "What just happened?" She pointed outside, oblivious of the mess she'd made. "That was Phil! And probably Lex his crappy partner!" She pushed her fist to her mouth. "Oh man! They're back!"

She started to collapse, but he caught her again and settled her on the chair. "I should have seen it coming."

He leaned closer to her. "Seen what coming?"

"I should have known." She straightened. "I bet the bike was from him, too."

"What? A bike?" He knelt on the floor and retrieved his phone. He tapped a couple times and looked up, phone at his ear. "Tell me. Tell me all."

# FORTY-THREE

"Jerk!" Phil pounded on the steering wheel. "I told you to bring beer. Remember?"

Lex smirked. "Is it for you, or for our implement buddy?"

"Me, of course!" Phil slipped his gun out of his back belt to under his leg. He wasn't about to tell Lex about losing his cool in that a girl's room. Beads scattered all over. Just floating in the air, suspended there. Weirdest thing. "Go down to the bar and get us some. And get some for our buddy. This gig is almost over and we need to keep him happy until we're gone."

"If I'm driving, you have to get out." Lex opened the car door.

"I'll drive. Dammit man. You don't know what I've been through. This has got to get done before something happens with Timmelsen."

Lex slammed his car door. "What could happen? He's locked up tight."

"I don't know. I just have the willies, like I used to before … " Like he used to get before Dad went on one of his rampages and things went flying, including Phil. Something about the air. What were those things? Frequencies? Wavelengths? He sure as hell didn't want to ever be on the same wavelength as Dad. Ever. Again.

He started the engine. There had to be a way to wipe memories. Like an app. Wave the app on his phone over his brain and wooop! Any memory of Dad? Gone.

Heh. Maybe that was Phil's million dollar idea.

Maybe not.

They drove downtown and parked in front of the bar. "Busy. Hey. Get two six-packs."

Lex opened his door. "What are *you* gonna drink?"

"Ha. Ha." Phil tapped his gun as he scanned who was in the bar. Man he had to get out of this town soon. The people here were starting to look familiar. And good.

Lex opened the door, the beer under his arm. A woman held it for him, chatting. He nodded and smiled. Those dimples pulled the girls in every time.

"What'd she say to you?" Phil watched her walk away through the glass door. "She want to meet you later? Cause I'm sleeping in this car, too."

Lex chuckled. "So what if she does?" He shoved a beer at Phil.

"All's I'm saying is this gig better work." He popped it open and chugged. "I need to get out of this town. Get Bea. And out." He drank again. "I don't care what happens with Clarence. Not even Warden." His jaw jutted. "Screw them."

## FORTY-FOUR

Clarence came to when something flopped over his body. He tried to move but could only turn his face sideways. Somebody had dropped a dirty towel over him.

He tried to roll over, but he slipped in ... shit. He was face down in the muck. Every time he tried to move to get up, he slipped. Every movement churned up the smell. He was sure his nose would never smell anything so rank, ever again.

Hands seemed to grip him from every point: his legs, his arms, shoulders. He was barely standing when hands tucked the towel around him and secured it around his waist.

He must have been beaten badly because he wasn't really seeing anyone, just feeling hands trying to move him, someone helping him.

Then he saw boots by his mucky feet. "Geeez, Clarence. You really got yourself in it this time." A deep chuckle. "Shit and all."

Seemed like about thirty people surrounded him, supporting him and wiping him off, but all he really saw were boots. One pair of boots. Dirty boots.

Clarence ventured a look up and what he saw startled him so much, he began sliding and falling.

Again, hands caught him and steadied him, keeping him upright and covered.

"Whoah there, Clarence." The voice choked. "You've been … you've been beaten pretty badly. Let's just take it easy and not fall. You don't need that."

Clarence found the voice with his eyes. Found the face belonging to the voice.

Lester.

For once, Clarence let the tears flow. The pain and humiliation, but the relief of seeing a true friend.

Lester.

He wasn't sure he was sane. Might be delusional because about fifty angels stood surrounding him and right in the middle of them was Michael.

"Michael." His voice was husky. He could barely get the name out. "Michael." He broke and slumped to the floor again, not caring what he was landing in or how he'd get back up.

When he came to, he was on his cot. His hair was damp and plastered against his head just like he'd had a shower. He was covered in several blankets. He had clothes on.

Cozy.

Must be how a newborn baby felt after its first bath and then was swaddled in warm blankets.

The whole morning came back to him and tears as well. The mess must have gotten up his nose because he could still smell it. He tried to rub his nose, but all he could feel were bandages.

He must have broken his nose when he was pushed onto the floor.

He wasn't sure he wanted to know what else was broken.

Then it all came rushing back. The threats. The guard stepping away. Brutalized.

Through the years, he'd gained a sort of respect among the ranks of inmates and had appreciated somewhat of a protection.

He helped them with their legal issues and they helped him stay safe.

The visual of the boots. "Lester?"

A voice out of recent past. "Lester isn't here right now, Clarence."

Clarence burst into tears.

Michael.

He reached out his hand, tried to make contact, but wasn't sure he'd ever had contact with Michael. They'd spent a lot of time together, but had they ever touched?

Clarence wiped his face. Ow. He tried to see, but his eyes were swollen.

There.

Michael.

The huge angel was in full-dress angel costume instead of work clothes and a plaid shirt jacket.

Clarence blinked.

Michael glowed. His wings reached up through the ceiling. Michael's head touched it. He guessed that if Michael stood up straight, he'd be taller than this building.

But those eyes.

He reached for his hand. "Michael."

Michael reached for his.

At that moment, he remembered another hand reaching for him.

Jesus.

Everything from that moment on the cliff rushed back at once. Crashed in. He remembered taking that step of faith off the cliff into Jesus. He didn't understand it all, he just knew.

"Michael. Jesus said come."

Michael leaned down on one knee, completely filling the cell. His glow softened but light still emanated from his face, his eyes. The angel nodded, his eyes watered.

"Michael, are you crying?" Clarence tried to lift his head but couldn't. "Michael."

"Clarence." The angel's hand clasped Clarence's. It was so huge that it covered his whole arm and hand.

Clarence wanted to ask him where he'd been, but something held him back. He didn't need to know. Just the fact that Michael was here now.

"Who were ... those other people in the bathroom? I saw thirty or more there. And whose boots were those?" Clarence closed his eyes. "They were right in front of my own feet."

Keys jangled in the cell door.

Clarence braced himself.

Lester.

"Hey buddy. You're awake." Lester approached with a tray. "Just a little something to build you up. You've had quite a ... a ... day." He wiped his face with the back of his hand. "Sorry to see you here again." Lester put down the tray at the foot of the cot. "Your old cell." He swept his arm around like he was showing off a new car. "Sorry this is all ... " He lowered his voice to a whisper. "And sorry these people are out to get you."

Clarence nodded, not sure how to respond. "It was your boots I saw in the bathroom. You helped me get up." He felt his hair. "You cleaned me up. I don't know how you did it but ... thank you."

Lester shook his head. "Oh believe me. I had help. Maybe not the kind of help most people would expect, but I had help." He held up a sandwich. "You need to eat—get your strength back. There's a glass of milk too." He held up a piece of paper too. "And a note from Sara in the kitchen."

"She helped me try to get away yesterday." He took a bite of the sandwich. "Was that yesterday?"

Lester chuckled and glanced at the walls. "You're going to have to start your calendar again aren't you."

"I tried but I didn't even know the day. I have no reference. I can't even start it."

"Well, this ought to get you started." Lester held out a pencil. "Hide it well. I'd probably get fired for just giving you that." He chuckled. "But I'm sure it hasn't been all that long, that you'll remember your hiding places and secret routines. Right?"

Clarence searched the walls. "The only thing I could remember was where I carved Annie's name—up there." He tried to point but let his arm flop back down on the cot. "What all is wrong with me? Is my nose broken?"

"Yes. I'm sure of it. Probably some ribs as well, your backside is really bruised up. You should be okay, but you are going to have to work hard and move like you used to—get back in shape." He held up his hand, teaching. "You need to get back on your feet as fast as possible. Even faster. You can't let them see you as weak." He shook his head. "That, I'm sure, is part of their plan. To weaken you until you give in." Lester stood straight, arms like they were holding weapons.

Maybe they were in some realm.

Had he really seen Jesus?

He checked to where Michael had been standing and he was still there, listening, but beckoning to—

Clarence gasped. There were about twenty angels, all lined up around the cell walls—side-by-side—not a gap between them. Angel insulation.

He could see them clearly, but also see the walls, the bars. Annie's name was still visible.

Amazing.

Since Clarence had stepped into Jesus, things seemed different. It was like he had needed to embrace Jesus so he could change. So things could change. He remembered the embrace. It was like hugging little Bea, her head on his shoulder, his on hers. But somehow he'd gone into Him. In Him. Inside of Him.

Become one.

He didn't understand. He only knew.

"Michael?"

The angel knelt again. "Yes, Comrade?"

"Comrade?"

Michael shushed him. "Rest, Comrade. We have to rest in order to ... "

Clarence must have passed out. When he came to, his eyes wandered over the walls. The bars. The ceiling and the facilities. Everything held memories. He had stared at each thing for sixty years.

He hadn't appreciated the nursing home for what it was. Freedom. Friendship. People who cared. Love.

And there was Annie's name carved forever into the concrete walls. He was surprised he could still read it, even with paint covering it.

When he had carved her name, there had been no one else in his life that he loved so much, that he had wanted as badly as her.

She had been his life. His world.

He had lived this long without her. In pain because she was gone. Because she had been taken from him.

But now.

He could still feel her. He still loved her. All these years and he would still embrace her and if they still had the chance, to spend whatever time he had left with her.

But she was gone.

He didn't understand it, but he could feel her pulling away from him. Not in anger, but in reality.

In love even.

Well, he guessed it was time—it had only been sixty years. He guessed no one could blame him for moving on after being faithful for that many years.

"Annie." He swallowed. "My Annie. Please forgive me."

And there she was.

Their daughter stood beside her.

Both beauties.

Both smiling sweet smiles.

"Clarence, my love." Annie touched his cheek. "It *is* time for you to move on and there is one who loves you like I love you. She is a faithful servant and is waiting for you. You are free to love another."

"But Annie—"

She shook her head and put her finger to his lips.

He looked from her beautiful face to their daughter.

She nodded.

And they were gone.

He shook his head. Since he'd met Jesus, he couldn't stop the tears. Wouldn't go well here in prison. But what could be worse than what he'd already been through?

Well. Dying.

Today that would be worse.

Because for the first time, he finally had something to live for.

Some*one* to live for.

The envelope with the adoption papers was back in his room at Hillcrest, but it was all done except the screaming and crying when he told the girls. He had done it without telling them, yes, but he knew it would make them happy. And he needed someone like them—young women and Bea—who would use the funds well and who would deserve it.

Katty and Bea had been through so much. He sighed. And right now Phil and Lex needed to die. He didn't believe Jesus would mind that. They were evil men and intended to do evil to Katty and Bea—maybe others.

Right now, someone needed to slam both Phil and Lex into a cell or better yet into a grave.

"Michael?"

No answer.

"Michael!"

He wasn't in the cell. Where had he gone now? He'd just come back into Clarence's life.

Where had he gone?

## FORTY-FIVE

Back home, Katty unpacked the groceries. She hadn't bought much, just milk and bread and the constant peanut butter. A cookie or two.

And ... she peeked at Bea. Already engrossed in the program on TV.

Katty pulled a small paper bag from the groceries, fingers trembling. Bea had been so excited over new peanut butter, she'd never noticed the small bottle of whiskey being checked out.

Mandy and John weren't working, so Katty didn't care what the checker thought.

She hesitated.

Not true. She did care.

She shoved the bottle, still in the paper bag, behind the sugar canister.

Click.

Katty held her breath.

The TV was noisy but she was sure she had heard a noise from in back.

She checked the window.

Nothing moved. She guessed she was getting jumpy what with seeing Phil and Lex at Hillcrest.

And probably because she had bought booze.

Just knowing they had been there and were in town made her uneasy and fearful. At least she'd talked to the cop—the cute one. He knew everything. He knew about Phil and their past, her past, but he also knew from Sheriff's point of view what Phil had done in Osceola.

The booze called to her. What if the cop came by?

There it was again. A sort of squeak. She checked out back again, then out the front windows.

Her imagination was going crazy, and who could blame her? *Phil was here. He was coming after them. He had a gun.*

Stop it!

She opened the bread and made a couple peanut butter and jelly sandwiches.

That was healthy, right? Bea loved them and so did she, if she let herself admit it.

There it was again.

A bug crawled across the screen. So that sound was made by a bug?

Man, she needed a drink. Fear piled on top of fear: Phil coming back to town, Clarence gone, Bea getting shot.

She pushed the flour canister in front of the bottle.

Must be a demon. After all that had been going on, she could believe it was more than a bug.

When she heard the sound again, she handed Bea's sandwich to her and walked outside, her own sandwich in her hand, nibbling as she walked. She stopped and just listened and watched. Pretty soon a cat crept out from under a bush and scared her silly.

She laughed but then stopped. What if Phil was sneaking around. Not only trying to scare her but trying to get her and Bea? What if he did get them?

She had begun to feel safe before Clarence had been hijacked to prison. She had even left her windows open at night for fresh air.

But now.

Would she ever feel safe again?

She went back into the trailer.

Bea stood by the sink … holding the bottle of whiskey.

Katty blinked. "Bea! What are you doing?" She grabbed the bottle from her.

Bea's chin quivered. "I know what that is, Mommy."

For as long as Katty lived, she would not forget the expression on Bea's face. Betrayal. Fear. "I'm … " Katty opened the bottle, her eyes never leaving Bea's face.

They stood there like that for at least an eternity, before Katty came to.

Bea's eyes told a million stories of a million nights spent hiding under the rocking chair while Katty caroused all night.

Shaking her head, tears threatening, Katty turned and poured the yellow liquid down the drain. She turned on the faucet and flushed it. She looked back at Bea.

Bea wiped her cheeks with trembling hands. Her chin jutted out as she nodded. "Good job, Mommy."

Katty rinsed the bottle over and over, then plunked it on the windowsill. She pulled a sprig of lavender from another bottle and dropped it into the whiskey bottle. "There. What was in it was evil, but now it's good." She leaned down and slowly picked up Bea. "I'm sorry, Baby Bea. I'm so sorry. I'm just scared right now. Scared of—"

"We'll be okay, Mommy."

Who was this wise child she'd been blessed with?

Another scratching sound. "Bea, we are going to have a party at the nursing home. Wanna come?"

Bea's eyes grew wide. "Yeah! Can I watch my shows?"

"Sure! We'll bring our jammies and toothbrushes and watch your shows."

Bea jumped up and down. "Yes!"

"So come on. We have to go." She dropped Bea's sandwich and what was left of hers into a baggie, and shoved some clothes into a bag. Grabbed her purse and dragged Bea out into the car.

Katty buckled Bea in and backed out of the driveway, knowing someone was watching. She tried not to panic. Didn't want to scare Bea.

She hadn't been this scared since Phil had left her. He had used her up, gotten tired of her and left. But she had hidden the fact that she was pregnant again—with Bea. He wasn't going to kill this baby.

She'd hidden out, delivered Bea by herself.

Tried to make a life—just Katty and the baby.

How Phil had found out she'd had a kid ... didn't matter now.

He knew.

He was back.

And he was going to do all the evil crap he could to get her, but to get Bea.

She pulled up at Hillcrest Homes. She didn't even try to find a parking place farther away. She parked in the Visitors Only spaces. Her eyes on the door.

*Just get inside. Get Bea inside.*

"What are we going to do here Mommy?" Bea kicked the back of Katty's seat but for some reason it calmed her. It used to make her so mad.

"We are going to see if they will let us stay here. Maybe they have a spare bed and you and I can have a slumber party together." She unbuckled Bea and grabbed her, bag and all.

No way she would let Bea even run loose. She wouldn't take any chances here tonight or ever again.

With every car they passed, she expected someone to jump out at them.

Her fingers trembled just like when she had been using drugs and needed a fix. When she needed a fix, every cell in her body screamed and shook until she could get more drugs or booze.

Whatever was going to happen, at least she would be among friends and people who cared about them.

She pressed the auto open button and stepped in. The receptionist had gone home, so Katty walked on down to the nurses station. Lisha was still on duty.

"Girl. You look like you seen a ghost." Lisha held out her arms and Katty ran into them. Bea got squished between them.

Katty fought to hold back the tears. She didn't want to scare Bea more than she already had. But those big beautiful arms around her made it feel like no one could ever hurt them again.

Lisha released them. "What's this about? Is it about those bastards that showed up earlier? What's their names?"

Katty nodded. "Phil and Lex."

"Did they come out to your house?"

"No. Well I don't think so. I kept hearing noises." Katty shifted Bea to her other hip. "I just didn't want to stay there. He knows where we live." She shivered.

"Well, I know just where you can stay for as long as you want." She winked. "And I don't have to ask permission. If the board has a problem with it, well they can just eat it!"

Katty smiled. Something about Lisha made her happy. Somehow she knew they'd be all right. It was comforting here.

As they followed Lisha to Clarence's room, dragging a pillow pet and bag, she felt so at home. They belonged there.

How was that for crazy? She belonged in a nursing home?

Lisha flipped the lights on and pulled down the shades in both windows, both rooms. "You both have your own bathroom. You have your own bed. But I reckon you'll end up together. You know which one Clarence sleeps in all the time, so I guess you can have this one." She checked for sheets. "Still made up, so have at it." She checked the closet in the office. "Full up with boxes but there's room on top for your bags. Need a toothbrush?"

Katty shook her head. "Could we call the sheriff and let them know where we're at? I told one deputy that I might do this and he said to call if I did."

Lisha pulled her phone from her pocket and dialed. "Who you want to talk to?"

"Um. Deputy Scott."

Lisha grinned. "Oh, the cute one. He's kinda short, but he'd be great for you. You're short too."

"Hello? Sheriff's Department. Deputy Scott speaking."

Lisha laughed and handed Katty the phone. "Handy."

Katty cleared her throat. "This is Katty Randolph. We talked at the nursing ho—"

"Hello. I remember you. Are you doing okay?"

She nodded. "Yes. I just wanted to let you know ... uh, let the department know that I decided to stay in Clarence's rooms at Hillcrest."

"Good idea. Glad you called. Need to make some rounds later anyway, so I'll stop by and check in on you. And your daughter. What's her name?"

"Bea. Her name is Bea."

"Like the buzz bugs, right?" Katty turned away from Lisha, who was doubled over laughing. "Well kinda. It's B. E. A. It sounds like bee though."

He laughed. "Okay. My bad. I'll be up in a little while. Got some paperwork here to catch up on and then ... I'll be ... there."

"Okay. Sounds fine. Thanks." Katty handed the phone back to Lisha.

"Well, that went fine, I think." She winked. "You have your own personal deputy. I'd say that's fine."

Katty shook her head. "Where can we get some washcloths?"

"Comin' right up."

Bea had already turned the TV on and was getting caught up on her shows.

Katty flitted through the papers on the desk, stacked them and sighed.

No work tonight.

She picked up Bea and sat, pulling Bea onto her lap.

Lisha returned with towels and washcloths and soap. She wrapped them both in a blanket—burrito style—and patted Bea's head. "Not used to having people so young here. Kinda nice to hear cartoons."

Katty smiled. "Oh, you'll get tired of it. Hey. How's Harold doing? He was pretty upset earlier."

"He's back to his self. Still upset about Clarence gone, but we finally got him settled down so he could rest. I think he was so intent on taking care of you two, that he just couldn't get the words out."

She headed for the door and closed it part way. "Do whatever makes you comfy and I'll be back in after meds to check on you." She peeked back in. "Doors auto lock at eight o'clock so we're locked in tight here. No one can get in."

Katty hung her head. "It feels so stupid to be scared."

Lisha came back in the room and reached for Katty's hand. "Now don't beat yourself up, Little One. My man used to beat me till my ears rang and blood dripped. I was terrified all the time." She blinked. "Never told anybody that."

"Oh, Lisha." Lisha too. She squeezed Lisha's fingers. "I hope Clarence is okay."

"He's okay. He's a stubborn old man. He'll be back." She waved and left.

Bea was already asleep on her lap.

Katty was glad for that because she felt that the emotional floor was dropping out. She tried to keep it quiet, but she couldn't stop weeping.

She stood and carried Bea to the bed. Wouldn't be the first time she had gone to bed in her clothes.

She brushed Bea's hair from her face and shook her head. She closed the door and sighed.

Would she ever be free of the memories?

She guessed not, but someday they might be safe.

Dreams of a simple man, a kind man made her feel better.

## FORTY-SIX

Noell wandered into the living room. She'd been in this room all her life. Maybe she was restless, knowing what she now knew about Katty and Bea being related to her.

It was the oddest thing. Almost as if something or someone—Clarence maybe—had drawn them all together.

She had some cousins!

There were so many stacks of junk, boxes, books that she'd never know if something here was valuable or not. Did Gamma have photos that were family heirlooms? Treasures?

She knew now what was in her mother's room and what those things meant. She hadn't come to a decision as to what to do with all that upstairs, but she knew whose it was and what it meant.

The rest of this she had no idea.

Where would Gamma had kept things that meant something to her?

Her bedroom?

She was restless right now.

The date with Fletch had stirred up emotion about her future.

The news that Katty and Bea were related to her had begun questions.

Some were the same old questions: like what should she do with the house—sell or keep it, if she kept it did she want to live here all by herself? She had fun with Fletch but was he the one? Was he a person that she would or could spend her whole life with?

How had Grampa or Gamma figured that out? She didn't have that time with her own mother to ask questions about life and love. Who could she ask? Who could she trust?

With Clarence in prison, she didn't feel she had anyone she could trust. She trusted Fletch, but right now he was part of the problem.

Gamma's bedroom had stayed the same as when she died just like Mommy's. The only thing Noell had done was change the sheets. She didn't even know why she had done that, but it seemed the right thing to do. Tough job to put everything back on the other side of the bed. Again. Seemed like the right thing to do.

Otherwise the room had stayed the same. There was a small private bath off to the left but that wasn't too cluttered. Gamma's bedroom had stacks and stacks of books—again was it her way to insulate the house? Wouldn't it have been better to have called a business to do that instead?

When she got the house all decluttered, it would seem huge.

Bathroom first.

Gamma'd had so many pretty perfume and lotion bottles on display but when Noell sniffed some, they smelled stale and rancid. She grabbed the trash can and dumped them all. Would they sell at the consignment shop? What would anyone do with these anyway? Maybe she should just pack it all up, except for real trash and take it down there. Let Mrs. Bertrand decide if it's worth anything. She'd know.

This was hard.

She was snooping.

She had to.

But she was snooping.

The closet made her want to scream.

Maybe the bedside table. Cute little piece of furniture. Three drawers in each one. Couldn't be too bad.

But the first one she pulled open was packed with little oil bottles. She knew Gamma had been into them but not like this. She didn't know a thing about them so she grabbed a box and started pulling them out. She sniffed one or two, wrinkled her nose at most of the others.

Done. She pushed the bottom drawer closed. She pulled it open again. It was actually empty!

Okay. Next drawer up.

Gah. Full again. Smelled the same. Looked the same. Full of little bottles of oils.

Same drill. She packed them all into the same box. If everything was this tiny, it'd take forever to go through.

Empty.

She braced herself for the top drawer. She just knew it would be full of tiny bottles again.

She pulled on the knob and got knocked back. Odd visuals of a man doing awful things to someone else flitted through her brain. Awful.

She pressed her fists into her eyes. What was that? Voices yelling obscene words. Who was that man and what was he doing in Gamma's bedroom?

Calm down.

She had been so engrossed in all that had happened to Clarence and hearing the news about Katty and Bea being related, she had forgotten to be afraid to touch handles and doors. And drawers.

But this. This was in Gamma's private stuff. She finally relaxed telling herself that it was just a fluke, that no one had been here. That man, whoever he was, had left Osceola and was long gone.

She also told herself that the top drawer would be either full of little bottles again or empty.

But it wasn't. It wasn't full of little bottles *or* empty.

It smelled like the other two drawers. The smell probably seeped from one drawer to the next.

Two book size notebooks were on top and a stack of letters underneath. The cover of the top notebook was covered in little drawings. They hadn't been printed on but ... drawn. Had Gamma been a doodler? They didn't feel raised or printed on by anything. She opened the journal and inside there were more. Really cute. Some were ... amazing.

Most pages had been dated. She checked the calendar on her phone. The most recent had been dated two weeks before she died. The handwriting was kind of messy but Noell guessed she had just scribbled down her thoughts as they came to her. These entries weren't probably for anyone to read but Gamma.

And here she was reading them.

The last entry was short. "Slept in till 6:30!"

That was sleeping in?

She had heard Gamma rustling around some nights but she figured she had needed the rest room or a drink.

"Every time I fell back to sleep, I slept <u>hard</u>. Felt like I worked hard in the night season. 'You did. You did all kinds of things.'"

Quotes. Odd.

It was like a conversation between Gamma and ... someone else. Who was it?

Huh.

She set the journals aside to read later. They would stop her momentum. She peeked at the empty drawers. Gotta keep going.

Letters. All tied in ribbons. She flipped them over and back again.

Were these love letters?

Naw. She'd never heard Gamma or Grampa talk about such things.

She untied the ribbon—a blue lace-edged satin ribbon—and opened the top letter. It was dated since Grampa had died so it couldn't be from him. Who would have sent her love letters? And why would she have tied them all up fancy like this if they weren't from him?

Did Gamma have a secret admirer? Or a secret boyfriend? Oh my. That would be awesome.

"Dear Father."

Her dad had to have died a long time ago. They had talked about when he died, in fact.

"Today I had to teach Noell about forgiveness."

What?

Noell slowly sat on the bed. She skimmed the page. "I remember this. It wasn't all that long ago."

Mr. Grimes.

She had long ago told Gamma about him being so creepy, but ever since then she had not talked about him very nice. Well, he wasn't very nice. But Gamma had been right—Noell had needed to get rid of unforgiveness.

She hated him. That was more than unforgiveness. Still working on that one.

The second page she skimmed again until the bottom.

"Noell doesn't seem to have the curse that I have lived with all my life."

Curse?

"Today I was at the store and checked out after an old man who had always flirted with me."

Aw. Cute. Gamma *did* have a secret admirer.

"I tried to avoid everywhere he touched but I missed the obvious—the credit card machine. I don't often use it but I didn't have enough cash for the groceries. So I checked out with that and could barely keep it together. Right away I heard heavy breathing and saw awful pictures from what looked like a magazine."

Noell dropped the pile of letters and backed against the wall. Gamma.

Gamma could see things too?

She grabbed the letters again and found her place. "When I went out to my car, Mr. Tate was standing by his car talking to another man. I avoided his stares, but when I got to my car, he scared the daylights out of me. Stood right next to my car and I didn't even hear him walk up. I still ignored him until he put his hand on mine to open the car door for me. Nice move, but I wasn't having any of him. When he touched my hand, I started trembling and I couldn't control it. He thought it was from his sexual aura. I told him to go away. That I wasn't interested in his filth."

Go Gamma!

"He went away, but not before touching my arm. Gonna go home and take a shower!"

Noell shook her head. Same things had happened to her, but she'd never told Gamma about it. "Oh, Gamma. Why didn't we talk about this?"

What if they had? They might have been able to help each other somehow. Maybe they could have grown even closer than they had been.

And did Grampa know? He had always been super protective of her. Super gentlemanly, too. They always held hands so she guessed Grampa was okay in the filth department. Gamma probably wouldn't have let him live here if he had been different.

Mommy. Had she had the gift?

She'd have to search her room better sometime.

Another pile of letters was tucked into the side of the drawer.

"My dear Gwendolyn." This one was definitely from Grampa. She read the whole thing, then two more. "Wow. Grampa, you were the best … lover. Such neat words." He had adored Gamma.

She sat staring out the window. Blinked a couple of times.

That's who she wanted to spend the rest of her life with.

Someone like Grampa. She hadn't known her dad, but it didn't matter. She wanted someone just like Grampa.

Fletch came into view out the window. He must have just gotten home from work and was chatting with his mom outside the back door. As Noell watched, he hugged her and patted her back.

Sweet.

She sat for a long time watching them, enjoying their obvious banter and love.

She realized something as she watched them. He reminded her of Grampa. She had always known he was like someone she had known or knew, but she had never realized it was Grampa.

## FORTY-SEVEN

Within fifteen minutes, Sheriff and his deputy knocked on Clarence's door.

Katty had been thinking about getting ready for bed. Glad she hadn't gotten that far.

Sheriff removed his cap. "This okay for time?"

Bea stirred on the bed.

"Oh, I'm sorry." He whispered and held his finger at his lips. "I woke her up. Will she go back—"

"Hi Mr. Sheriff." Bea rubbed her eyes and slid off the bed.

"Guess not. I'm sorry."

Katty shook her head. "It's okay. We'll have a slumber party after you leave."

They all sat down around Clarence's desk. Bea climbed on her lap.

"How are you doing, little Bea?" Sheriff leaned over the desk. "We didn't get to talk much the other day."

Bea looked up at him from under Katty's arm. She looked from his face to the deputy's face. She smiled, then tucked herself under Katty's arm.

"Just a little shy." Deputy Scott walked his fingers toward her on the desk.

She giggled and pushed his fingers away.

Katty knew Bea still wasn't sure of any man's touch other than Clarence's. She was all over *him*. He could tickle her, kiss her, hug her and paddle her little bottom. He'd only done it once, but Katty guessed that was the only time he'd have to ever spank her. She'd remember it for life. All he'd have to do now would be to remind her of it and she'd behave.

"Is it okay if she is here for this?" Sheriff pointed at Bea. "I don't want to upset her if—"

"No. She's okay. She knows it all anyway." Katty glanced down at Bea. "At least I think."

"Well, if she does get upset, maybe I can take her for a walk or something." Deputy Scott made it known that the something meant ice cream as he pretended to hold an ice cream cone and then lick it.

Katty grinned. "That would be fine." She rubbed Bea's back. "It'd only take her seconds to warm up to you."

Sheriff opened his notebook and clicked his pen. "Well, I'm glad Lisha called us. This whole thing has gone on far too long. About what time did you hear noises at your trailer?"

Katty checked the clock on the wall. "Maybe about six o'clock? Something like that. We'd just gotten home from the store. And before that, we were here when people saw Phil and Lex hanging around. Or rather hiding around."

"Okay." He scribbled in his notebook. "So you saw them here, then left for the store and got home. What noises did you hear at home?"

"Just ... noises. Like something hitting against the trailer. Or something slamming. Or scraping. I ran out and saw a cat, and it could have been that. But after seeing Phil and Lex here earlier, I was scared already, so maybe it was just a cat. But I thought of Phil right away."

"Was there any contact when you saw them here before?"

Sheriff glanced around the room. "They didn't come down here?"

Katty shook her head. "No. We didn't talk to them and they didn't come down here."

Bea peeked out from Katty's arm. "They wanted ice cream 'cause that's where Mr. Harold saw them."

"Right." Sheriff got busy with his notebook. "Let me write that down." He dictated as he wrote. "They. Wanted. Ice cream." He tapped the pen on the notebook. "I got it down."

Bea grinned. "But they didn't get any. You were too fast for them."

He diligently wrote that down. "Well I'm glad you called. We need to know every time you see them or hear from them."

Katty nuzzled Bea's head, pursing her lips. "Well, when you say it like that, there have been a couple other times."

Sheriff straightened. "Really. When?"

Deputy Scott tapped the desk in front of Bea. Probably trying to distract her. He walked his fingers over to her and tried to tickle her.

"Well, we got a bike left at our place."

Bea sat upright on Katty's lap. "Yeah. It was red and bright and shiny. It had handlebars and a basket. And pedals. And a great big bow on it."

"How big was the bow?" Sheriff was ready to write it down.

"This big!" Bea held her arms wide. "And Mommy wouldn't let me keep it."

Katty shrugged. "I figured it was from Clarence. He's been like a grandpa to us—to her. So I called here and that's when they were picking him up to go prison. I heard the whole conversation and we rushed down here. But Clarence hadn't left the bike. He told me so over the phone, before they got him."

"That was just before he and Bea were shot, right?" Deputy Scott folded his hands on the desk in front of him. "Why did you think Clarence had left it?"

"Because he was always doing something like that. Nothing so expensive as the bike, except for when he pays me and he helped with our new deck."

"He bought me a new car seat so I wouldn't fall out of the car." Bea nodded, her face serious.

Sheriff and Deputy Scott glanced at each other.

Sheriff bit his lip.

Deputy Scott wiped his eyes.

"So you don't have any proof that it was Phil who left the bike for her, then."

"No. Except." Katty hesitated. "Yesterday, I got the mail and there was a note in there for Bea."

"There was?" Bea jumped down, holding her side. "Where is it? I didn't see it!"

"You didn't see it, because I didn't show it to you." Katty reached for her purse and pulled the note out. She held it for a second, but when she looked at it again, she was afraid she would get so mad that they would arrest *her*. She handed it to Sheriff.

He took time to look it over and to read it before passing it to Deputy Scott.

He read it and gave it back to Sheriff. "What makes you think this is from him?"

Katty was almost jumping out of her chair, she was so sure of herself. She showed them the envelope. "I'd know this handwriting anywhere. It's his."

Bea craned to see.

Sheriff and the deputy exchanged looks. "If you can give us some sort of example of his handwriting that is his name for instance, or has something written and signed by him, we could compare them and send them in for analysis."

Katty shook her head. "I hated him so bad, that I burned—" She tapped her finger against the notepaper. "I have ... " She got her purse and opened her wallet. She pulled out a piece of paper. "I don't even know why I kept this." She opened the note and pushed it to Sheriff.

He skimmed it and glanced up at her. "Why? Why did you keep this?" He pushed it over to the deputy.

She fumbled with the latch on her purse and shook her head. "I thought ... I thought he loved me. When he sent me this, I wanted to leave my parents so bad. They ... ," she glanced at Bea, "they weren't very nice people."

Bea crawled on Katty's lap. She looked at the note, then searched Katty's face.

"When he sent me this, it was a way out." She shook her head. "I didn't know what he was really like." She bit her lip. "It started the minute we got to his place. I didn't have a chance."

Awkward.

She'd never told anyone that. Never showed the note to anyone.

Deputy Scott handed the note to Sheriff and he compared the signatures. "Looks the same to me. Okay if I keep these? I can send them in and get an official assessment."

Katty nodded. She had loved him once. "I don't ever want it back, Sheriff." Good to break ties to her past.

Sheriff stood and pushed the chair up to the desk. "Okay. I guess until we get the samples back, we're done. And, like I think Lisha might have told you, they automatically lock up here at eight. No one comes in. No one goes out." He checked the clock. "Except us. In an hour."

"Okay." Kathy looked at Bea. "Maybe we'll go down for ice cream before we go to bed, huh Bea?"

Bea hopped down. "Let's go, Mommy!" She dragged Katty out to the hallway and gestured to the men. "Come with us."

The men laughed.

"Feel free, Deputy. I want to get these in." Sheriff tipped his hat. "Another time." He bowed to Bea. "Thank you, Ma'am." He straightened. "And Katty, I assure you, we will do everything we can to keep you two safe. I wish I could say the same thing for Clarence."

FORTY-EIGHT

Phil parked the car at the implement company and walked across the highway to the park. He guessed the employee would be okay with him parking there since he'd left a six-pack for him in his vehicle a couple times. This evening produced the grand prize of a bottle of whiskey in a paper bag on the drivers seat.

No traffic on the highway. He didn't even look both ways. Bad boy. These small towns were such a joke. People just lived in them to hide from life.

He raised his eyebrows. Maybe that's what he should do—hide. He guessed that just like ole Jessie James though, his past would catch up with him at some point.

As he stepped across the railroad tracks and into the park, he spied Katty and Bea outside the nursing home eating ice cream with a deputy. He dipped down behind a tree. What a coincidence. He definitely planned to kidnap Bea and whatever he had to do with Katty, he'd do. But not in a public place.

He had found their crappy trailer park. Katty was such a loser, but he'd always known that. Why they had hooked up years ago, he couldn't remember. Probably because he was just his usual horny self.

He smiled. Yeah. He lived life through testosterone.

He ducked. Had she seen him? She didn't grab Bea and run inside, so maybe not.

He shifted behind a closer tree for a better look.

Closer to that old slide.

Still there. He got a rush just looking at it. He'd had Bea back then. He should have kept on driving with her in tow and not given them a chance at her. He never once figured old Timmelsen would be able to rescue her especially when he lit it on fire.

If he himself couldn't have Bea, then he didn't want Katty or Timmelsen to have her either. Something in him rose up that day. He had not forgotten that moment when he knew he'd kill Bea by duct taping her to the slide and then setting it on fire.

He didn't understand what that something was—that moment—but he knew it well. It was the same as when he'd gotten rid of a few babies for Katty. And when he'd beaten Timmelsen. And when he touched Bea's cheek—so tender and pure. And when he'd almost killed Katty.

As he watched Katty wipe Bea's face, that something rose up in him again. Powerful. Terrifying. Growling.

Damn, he knew what it was and still, after all these years, he wasn't ready to admit what it really was.

A demon.

And not just one.

He remembered moments when he'd watched his dad drink blood. Dad had been a meat cutter and had plenty of access to the stuff.

When he drank it, his face changed. Phil hadn't understood it then. It had been terrifying yet fascinating at the same time. There was something in that blood—some power—that could actually change a person's skin and structure.

Crazy.

Even crazier was one time when his dad had set down the paper cup, his eyes were almost delirious—the guy used knives to cut meat for Pete's sake—he looked at Phil and filled the cup back up and shoved it to Phil.

Like he would drink blood.

But sweet dad, when Phil said no way, picked up a knife and grabbed his hand, ready to inflict pain if he didn't drink.

He drank.

That day something changed in him. Something was different. He almost felt that someone had taken up residence in his body. Back then, he didn't understand that stuff and he wasn't all that sure he really understood now, but every time he inflicted pain or drew blood, power grew and surged into something even he couldn't control.

Katty laughed and smiled. That deputy was chasing Bea around Katty's legs. Did they have a thing?

Phil was shocked at the jealousy growling inside him.

Bea didn't seem to have as much energy as she had months ago when he was trying to tape her down. She held her belly.

Oh, right. She'd been shot.

Something Phil didn't understand flickered inside. When he had taped Bea to the slide, he hadn't cared that she might die, but now he gets all soppy because someone else shot her?

She was cute.

Katty picked Bea up and snuggled her.

Even seemed like *Katty* had changed.

She nuzzled her nose into Bea's neck and hair.

Sweetness.

He peeked around the other side of the tree.

Katty *had* changed. She seemed … more tender. Nice.

Too bad she hadn't been that way back … why was he wanting to kill them or even kidnap Bea when they could be a family?

Holy shit! Where had that thought come from?

A slow growl rose from his very toes and surfaced in a snarl.

Look what he could have had back then but … even now. He could have had a family: a wife and kid. They could all be playing together, instead of that deputy. Damn, he had been robbed.

Katty laughed as Bea tickled her neck.

Why should Katty get all the love? Why should she get all the snuggles from that sweet pure little girl?

At the thought of how perfect Bea was, more rose up within him. He could feel it where you couldn't scratch in public.

It was a demon and it began its stinky progression up his torso to his chest. Every part of him wanted what Katty had.

That little girl had to be his.

Oh-oh. He ducked behind the bigger tree and peeked around it. The deputy patted Bea's head and walked to his squad car.

What was this? Phil wanted to growl. Did they have an admirer? A boyfriend? Or more. A lover.

The thought pushed Phil over the edge.

This had to stop.

He had to get his little girl.

# FORTY-NINE

Clarence tried to lean up off the bed, to check the cell door but could hardly move. All he could do was roll to his side and let his head lift.

The lights were dim, but he couldn't see anything or anyone.

He needed to move around. Who had told him that recently? Lester.

Was Lester real? Was he an angel?

Lester had given him good advice to just get moving.

He gripped the sides of the cot and tried to sit up. Oh God, he couldn't do it.

He rolled to his left side and grabbed the metal bed frame.

He was able to slide his legs to the edge and barely get them over and toward the floor. He pushed up with his right hand and set his feet onto the floor at the same time.

Luckily, the bed wasn't far off the floor so his feet touched.

Man, he hurt. He had been beaten to the very end of his life before. But before, he had been a hundred years younger.

He leaned, his arm supporting him and almost sat up. He pushed harder and sat up right. Felt like he'd run a marathon, instead of just sitting up in bed.

"I see you're back to your old self, Mr. Timmelsen."

Clarence jumped. He almost fell back against the wall. Still on the cot, but he would have hit his head which had taken enough hits.

Warden stood on the other side of the bars with five fully armed guards. "Glad to see our welcome committee didn't keep you down."

Clarence could only growl. Welcome committee my—

"You better get used to that kind of treatment." He smirked. "I'm sure you know you'll be here till you die, so get used to it."

One of the guards looked familiar now that his eyes had adjusted a little to the dark.

Randy.

How could one man change so quickly? On the trip to Osceola, Randy had been almost a friend. Said he'd wished he could buy Clarence a steak supper instead of the fast food they had eaten.

What would have changed a man so quickly?

He seemed to avoid Clarence's stare.

"Randy." Clarence's voice was almost gone. He coughed. "What are you doing following this man?"

Randy flinched.

Warden roared. "You shut up. He doesn't need to listen to you. He reports to me now."

"Maybe so. But Randy is a good man. And you have changed him. You have lured him into the devil's snare and now he is one of you."

Where had that come from? The devil's snare?

Something had changed in Clarence and he suspected it had something to do with when he'd stepped off that precipice last night into Jesus' arms.

"Randy, there is another way. You have another chance to be free of this man. You can be free of this evil."

Wow. Those words were not from him! Out of his mouth

maybe, but not his.

The warden stepped closer to the bars. "No, you shut up, Timmelsen. He is just fine doing what he's doing. He has served me well." The warden roared. "Shut up!"

Clarence had never been so aware of evil and good. Of the difference in people. He could hear it in Warden's voice. In Tay Ralston's voice. He could see it in Randy's eyes.

"You know I didn't kill your brother in cold blood. He drew a knife on me and it was all in self defense. You know that. You know that's the truth." Clarence stretched to full stature. "Randy, you know that's the truth. It was self defense. Get the old files. See for yourself. This man who calls himself the warden is a liar. He's willing to cheat, lie and steal from people like you and me. Just to make himself look bigger."

Randy wouldn't look at Clarence. He just kept his eyes downcast, his hands at his sides.

"Go to bed, Timmelsen. We'll deal with you tomorrow. We have some surprises for you then. Maybe some reunions between old friends. We're bringing guys in who were there when you killed Lewis. They have a few things to say to you, too. They'll set things straight."

Clarence shuddered.

Randy stared at him from between the warden and another guard. His eyes had changed from just minutes before. He shook his head and prepared to leave with the others.

They started to march off down the walkway, when Warden turned and stared at Clarence. "I just want to thank you. Because you signed all your property over to me, I can afford to take a little trip." He squinted. "It seems the government doesn't like my little family dealings, so we will be leaving soon. Phil left to take care of your girls—all of them—and tomorrow, you'll get repaid for killing my brother—firing squad style." He glanced at Randy. "I don't think anyone does that anymore, so it should be," he leaned closer, "spectacular."

He turned and walked on down the hall.

Clarence was left alone.

He shook and shuddered at the thought of what tomorrow might bring. Warden must be bringing in the very guys who had fought him that fateful day and lost.

Clarence had never been a fighter, but he figured he had enough anger in him at losing Annie and being robbed of his life, that it must have given him power. Fueled the fight so he could defend himself against those monsters.

He moved around the cell as good as he could. Shuffled back and forth. From bars to the facilities. From his cot to the other wall.

It was painful but the more he moved and walked back and forth, the easier it got so he could almost walk right. He made himself stand up straight—head up—shoulders back. He willed himself to walk up straight instead of leaning over and bent like an old man.

He would fight. He had no idea how he would get out of here, but he would.

Even though the guards and Warden had left, the evil was still there. Clarence looked in every corner. Under his cot. Behind the toilet. He could see nothing.

But he would bet his life's savings and holdings—he actually had some now—that there was evil present. It made his skin crawl. He needed to find a way out. Out that tiny barred window. To get away from this evil, this madness.

He didn't understand what it was, but he felt it with every cell of his body.

He made himself walk more. Stretch more.

Even as he tried ignoring the presence, it didn't go away.

He bent over at the waist. Tried to do squats. That hurt too much.

He knew he'd lost a lot of blood because he was so weak.

Another circle around the cell.

Another.

And another.

More stretches.

Leg lifts.

Arm lifts.

He moved every way he could think of without crying out.

The evil persisted.

Dammit. Enough.

"In heaven's name go away." He tried some words he'd heard Mrs. Hatly say at Hillcrest.

"In Jesus' name."

Some song he'd heard—didn't even have to be Christian.

"How Great Thou Art."

Where had he heard that from? They'd hardly gone to church after his mother died. Must have heard it on the radio or TV. Or Lisha had been singing it.

"Help me, Jesus."

The evil would not go away and Clarence wouldn't have admitted to anyone but he was afraid to try to lie down and sleep for fear it would overtake him and kill him as he slept.

"And the roll is called up yonder."

That was stretching it.

He lowered himself onto his cot. At least he could move. Somewhat.

"That's it, whatever you are." He spoke to the evil and then thought a minute. "You are a someone. Aren't you. You are real."

Something rose up in Clarence. A righteous indignation. Anger so powerful. A knowing that he was on the right track, he just didn't know the right words to say.

"You know what, devil?" Clarence gathered force. "I'm not giving up."

Another breath.

"And I'm not giving in."

"For nothin' or nobody."

FIFTY

Noell opened the back door. Somedays—like today—she just wanted to come home from work and not face the mess. It had been a good day; everybody bantered and joked as they filled potholes—a never-ending task. Steve Ivertson, her boss, had brought a case of soda for them all to share. Just made the warm day go a little better. Maybe he was also feeling a little sheepish over the fact he had been gone all morning, taking care of his grandma at the nursing home. It worked. The soda had invigorated them all.

Stacked boxes had the usual effect as she dropped her lunch cooler on the floor. She shook her head. There was much to do.

The keys to Grampa's shed dangled in the sun, hanging from the crazy key closet on the wall beside the back door.

Thank God they had been diligent in keeping track of keys. There were still things that Noell couldn't find. She guessed that there were legal papers Clarence might need to sell this house, but maybe she'd still find them. And she could go to the court house and check there too.

The keys beckoned. Unpack more stuff or go outside and explore Grampa's shed?

No contest.

She grabbed them and stepped out the door. Beautiful fall day. The rains lately had turned the grass a lovely green. Leaves falling on the lawn were golden yellow and rust against the green. A bush by Grampa's old shed was a beautiful rose red.

She checked the camper. Still locked, but weird vibrations ran up her arm from the knob. She shook her hand. That was crazy. No one came back here. Not even her until now. Gamma hadn't even been able to get here for years she guessed.

The shed wasn't a falling down shed. It had been kept up through the years by Grampa. She used to love being out here when he was working. He had always been tinkering on some little thing. She would play at his feet with her ... what? Noell couldn't remember any dolls out here. He had given her tools, all her own. She remembered them but what had she done with them? Were they still in here?

Now that became the most important thing in this world to find: her tools and what she had made with them. More than anything in the house, this became the piece of gold that she needed to dig up.

She grasped the doorknob and the jolt she got from it knocked her flat. A grumbling, growling voice ran through her mind, her being. She could almost hear this voice audibly.

The pictures that scrolling through her mind were terrible. She closed her eyes, but they only became worse—even more graphic. Awful bloody pictures. Babies. A woman.

Katty?

Awful things with her. Awful.

Noell covered her face with her hands and wanted to scream but she was sitting in her backyard, exposed to the world of her neighbors.

This wasn't Mr. Grimes or his stuff.

This was someone else.

Something totally different.

She couldn't do this. If she was to get into Grampa's shed, she'd have to get some kind of bulldozer or little skid loader. Maybe even back the old pickup into it so she didn't have to touch the doorknob again.

Ever again.

She turned away and walked toward the house, wiping her cheeks. When had she cried? That jolt had been so powerful it must have jarred tears lose.

She looked behind her at the shed. Who had been here? Who had been back here and when?

More steps toward the house.

Each step slowed until she stopped mid yard. Right next to the clothes line she never used.

Wait. This was her property and just like the nightmares and the pool, she would not let it scare her away. She would rise up and claim what was hers.

Tears ran down her cheeks and her neck.

This must be another one of those moments when she had to face her fears.

And face them she would.

She turned back to the old shed.

One step.

Another.

And another until she was standing at the door.

She swallowed, aware now of someone farther down the block in their back yard.

Kids. Kids were swinging and singing.

She braced herself.

Hand on the knob.

She would not let go.

She made herself keep holding onto it.

The voices and visuals swam around in her mind, mixing with others there. Screaming. There was blood.

But somehow there was Grampa.

And a sweet child's voice.

Hers!

Her voice.

Her whole body vibrated. Trembled with the frequencies of the voices and all, but she forced her hand there on the knob and inserted the key into the keyhole.

At first she couldn't hit it right. She turned it upside down and it fit in.

One turn and the lock inside clicked and it opened.

Even in the darkness, she sensed Grampa. Even after all the voices and such, his presence was so much stronger in here.

She found the light cord and pulled, expecting it to break or not even work, but the light came on.

Not just one light bulb but a series of shop lights that illuminated every corner.

Her whole being wanted to burst.

Everywhere she looked she sensed him. She walked farther inside and she could smell him.

Trailing her fingers along the tools still on his workbench, she remembered. Things had been left as if he had just walked into the house to eat. He loved his food.

She remembered where she had dropped one of his prize roses.

She clapped her hands.

*He* had been the gardener, not Gamma! All this time she had thought it had been Gamma who had kept up the gardens until she couldn't anymore. She probably had done it for him—to keep up his memories. Just like she had kept up going to auctions, only at some point it had turned into an obsession that neither had foreseen.

She touched the router and waited for any voice or picture. Several popped up. Grampa had been making cabinets for inside. She could see the lines he made with the machine, the beautiful carvings he had done. Carvings of flowers.

Of course since he had been the gardener.

Interesting.

If she didn't shy away from touching tools or door handles, she could maybe learn something, see things that could help her. Help other people.

She picked up a hammer and immediately she sensed many men and women using it. Heard familiar voices. Grampa's distinctive voice—his voice had always soothed her with its melodic, deep smoothness. Some older men had raspy harsh voices but his was like a river or like caramel or smooth wood that he so beautifully finished.

But there was another voice that was familiar from this hammer.

She rubbed the wooden handle. Almost lovingly. After the blast from the doorknob outside, this was soothing and peaceful. Calming.

Who was the other voice?

Sounded like Clarence but couldn't be. He wouldn't have been around ... unless.

She froze. Skitters of inspiration and even joy ran up her spine.

Grampa always bought a lot of tools at auctions.

What if he had bought some tools of Clarence's dad's and Clarence had used it before he went to prison? When he was still at home as a boy and helped his dad.

She began to touch everything in the shop.

She didn't hear anything from some tools or items she picked up, but some almost yelled at her.

Rat?

The guy from work at the Roads Department?

When had *he* been out here?

She'd have to see if her gift helped her find a timing to the visuals.

Like had he used a tool that Grampa had purchased at an

auction or had Rat somehow stolen them or broken in here? And when?

She had discovered things in here. Things that had scared her as a child and possibly would scare her now, but she knew she had to go back there and remember.

Had this guy who knocked her back at the doorknob wanted to cause her pain?

Rat had. He was a creep. If she hadn't have stopped him, he would have taken all she was. In one night. In one action that would have closed her to ever being or finding herself.

She found herself getting excited and drawn to this shop—to discovering everything here and how it spoke to her.

Just like in the camper. Some things just pulled at her and she knew she was to follow.

She hated to go back inside, but now she knew there was nothing she wanted to get rid of out here in the shop.

With a deep sigh she opened the door, at first careful to avoid the doorknob, but she touched it almost without thinking, knowing she needed to.

And braced herself once again as she locked it.

The voices were as clear as before, but this time she saw a man driving past Gamma's house in an older model car. She'd seen this before. When Gamma was still alive.

Was the man in the car, the same man who had touched the doorknob?

As she walked to the house, she felt someone watching her.

Sure enough, Mr. Grimes waved at her through his window.

Gross.

She wouldn't wave at him if he was going to get run over by a truck.

She continued inside the house and randomly touched things to test her gift. Most things she didn't sense anything from— voices or otherwise.

She walked upstairs, taking the steps two at a time.

The railing didn't give off anything.

Oh, don't let him have touched anything from Mommy's room. The doorknob didn't give off any vibes.

She turned to the doorway to her room.

Don't let him have gone in there.

She touched the doorknob and got knocked back almost as violently as she had outside the shed.

God. He had been up here.

She should report this to the police, but how would she ever say it? They would never buy the fact that she could *feel* and *hear* the people.

In her own room. How that was any different than all over the rest of the house she didn't know. Thank God he hadn't gotten inside the shed. She had locked it up right so no one could ever get in there except her.

The doorknob to her bathroom was quiet. Just her.

Whew.

Her bed frame was fine. Nothing.

When she touched her Bible, she felt something but not him. She chuckled. Could her Bible speak to her? Could she discover or hear voices from it? See visuals? She'd have to test it sometime.

The little cup from Gamma was sweet. There were voices that she'd never detected before. Little kids laughing and playing.

Deep breath. Such peace from the Bible and cup. So thankful Gamma had given that to her before she died. It gave her peace.

Another deep sigh.

She knew Gamma had kept and hung onto too many things. She stared out the window. She could forgive that as she was learning so much more about her Gamma since she had died.

But her baby bracelet was gone—wait! The tiny beads and pearls were scattered all over the floor! They hardly showed up against the old painted wooden floor.

She screamed and fell to her knees.

As she picked up each one, she screamed again and again with the visuals that hit with each bead.

Awful pictures of a little boy and a man who hit the boy repeatedly. The boy hiding in a closet with creatures all around him as he cried and raged. Babies. Babies mutilated.

That man!

God, help!

Noell couldn't help herself. She was compelled to pick up every bead, each pearl, but with each one came horrible and gruesome pictures and sounds.

She finally sat with her hands cupping the remains of her baby bracelet, sobbing.

Who was this man?

Murderer.

Violator.

Defiler.

Destroyer.

He had broken one of the only direct connections to Mommy that she had left. Maybe Mommy had been the first to touch it. Maybe she had even put it on Noell's own wrist.

That man had desecrated that purity, that sweetness.

Noell had always reached for it anticipating Mommy in a sweet moment before the drowning. It had comforted her.

Now as Noell held every bead cupped in her hand, the culmination of evil now on each one threw her back against the closet door.

The same voice from her bracelet was the same voice and visuals at Grampa's shed doorknob.

That man had been on her property.

He had been inside her house.

In her room.

He had touched—and destroyed—her bracelet.

## FIFTY-ONE

Harold pushed his walker to the sink and grabbed his tooth-brush, squeezed some green toothpaste out and paused.

What was Clarence doing about now?

He glanced behind him at his alarm clock. Nine a.m.. He could see it from clear across the room—nice big numbers. He'd had breakfast and a sweet conversation with Mrs. Hatly. They had lingered over coffee, both worried about Clarence.

Harold was just as worried about her. She seemed even more frail than before. Her hands shook a little and the twinkle in her eyes wasn't as … twinkly.

He started brushing and spit. Mrs. Hatly and Clarence had something so sweet and deserved—

Ring!

Dang. Where was that phone?

He grabbed his towel and took a step. Forgot his walker. Dilemma. He needed his walker.

Ring!

"I got it, Harold!" Lisha burst into the room and stumbled. "Wait. Where is it?"

"Oh ... I ... there!" He pointed to the pocket attached to the arm of his wheelchair. "I left it there."

She fished it out and tapped it on. "Hello?" She turned and faced him. "Harold's phone."

Harold wiped his mouth and reached for it, only she didn't give it to him. Her eyebrows twitched and her brown eyes opened wider.

"Um." She straightened. "Yes, Sir. He is." She nodded and pointed at Harold. "He's right here, Sir." She leaned into Harold. "It's the governor's office."

He cleared his throat and took the phone. Glad he'd brushed his teeth. "Hello?" The professional detective kicked in. "This is Harold Dexter."

Lisha clapped her hands together against her lips.

"Yes." He slid into the wheelchair and searched for his notepad. Where was his pen?

Lisha patted the newspaper and papers on the table. No pen.

Damn. What had he done with it? "Yes. I do have time." He tapped Lisha's shoulder and pointed to her pocket.

She whipped her pen out and handed it to him then tapped his phone speaker on.

Harold hovered his hand over the phone and accidentally hit the "end" button.

"Oh! Harold!" She picked the phone up. "You cut him off!"

"Damn it! I'm ... he was just getting to the phone. He'd had his secretary or somebody dial and he was just—"

Lisha hit redial and handed it back to Harold.

He carefully placed it on the table and picked up her pen, poised over the notepad.

Ring!

An aide waved from the open door. "Want juice, Harold?"

Lisha shushed her. "He's talking to the governor."

Hand at her mouth, eyebrows arched, the aide backed away and swung her noisy juice cart to the other side of the hallway.

Good. He needed quiet. He used to be smooth and together—even with distractions when he talked to people, but now he couldn't concentrate.

"Hello? Governor's office."

Cleared his throat. "Hello? This is Harold Dexter, again. I apologize for hanging up on ... er, tapping off, er, the decline button on you."

A deep voice came on, laughing. "That's okay, Harold. I've done that too."

Harold, hand half covering his mouth, whispered, "It's the governor." Back to the phone. "What can I do for you, Sir?"

"First of all, where do you live, Harold? What town and all?"

Lots of noise on the governor's end. "I live at Hillcrest Homes in Osceola, Nebraska. The nursing home."

"Okay. So, you knew my dad? Did I get that right?" Phones ringing. Voices. Busy office.

Harold nodded. "Yes. Yes I did. We worked together on several cases, but I lost touch with him after I retired."

"That's what he said." Governor chuckled. "I talked to him last night about you. He had great things to say about your work and how you used to go out of your way to help people out. Sounds like you are the same man today, with the way you want to help ... uh, Clarence Timmelsen? Is that his name?"

"Yes. He is one of my best buddies here and has been dished a hard road. All his life." Harold blinked. "All his life. And now they took him back to—" Harold choked.

Lisha rubbed his shoulder. Her eyes filled, too.

"Hmm. I've had a friend like that. They don't come along very often, do they?"

Harold swallowed. "No, they don't."

"Well, I just wanted to thank you for calling the office. You have no idea the ruckus you have caused here." He chuckled again. "I can't tell you all the details right yet, but because of your call, you have given us the missing link of a huge ... well, I can tell you and know you are a professional. Just keep it under your hat, okay?"

"Yes, Sir."

Gasps came from the doorway. Four aides stood there, hands over their mouths. One was noiselessly jumping up and down.

"You have helped open up one of the nation's largest drug ring and sex traffic dynasties. It seems to be based in Chicago—at that prison. If you're a praying man, teams are organizing. The timing has to be just right, so prayers are needed. There is unusual resistance right now, but when we are able to put this last piece of the puzzle in, we will be able to free many people, including Clarence."

Lisha walked to the door, her arms wide, pushing the women back and shushing them.

"Yes, Sir, Mr. Governor." Harold blinked. He couldn't believe what he had just heard. First of all to get Clarence out, but to break up something that big! He'd just told them what he knew, in order to get Clarence home. He wanted to salute, just like back in—

"Well Harold, I'll let you go. I need to get to work. Okay if I call back, if we need more information?"

Someone must be talking to him. Lots of noises: more phones ringing, voices. Something dropped.

"Yes. Yes. Anytime." Harold held up his finger. "Say. Would you greet your dad for me? Tell him hello?"

Governor paused and shushed someone near him. "Harold, I would love to do that. It has been a pleasure talking to you. And I'm not joking. This is a huge deal. We even traced something going on out there in Durant, a non town out there by you." He stopped. "There. I've said too much. I'll keep in touch, Harold."

"Thank you, Sir." Harold blinked. "Get Clarence home!"

## FIFTY-TWO

There he went. Clarence counted five times Warden had circled around the cell block.

Didn't he have security to make rounds?

Pacing. Up the steps. Past all the cells on that level, across to the other wall and down the other side.

Again and again.

After the fifth time when Warden passed Clarence's cell, Michael appeared.

Ever since Clarence had stepped off the cliff with Jesus, Michael had been around.

Clarence guessed one had something to do with the other. Him stepping into Jesus and Michael being released to help Clarence or even appear to him. He didn't understand, he just kind of knew.

Michael leaned out the cell, watching Warden.

Dear Father, he loved this guy—this big angel. All the moments they had shared. Grinding gears in that old pickup. Times in that pool.

God. Osceola.

Clarence watched the warden march across the commons area on the opposite cell block, exactly across from him.

Stomp, stomp, stomp.

"Michael." Clarence reached out a hand to him. "Michael. Are my girls okay?" He shook his head. "You know I can call them that now, right?"

Michael didn't turn his head. He didn't even flinch.

Louder this time. "Michael. Can't you hear me?"

He wasn't paying a bit of attention to Clarence. Like he was deaf. Like he didn't even want to talk to him. Or was a statue.

Michael stomped his foot once. The whole cell block shook.

Clarence's cell door swung open and when he looked down the block, all the other doors flew open too. On both sides.

Warden had just gotten to the left of Clarence's door. He started yelling for the guards to come and trap the prisoners who had started to run out.

Michael grabbed the warden by the neck and held onto him while Clarence ran out of his cell.

He flung the warden inside the cell and slammed the door.

Warden rushed to push his way out, but he smashed his head into the bars.

Locked!

For a moment, Clarence was just as shocked as Warden appeared to be.

The bars had always separated them. But Warden was always on the outside and Clarence was always on the inside.

Clarence grinned and ran his fingers against the bars as he walked past, tapping each one for effect. "How do you like it from the inside, Warden? Feels just like home, right?"

Warden roared. "You can't do this!" He saw the other inmates running down the steps—yelling and jumping and thundering. "How did you do that? You are a bastard! I'll get you back."

Clarence calmly walked to the bars again. "You—"

Michael hooked Clarence's arm with his huge hands. Full on angel costume. Wings spread up and out as Clarence watched.

Breathtaking. So much so that Clarence couldn't breathe. Couldn't finish insulting Warden.

A door slammed downstairs and gunshots echoed across the block. Security entered and ran upstairs both sides and trapped some of the inmates. Several were caught and cuffed.

Randy led two more guards up the steps to Clarence's side. He stumbled when he got upstairs and saw the Warden inside a cell.

Clarence's cell.

"Get me out! Get me out!" Warden yelled and rattled the door.

"You scream like a girl, Warden." Clarence loved it.

Randy just stopped where he landed and stared at Clarence. "How'd you do that?"

Clarence shook his head. "Randy."

They stared at each other for what seemed like hours.

Michael leaned down then. He was ten times taller than normal. "You want to stay and taunt the warden or do you want to go home to your girls?"

Clarence blinked. "Home. Michael, home!"

As soon as he closed his mouth, he landed outside the prison.

Clarence turned in circles. How on Earth?

Cars and TV trucks whizzed past him. Some other inmates ran down into a gully, guards chasing them.

A siren blared but no one followed Clarence. He had the prisoner uniform on and everything, but no one even looked at him.

It was like ... he was invisible.

Michael and several angels walked right in front of him, some surrounding him. He could see them now. Were they hiding him? Why not the other prisoners?

Wait. He looked over beyond the gully and one other prisoner was surrounded just like he was. He waved.

"Michael! Who is that? What is he?"

Michael looked up. He was concentrating so hard. "Where?"

Clarence waved back at the man. "There."

"Oh. You might get to meet someday." He grinned. "It'll be a surprise. Sort of."

Someone was on the intercom from inside and it blasted all over the grounds.

Screaming, "Find him! Now!"

Warden.

# FIFTY-THREE

Katty brushed her teeth. She tried not to invade Clarence's space, so she just kept her private stuff like toothbrush and female things in their bag. She had packed so fast. She had her jammies and her robe and right now that was all she cared about.

Bea was already crashed. She'd let her watch a TV show, but she'd fallen asleep right away. Carol and Lisha said she would be that way for awhile. She was still healing.

Katty shuffled in her nursing home issue slippers to the window.

Clarence.

He was in great shape, but it couldn't be good. She had never spent time in prison, just a few nights in the local jail but prison was way different. When she had spent time in jail, women there had talked about the brutality—even in women's prisons.

Katty cringed thinking of what Clarence might be going through.

Nursing homes didn't seem so bad. If a person had a car. She had no idea how much it cost, but bet it was expensive.

Well she was going to enjoy it while she could. She had all kinds of service. Meals. Housekeeping. Nurses at her disposal.

She loved the place because of the people but never would she be able to give a stranger a bath or do those other things they had to do.

She'd heard Lisha make a comment or two she wished she'd never overheard.

"There you are!"

Katty turned to see the administrator standing in the doorway, her hands on her hips. Frizzy, dyed hair framed her full face. Eyes seemed stern. Couldn't this nursing home ever find nice administrators?

Maybe the free ride wasn't so free.

"Uh, hello." Katty glanced over at her sleeping Bea. Dang. Where would she go now? "I'm sorry. I forgot your—"

The woman tapped her name tag. "Miss Oster. And you need to clear out. This is totally unorthodox."

"Isn't it paid for?" Katty shuffled some papers around on Clarence's desk. Where were his bills? "I mean, he already paid, right?"

---

"HEY GIRL. YOU OKAY?" Lisha framed the administrator by a foot, above and both sides.

Lisha. Thank God.

She pushed around the smaller woman, bumping her aside, and stood between them. "Ain't this awesome, Mizz Oster? Clarence isn't using his rooms right now, so Katty and her baby girl might as well, since they going through some stuff." She held out her arms wide. "Ain't it great?"

Miss Oster squinted and shook her head. "I suppose. As long as—"

"They don't drink as much coffee as Clarence or won't eat here," she glanced at Katty, "so the home saves money, actually. We won't even wash their clothes."

The administrator threw up her hands. "I suppose." She glanced at Bea sleeping on the bed. "Nice to have little ones here." Back at Katty. "I suppose." She turned. "Have a good night."

Lisha bit her lips.

Katty raised her eyebrows.

Silence, except for the sound of heels clomping away, down the hall.

Lisha covered Bea up and brushed her hair off her face. "How you really doing?"

Katty stacked the papers. "I'm okay." She hugged her arms. "Just thinking about Clarence and wondering how he is. I've heard awful stories of prison and—"

Lisha held out her arms and Katty walked into her. This woman's heart was as big as her body. And Katty loved every cell of her. "I know, baby. Carol and I pray all the time for him. We ... " She shook her head and blinked. "God keep him safe and bring him back home."

Katty nodded

"Look." Lisha pointed outside. "Ain't that the deputy man?" She tapped on Katty's nose. "Bet he's coming to check up on you."

"Me?" Katty backed away and shook her head. "No way." She pointed at the car. "He's coming to check to see if those—"

"He's checking up on you." Lisha grinned.

"So what if he is? I can't stop him, right?" Katty smirked. So what if he was?

Lisha left and laughed all the way down the hall.

There had only been one man in her life that she would have cherished and that was Tommy Sand. When they were both twelve, he used to ride his bike by her house everyday on his way to school. He'd ride past even though it was blocks out of his way. And then back home from school. Summer was the worst. She almost got tired of it until her mom figured it out.

Reliving that day was awful.

Katty had been hanging out on the porch, reading, waiting for him actually. He always waved and smiled. With what she had going on inside her house, he was a breath of the air that had been sucked out of the house.

That day—here he came, pedaling for all he was worth—up a small hill. You'd think he would have been used to it. Built up his muscles.

When he was even with one corner of the house, Mom stepped out from behind a bush and threw a log at him.

A log.

Not a twig.

A log that you would burn in your fireplace.

It knocked him over. Mom was a strong woman. She had built herself up beating her kids.

Blew him over like he'd been hit with a battering ram like on the movies.

He didn't get up right away and Mom had started laughing.

Katty had screamed and started to go help him, but Mom caught her by the arm. All she could see as she was dragged away was Tommy stumbling, trying to pick up his bike. Terrified. Horrified.

He had been a sweet kid.

Wonder where he was now. Could be living in the same town as her, but he'd never again acknowledge her.

Knock, knock.

Katty turned and there was Deputy Scott.

He waved. "Hi. How're you doing?"

She smiled and nodded. "Better."

He glanced at Bea all snuggled in one of Clarence's beds. "How is she?"

Katty nodded. "She's better. She gets really tired though."

"A gunshot wound takes a while to heal."

Lisha rumbled in with her cart. "Anybody for coffee and cookies?" She glanced at Bea then shushed her mouth. "Oh, sorry. I forgot. Most people here are deaf so—"

"She's fine. Sleeps like a little log." She looked at the Deputy. "I'd like coffee … if you have time."

Nursing homes had great dating services also.

Catering too.

He checked his phone. "I have a few minutes. It's okay. Thanks."

Lisha served them and snuck a cookie for herself. "Yum. I love it when they make macadamia nut." She winked and pushed her cart away and partly closed the door.

A set up.

He smiled. "This is a nice break. Usually I just roll up to the corner convenience store and grab a slice of pizza." He patted his stomach. "And it shows."

She laughed. "I know. I used to be a beanpole but now I have a donut roll." She didn't say that she used to be a beanpole because Phil would never spring for food. It was always booze and drugs. Maybe a pizza thrown in once in a while.

They'd barely gotten to speak five words and taken one bite of the cookies when he got a call.

He shook his head. "It never fails." He checked the read out. "I better go."

"Aww. You can take the coffee and cookies with you for later if you want."

He helped himself and stuck two in his pocket. "This'll make the rest of the night go better." He reached to shake her hand, but then hugged her.

Oh my. The old Katty rose up and embraced him hard and kissed him hard.

He pulled away and looked her in the eye. "Uh. I better go." Then he pushed her away.

"I'm—" She didn't know what to say. "I'm—"

"It's okay. I better get back." His face was different. "Duty calls. Hope you both have a good night."

And he was gone.

It had all happened so quickly.

She was so stupid. He must hate her. She should have known better. But she didn't. That was how she'd always been with guys because that was what they wanted.

Every one of them.

FIFTY-FOUR

Clarence walked on, angels on every side—some as tall as the three stories of the prison, many with weapons he'd never seen before and had no idea how they would be used. How long this could go on he didn't know. He just knew that Michael had set him free.

"Michael."

The huge angel slowed down and turned toward Clarence. They were well hidden by the huge beings surrounding them. Some were even bigger than Michael. Although since Clarence had known him, he had seen Michael grow through a three level building before, so he was sure that Michael was shorter right now just for him.

"Michael. Thanks."

Michael clapped him on the back. "All part of the plan. Buddy." He grinned. "You used to put up with me grinding the gears in that red pickup."

Clarence chuckled. "Buddy? You've never called me that. Yup. If you can't find 'em, grind 'em." He must be dreaming. How did an angel stomp on the floor and all the cell doors fly open?

Whatever.

He was happy to go along with it, just as long as he didn't wake from this dream and find out he was still in his prison cell. Or worse.

The sirens went off again and didn't stop this time.

"Do you figure Warden is out of my cell by now? That was pretty slick, shoving him in there." Clarence slowed. He'd never forget looking into his prison cell—*his* cell—and seeing the warden looking out at *him*. "I'll never forget that as long as I live."

Michael smiled. "It just seemed to be a fair swap. Him for you. Or you for him." He grinned. "I wish we could have gone further with him."

"Further?" Clarence stumbled and tried to catch up with the angel's huge strides.

Michael shook his head. "I shouldn't even admit this, but several of us wanted to torture him the way he tortured you."

Each warrior surrounding him nodded in agreement. They lifted their weapons above their heads and roared. "Onward for the King!"

Clarence shuddered and stumbled again. These beings were ... they would have ... paid Warden back for the pain he'd caused Clarence?

Michael gripped Clarence's elbow and another angel on the other side did the same. Even lifted him off the ground a little as they crossed railroad tracks at the edge of the prison grounds.

Whew.

He blinked and turned to look at the prison. He wiped his wet cheeks and crumpled onto the grass in the ditch.

Immediately angels moved in tight around him, backs to him, facing any outside danger.

Clarence could still see the natural dimension through them clearly.

Overwhelmed.

Michael rustled behind him and lifted him up. "We must go, Clarence."

Warden must have been rescued and sent out word—sent out the troops. A prison break wasn't good on a warden's resume. Judging by the numbers of prisoners that had already escaped, the warden would be in deep trouble with his backers. That possible loss of revenue would close the prison for good.

Clarence seemed to cover the steps, then miles quickly. The angels were still surrounding him, but not as close as before. He had no idea of where to head, just west. Then southwest.

Osceola, Nebraska.

Truck stop. He didn't remember how he got here, but it was a place to start.

He wasn't even tired. He glanced down at his shirt as he opened the entrance door—no blood. He still had the inmate uniform but people who held the door for him and others he met, didn't even look at his clothes. They just smiled at him and said hello.

"Michael? Do they even see me?"

Michael smiled and pushed him forward, his hand on Clarence's back.

Clarence passed behind the people standing in line to pay and his stomach growled. He patted his empty pockets. He had no idea how to get something to eat or what time it was. But his stomach said it was time to eat.

The last man in line, a huge mountain of a fellow wearing a crunched straw cowboy hat looked down at him. The man was almost a big as the angels. "Hey, Buddy."

Clarence glanced to make sure Michael was still beside him. "Uh, yes?"

"Need something to eat?"

Clarence nodded. "Yeah. I guess." He didn't have any money. He didn't have his wallet. No identification. Where was his wallet? Probably back at Hillcrest. Hopefully Katty found it and put it away. Better yet, she took it with her. They had grown to trust each other in the short time they had come to know each other.

The trucker didn't even have to get out of line to grab a banana and some packaged muffins. And he was next in line.

"Is this all for you?" The cashier began to ring up his purchases. "Er. Did you find everything you need?"

The man chuckled. "Well, to answer your first question, it takes a lot to keep a man of my size going." He patted his chest then handed off the banana and muffins to Clarence as she rang them up. "Here you go, Buddy."

"Th-thank you." Now he was taking handouts. "Really. Thank you for your kindness."

Michael was bowing his head to honor the angels with the trucker. They did the same to him.

When Clarence saw him do that, he bowed his head to the man. "You are an honorable man to help out a stranger."

The man laughed out loud, and his big belly shook. He held out his hand for the change and stuffed his purchases into his pockets. "Hey you need a ride somewhere? Can I give you a lift?"

Clarence couldn't even think. Why was this man being so kind? "Uh. Well, if you are going my way."

"Where are you headed, Old Man?"

Clarence had been called many things in life and old man was one. But this man said it with respect and kindness. Were his ears and eyes open more now or had others spoken in the same way, but his heart had been so hard, he couldn't sense it?

"Nebraska?"

"The man nodded. "Where in Nebraska?"

"Osceola."

The man next in line turned. "I had family that used to live in Osceola, Nebraska. Nice little town."

Clarence couldn't believe what was happening. First an angel breaks him out of prison and a whole raft of angels hide him from the guards. Then somehow they get him to this truck stop in record time. And these truckers treat him like he was their long lost uncle and fed him!

Never, ever—

"I'm going that way. Or rather near there. I could drop you off anywhere near there."

"Why are you being so nice to me?" Clarence bit into the banana. "You don't know me." He threw the peel in the trash, cupping the muffins in his other hand against his chest.

"Well, if you don't want to ride with me that's okay." The man turned the key in the door lock of his big rig. He faced Clarence and waved his hand toward his own chest. His face was kind, eyes were soft. "Come."

Clarence was transported immediately to the top of the precipice with Jesus. He had beckoned to Clarence in the same way, used the same word.

He wiped his eyes. Guess he could trust this guy too.

He nodded. "Thanks man. I could use a ride if it works for you." Locks clicked on the passenger side door and the man started to walk around to help Clarence up and in, only Clarence was already climbing into the cab.

The man smiled. "Guess you don't need my help to get in." He climbed onto his drivers seat and held out his hand. "Names Bender. Robert Bender."

Clarence shook hands. "Clarence Timmelsen." He checked around him for the angels or Michael. They were nowhere to be … wait. Was that a wing sticking out from behind the cab?

Michael leaned out and grinned. Three others did the same.

Clarence never realized what a comfort those guys or angels had become. When they were around—

"Glad to meetcha, Old Man." The huge truck roared as Robert pulled out of the parking spot. "Ever ride in one of these?"

Clarence shook his head. "I don't think I have." He checked behind the truck for wings. Still there.

"It's okay, Old Man." The driver cleared his throat. "They're still there."

Clarence blinked.

FIFTY-FIVE

Noell began packing her bags. That madman might come back when she was here. She had to move. Had to get away before ...

She sat on her bed and spied her baby bracelet, now all together in a small bowl. So tiny.

She picked up the bowl and braced herself for the voices and visuals to come back.

She made herself sit and listen and not throw them down. She willed herself to focus on the voices, the words, the pictures, no matter how awful. Maybe she could learn something about the man that would help her find him.

She sat upright. What would she do if she found him?

Maybe she should go to the police.

They'd never believe her. They'd think she was crazy.

And she sometimes wondered if she was.

Just one bead at a time.

She grabbed a notebook and pen, then carefully picked out one pearl.

Once she got past the painful parts, she waited for pictures of the man as an adult. What did he look like? What did he sound like? Were there any pictures of a place she might recognize?

She shook her head. She'd have to work on that. It was too hard to try to get past the bad stuff to find anything helpful.

What if Katty had these same gifts?

Did Bea?

She stood and tried to envision them all living here.

If she could get it all cleaned out.

Katty could even have Gamma's bedroom downstairs. Or Mommy's room. It didn't matter that it had been her mom's room.

What if they could all live here—one big, well, small, happy family.

Her heart started to soar.

Remembering that man made her even more determined to offer Katty and Bea a home with her.

Wait! One of the pictures the first time she had touched the bracelet ... had it been of Katty? A younger Katty?

What if this was the man who had been after them?

What if this was the same man?

She stood abruptly and grabbed a trash bag, ran out into the upstairs hall and pulled open the closet door. All she saw were toys and games and dolls. No. She couldn't throw all that away. Bea might want some of it.

She slammed the door and ran down to the door at the end of the hall.

She had never ventured anywhere but where she had to be: her room, the kitchen, porch, living room. Not even Gamma's room much. Just like Mommy's room, she had never opened this door—always afraid of the clutter and stacks of stuff.

Opening the door, she ventured a look as she held her breath.

Grampa's stuff?

It was all placed just so. Books and books, but all on bookshelves. A lamp glowed on a square oak table that warmed the room. She had never realized the light was on. She'd never seen it from outside through the window or under the door.

Wait. How long had that light been on? How long did light bulbs last anyway?

She bent and examined the door. A small rubber strip like weatherstripping followed the bottom edge.

Huh.

Once again she felt like an intruder—like that evil man that had been in her room.

But this was Grampa's. There were framed pictures of old buildings. Was that ... was that the old drug store? People posed in front of it. Interesting. She followed the pictures along one wall and onto the next. Then backed up. The whole room was a museum. Shelves across from the bookshelves had old guns, old helmets.

She picked up a tool of some sort. She had no idea what it was. She needed someone to come in here to show her around and tell her what everything was.

She pulled at a metal knob on an old oak cabinet. Locked. Through the glass she could see little drawers. Some little shelves with parts. Metal. Old. Not really rusty but really old. Some type of collection but she had no idea what it all was.

She looked around for a key.

That was a mystery. Maybe whatever was in there was dangerous and he had kept it locked up so she, as a little girl, wouldn't get into it.

An old patterned rug covered the wood floor. She picked up one corner. Maybe the key was under there. Interesting floorboards, too.

No key.

Noell slipped out and quietly closed the door. Something in her wanted to respect the privacy and memories until another day.

On downstairs.

She still had the trash bag in her hand and while on the front porch, she pushed everything within grasp into the bag. No matter what it was. She couldn't stop herself. It was almost as if her hands were disconnected from her head.

As she worked, all she could think of was, there were two museums upstairs—Mommy's room and now Grampa's. She didn't want to mess with them, to tear things out of there, but then she would be acting just like Gamma.

She needed to find someone who could appreciate what Gamma had hung onto. What she had not wanted to part with for so long.

Doorbell.

Noell jumped. No one ever rang that!

Fletch just opened the door and yelled. And no one ever came to visit.

She dropped the now full bag and ran in time to see Katty turn away to her car.

Noell rushed to open the door. "Katty!"

Katty turned. She'd been crying. Her eyes were puffy and red.

"What's wrong?" Noell looked behind Katty at the car. Bea waved from her car seat. "Is she okay?"

Katty nodded. "I don't even know why I'm bothering you. I just wanted to know where you lived and—"

Noell waved to Bea. "Go get her and come in. Please."

There were some cookies left in the freezer if Fletch hadn't gotten to them all. And she could make tea. Maybe even peanut butter sandwiches. Wait. Did she have any bread?

Katty had Bea in tow.

No time like the present for them to see it all. Like, in all.

"Come on in." She opened the porch door farther and by the look on Katty's face, she saw it all. "Well, this is where I live."

"Uh, it's nice. Nice. Isn't it Bea?" Katty's eyes bounced around on every pile and stack.

"No it's not. But *you're* being nice." Noell dropped the trash bag. "It's awful but I just started again to clean out." She pointed the way. "Come into the kitchen. I'm not sure what I have, but we'll find something."

Bea jumped up and down. "Mommy! Look at the red couch. Mommy she has a TV too."

In the kitchen.

Even Bea's face was surprised at all the stacked cookbooks lining each and every wall.

Noell laughed. "I know! Lots and lots of junk, right?" She picked up Bea, then remembered the surgery and gently lowered her to a chair. "Let's see what I have." She opened the cupboards. "Looks the same inside and outside." She swung her arms around the room. "I am sorry for the way this looks. Still freaks me out."

Katty had wandered into the room. Her face was appalled, but when she met Noell's eyes, she smiled. "Is this all yours?"

Noell started to shake her head no. "Well, when Gamma was alive, it was hers." She shrugged. "It's mine now." She glanced around the room. "Every cookbook. Every box. Every ... you get the idea." She pointed to a chair beside Bea. "Sit. Please."

Katty nodded and sat.

Bea couldn't keep her hands off the little sugar bowls and salt and pepper shakers on the table.

"No, Bea." Katty shoved them away from little fingers.

"Oh, she's okay. She can look at them." Noell pulled two glasses and a cup from a shelf and filled them with water. "I don't keep much here. Just lunch stuff for work."

Bea dropped a salt shaker onto the floor, scattering salt all over.

Noell had an awful visual of the beads on the floor upstairs in her room and her face must have showed it.

Katty jumped and slapped Bea's hand.

"Oh, no! It's okay. She didn't mean to. It was an accident." Noell sucked in a deep breath. Katty had been in the visuals.

Oh, dear Lord.

She picked up sobbing Bea carefully and hugged her. They

just swayed back and forth. She reached her hand to Katty and Katty burst into tears.

Slowly she sat down, still holding Bea and still holding Katty's fingers. "What is going on?"

Katty opened her mouth, but Bea beat her to it. "There's a bad man after us. He keeps sending me bikes and notes and scaring us." She hiccuped. "He's a bad man."

Noell glanced at Katty.

Katty met her eyes and nodded. "That's pretty much it."

"And Clarence is shot. He's gone." Bea burst into tears again.

"Wow. We all need each other, don't we." Noell sighed, her cheek against Bea's head. "Bea, do you like peanut butter? Cause that's all I have. We could have some on crackers."

Bea sat up, wiping her face. She could put on an especially sad face, but this one was real. She nodded.

"Gamma used to keep some bottled juice around here someplace. Cranberry I think for when she got a bladder infection." Noell sat Bea down and checked the pantry.

Bea immediately followed her, pointing at the donkey salt and pepper shakers along one shelf. "Are those toys?"

Noell laughed. "Nope. But they're cute, huh." She found the juice and checked the date. "All good. You want some Katty?"

Katty straightened. "Yeah. Sounds good. Peanut butter and cranberry juice." She smiled. "Sorry but you'd have a hard time beating coffee, cookies, juice, a full meal where we are staying right now."

"What? Well we better go there."

"We get to live in Clarence's room!" Bea took a sip of the cranberry juice. "I don't like it." She wiped her mouth with the back of her hand.

Noell laughed. "I don't either. My Gamma used to make me drink it so I didn't get sick."

"Do you have any toys?" Bea leaned over into Noell's face.

"I do! But you have to follow me up some steps to get them."

They started up the steps, Katty following behind. Bea crawled up one at a time.

"Where? Are there dolls? Do you have a stuffed monkey?" Bea badgered her with questions until they got upstairs and Noell opened the hall closet door.

Bea stopped. "Ohhh. Y-you have lots of toys, Noell."

Noell giggled. "Yes, I do! What would you like to play with first?"

Bea looked up at Noell, eyebrows raised, a half smile on her lips. "Really?" She got down to business. "Can I play with that?" She pointed to an old doll, one eye was open and one eye shut.

"She's kind of broken. I think she's winking at you, right?" Noell handed it to Bea along with a little truck. She hadn't even thought about voices or visuals. They were all ... hers, from the past.

"Is this your house now?" Katty pointed at the doors.

"Yes. And I was just thinking that I need to sell it."

"You'd get rid of this? This is a great house." Katty peered at the pictures on the walls.

"Well ... really ... what I was just thinking before you came over was, since we are related now and all ... you and Bea should move in with me." Noell stopped and bit her lip. "After I get it all cleaned out anyway."

Katty burst into tears. "Oh, you wouldn't want us here."

"Katty." Noell hugged her. Maybe they didn't want to move. Maybe this wasn't the right thing to ask. Maybe they didn't like her.

Katty held on, still sobbing.

Bea carefully put the doll on the shelf and hugged their legs. Then she looked up at Noell. "Mommy's scared. The bad man who tried to kill me on the old slide is back." She was so grown up right then.

"Bad man?"

Katty lifted her head and looked into Noell's eyes. She

nodded. "If we moved in here, he'd just follow us and hurt you, too. We can't."

"Mommy."

"Shush, Bea." Katty swallowed. "That would be so cool, but this is your house."

"I'll clean it up. It's not too bad up here, but downstairs." Noell winced, thinking of her baby bracelet and all she'd learned about the bad man.

Something felt so right about this.

Bea jumped up and down. "We'd help, right Mom?"

Noell slowly looked around the upstairs, and visualized the rest of the house, the lot and came back to Katty and Bea. "Gamma was your family, too."

FIFTY-SIX

The trucker shifted gears. One gear after another. Clarence guessed he had been in prison so long that he'd never learned about semi truck driving. The engines and how they needed to be shifted. "That must take a lot of practice."

Robert looked over at him. "What?" He continued to shift almost without thinking. "You mean shifting?"

Clarence nodded. "Yeah. That looks complicated."

"It's not. You just have to know how." He shifted again. "See, there are different levels to it." He checked his rear view mirror and shifted again. He chuckled. "Lots of levels. I'll teach you sometime if you want. You could do it."

Clarence had no clue when that would be. He was interested in how it worked, but he was more interested in getting back home.

The engine droned on.

Clarence must have dozed because the brakes were loud. They were pulling off interstate. "Gotta get gas?"

"Gotta take my half hour off, so I figures we could stop here and get a bite to eat. Okay by you?"

Clarence once again patted his pockets. "I don't have any money with me."

"S'kay, Old Man. My treat." Robert eased his truck into a space and stopped. He filled his trucker log out and checked with Clarence. "You ready?"

"Sure. Thanks Robert. This means a lot."

"No problem. I believe in paying it forward or whatever that saying is." He opened his door and hopped out. "You need h—"

Clarence was already on the ground. How was that possible, since this morning ... just this morning ... he couldn't move off his bed?

"Guess not." He locked the truck and met Clarence in front. "Lots of troopers out today."

A state trooper pulled into the parking lot.

Clarence had almost forgotten he was an escapee. They had to be looking for him. He held back behind Robert. Good thing the man was big. Did Clarence imagine that Robert stepped in front of him at the same time?

The trooper drove on by and waved.

Robert waved back.

Clarence blew out a breath. Somehow the truth had to come out about how evil the warden was and his illegal dealings, so Clarence could be free and not constantly looking over his shoulder.

But probably not today.

"Nice guy. Lots of them around—must be because of the prison break. They said on the radio earlier, that thirty guys or so had escaped. A couple even were killed." He smirked. "The ones that got away must be really bad guys to send this many troopers out looking. If I heard right, they said that one had been in maximum security—the really bad ones."

Clarence peeked up at Robert. His side-long glance was with a smile.

What did that mean?

Clarence didn't let on but walked on beside him. He opened his mouth to say something.

Michael shook his head and kept on shaking it all the way to the entrance.

Guess that meant, "Do. Not. Talk."

Same as at the last truck stop. Everyone looked him in the eyes and smiled. Didn't even see his prison clothes.

He looked down. Still there. Just checking in case angels could make his clothes look different. He should ask for a Led Zeppelin shirt.

Clarence hit the restroom. He was hurting still from the beatings but made it inside. Doors were even heavy today.

Did his business. He didn't know how far he'd get to travel with Robert. He didn't know the next miles. He didn't even know if Robert would be waiting for him in his truck to take him farther down the road.

His stomach growled. He did know he was hungry, but even that could wait for a long time to get back to Osceola.

He pulled the door open and came face to face with Randy.

Randy slowly drew his gun, keeping his eye on Clarence.

"Randy." Clarence slowly raised his hands. "Randy."

Michael stepped between them.

Clarence took a step to the side so he was clear of Michael. "We have to do the right thing, Michael."

"Michael. Who's Michael?" Randy shook his head and lowered the gun.

A state trooper came along beside him. "Is this your man?"

A man from inside gasped and slid alongside Clarence and then Randy. He practically ran. So easy to escape when you weren't wanted.

Randy stared at Clarence for a long time. He didn't speak right away. "No. No it's not. Looks like him, but I'd know the guilty man anywhere." He holstered his gun. "This man is innocent."

Randy.

Clarence had always said no crying. And he'd kept to that rule for a lot of years. But right now when he was on the receiving end of grace, he wanted to bawl like a baby.

"Okay. You know your man." The trooper saluted both Randy and Clarence. He picked up a package of chocolate morsels and went to wait in line.

Clarence stepped forward and held out his hand.

Randy didn't hesitate. He shook Clarence's with vigor.

"Clarence. I ... I can't apologize enough." He checked around him and pushed Clarence into an empty aisle. "Warden had us all snowballed into believing his lies." He shook his head. "Only Lester kept the faith that you were a good man. And thank God he did. Otherwise—"

"Otherwise I'd be dead." Clarence wiped his face. He almost asked about Warden but didn't. He had to keep moving forward. To his girls. "And thanks, Randy."

"How about I try and make it up to you and give you a ride home." Randy looked dead serious.

Robert stepped up beside Clarence.

Clarence searched Robert's face then looked at Michael.

Both nodded yes.

Who was this Robert?

Michael knew he wanted to ask. Maybe later when this was all over.

"Hey, I think I'm out of a job at the prison." Randy shook his head and looked like he wanted to cry. Then he chuckled. "My wife would love for me to get out of that line of work. Maybe they need a maintenance man at Hillcrest." He cleared his throat. "Anyway. Let me take you the rest of the way."

Clarence slowly nodded. "Thanks, Randy. I'd be honored."

Randy bowed his head. "No. I'm the one that would be honored."

Clarence turned to Robert and shook his outstretched hand.

"I can't thank you enough, Robert. You took a chance on a man. Thank you!"

"S'okay, Old Man." Robert faced him, his massive body blocking out most of the convenience store. He still held onto Clarence's hand and bent his head down. "You go back home and make one tiny lady happy."

Clarence raised his eyebrows. He hadn't talked about the girls to Robert. How—

"No. I mean Mrs. Hatly."

Clarence froze. Especially Mrs. Hatly. "How—"

"You don't miss this, all right? So many don't take the chance for love. So many let love slip through their fingers." Robert withdrew his hand from Clarence's and held his Get This finger in Clarence's face. "Don't let your testosterone get in your way— even you as an old man know what I mean. Go home and marry her."

Clarence cried out.

Marry Mrs. Hatly?

Robert nodded.

Clarence nodded along with him. He had barely been married long enough to make a child with Annie and then she was dead and he was off to prison. He guessed he wouldn't be making babies this marriage, but ... marry Mrs. Hatly.

Robert stepped away. "Well, I have to get going to my next gig, so good to meet you and I know you'll be just fine in this man's care." He pointed to Randy and turned to go.

"You ready to go, Clarence?" Randy brushed off his round tummy. "We can grab something to go, if you're hungry. I'll get gas and we could get you home in four hours. If we're lucky."

Clarence nodded and started to look around.

Randy tapped him on the shoulder and slipped him a twenty. "I'm sure you didn't get back your property before you left." He smiled.

Clarence nodded. He hadn't taken anything with him. They'd

just ripped him out of his room and shot him and he was gone. No wallet. No pictures. Nothing. Just like the first time. Except for getting shot.

Randy walked away. Clarence sighed. This moment. Something was going on. He could feel it. Right here, but back at home, too.

He didn't understand how, but something real moved inside of him. It was like how it had felt when he'd had a soda with Annie and they would sit back in his old car and watch the world. Together. Not saying anything. Just ... sigh.

He grabbed some candy bars—made him think of home— the grocery store and Mandy and Stupid John. He needed to be a nicer person to them.

Robert had stopped by the exit and was ... talking ... to Michael? Was Robert ... ?

Clarence slipped closer. They were face to face, opposite arm locked between them. Heads bowed. Quiet.

Were they—?

He could still see people coming and going around and ... through them?

Robert grinned. "And brother, somewhere in our training, we need to learn to drive those stick-shifting trucks."

Michael laughed. "If you can't find 'em, grind 'em, right?"

High five.

Did he really hear Michael and Robert tease each other about grinding gears?

Then Robert stepped away and ... first his head disappeared, then his chest and upper body, then ... he was gone. Like he walked into a waterfall and disappeared.

Clarence gasped.

Michael met eyes with Clarence and smiled.

# FIFTY-SEVEN

What was that sound? Things banging. Metal on metal.

Katty rubbed her eyes.

The nursing home.

Oh.

Bea was snuggled into her side just like a kitty would. Still sleeping. So sweet.

Katty just watched her. This moment. She had never done this. Never woke up and just watched Bea sleep.

Pain. Regret. Hot tears. Her chest burned with grief over what they both had lost.

She swallowed.

Lisha peeked in and smiled. She tip toed in and set a steaming cup of coffee on the bedside table and stroked Katty's hair. "You good?"

Katty nodded and stretched.

Lisha leaned close to Katty's ear. "Mrs. Hatly is sick. Think about her while you can."

Katty started to lift her head, but Lisha pressed her back down.

"Nothing you can do, but she needs prayer." Lisha's chin quivered. "I think she's just heartbroken over Clarence being gone." She hovered her hand over Bea's head. "So sweet." And she started for the door.

Katty lifted her head and whispered, "Thanks for the coffee."

Lisha nodded, threw a kiss and left.

Bea blinked and rubbed her eyes. She smiled a sleepy smile and rolled to her side, spooning with Katty.

Katty put her head down next to Bea's. Tonight they'd have to try the showers here. Bea hadn't had a bath since the hospital. Hospitals had to be clean so she guessed Bea was cleaner now than if she'd just had a bath at home.

Bea stirred again. When she turned her face toward Katty, she had the sweetest smile on her face.

"You doing good, little Bea?" Katty traced Bea's face, around her eyes, over her nose and circled her mouth.

Bea giggled. "That tickles, Mommy."

Deep sigh.

"Do it again."

Katty smiled, laid her head back down and traced Bea's ears.

Belly laugh.

Giggles filled Katty too.

"I have to go potty." Bea pushed the sheets off and jumped out of bed. "Mom. My shot place is better." She held up her jammie top. The tape had come loose and the bandage was hanging off to one side. Sure enough the incision was very smooth.

"It is!" Katty gave her a love pat on her behind. "Now go potty!"

Bea giggled and ran.

Katty knew there were some days she'd get busy and forget, but she was determined to forever appreciate and cherish this little girl she'd been blessed with.

It felt like they were in a motel—a motel with extremely great service. She sipped her coffee. This wasn't the usual resident coffee. They must have a pot just for the staff. She rotated.

Clarence had his own coffeemaker right here. But it hadn't been brewing.

She sipped again. This was good stuff!

She set the cup down and pulled their clothes out of the bag. Hers would do another day. Bea's not at all. There was dinner, all over the front of her shirt. Dang.

It wasn't really Bea's fault, because Mr. Harold had tickled her from behind, making her drop her spoonful of spaghetti. It slid all the way down her shirt to her jeans and onto the floor. Thank God it was that polished wood or vinyl flooring. Easy to wipe up. Not so easy to wipe off Bea's shirt.

She needed to go home for more clothes. And to wash this.

Knocking at the door.

"Yes?"

The door pushed open and a coffee carafe appeared. "You proper?"

Bea pushed out of the bathroom just at the same time and gasped. "What is that Mommy?"

Harold peeked in.

"Mr. Harod!" Bea jumped toward him.

"Bea! It's hot! Be careful!" Katty jumped just in time to rescue Bea and the coffee and Harold.

She sat it on the desk. "Can you stay for some?"

"No. I have baking right now." He smirked and wheeled his chair to face the door. "Like I need cookies to feed this pot belly." He hugged Bea and started to leave. "You two doing okay?"

Katty nodded. "Yeah. We just need to go back to the trailer for some more clothes for Bea."

He grinned. "I made her make a mess, didn't I."

"Yup. You did."

"Are you sure you should go back there?" He shrugged. "Maybe alert Sheriff you are going and one of the deputies can meet you there." He winked.

Did everybody know something she didn't? "Good idea. I'll

give him a call as soon as we get changed." She poured more coffee. "And thanks for the coffee."

He hesitated. "You hear anything about Mrs. Hatly this morning?"

She shook her head. "Just what Lisha said. That she's sick and probably missing Clarence. Right?"

He nodded. "She's really sick. He has to get here. He has to."

She slowly sat on the bed. "She's that sick, like in ... " She glanced at Bea who was trying to pull her jammie shirt off. "Wait Bea. Man in the room, remember?"

"Oh. Sorry." She pulled it down over her wound. "Wanna see my surgery?"

Harold laughed. "You two can live here for a thousand years if you ask me!" He nodded at Katty. "Just letting you know, Katty." He headed for the door. "Maybe go see her. That might cheer her up."

"We will Harold. Thanks." She jumped. "Thanks for the coffee."

As soon as the door closed, Katty pulled Bea's top off and pulled the dirty one back on.

"Ick Mommy. It's all smelly."

"We'll get some clean clothes for both of us when we go home."

"I don't want to go, Mommy." Bea looked up at her. "Will it be okay? I mean will the bad guys be there?"

Katty shook her head. "Thanks for reminding me. I'll call Sheriff right now and check in with them. Maybe the bad guys are locked away in jail and we don't need to worry where they are, right?"

"Right, Mom."

"Where is this Mom stuff coming from? Aren't I Mommy to you?"

Bea sighed and zipped her jeans. "I guess I'm just growing up,

Mom." She grinned. "Big girls can call their mommy's Mommy, right, Mommy?" She laughed. "Mommy?"

"You!" Katty swatted her behind with her clothes as she opened the door to the bathroom. "I'm getting dressed. Oh. First call the Sheriff." She tapped her phone.

"Hello? Sheriff's Department."

She tapped speaker. "Hello. This is Katty Randolph. Is Sheriff there? Or—"

"Deputy Scott?"

Katty held the phone away from her. Did everyone think—

"Hello this is Deputy Scott. How may I help you?"

"Hi. Hello." She swallowed. "This is Katty."

Bea jumped and knocked the phone out of her hand. "Hi Scott. Hi!"

"Bea!"

He laughed. "Sounds like everybody's awake."

"Yes." Katty tapped the speaker to off and held the phone to her ear. "Yes. We are." Pictures of her foolishness from last night stopped her.

"You there?"

"Uh, yes." She cleared her throat. "Yes. Sorry to bother you, but Harold thinks I should let you know that I need to go home for more clothes and things. He said you should at least know I was going there."

"Good idea." Deputy Scott seemed to be smiling through the phone. "When were you thinking about going?"

"Well, right away. Or as soon as we can brush teeth and get shoes on."

"Okay. I'll meet you there. Will that work?"

Katty sighed. "Y-yes." Oh man. He wasn't mad. And she didn't want to be there alone. "If that's not too much trouble."

"No trouble. I'll leave right now. That way when you arrive, I'll already be there." He paused and lowered his voice. "Last night was okay, Katty. I'm not mad. It just took me by surprise."

"I'm glad. I'm so sorry. I won't do it again. Promise." How could he read her mind over the phone?

He laughed. "Well, we can figure that out."

Katty blinked. He wasn't mad. And ... figure that out?

"So I'll meet you there so you don't have to worry about the bad guys showing up when you're there. Okay?" Someone must have walked past him.

"Thanks, Deputy."

When Katty put down the phone, Bea was singing. "Mommy likes Deputy. Mommy likes Deputy!"

A laugh burst from the phone

"Oh crap! I didn't hit end." Katty hit end and made a face at Bea.

Bea's eyes were wide, her hands covered her mouth. "Oops!"

Katty shook her head. "Get your teeth brushed and I'll get dressed. Quick! Quick!"

## FIFTY-EIGHT

Clarence hesitated.

Same big white van they had dragged him into and shackled him to take him back to prison, bleeding and broken. Fearing for his own life, but even more for Bea and Katty's lives.

Hard not to go back there right now.

He tried to breathe but could only get out a short gasp. The memory of that day, the sounds, the voices, the pain, the fear, tried to wrap themselves around his windpipe and pour into his belly. They all needed to get pushed down. This day was a new day and he would see his girls and if he had to, he would fight for them.

Randy was watching him through the van, from outside the driver's door, his beefy hand on the door handle, three large candy bars sticking up out of his uniform shirt pocket.

He was reading Clarence's mind. He must have been thinking of the same thing—that awful trip from Osceola to prison.

Maybe. And here they were again, Randy driving him to Osceola—once again.

Clarence nodded at him across the van and opened the door.

Randy slid in at the same time, his hand on the candy bars in his pocket so they didn't fall out. Doors slammed at the same time.

"All gassed up and ready to go. One last tank on the prison's card." He started the van and tapped the steering wheel.

"What are you going to do now, Randy?" Clarence strapped himself in.

He immediately thought of Katty and Bea. Katty never used to buckle Bea in at all. She used to pretend to, but never did. Now she consistently buckled Bea in and was always nagging him to buckle his seat belt.

There was that feeling again.

He needed to get back.

Something didn't feel right.

Something was wrong.

There was a yearning or foreboding.

Something wasn't right back home.

He checked behind him. It was a huge van with three bench seats. All three were filled with angels, Michael right behind him. They seemed different this time. Dressed different.

He faced the front. Angels were different. He himself felt different.

He turned to look back at Michael and realized the difference. Each angel had battle gear on—armor and weapons.

Michael was watching him. They met eyes and he nodded.

Clarence blew out a breath and nodded back. This could get bad. Maybe it already was.

"What's the matter? Someone following us?" Randy checked his rear view mirror. "It could happen." He gripped the steering wheel. "It could happen. I'm sure the warden put out an APB on you, if he's still alive. Especially to your Sheriff—what's his name?"

"Sheriff Dennison." Clarence nodded. God, what was Sheriff thinking right now? The man had to do his job, but—

"Yeah, that's right." Randy was quiet for a minute. He shook his head and wiped an eye. "That must have been a rough day for him as well."

Clarence stared ahead.

That day. So many visuals and sounds.

Don't go there. Focus on what was ahead.

Focus.

He glanced behind him, knowing Michael was right there. But there was something different even in that. He searched the landscape around I-80 as they headed West from Des Moines. Trees. Fields. Farmland. Small towns. Signs.

A short movie played in his mind. "Come." Jesus holding out a hand to him. He had let it all go when he had jumped.

That.

He didn't know anything about Jesus except what he had learned when he had spent a year or two in Sunday School.

He searched the blue sky. Little songs—kids songs—about lights and bushels and love rainbows filled his hearing, his being. Little voices all rejoicing.

He shook his head.

Hearing things now.

He *was* crazy.

Randy looked over and held out a candy bar. "Want one? I shouldn't eat them all."

Clarence took it. "Thanks."

Baby Ruth. He tore open the wrapper and it made him think of Mandy and John again. He was going crazy with all these thoughts and sounds.

Candy might help.

## FIFTY-NINE

"There. I think that's him." Phil pointed at Deputy Scott. "That's your man."

Lex gunned the engine. Then backed it off a bit.

They watched as the cop car drove a little closer. Didn't want to tip him off.

"Now!" Phil yelled.

Lex gunned the car forward, letting the tires catch on the pavement, then hit the gas. The car swerved, but he kept control.

"Good driving, Cowboy!" Phil slammed his hand down on the dash. "Get him!"

The deputy was gripping the steering wheel, giving it a hard yank to avoid hitting them.

Lex jerked his steering wheel again, putting them right in the car's path.

Deputy's eyes popped. He leaned into the steering wheel and swerved hard.

Lex turned just in time.

Bam!

The cop lurched forward in his seat just as Katty could be seen pulling into her driveway, behind him.

"Right on time!" Phil pounded Lex on the shoulder. "See you soon. Stay on him."

Lex pulled his gun out from under the seat.

The deputy ran to Lex's car door. "What the hell do you think you are doing?" His hand was on his weapon. He had unsnapped the leather strap. "You are under ar—"

Phil didn't hear any more. He pushed the car door open and ran for Katty's trailer. One look back. Lex had pushed the car door open into Deputy Scott and knocked him to the ground.

Dork Deputy! Damn Dork Deputy!

Phil poured it on to Katty's car. She had seen the crash so was already grabbing the doorknob to the trailer house. She had hold of Bea's wrist.

Bea was crying. "No! No!"

She remembered him.

Katty got inside and slammed the door in his face.

He kicked it open and pushed himself inside. Katty faced him. Bea peeked from behind Katty.

"Bea! To your room! Get under your bed. No! Run to your hiding place."

What? Phil tore at Katty and knocked her down. He grabbed Bea and started to the door with her in his arms.

Score! He hadn't thought it'd be this easy.

She screamed and cried. Didn't matter. She'd be his. He'd show her how a daddy could treat his daughter.

What was that? He looked down at his arm and shirt. "Did you pee?" He brushed at his shirt. "You did! You ungrateful little shit!" He threw her against the wall, knocking a lamp off a table. He wiped his arm against his chest and looked up.

Katty had a gun. Trained on his head.

"Now, Sweetheart." Phil slowly raised his hands.

"I was never your sweetheart. I was your punching bag. Your surgical experiment! Your bitch!"

He stepped toward her. "Now, now. You probably have never

shot a gun in your life. Just put it down and no one gets hurt." He pointed to where Bea lay on the floor. "Especially our sweet daughter." He took another step. "Why didn't you tell me about her?"

Katty took a step back, bumped into the table and stumbled.

He rushed her, but she recovered sooner than he'd expected.

Blam!

Just missed his head! The bullet whizzed by his ear.

He took another step.

Blam!

God! "My leg!" He fell, clutching his thigh. "You shot me."

Gunshots from outside. Good. Lex must be cleaning up the deputy. He'd be here.

Blam!

"Don't shoot! Don't shoot again!" He collapsed to the floor.

Katty raced to Bea and gathered her in her arms. As she passed him, he grabbed at her foot.

Missed.

She kicked him in the thigh and ran out the door.

God! Right where the gunshot wound was.

Lex would get her.

He limped to the door.

She was already in the car, strapping Bea in the car seat in back. She was struggling to buckle her in.

He stepped out the door and almost collapsed to the deck. The railing saved him, but he still tripped. Where had she learned to shoot? He'd never allowed her to have a gun.

She slammed the driver side door and started the car.

He searched for Lex. The deputy sat on Lex's chest, straddling him. He clocked Lex on the head with his gun.

*Ow.*

Katty backed out of the driveway, tearing up grass and throwing gravel at him. She squealed onto the pavement and took off.

There. An old red Chevy pickup. He limped to it. Hope for the keys.

Score!

He hopped in, trailing blood over the seat. He slammed the door and turned it over. Please have gas. Please start.

He pumped the gas pedal and turned the key.

Vroom!

## SIXTY

Katty could only hope Deputy Scott was okay and that she was far ahead of Phil or better yet, he couldn't move because she had shot him—because she was out of gas.

The blasted E on the gas gauge was bright red, screaming at her. "Why didn't you fill the tank?"

*From now on, keep the gas tank full.*

"Mommy. Mommy."

"You're awake!" Katty checked her rear view mirror. "Are you okay?" A huge bump was already on Bea's head. She pushed down on the gas pedal. It sputtered. "Car get us to the gas station."

It lurched.

"God, please!"

It caught. Somebody must have poured gas in because it was running like a race car.

She checked the gas gauge. Still empty.

She knew Phil's car had to be out of commission. He couldn't follow them right away. But her chest felt tight like an elephant was sitting there, when she thought of him.

Too many awful memories.

She turned a corner and a picture blinked into her mind. Slap! Phil's hand was powerful across her cheek.

"Mommy. Mommy! He's coming!"

Katty blinked. No!

She drove through the intersection by the old school. Another visual—a boot kicked her belly. "The baby! Phil! The baby!"

She almost doubled over now with the memory.

To the highway. Stop sign.

"Stop Phil! You're hurting me!" She could never get free from him. He was too strong.

Bea kicked her seat.

*This* baby was alive and kicking.

"It's gonna be okay, Bea. Hang on."

The traffic blurred. A truck zoomed by. A white van followed. Another car. She blinked again and wiped her eyes.

A nurse's face from the past was in hers. "Hang on, Katty Randolph. We gotta pump your stomach." She'd never forget those concerned brown eyes—that moment. The nurse knew everything—in that moment. Katty had been sure she would die.

She blinked. She could face dying again, but Bea ... never!

She panicked and froze.

A picture in her mind layered over highway traffic.

She'd had flashes since she was a kid—some freaked her out and others she hardly acknowledged. They flew in and flew out.

This time the visual was a red truck cutting the turn and slamming into her car head on. Glass exploded everywhere. And that was it. End of vision.

What *was* that?

Red truck just like her neighbor's truck.

She skipped the highway and turned into the implement company drive and almost hit a sign that read, "This is not a driveway."

She wiped her face again and zoomed through the Dive-Inn's

back employee parking lot, bouncing over the breaks in the concrete. They would be mad. Almost hit the owner's car.

She stopped beside an unoccupied pump at the gas station. They were busy. Cars and pickups parked everywhere, across the highway even, blocking the entrance. Old guys sat at the tables inside, drinking coffee, looking out of the windows, like fish in a fishbowl checking out the world.

The gas pump. She panicked. She never had any money. Phil aways kept it so she couldn't buy food.

No. Not back then.

Now. She reached into her purse and pulled out the debit card.

Just as she turned and faced the windshield to open her car door, an old red truck appeared out of nowhere, roaring down the hill, and turned into the gas station.

Phil!

For a split second, their eyes met and raw emotion traveled between them. Hatred both directions. A growl rose from inside Katty.

"Shit! He's not stopping!" Katty was still buckled in. "Bea. Hold on!"

Bea screamed the same time Katty did.

The truck slammed into the front of her car, shoving it way back into old gas tanks behind them.

Katty's head was thrown back hard against the headrest and the world went black.

She didn't know how long she'd been out, but when she came to, people were screaming and running. Pointing.

What could they see that she couldn't?

"Oh shit!" Gas sprayed into the car through the broken windshield. Katty's clothes were wet and she guessed Bea's must be too. Gas fumes leaked everywhere. Smoke and steam rolled from the front of the car and the old truck. Broken glass was everywhere.

The vision!

She could barely see Phil. His head and body had broken through the windshield and had landed on the hood, blood oozed from his face, his nose was smashed to the side. Unconscious.

An emergency truck screamed down the hill, into the gas station along with two fire trucks.

Fire trucks!

"Bea!" The rear view mirror was broken and on the seat beside her. Katty tried to turn her head but met with horrible pain. Her eyes blurred and the world started to spin. "Bea!" She tried to unbuckle her seat belt. Her right arm was fine, but her left arm was smashed against the car door.

Trapped!

She tried to raise her good arm over the back of the seat, when her door was jerked open. Hands reached in and pulled her out.

She screamed. Her left arm must be broken, the one they dragged her out with. A man—it was the deputy— tried to help her to stand, but her legs gave way beneath her. Intense pain spiked through her left leg. "Don't worry about me! Get Bea!"

Flames burst up from the old pickup and a fireman carried her back against the building. "We will. We'll get her."

She could barely see Bea through the smoke. Her head was slumped against the car seat.

"Bea!" Katty started sobbing and screaming. "Help my Baby! Get her out!"

## SIXTY-ONE

Clarence always liked the curves coming into Osceola. He needed to get to Katty and Bea to make sure they are all right, but he was coming back.

His home town.

Just a few months ago, he had been so angry about being shipped off to Osceola. He swallowed. If he really took time to admit it, he had been an asshole. He shook his head. To everybody. Carol and everybody at Hillcrest. Mandy and John at the grocery store. Lisha. The Oust Clarence Brigade or whatever they called themselves. They probably had disbanded since he'd been gone.

He'd have to make things right somehow.

The vet clinic. Maybe he should get a dog. Or get Bea a dog.

Good to be back.

The old ball field. No body ever used that. Nice piece of grass. Close to the tracks though. The town should do something with it. Somebody had to mow it. They should just expand the park to here. Plant some trees. Or sell it. It'd make a great business opportunity. Maybe he and Harold should build a little office there for their detective business.

"Wait. Let's turn here." Clarence pointed to the street almost too late. "Go past the cemetery and down to the trailer park." He nodded when Randy made a sharp left. "We can start there and see if they're home."

"Ya coulda told me a little earlier." Randy chuckled. "This is a pretty little town, Clarence." He slowed. "That's a nice cemetery —got your plot?"

Clarence grinned. "As a matter of fact I do. Thanks to Dad. I have a couple plots there—besides where Dad is buried anyway." He'd never thought about that before. Guess that's where he'd go when he died. Funny with how old he was, he'd just never thought about it. Most geezers his age had it all planned out. He should go visit Dad's grave ... sometime.

"One ... two more blocks I think." He chuckled. "You'll find it. It's not too hard to find—" He pointed. "There. The first trailer on the right. Her car isn't there, but I'll jump out and knock on the door. Maybe she's having the car worked on."

The new deck looked so nice. Made the old place look better. They'd have to do something about the trailer itself when he got settled at the home again.

He knocked and the door pushed open. Unlocked.

Not like Katty.

He started to step inside when he noticed something on the floor. He pushed the door open farther. The room was a shambles. A chair was overturned and the sofa lamp was broken on the floor.

A trail of what looked like blood led him back to the deck.

Blood on the deck.

"Randy!" Clarence roared. "Something happened." He tripped down the deck steps. "Nobody's here and there's blood on the floor and the deck!"

Sirens went off.

Goose bumps skittered up his arms. He rubbed them, searching the sky, the trees, toward the town.

Smoke.

He met eyes with Randy and moved.

Randy shifted into reverse before Clarence opened the door.

Clarence barely got in, when Randy gunned the van back onto the street.

"Where to?" Randy swerved, just missing the mess on the street. "Holy cow! Want to stop?" He slowed to inspect the scene. "Cop car head on with that old Buick." He sped up. "No blood there anyway."

Clarence craned his neck as Randy drove past. "I don't see anybody. That might be Deputy Scott's squad car." He shifted to the front. "Where would the girls be?" He shook his head. "I guess try the nursing home. Remember how to get there?"

"Really? This ain't Chicago, where I'm from." He drove back the way they'd come. "Keep an eye out for anything. Smoke. Cops."

This might be about Katty and Bea. There were lots of reasons for sirens, but he knew in his gut that the siren was about his girls.

At the highway. "Turn left." Smoke and fire billowed at the gas station. "There!"

Randy poured it on and they pulled in.

"Katty's car is on fire!"

# SIXTY-TWO

Every angel was in place.

But so were demons.

Michael rose above the chaos along with other angelic beings. The host was with him. He glanced on every side. Angels in heavenly armor glowed, each reflecting the Father's love. Swords reflected the light in their eyes, clanging against each other, as angels prepared for battle.

The scene below was normal from their point of view.

Humans being humans.

Hurting each other.

So much pain caused by so much pain.

Demons hovered with Phil and the truck, not willing to let go of the man's body. The man looked to be horribly mangled. Smashed through the glass in the windshield, his face was undistinguishable.

Angels were posted at every corner of the property and lined the rooftop. But demons badgered them from every direction—just like sparrows pestering an eagle, the demons picked and slapped and poked but that seemed all they were able to do.

They knew they were defeated in this battle.

Michael nodded to a huge angel—Mrs. Hatly's intercessory angel—and he flew off to stand with him.

The angels rose higher into the Light.

Another angel tipped his sword and hundreds flew off in response to stir others to pray. To houses, the school, businesses. Inspiring people who would hear and listen and bow their hearts.

All was ready. All were in position.

Michael nodded.

Only the Father knew the outcome, but they had done all they could. Now it was up to the humans to press in, to push forth and not give up the battle.

# SIXTY-THREE

There! Before Randy had the van stopped, Clarence was out the door. He rounded a pair of old dump trucks parked beside the service station and stumbled to a stop.

His girls. He finally knew who he was meant to be. Once it had been for him to be Annie's husband, but now ... Katty and Bea's family. Mrs. Hatly.

Katty's car was sandwiched between a pickup into the front end and gas tanks at the rear. The hood was crumpled and pushed up. Smoke poured from the engine compartment. Steam rolled and hissed from both the car and pick-up as they sat, hood to hood.

Fire trucks roared onto the lot, horns blasting, as Clarence skirted between them. Firemen leaped off the trucks and ran hoses from the tanks. Police roped off the area. Radios blared for additional help. An ambulance backed in beside a fire truck. People stumbled to get out of the way.

Clarence ran. No one noticed an old man darting about, in all the confusion. He skidded to a stop.

A man was draped over the hood of the pickup, bleeding and unconscious.

Phil! The bastard! "Die Phil!"

There. Katty was being detained against the building. She pointed to the car, screaming, crying. "My baby's in there! Get her out!"

A cop pushed her from the wreck, but she kept breaking away from him until another cop grabbed her.

The Deputy.

Where was Bea?

Clarence stopped beside the passenger door of the car but was knocked off his feet by a fireman, who pushed him away. "Not now old man." The fireman took a second glance at Clarence and growled. "Get away you ... filthy jailbird. How'd you get out? Go back to prison where you belong!"

Clarence struggled onto his feet and fought his way between the two firemen, only to be pushed back again. The fireman turned away to yell at a cop. "Get this bastard out of here."

Clarence saw his chance and dove under him, pushing himself into the back seat.

Bea. Unconscious. Bleeding.

He reached for the car seat. Buckled. He'd never buckled or unbuckled a car seat in his life.

Boom!

He looked behind him to the front of the car. Flames burst from the engine, rocking the car.

"She's gonna blow! Get out! Get away!"

Clarence fumbled at the straps. His eyes watered. Smoke filled his lungs.

If he had to die trying, he'd go with her.

But she had to live.

Moments collided and Clarence couldn't tell whether he was in his past with Annie and that accident or the present with Bea, but he screamed and wrenched the straps, breaking them, shredding them until Bea was free. He gathered her in his arms and backed out, tucking her into his chest.

As soon as he was free from the car, arms pried her from him.

Someone pulled him to fresh air. They pushed him onto a gurney and rushed him away from the burning car, bumping, jarring him.

"Bea. Bea." He reached his arm out. "Where is she?"

People hollered. "It's gonna blow!"

Engines gunned. Tires squealed.

Ka-boom!

The ground shook as someone laid on him, covering him. "It's okay, buddy. You—we're gonna be okay."

Debris and shrapnel bombarded them.

"Feels like a war zone."

Someone covered his eyes. An oxygen mask lowered over his mouth, but he ripped it away.

"Where's Bea?"

The mask was forcefully strapped on.

"Leave. It. On. Jailbird. You breathed in too much smoke back there. Don't you dare take it off." A female voice growled.

A blanket of sorts draped over him. He fell back onto the gurney. A strap tightened around his middle.

Someone forced his hands together in front of his stomach and handcuffs clicked.

# SIXTY-FOUR

"No! No!" Katty fell again. God, help! "You've got to get her out!"

Ka-boom!

The car and truck exploded.

Everything slowed. Debris hung in the air. People moved their mouths talking or screaming.

Deputy Scott moved in front of her, shielding her.

She was caught in another realm. She watched people move. She could hear them scream. She could feel the heat even through the Deputy.

Her heart pounded. Beat. By. Beat. She could feel it in her chest—hear it in her ears.

She didn't even feel pain from her arm or her leg.

She was gripped by another pain much deeper than any broken bones or torn flesh.

Nobody had gotten Bea out.

She pushed at the Deputy only he wouldn't let her go.

She pounded on his back.

He was too strong.

Visuals took her back to Phil and she pounded on his back to get away. She had to save her baby. He always killed her babies.

"No. No. No!"

People seemed to hold their breath collectively. No one moved.

Until they saw a fireman grab a tiny girl from a bent old man and run to the emergency unit.

## SIXTY-FIVE

Clarence jumped and tore the oxygen mask off. "Michael, tell them! I'm innocent. You broke me out of prison."

Sheriff grimaced. "I'm sorry Clarence. Whether Michael is real or if he's an angel—"

"Others see him, too. I'm not crazy. I'm innocent." No one in the room but Clarence and Sheriff ... and angels—all lined up around the walls of his hospital room.

"Clarence. The law is the law. You broke out of prison." Sheriff blinked. "That's a federal offense. You will go back to prison and I can't do a thing about it." He flipped the papers in his hand. "I'm bound by the law. When they release you here, you're going to jail to await trial."

John burst into the room, followed by Mandy. "Sheriff. Governor. The governor!"

Michael slid behind them against the wall.

Mandy shoved John aside. "He's here."

Sheriff walked around Clarence's hospital bed. "Who's here? And this is a private conversation." He shoved the door, but stopped just before slamming it on the governor. "Whoah. Governor!" He glanced at John and Mandy, then backed away. "My apologies, Sir."

Governor chuckled and shook his hand. Then slapped John on the back. "Nice job, my man." Nodded at Mandy. "You too. Great work." He stepped closer to the bed, reaching his hand out to Clarence. "So is this the man?" He shook his head. "Where do I start?"

John leaned in. "Maybe we should turn up the TV." He pointed.

The TV was on, but no sound. The news.

"That's him!" Clarence pulled the mask clear off and handed it to Michael, who slid it to John. "Turn it up! That's Warden."

Mandy found the button.

The announcer looked directly into the camera. "This is the man behind several incidents in recent news." The camera showed Warden being escorted out of the prison, hands cuffed behind his back. He tried to hide, ducking into his sleeve.

Where was the cocky, evil warden now? Clarence closed his eyes, holding in emotion. Rage. Terror. Pain. Relief. All flooded him now.

Something touched his hand. He blinked his eyes open.

Mandy. She gently rubbed his fingers.

He blinked. He wanted to hide his face too, but for way different reasons than Warden just now. God he hated that man. What he had suffered because of that man. Others, too. If only he knew Warden would get what he deserved.

"Look!" Clarence pointed at the TV. "That's the guard that shot ... " Clarence swallowed. "That's the one that shot my Bea."

Right behind Warden shuffled Tay Ralston. His eyes glanced up at the camera, then quickly down at his feet.

Clarence blinked and wiped his eyes. His fists clenched, balled into fists.

Mandy kept on caressing his hands.

*Breathe.*

"You okay, Clarence?"Governor cleared his throat. "I have driven all this way to inform you—"

Mandy gasped. "No. He's a good man. He doesn't deserve jail." She patted Clarence's chest. "He doesn't deserve to die."

"Oh, Clarence. How blessed you are to have such great friends." Governor swallowed. "No I'm here to inform you ... that you are a free man. You have been exonerated."

Clarence pulled himself upright.

Mandy pushed the pillow under his shoulders.

"Did ... did you just say exonerated?" A legal term Clarence understood. He'd helped a couple inmates achieve that status, but only through hard work and more evidence. He searched the governor's face.

The man appeared serious. "I did. I said exonerated. You, as a lawyer, know exactly what that term means."

Clarence slowly nodded and leaned back onto the pillow. "How?" He glanced at Sheriff. "We have tried and—"

The TV announcer. "Durant, Nebraska is being investigated as the local hub for this huge operation."

Governor pointed at the TV. "Mandy turn it down for me, please."

She raised the remote and punched the button.

Governor pointed at the screen. The picture showed run-down buildings formerly used for grain storage. As the camera panned inside, a high-tech world was revealed—rows of computers, lockers of guns, dorm rooms. "That. That was the ... he said it ... the hub for Warden's family business. Drug running and sex trafficking. The outside of the buildings never let on what was really going on inside. No one ever knew. Local people. Railroad —it's right on the tracks. Farmers? No one had a clue."

The screen picture shifted to a photo of Clarence.

Mandy punched the button.

Clarence froze. Felt like Michael was sitting on his chest. What now?

"This man." The announcer continued. "His name is Clarence Timmelsen. He had served time for a crime he didn't commit and released to a nursing home in Osceola, Nebraska.

"Knock." Bea peeked in. "Knock, knock." She looked behind her, pulling at her hospital gown covered in ducks. "Mommy. Clarence is home." She looked into the hospital room. "He's having a party."

Katty reached for Bea, just missing her. Her eyes bounced from one person to another. "I'm sorry. We'll come back."

"Hi Mandy." Bea crawled under John's legs to Mandy. "Hi Clarence." When Mandy lifted her onto the bed, she pointed at the TV. "Look, Clarence. You're on TV."

Clarence reached for her. "I know." Startling to look up and see his own grizzled face on the screen.

"Did you win?" Bea snuggled down next to him.

Clarence glanced at the governor and raised his eyebrows. "Did I?"

"You did win, Clarence." Governor nodded.

The announcer continued. "He was incarcerated again, for allegedly murdering Warden Ralston's brother during his first stint in prison. When two guards stepped forward to testify against the warden's family accusations, the truth came out. Clarence Timmelsen had acted in self-defense and will be freed of all charges, according to the governor of Nebraska."

Governor raised his eyebrows and nodded. "That's what I was trying to tell you, Clarence. The guards testified that you acted in self-defense."

Bea pointed. "Michael's here."

Katty stepped to the bedside and started to lift Bea.

Clarence closed his eyes and held onto her. He grabbed Katty's hand. Oh God. Savor this moment. "How?" He cleared his throat and opened his eyes. "How? Who? Who were the guards?"

Governor shook his head. "I don't ... I don't remember names, but—"

John dropped the mask on the bed and pointed. "Was it them?"

The screen showed two men in drab brown guard uniforms.

Clarence leaned up. "That's Randy and Lester." He looked over at Governor. "Them?"

"Yup." Governor nodded. "When your friend called us, certain things seemed to fit together with other crimes that were unsolved. This man, William Ralston, was the missing piece to tie it all together."

A man in a suit stuck his head in. "Governor." He waved. "Sorry to interrupt, but we need to get back to Lincoln."

Governor nodded. "Yup. I"d love to stay and enjoy the news with you all, but I'm sure you don't need me to do that." He stepped close to the bed. "I assure you that all your property, finances, real estate is safe. Titles had not been changed over. Luckily, Ralston was kept pretty busy trying to track you down, Clarence." He reached his hand to Clarence. "You're a good man. Never forget that. In tracking down the details of the case, your name came up many times because you helped people—stuck your neck out for them."

Solid handshake. "Governor. You'll never know what—"

"Oh, I think I have an idea. These people are your friends."

"Family." Bea piped up. She tapped Clarence's chest. "He's my grandpa."

Katty shushed her.

Too late.

Clarence lifted his head to see Katty. "Did you ... did you find it?"

All she could do was nod and bite her lip.

"Ha. I'll let you all enjoy the news." Governor bowed and headed for the door.

Sheriff followed him out. "I'll walk you out, Sir." He turned back to Clarence. "I'll be back."

Clarence jumped. "Say, Governor?"

Sheriff hooked the governor's arm. "He wants to ask you something, I think."

"Yes." Governor stepped in.

"You said a friend of mine called you?"

"Yes. In fact he knows my dad. Name is Harold ... Harold Dexter." He nodded. "A good man. And a good friend to you."

"Thank you." Clarence sank back down in bed and blew out a breath. "Yeah. A good man." He nodded. "A good friend."

## SIXTY-SIX

Clarence checked himself in the mirror. He'd really wanted to wear his Led Zeppelin T-shirt for this important day, but he knew she would look so pretty that he had to gussy up a little.

He brushed his teeth and spit into the sink. The morning's conversations at breakfast had been so funny. The threesome—Harold, Mrs. Hatly and Clarence had lingered over coffee. Harold had been teasing Mrs. Hatly about marrying a young stud.

Clarence inspected himself in the mirror now. Well, he was a stud, but an old one for sure. He'd earned every wrinkle, every scar, especially the latest ones.

Then Harold had wheeled away, chuckling.

Still sitting next to her, Clarence had held out his hand. "Mrs. Hatly."

She chuckled. "Not for long." She took his hand in hers and pressed it against her soft cheek.

He paused. "You sure? You've been Mrs. Hatly for a long time."

She smiled sweetly at him from her wheelchair. "I'll be Mrs. Timmelsen for eternity. Oh, and you can call me Violet."

Clarence blew out a breath. Tears stung. He was such a cry baby today.

Flashbacks to the prison beatings. Only one way he could have lived through that. He blinked. Swallowed. All for today. This day.

He stepped back against the bathroom door in order to see most of himself and smoothed back his hair. She liked it long so he'd just had it trimmed.

"Pretty slick, Buddy." Harold knocked at the door and wheeled into the bathroom. "Lookin' good."

Clarence adjusted the bowtie and turned to him. "You sure about this? I've never worn one of these in my whole life."

"You've never even worn a tie in your whole life." He chuckled. "You said yourself, she's a bowtie kinda girl." Harold nodded. "Looks good."

"I think I must have worn a tie to my mom's funeral back then. I think." Clarence nodded. "Yeah." He followed Harold into his office and picked up the jacket. "Never worn one of these either. Thanks for loaning it to me." He pulled it on. "Buttoned or not?"

Harold nodded. "Buttoned."

Clarence buttoned it and turned the American flag pin right side up. He stepped back.

Harold shook his head. "Not."

Clarence unbuttoned it and laughed. "Yeah, I've eaten too good here lately. Gained some weight back." He adjusted his bowtie again. "I think I'm ready. How's the time?"

Harold checked his watch. "Time to go. It's almost three o'clock. Everybody's had their naps and the dining room guy has set things up. Hillcrest even supplied the preacher—Pastor Anderson—from down the other hall." He grinned. "Everything looks ... well, I'll let you find out."

They made their way to the dining room. Residents were too.

Everyone had been invited—the perky and the bedridden and all in between.

"Excuse me, Harold." Staff wheeled beside them. "Oh the groom! Don't you look snappy!"

Sheriff Dennison looked smart in his uniform. He edged around the wheelchairs and walkers to follow Clarence and Harold.

"Hey Sheriff! Glad you could make it." Clarence patted his shoulder.

"Wouldn't miss it." Sheriff bent between the men, his mouth close to their ears, pulling them to the side. "Just relieved everything worked out."

Clarence locked on Sheriff's eyes. *Yeah.* "Yeah. Me too."

Harold held up his finger. "Well, hello Mrs. Brandon. You look nice today."

The woman took one look at Clarence and the sheriff and shook her head. "Clarence, I might have been wrong about you."

"It's okay, Mrs. Brandon. We all make mistakes." Clarence smiled.

"Well, Mrs. Hatly has been my roommate for a year and she ... well, she is a good woman. She helped me see who you are." She fiddled with the brooch at her neck. "I'd better let you get to your wedding. You don't want to hold up the bride."

Pastor Anderson peeked around the corner.

"I need to let you go, Clarence." Sheriff patted his back. "Just wanted to update you. There will be TV coverage about the prison later. Warden is all locked up."

"Pretty convenient right there at the prison, right?" Clarence chuckled. "Hey, before they kidnapped me back to prison, Harold and I were talking about starting our own detective agency. I hope we can work together."

Pastor Anderson beckoned.

"Guess we'd better get, Harold." Clarence grinned. "I don't want anyone else marrying my bride."

"I'll let you go. We can talk later ... or tomorrow—next week." Sheriff laughed. "I suppose you'll be pretty busy for awhile."

Clarence let his eyes close for just a second, relishing the thought, smiling. He had no idea what marriage was like. But he was excited to try it out. He ushered Harold to where Pastor Anderson had been standing just inside the dining room.

Clarence's breath caught. Tears threatened. He couldn't start now.

Streamers of gold and silver were strung from light fixtures and draped along the top of each wall. Every table had a small bouquet of white roses. Tables had been rearranged so there was an aisle down the middle, from the back to the front, where the minister stood with the guy running the sound system. Tech guy.

They both looked up when Clarence entered the room and waved. It was hard to believe this was all for Mrs. Hatly ... Violet and him. He chewed on his lip to keep from crying again.

The preacher talked into a nursing home radio and nodded. He held his thumb up. The bride was ready.

Preacher Anderson motioned for them to walk down the center aisle.

Mindy and John! They waved. Would wonders never cease? John had a tie on. Mindy had pink hair, probably in honor of Mrs. Hatly, and a pretty black dress. Hid her tummy rolls well. Very pretty.

Clarence waved back and mouthed, "Who's running the store?"

They grinned. John shrugged. "We don't care."

Mrs. Margin piped up loudly. "Aren't we going to have our afternoon coffee?"

"Shush." The woman next to her shook her head. "We're having a wedding today. See all the decorations? We'll get coffee later." She licked her lips. "Maybe cake."

Randy.

Clarence nodded.

Randy closed his eyes, patted his big chest and almost bowed.

The preacher showed them where to stand. Harold had been stubborn about not using his wheelchair. He wanted to stand with his buddy on this important day.

The tech guy started the music. People turned toward the front, some snoozed. Even had beds rolled in and lined up in back. Mrs. Bernadine was wiggling all over, babbling.

Clarence held up his index finger to the preacher and rushed back to her. She calmed as soon as she saw him approach. "Hi, Mrs. Bernadine. I don't think I ever thanked you for hiding me from Pete back then. I interrupted your breakfast and everything." He bowed to her. "Thank you."

A tear slowly tracked down the wrinkles of her cheek.

He wiped it away and patted her hand. "Well, I better get back up there." He adjusted his bow tie. "I'm getting married today!"

She babbled back.

"I know. And thank you for being here." He turned and made his way back up front just as the music started.

Sounded like "Here Comes the Bride" but in piano. Nice. Harold stood like a soldier next to him. He glanced at the people in attendance.

Katty. Bandages and cast on her arm. Oh Katty. He couldn't lose it now. He hadn't even seen the bride yet. Noell sat next to her.

They were both beaming and beautiful. He hadn't gotten a chance to tell them about the adoption. He straightened. Had been the right thing to do. He especially knew it now.

Lisha was first to come out and down the aisle. She was beautiful in all her … she was beautiful. Her dreadlocks were all caught up at the back of her head. Ribbons or something had been woven through. They matched her gold, sparkly dress. She walked proudly, looking straight at him. She caught his eye and stuck out her tongue.

He lowered his head, shaking it, biting his lips. Can't laugh. Not going to laugh.

Next was Carol.

Oh, he was gonna cry now.

She looked beautiful in her gold dress. Different from Lisha's. Her hair had sparkles in it, but her smile wobbled. She was already wiping her eyes and she nodded, her eyes on him too. Such a good friend. Probably his best friend in the world. Next to ... Violet. Next to Harold. Next to—

They both stood on the bride's side.

The music got a bit louder.

This was it.

Oh, Jesus.

Jingle. Jingle. Clarence's fingers had found the coins in his pants pocket.

Preacher Anderson tapped Clarence's arm and shook his head.

Oops. In trouble at his own wedding. He clasped his hands in front.

Bea walked out, knowing she was pretty. Oo's and ahh's—even from this sleepy crowd. Clarence had never seen her act shy before, but she was now. She wore a gold dress too, her hair in skinny braids, gold ribbon woven in each one and swooped into loops to the back on her head. Almost like Lisha's. And a Band-Aid on her hand.

A hush fell as Violet appeared at the back. Her grandson, Steve Ivertson, was at her side, standing tall, a huge grin on his face, eyes shining.

Ohh.

They took the first steps toward him.

At first, when Clarence looked down the aisle, he only saw Anne. She had been beautiful back then, in her white dress, veil, her eyes sparkling with love. He could even erase Judge Green, walking her down the church aisle.

But today, he knew he needed to set Anne aside—he would always love her and honor her—remember her. But today his heart focused only on Violet.

Her eyes twinkled with love too.

*Breathe.*

Harold leaned in. "She's beautiful." He chuckled. "You okay, Buddy?"

Clarence had tried to be so strong—all those years in prison through everything—not gonna cry.

But now. His chin quivered.

And he let it.

Tears ran down.

And he didn't wipe them away.

This precious dear woman had watched him repeatedly sneak out and escape from the nursing home. He had kissed her, surprising especially himself and she had not bashed him with her walker. She had fought Pete off with her wheelchair, ramming him down.

She had never doubted him. Never joined the Oust Clarence Brigade.

She had *prayed* for him.

And now here she was before him, going to become his wife.

Those eyes twinkled underneath a short veil of soft rose netting attached to a pretty ivory wide brimmed hat. Her ivory suit was simple and perfect, although he was sure he wouldn't remember what she wore tomorrow.

Steve patted her arm. She was walking without her walker.

They all turned to the front and the preacher started the dearly beloveds, and the we are gathereds.

Thank God it wasn't the same preacher that buried Noell's Gamma. It was Preacher Anderson, who lived at Hillcrest. Nice guy, even when the Brigade ladies were being their worst. He had welcomed him home after prison this time.

The wedding was all a dream or felt like it. Clarence didn't come to until the I dos.

And the rings.

He wept all through it.

Openly.

Unashamedly.

And he kissed the bride—his bride—Mrs. Clarence Timmelsen. Sweetest moment in eternity.

Some country guy started singing the walk out song, only they didn't. They just stood, facing each other, eyes locked and holding hands.

Finally they broke free and started down the aisle as man and wife.

Mr. And Mrs. Clarence Timmelsen.

Even halfway there, they stopped and turned to each other. Just gazed into each other's eyes and listened to the last verse and chorus of "How Great Thou Art."

Had he ever imagined this would be how he could spend the last part of his life? After sixty years in prison and then being kidnapped and back to prison. Beaten. Cut.

Yet, here he was.

He'd dreamt of years with Annie. Children with her.

But that wasn't meant to be.

Here and now, his wife at his side, they had many children. Bea bounced toward them. Katty and Noell hugged them. Lisha. Steve.

Carol.

He hugged her. Never a truer friend.

A dark curly head towered above all.

Michael.

In a tux.

Stud.

Clarence drew his arm around Mrs. Timmelsen.

She searched Clarence's face and followed where his eyes gazed.

Michael bowed his head and wings grew out of his back. A gold belt held weapons and a sword.

Tux stayed.

He opened his eyes and looked at the newlyweds and smiled, nodding.

She hugged deeper into Clarence's side.

He rested his chin on the top of her head.

Michael lifted his arms, closed his eyes again and disappeared.

"Where'd your angel go, Clarence?" Bea tugged on Clarence's pant leg.

He picked her up and wrapped his arm around his wife again. "He'll be back. He has to report in to Father."

He didn't know why he said that, he just knew.

"We'll see him again."

# BOOK CLUB QUESTIONS

1. How would you clear out Gamma's house?

2. Hoarding is a tough thing. My mom kept used envelopes with her name on them from her own Birthday cards. She grew up in the Depression. Is that hoarding?

3. What things do you tend to hoard? Too personal?

4. If you knew a neighbor had addictions and an abusive background, would you reach out to them? How?

5. You have heard things about a certain person in your small town or community—even your church. Maybe they are a sex offender, an ex-con, or gotten in obvious trouble. Would you try to help them? Would you even talk to them? How?

6. If you saw a neighbor abusing their child, would you report them or somehow intervene?

7. What are you most prone to do for someone who has had surgery or a new baby?

8. Would you be okay with welcoming an ex-con to your Bible-study or church or book club or senior center?

9. Are you okay with reading fiction about your community or somewhere close to you? What if the author has made up awful

things to take place near you? Do you like driving past where the author placed a crime that didn't really happen?

10. Would you like to see more of these characters in future novels?

# AUTHOR NOTES

Where does a story come from—other than the awesome, but strange brain of an author? So many things and experiences draw an author to an idea.

You know how there are days when you repeatedly see a person, or hear a song, or think of a word? The common saying, "We are on the same frequency," intrigues me.

So, were we? Were we on the same frequency, when you called me, the other day? Or when we both ended up at the same store at the same time?

And what is a frequency, anyway? A wavelength?

The dictionary defines frequency as "the rate at which something occurs or is repeated over a particular period of time or in a given sample."

I don't pretend to understand this stuff. I love it. I just don't understand it ... yet.

When I wrote book two in The Great Escapee Series, I saw sink holes everywhere! On the news. On vacation. Crazy. And caves. And underground pools.

You remember when you were wanting to have a baby, and

everywhere you went—the grocery store, restaurants, church—there were prego ladies everywhere!

Or when you were looking a buying a new car? Yeah. You noticed every vehicle—every make and model.

What is that?

So, in my writing, I mean to explore those wavelengths that draw us together.

Are they God?

That'd be cool.

Anyway, enough of my wonderings and wanderings.

My editor, Kathy, called me out on letting Clarence just drift along, never being held accountable for the prison break, so I added three chapters and scenes elsewhere. Funny how my main beta reader, my sister Jan, has comments and recommendations very close to my editor!

Our nursing home. A great place to work, to live. I have to write this—there is no way our administrator, or staff or residents are anything like in this book. Anything from a flawed character's point of view (like Clarence—he's still stubborn—or Phil) might be one-sided, critical and snarky!

Our court house is a wonderful building and the people working there are even more wonderful—helpful, knowledge-able. Even though information held there is public knowledge, they still would protect it from an evil guy like Phil!

Again, the comment somewhere in this story, "Small town grocery store." We used to own that small town grocery store, here in Osceola. I loved the customers who blessed us with their trust and business and friendships. Again, I write a disclaimer that any current business or hospital or nursing home we enjoy in our small town, is appreciated and supported. Just because the character has a problem with some entity doesn't mean this writer does! Doesn't mean it's true!

Phil hates small towns. I love them. Especially Osceola. Quirks and all. Negativity and all. I love the old buildings— falling down and all. Phil is Phil—an evil man. What he loves and what I love are two different things.

So, if you are a resident of a small town or even Osceola, Nebraska, please don't take offense at his attitude. He. Is. Evil!

Oh, yeah. The Dive-Inn? Whose opinion do you suppose that is? Right! Phil and Lex's from Released, Book One. My opinion? We love Terry's Drive In. It's our favorite place to get ice cream, then take a drive through town. Or a burger. Or broasted chicken. Or …

So … just in case I didn't make this clear … any negative comments in the book about the town, any businesses, the nursing home and any staff or residents are purely from the bad guys. This town is a great town. The people are great!

But, I might want to keep Lisha and Carol. They are sweethearts.

---

I am taking a couple of courses to help me with marketing and website maintenance. One asks what my usual themes are in my books. Well yeah: sink holes, demons, angels, caves, prisons, sweet little girls, drug abuse. And more. But even more: faith, hope, surrender.

And as authors write, Someone takes us through the darkness to where we are free. Or freer.

Hence this book.

Clarence in taken back to prison.

Don't we go back into those dark places again and again? Heartbreaking, but true. When I do, I know God is leading me there for a reason; he wants to take me a little deeper, so I can get ... a little freer.

Clarence went to the very end of himself (and the edge of the precipice).

Me, too.

When Jesus says, "Come," it's over. We are at the end of ourselves and if we step off that cliff, we will never be the same. Is life perfect then? Naw. But at that divine moment, we have been given the power to become the sons of God (John 1:12.). New family. New life. New mind. New faith.

# ACKNOWLEDGMENTS

Thank you to my editor, Kathy Tyers Gillin, for putting up with my comma messes! I learn so much from her and appreciate her! WE KNOW!

---

Jane Dixon Smith is my cover designer. I give her a short synopsis and she gets it. I never stress over them. Ever. Forever lovely to work with. Thank you, Jane!

---

Thank you to my beta readers, Jan and Jo. You keep me sane by catching the mistakes. It is a huge deal to take the time to read my manuscripts in the middle of your busy lives. Thank you!

---

Jan. You have read my words. And reread them. And again. Either you are terrified of what your sister will put out there, or you care deeply that it's well done. Either way, you're my Boss and I love you. There are so many cliché ways to say that. They are almost meaningless. I love you says it all.

I kept hearing as I pondered this book: "Pull out all the stops. (A musical organ term meaning blast it out!) Go where you don't want to go. Take the story to the dark places, the hard places." God usually does that because he wants me to personally go to those places—to face my messes. To God, I give eternal thanks.

Speaking of messes, if there is any part of this book that is not quality writing, it's mine! My editor and beta readers made it shine!

# OTHER BOOKS BY BONNIE LACY

Thank you so much for reading my books! If you have a minute, would you consider leaving a review anywhere you purchase books? This is a huge help to any author!

---

Did you like The Great Escapee Series?

---

Do you want to read more about Katty and Bea? There is a trilogy coming!

---

About Clarence and Harold's venture into detective work? Yes. They have their own trilogy! Michael is in it. Yes, I sprinkle Katty and Bea in. It will be fun to see what those two codgers are up to!

---

What happened to Phil? I know. Ugly, evil man. But what if ...

---

Why is Noell drawn to the pool? What are her other gifts? She goes to strange places in her own trilogy!

---

Find out by going to www.bonnielacy.com

There, you will find an annoying pop-up window asking you to sign in
with your email address. You will be added to my email newsletter list
and when I have news about upcoming books, or cover reveals, or any
new strangeness like sink holes or weird places I have explored, you will
be the first to know! I won't explode your inbox!

---

Be blessed. No. Really. I don't just say that. I'm praying that you are
indeed blessed by the One Who gives freely as we learn to receive!

---

Keep in touch! No. Really. There is a contact page on my website. Or
reply to my email newsletter! I'd love to hear from you!